BURNED & BOUND

Copyright © 2024 by A. Winchester

All rights reserved. No part of this book may be reproduced in any form or by any electronic or mechanical means, including information storage and retrieval systems, without written permission from the author, except for the use of brief quotations in book reviews.

This is a work of fiction. Names, characters, businesses, places, events, locales, and incidents are either a product of the author's imagination or used in a fictitious manner. Any resemblance to actual persons, living or dead, or actual events is coincidental.

The author acknowledges the trademark status and trademark owners of various brands, products, and/or restaurants referenced in this work of fiction. The publication/use of these trademarks is not authorized, associated with, or sponsored by the trademark owners.

Cover Design: Winchester Publications

FOR MY HUSBAND,

WHO TAUGHT ME THAT MY NEED TO
BE LOVED DIFFERENTLY

NEVER MADE ME LESS WORTHY
AND DESERVING OF BEING LOVED.

posuere, metus
nibh, vitae scele
massa eget pede
nterdum
bus at, q
onsectetu
at quis, te

In in nunc. Class
taciti sociosqu ad li
torquent per conubi
per inceptos hymenae
ullamcorper fringilla
Fusce in sapien eu pur
dapibus commodo. Cu
natoque penatibus et m
dis parturient montes, n
ridiculus mus. Cras fauc
condimentum odio. Sed a
ligula. Aliquam at eros. E
at ligula et tellus ullamcor
ultrices. In fermentum. lore
non cursus porttitor, diam
urna accumsan

que
et malesuada
egestas. Nunc
Maecenas odio
ulputate vel, auctor ac,
umsan id, felis.
Pellentesque cursus sagittis
felis. Pellentesque porttitor,
velit lacinia egestas auctor,
diam eros tempus arcu, nec
vulputate augue magna vel
risus. Cras non magna vel ante
adipiscing rhoncus. Vivamus a
mi. Morbi neque. Aliquam erat
ultrices

YOU ARE NOT
THE DARKNESS
YOU ENDURED.

YOU ARE THE
LIGHT THAT
REFUSED TO
SURRENDER.

JOHN MARK GREEN

PLAYLIST

Music got me through writing Burned & Bound. It helped me breathe and get through each chapter, especially the difficult ones. Each of these songs has weaved a special place into the pages of this story.

Songs That Inspired

Burden — Citizen Soldier
Boys Don't Cry — Jake Banfield
I Am Not Okay — Jelly Roll
Pain Killer — Warren Zeiders
Where You Need To Be — Blake Proehl

Songs In The Book

Chasing Cars — Noelle Johnson (Prologue)
Devil You Know — Tyler Braden (Chapters 02 & 80)
Simple Man — Jensen Ackles (Chapter 08)
A Bar Song (Tipsy) — Shaboozey (Chapter 11)
Just Pretend — Five Finger Death Punch (Chapter 12)
Losing Hold — Esterly & Austin Jenckes (Chapters 14, 72, & 73)
Hell or High Water — Bailey Zimmerman (Chapter 16)
Wildflowers & Wild Horses — Lainey Wilson (Chapter 18)
Burn It To The Ground — Nickelback (Chapter 18)
Let It Burn — Citizen Soldier (Chapter 19)
I'm Not For Everyone — Brothers Osborne (Chapter 24)
Truck Bed — Hardy (Chapter 27)
Porch Light — Josh Melody (Chapter 33)
Fix You — Dean Lewis & Daniel Seavey (Chapter 37)
Hold Me — Teddy Swims (*Chapter 40*)
Iris — DIAMANTE & Breaking Benjamin (*Chapter 41*)
Tomorrow — Trevor McBane (*Chapters 43 & 44*)
Home Sweet — Russell Dickerson (*Chapter 46*)
Up To No Good — Warren Zeiders (*Chapter 48*)
Breathe — Through The Fire (*Chapter 51*)
Burn It Down — Warren Zeiders (*Chapter 52*)
I Had Some Help — Post Malone & Morgan Wallen (*Chapter 53*)
A Bit Of Lightning (Acoustic) — Flat Black (Chapter 58)
Wanna Be Loved — The Red Clay Strays (Chapter 61)
Addictions — Warren Zeiders (Chapters 62 & 63)
Son of a Sinner — Jelly Roll (Chapter 68)
Dark Night — Warren Zeiders (Chapter 79)
Stetson — Hunter Hayes (Chapter 84)
Hard to Love — Lee Brice (Chapter 87)
Country As Fuck — Shaman's Harvest (Chapter 89)
Something's Gonna Kill Me — Corey Kent (Chapter 91)
Hold On — Chord Overstreet (Chapter 93)
Death of a Cowboy — Warren Zeiders (Chapter 95)
Heartbreaker — Warren Zeiders (Chapter 96)
Broken Things Break Things — Austin Williams (The Letters)
Wait For You — Myles Smith (The Letters)
Happier — Marshmello & Bastille (Chapter 98)

Happier — Marshmello & Bastille (Chapter 98)
My Home (Acoustic) — Myles Smith (Chapter 100)
Tough Ones — Cooper Alan (Epilogue Pt 1)
Stargazing — Myles Smith (Epilogue Pt 2)

Songs I Kept On Repeat

My Demons — Starset
Perfect For Me — Bradley Marshall
My Fault — Shaboozey & Noah Cyrus
Last Rodeo — Restless Road
All I Ever Wanted — Dean Lewis
High Desert Road — Warren Zeiders
Fight Like Hell — Warren Zeiders
Unsteady — Transforming Duke
If You Love Me, Leave Me — Through Fire

CONTENT WARNING

While Burned & Bound isn't a dark romance by any means, this story is very mental health oriented. There are heavy themes explored as well as hard-hitting emotional scenes.

The core of this story is the journey of living with violent sexual trauma and undiagnosed complex PTSD. Please read with care and know the following are things you will encounter in order of relation to sexual assault, mental health, and others.

mentions of violent group sexual assault
mentions & description of victim branding
on page unwanted non-sexual touch that triggers trauma response
on page discussions of inability to engage in sexual activities due to trauma
on page unwanted physical arousal
on page uncomfortable attempts at physical affection
on page panic spiral due to consented sexual contact
on page emotional breakdown due to sexual trauma
on page discussions of navigating sexual trauma as a couple
on page reassurance through sexual activity geared toward a trauma survivor
on page discussions of consent
on page uncertainty about sexual activities
on page internal change of consent during sexual activity without informing partner
on page emotional breakdown during sexual activity

on page general panic attack
on page trigger-based panic attack
on page anxiety attack
on page self-deprecation
on page PTSD blackout
on page self-harm as a grounding technique
on page panic attack amnesia
on page disassociation
on page partner uncertainty handling trauma survivor's trauma responses
on page struggling with partner's PTSD & inability to "fix" it for them
mentions of attempted suicide
on page assault of partner during a PTSD blackout
mentions of diagnoses
mentions of inpatient therapy
on page prescription medication use

mentions of child abuse by parent
on page alcoholism
on page use of alcohol to cope
on page relapse
on page alcohol withdrawal symptoms
on page physical assault of an adult child (he is 18 but attacked by his father)
on page homophobia
on page homophobic remarks
mentions of parental death
on page violent bar fight
mentions of murder
mentions of prison time
on page arson
mentions of parental suicide
mentions of spousal abuse
discussions of third-party responsibility to intervene in child abuse
on page threats between main characters
on page sharing of old prescriptions
mentions of drug use
mentions of gambling
mentions of a robbery
mentions of a shooting
on page blood & injury
on page graphic injury of a main character
mentions of physical therapy & body rehabilitation

This is not your standard kind of romance.
If you're looking for a super spicy romance with a hot biker & a cowboy... this isn't it.
If you're looking for a dark romance... this isn't it.
If you're looking for a sweet and swoony romance... this still isn't it.

West is a survivor of a violent sexual assault and has never processed his trauma. He can't connect with others in a way that is considered "normal". He can't maintain relationships in a way that is considered "normal". He can't experience intimacy in a way that is considered "normal".

But you know what? *Fuck normal.*

West's story is a raw journey about learning to accept love and figure out intimacy as an assault survivor. You will hate him at times. You won't understand him at times. You may want to throw shit at times because of him. Trust the process. He's crossing barbed wire to get out of his own personal hell and unless you've been there... you may not understand. And if you have been there, this journey looks different for each person.

Jackson's story is a raw look at what it means to love someone who has experienced trauma. The patience, the education, the gentleness, the emotions. You may find yourself wondering why he's still there... why he's sticking around as West puts him through the wringer, but true love isn't always pretty and wrapped up in a lovely bow with that dreamy happily ever after. It can be a messy, raw, and utterly beautiful experience that tests your fortitude, your resilience, and your understanding. Jackson doesn't see West for his trauma and the resulting trauma responses. He sees West for the man underneath... the man all of those responses are trying so damn hard to protect.

Trust the process.

I've cried more times than I can count writing and editing this story. West has my heart and soul. I hope it moves you the way it did me.

PROLOGUE

WEST

"Shut the heck up!" Jackson hissed when I tripped over a metal bucket. *Again.* I broke down laughing. "We're going to get caught! You and your massive dang feet!"

I laughed harder—practically giggling. Jackson Myles wouldn't swear if someone paid him all the money in the world. No, Sir. He was a good country boy, and good country boys didn't swear. *But me?* I didn't give a flying fuck. I, Dakota McNamara, was eighteen years old. I was a man. No one could tell me to do a damn thing.

Except my father. But that was a different story.

When I ran into a shovel, the horses stirred in their stalls. *Grace was not my middle name.* West was though, and everyone called me West.

Except my father. *Again.*

"You might as well set off an alarm, you know." Jackson sighed dramatically. "There's no point in sneaking out with you ever."

"It ain't my fault the stable hands suck at fucking cleaning," I muttered. "Who the fuck let James run the stables anyway?"

"Our dads, that's who," he reminded me. *Oh, yeah.*

1

The Myles and the McNamaras had a long history together. Our great-great-great-too-many-for-me-to-fucking-remember-grandpas bought a plot of land with all the money they had in their pockets. They named it Double Arrow Ranch—for some reason or another—and then worked their asses off until that small plot of land became a thriving ranch. We were the largest cattle ranch in all of Oregon with connections all around the country for bull breeding. Some of the best bulls in the industry came from our ranch.

We also had horses, but those seemed to be more of a hobby than anything else. Jackson's mom called the herd her babies. She had them named, spoiled, and looking just fine. Every minute I had, I helped her with them.

Jackson and I grew up on this ranch together, and one day, we'd run it together. His family had their house, and mine had ours, but I couldn't remember a time when we weren't together. Even at night, when we should've been sleeping, we'd sneak out to take our horses for a ride.

"Just watch your feet, Bigfoot," Jackson teased. He took the lead, moving through the barn like he owned the place. *Maybe he did. What did I know?* Jackson belonged on this ranch. It ran deep in his blood. Me? Yeah, I was born and raised here just like him, but I didn't feel it. I didn't want to be a rancher. Honestly, I didn't know what I wanted to be. Or what I wanted to do with my life.

"Look at you, pretty girl," I whispered as I slipped into my horse's stall. Bailey was a gray leopard Appaloosa and a gorgeous one at that. She'd been a gift on my fifteenth birthday from Mrs. Myles. My father thought getting me a horse was a bad idea—too much responsibility for a kid who couldn't wake up with his alarm. But I'd do anything for my girl. I liked her a hell of a lot better than I liked my father.

I brushed my hands over her snout and doted on her. Even if we did get caught, I was still taking my time. Bailey deserved my respect when I saddled her. Hell, I knew Jackson was doing the same with Lucky across the stables.

By the time I guided my girl out of her stall, Jackson was waiting for me with Lucky and wearing that soft brown cowboy hat of his.

"You and that stupid hat," I scoffed. I made fun of him only because it looked so goddamn good on him. Jackson looked the part of a rancher from his sunkissed chestnut hair to his tanned skin that made his blue eyes stand out in an unnerving way. I gave him shit for it but that didn't stop me from admiring.

The real problem was that I was in love with Jackson Ford Myles. I had been for years. Boys like Jackson chased after the girl next door types while I just pined silently after my best friend. While it fucking hurt sometimes, I'd come to accept that this was my reality.

"Better than that tattoo you got," he shot back. I grinned. On my eighteenth birthday, I'd gotten a tattoo—four simple words: *no fear, no regret*. It was small and technically two tattoos since I had one phrase on the inside of each wrist but still.

I followed him outside. As soon as we cleared the side of the barn, I mounted my horse and took off at a gallop. It was seconds before Jackson caught up. Lucky was a bay Thoroughbred and a fast one at that. Jackson could've turned him around and made some damn good money racing him, but the closest thing to racing Lucky would ever do was our late-night adventures.

Double Arrow fell just shy of thirty thousand acres. It gave Jackson and me a hell of a list of places where we could hang out away from our parents. Our favorite spot was just over the northern ridge—far enough to be alone but close enough that we could get back fast enough. The cows never ventured there and neither did the horses, leaving it untouched. *I kind of had a feeling that Jackson's mom had something to do with keeping the space for us.* She was just that kind of mom.

We rode in silence like we always did. Mostly, we just wanted to make sure we got the hell out of dodge before we drew too much attention to ourselves. The twenty-five-minute ride always passed with ease.

Letting go of a heavy breath, I tipped my head back and enjoyed the rush of wind over my face. I loved the outdoors. I'd never go inside if I didn't have to. There was something comforting about a clear night sky overhead and the pounding of hooves underneath me. I had no love of ranching, but I did love being on the back of a horse.

We hitched the horses and dropped down into the long grass. Jackson stayed close like he always did, and I was all too aware like I always was. His arm brushed up against mine, his knee knocked against my thigh. The contact had my heart galloping in my chest.

"I'm thinking of trying my hand at bull riding," Jackson said.

"Didn't your dad tell you no?" I replied. It was no secret he wanted to be a bull rider. He'd been dreaming of it since we were kids putting fake horns on calves when we played.

"Yeah, but I'm eighteen next month. Nothing he can do about it then."

"Your mom's going to have a heart attack, you know that, right?"

"Nope." I could hear the smile in his voice. "You know those meetings she drags me to twice a week? They're with Buck Hartley."

"You fucker." I laughed. Buck Hartley lived across town, kept a small ranch, and kept to himself. He also happened to be a retired bull rider—and one of the best too.

"He says I've got real talent," Jackson beamed.

"I bet he says that to all the boys with money," I retorted.

"Shut the heck up!" He elbowed me. "Mom ain't paying him. He wouldn't take it anyhow."

"That's cool," I said. "Isn't it a little late to just get started? The season starts in like a week or two."

"Yeah, but Mom made a whole plan with Buck about ways I can ride through small summer festivals. Make a name for myself and all that," he replied. "He thinks I've got a good chance at coming in strong as a rookie in the next year or two."

"Your dad's going to be pissed," I told him. *Shit, I couldn't imagine pissing my father off like that.*

"It won't be so bad." I felt him roll on his side and did the same. It was damn near impossible to see him, even though we were practically nose to nose. I held my breath, my heart pounding wildly. Sure, this was nothing for him, but it was so much for me. "Mom says I just need to prove I plan to make the ranch important too."

"I'll help," I volunteered a little too quickly. "With ranch stuff and all that."

I didn't want to do it but for Jackson, I would.

"Will you be there when I do my first ride?"

"Will I be there to watch you fall flat on that ugly face of yours?" I chuckled. "Hell yeah, I will."

"You suck." *But he was laughing.* The sound did things—stupid things—to my brain. Enough so that I didn't realize what I was doing until it was too late.

Closing the distance, my lips barely touched his, and I froze. Alarms and red flags fired off in my head. This was such a horrible idea. There was no coming back from it. How the hell did you fix kissing your straight friend?

The truth: you didn't.

I started to pull back, but to my surprise, he followed. His mouth latched onto mine in an awkward kiss. Between the angle and my retreat, it was a mess. I'd never kissed anyone. I didn't know what I was doing. I chuckled awkwardly, unable to get out of my head as I broke away from him.

"I'm sorry," I managed to say pathetically.

"Don't be," Jackson said, his voice thick as gravel. His fingers brushed through my hair, sending a tingle down my spine. "But I ain't done kissing you."

That hand anchored at the back of my neck and dragged me closer. His lips slid across mine, and I followed his lead. *Soft and warm.* That's what he was. Despite his whole rough cowboy thing, Jackson was soft and warm. He kissed me gently as if afraid to break me. My tongue flicked over the seam of his lips, and he opened, meeting me in a greedy battle for control.

Kiss after kiss, we grew bolder. My hands ran down his sides, his leg wrapped around mine. *The feel of his hands, the taste of his mouth, the warmth of his body.* I was fucking flying.

"What're we doing?" I asked in a lull as we both stopped to catch our breath.

"I don't know," he admitted. His head shook slightly. "I don't..."

"Tomorrow," I suggested when he faltered. "We can figure it out tomorrow."

"Yeah," he agreed. "Tomorrow is good."

And then his mouth was on mine again. I melted into the cool grass as I made out with my best friend under the stars.

We stayed out way later than we usually did, but neither of us wanted to leave. Somehow making out in a field until we were both rocking the most painful boners of our lives was better than anything else. Also, riding a horse with a boner wasn't comfortable.

Hours later, I snuck in through the backdoor and practically tiptoed through my house. My father wasn't a fan of me sneaking out, so I tried to keep it down. With any luck, he'd passed the fuck out with the help of whatever drink he picked for the night.

"Where the hell have you been?" *That gruff voice stopped me dead in my tracks when I tried to pass through the living room.* The light flipped on and my dad sat in his favorite chair, empty drink in hand and an empty bottle on the table next to him.

Shit.

Harrison McNamara was a beast of a man—something I wasn't, much to his disappointment. Granted, everything about me was a disappointment. I took after Mom, which made me a reminder of her that he was stuck with. My dark hair contrasted his light hair, my gray eyes didn't match his brown ones, and he was tall while I was average at best. *Yeah, Harrison McNamara would've been happier with anyone else for a son.*

"I went out with Jackson for a ride." I cleared my throat as my voice cracked. "We talked. I promise we didn't mess with the herd or break anything, Sir."

He grunted, and my heart lodged in my throat. That wasn't a good sign. Neither was the way he pushed to his feet. I remained rooted where I was, knowing that turning my back was the worst thing to do. Sometimes it was just easier to take my father's wrath than try to avoid it. That always ended worse. I could take a hit or two. I was tougher than he thought I was.

He reeked of alcohol as he stomped close. My stomach rolled at the stench. I didn't move—could barely breathe—as he glared down at me. I hoped to hell he just decided I wasn't worth his time and went back to drinking so I could go to bed.

"What the hell is that on your neck?" he demanded loudly. Before I could say a word, he grabbed a fistful of my hair and wrenched my head hard to the side. "Is that a goddamn hickey on your neck?"

My heart stuttered in my chest, and my ears burned. I definitely remembered Jackson's mouth on my neck, but I hadn't known he left a mark.

What was I supposed to say? He knew I'd been out with Jackson, and the evidence was right there.

"Dad, I..." I swallowed hard, struggling to say the words. "I love him."

I barely had time to register the blind rage in his face before the first hit came. The blow to the side of my head sent me stumbling backward.

"The hell you do!" he screamed. The ringing in my ear distorted the sound. I pushed back the urge to run.

I could take a hit. I just kept reminding myself that. A few hits and he'd be done. He always got bored with me.

But each hit got harder, and I crumbled. I didn't mean to, but I did. When his fist connected with my jaw, I went down. Blood coated my tongue, and I hurt everywhere. I covered my head but that didn't protect my stomach from the toe of his boot. Something cracked and pain exploded in my side. I cried out and scrambled across the floor. He grabbed the back of my shirt and dragged me to my feet.

"Please, stop!" I begged, fighting off his hands.

More words were shouted at me but I couldn't hear them over my own screaming and the sounds of his fists on my skin. When he grabbed me by the throat, he lifted me clean off the floor. I clawed at his hand and kicked with my feet. My throat burned, and black spots blotted my vision.

In a desperate move to get free, I kicked him in the balls as hard as I could. My steel-toed work boots made all the difference. He dropped me as he collapsed to his knees. Gasping and sobbing, I put as much distance between us as I could.

"You get out!" he hollered, his voice tight. "You get the fuck out of my house! I won't have some faggot for a son! You get the fuck out! Get out!"

I ran up the stairs two at a time and stormed through my room, tearing it apart as I grabbed whatever I could stuff in my backpack. The stash of money in my desk drawer, some clothes, the leather cord from Mom. It wasn't much. I didn't have much I could take with me.

The picture of Jackson and I on my desk stopped me in my tracks. Maybe I could go there? Maybe I could—

Heavy boots stomped up the stairs, and my heart lurched into my throat. *I had to get the fuck out of here.* I wasn't sure I could handle much more from him. I frantically took apart the frame and stuffed the picture in my bag before darting through the window onto the small overhang.

I'd snuck out this way more times than I could count. Getting from the overhang to the tree and dropping down was second nature. Even beaten, broken, and bloodied, I still managed to do it.

I was halfway down our drive when I dared to glance over my shoulder. He stood in the window. *Just watching.*

I couldn't stay here. He'd kill me. And I couldn't run to the Myles family house. I couldn't stay that close. My father would never hurt Jackson, but I suddenly understood that he'd have no problem killing me. Maybe not intentionally, but it'd happen. If I stayed, it'd happen.

I ran away and refused to look back.

CHAPTER 01

WEST

seventeen years later

"So, tell me, Jackson," the reporter—some woman named Sadie or some shit like that—said on the crappy bar TV, "*how does being the League's first openly gay bull rider affect your experience?*"

"Jesus fuck," I muttered into my beer. Who the fuck thought that was a goddamn good question?

"*Well, the only one who matters in this whole thing is the bull, and he only cares about two things as far as I'm concerned: tossing and trampling me. I think that's all there is to say about that,*" Jackson replied. I snorted, shaking my head.

Jackson Ford Myles: the League's poster boy for gay inclusion. What a fucking joke. Who cared where he put his dick?

Maybe I cared a little. It was a mix of resentment and interest if I was being honest with myself. Jackson was nothing but a bad reminder of what got me into this miserable fucking life. I glanced around the dingy, questionable biker bar. *Yeah, I was living it up.*

And yet, that didn't stop me from sizing him up every time I saw him on TV. He really leaned into the whole cowboy thing, except now it worked for him. That wayward chestnut hair was damn near blond from the sun while those bright blue eyes stood stark against his tanned skin. The full beard he had did nothing to hide the chiseled jaw. Head to toe, he had broad shoulders, bulging biceps, and a toned physique. Working the ranch did something for him.

The mention of *that* place soured my mood even further. I tipped back the rest of my beer and pushed away from the bar.

"He leaves the bar!" Vinnie shouted as if it was some great feat to get me to leave the bar. Vinnie Barton was about the closest thing I had to a friend, but I wouldn't call him that. I scowled as his scruffy face lit up with a laugh. *Douchebag.* "You going to come play cards with us or watch some more bull riding shit?"

"You know he's obsessed with that shit," Deaton commented. I hated Deaton Marcus—okay, I hated most people. But Deaton was President of the local Club and a special brand of asshole. I wasn't a member despite my leather and bike, but I ran into his crew. A lot. Most of them didn't like me but never took issues. *Except Deaton.* That might've had something to do with me accidentally picking up his girl one night. The only reason he hadn't killed me was because I was new and didn't have a fucking clue who anyone in town was. That didn't stop him from trying to create a reason to drag my ass out to the desert and slit my throat.

Which was why I never played fucking cards.

If only he knew I hadn't touched his girl, but that was a me problem.

"Like I've got a damn thing to do with what the fuck Mack puts on the TV," I snapped gruffly. I fished out my pack of cigarettes and propped one between my lips. "Maybe next time."

I wouldn't fucking play next time. They all knew it.

"I think you're scared I'll win," Deaton replied.

"Ain't fear if I know for a fact you'll fucking win. I like my money where it is." What little I fucking had anyway. Part-time work and a tiny ass trailer weren't getting me far in life. "Later, Vin."

"You coming out drinking tonight?" he asked—a little too hopeful. Vinnie and I always got into stupid shit when we drank too much. *Which was every time we went drinking.*

"Nah, got work," I told him. That wasn't a lie. I managed to pick up an extra shift on the late-night tow line for our area. It didn't pay much, but as a felon, I couldn't be picky. Work was hard enough to come by without doing shady shit. There were moments I was tempted—money was a big fucking motivator—but I was trying my damnedest not to fall out of line. Jail was the last fucking place I wanted to go.

Outside, I took a deep breath. *Fuck, I loved the fresh air.* It beat the stench inside the bar. I lit the cigarette and wandered across the parking lot, trying to think of ways to kill a few hours before my shift started. I could get something to eat, or I could go back to my trailer and make something. Both weren't appealing.

Truth was, if I went back to my trailer, I'd sit around thinking about Jackson, and I'd drown in a bottle all over again. *Some memories just haunted you.* I couldn't afford that shit. I needed this fucking job.

My phone rang—thankfully. I needed the fucking distraction. Except, I didn't recognize the number. *I did recognize the Oregon area code, though, which made my blood run cold.*

It wasn't Harrison's number, which was something at least.

"*Mr. Dakota McNamara?*" the man on the other end asked when I answered.

"Who the fuck is asking?" I demanded. I didn't like unsolicited phone calls, especially from people who used my first name.

"*My name is Charles Hart,*" he replied, completely undeterred by my attitude. Good on him. Still a fucking douchebag for calling. "*I represent the McNamara family in the Double Arrow Ranch estate.*"

"Yeah, I don't give a fuck about that shit," I told him. "And I don't handle that shit. You want my fucking father."

"*That's what I'm calling about. I'm handling Harrison McNamara's will.*"

My heart damn near stopped in my chest.

"My old man is dead?" My stomach rolled even as I asked the question.

"*Did no one contact you? I'm so sorry,*" Charles rushed to say. "*I thought someone had informed you of your father's passing. Had I known—*"

"Harrison McNamara has been dead to me for the better part of seventeen fucking years," I interrupted gruffly. "I didn't give a fuck about the old man then, and I sure as fuck don't give a fuck now."

That was mostly true. I didn't have nightmares about him finding and killing me no more, but I still found myself looking over my shoulder every once in a while. That man fucking destroyed me. Me. His own flesh and blood.

"*Well, there's the matter of the Double Arrow Ranch,*" he continued.

"I don't fucking want it," I said. "Sell it to the Myles. Give it to them for all I fucking care. I don't give a fuck."

"*Unfortunately, it isn't that simple—*"

"It is that simple. I don't want a fucking thing to do with that goddamn place."

"*I understand that, but—*"

"No buts," I growled.

"*In order to sell the place, Mr. McNamara, you have to come here personally to handle it. All of your father's affairs need to be handled,*" he explained. *Fuck, fuck, fuck.* I drew in a sharp breath. That unsteady clawing feeling weaseled its way into my chest as I tried to focus on my breathing. I didn't want to go back there. "*We just need a single meeting to handle it all. That's it.*"

"We?" I managed to ask.

"*The estate needs to be gone over with you and Mr. Myles—Jackson Myles,*" he told me.

"Fuck," I snapped. I ran a hand over my face. I couldn't go back, let alone be in the same fucking room as him. "Fuck!"

"*When should I set up this meeting?*" Charles continued without hesitation. This guy really did just fucking plow on forward.

"I can be there next Monday." I heard myself say the words but could barely comprehend them as they came out of my mouth.

The attorney kept talking, but I didn't hear a fucking word of it. I folded over and did my best to breathe while my stomach tried to empty itself and something awful tried to crush my lungs.

Double Arrow Ranch.
I didn't want to go back there.
And I certainly didn't want to see Jackson Myles again.

CHAPTER 02

JACKSON

F UCK BEING IN A good mood.

Fuck this goddamn meeting.

And fuck West McNamara. Maybe I'd call him Dakota just to piss him off. *Yeah, I was still bitter about the whole damn thing.* I loved him—I had for a long time—and I'd honestly been fooled into thinking he loved me too. That night in the field was supposed to be our turning point. But then that selfish asshole just walked away from it all. From the ranch. From his dad. From me.

There was no denying that Dakota West McNamara had broken my heart.

I would've been just fine—maybe a little hurt—if he'd told me that night had been a stupid fluke. A thing he didn't want. But to just leave without a fucking word? That shit fucked with my head.

I leaned against the only window in that tiny as fuck mediation room, arms crossed, boots crossed, and head tipped down. It made it impossible to see a damn thing over the brim of my Stetson. Not that I cared. Being stuck in a room with Charles Hart and Maggie Lawson wasn't how I wanted to spend the morning. Hart represented the McNamaras when it came to the ranch while Maggie represented my family. Why the hell my parents split the legal representation was beyond me. Dad died without ever telling me, and Mom's memory wasn't real great anymore. I learned early on to not ask questions unless it was dire to the function of the ranch. Maggie seemed to have all her shit in order, so I trusted her.

"I thought you said your client would be here, Mr. Hart," Maggie quipped once more, her tone tight.

Yeah, West was a good hour late. Color me fucking surprised.

"I have Mr. McNamara's assurances that he'll be here soon," Hart said.

"You've been saying that same fucking sentence for the last hour," I chimed him. I lifted my head, leveling my glare on him. He swallowed hard. That was the thing about me. On camera, I was a hell of a personality. Everyone loved the happy-go-lucky gay bull rider persona. What wasn't to love about that? But anyone who knew me outside of that? Well, they all knew it was a fucking smoke show. I was a mean son of a bitch when I wanted to be, and no one fucking messed with me. Gay didn't guarantee I was happy. It just meant I liked dick. I could be as grumpy as I fucking wanted. "I don't like my time being wasted. Is he showing up or not?"

"He'll be here," he insisted and then got right back on his phone. Pushing away from the table, he stormed out of the room. Apparently, Hart was none too impressed with his own client. *That made two of us.*

"I ain't staying much longer, Mags," I told her. "I got shit I need to do. A ranch don't run itself."

"I know," she replied. She leaned back in her chair and sighed. Maggie was older in a way that reminded me of my mom. Dark gray hair, crow's feet at the corners of her brown eyes, and a smile laced with cyanide. She looked as ready to rip West a new one as I was. Hell, I considered sticking around for just that. "And no one would blame you. I told Charles after everything it took to find Mr. McNamara that we shouldn't have set this damn meeting until we had him in the state."

"What the fuck does that mean?" I demanded.

"Let me just say that you dodged a bullet with that man wanting to sell," Maggie said. "It took two private investigators to even find him. His parole officer all but told us to just give up because keeping track of West McNamara is... in his words, a fucking feat."

"What the hell did he go to jail for?" I asked, frowning. I didn't need to know, considering how quickly I planned to forget the man, but we'd call it morbid curiosity.

"Armed robbery when he was nineteen. He never fired his weapon and he gave up real fast, which is probably the only reason his sentence was so short. But his behavior in prison was questionable at best." She rolled her eyes. "Should've kept him longer in my opinion with the number of drunken disorderlies and bar fights that man has racked up over the years. It's a miracle he's not back in jail."

Jesus fucking Christ. I ran a hand over my face as I tried to process all of that. I'd convinced myself that West was off living his best fucking life, but it sure as hell didn't sound that way. Not that it fucking mattered.

"Finally found him in a biker town in Colorado. He rents out a crappy trailer by the week, pays cash for everything, works under-the-table jobs, uses a burner phone," Maggie continued. "It's like he didn't want to be found. The man could've died and no one would've known."

"If we're entirely done with the gossip, Maggie," Hart interjected loudly as he rejoined us. "I told you my client would be here."

My gaze snapped to the door where West McNamara stood. *Fuck me.* He looked good—dangerously good for a man I wanted nothing to do with. Unkempt dark hair flared around his ears and off his neck and stuck out around the aviators atop his head. The thick beard on his face matched the unruliness of his hair. He'd filled out with broad shoulders and muscles in places no man had a right to be showing off in a shirt that fit that tight. The pushed-up sleeves on his Henley showed off ink on both arms and hands. He still wore the leather cord from his mother around his wrist, and the rest of his clothes looked just as old and worn as the cord—dirty work boots, faded jeans, and an old leather jacket that he carried.

But those gray eyes. Shit, there was a void there. Broken. Haunted. I couldn't quite explain it, but he looked every bit the invisible man he was trying to be.

His chin lifted slightly when he caught me staring.

"Jackson," he greeted without an ounce of emotion in his voice.

"About fucking time you showed up," I growled. "Next time you set a fucking meeting, you show up for the goddamn meeting. No one owes you shit here, and we sure as hell don't need to be waiting around for your ass to decide to show the fuck up."

The tension in the room skyrocketed as Hart and Maggie held their breath, waiting for whatever retaliation would come. The West I knew was a fucking fighter. There was a reason we needed lawyers and a neutral location to hash this shit out. Once he got started, there was no stopping him. *I wanted that fucking fight with him.*

"Let's just get this shit over with so I can get the fuck out of this state," West replied, giving in much to my surprise. And a little to my disappointment. He found a chair at the farthest end of the room and sat, putting his back to a corner.

"It's what you're fucking good at," I quipped just to be an asshole. His jaw ticked, but he said nothing.

"It's not going to be that easy," Hart said. Like the good attorney he was, he moved his chair to sit next to his client. I didn't miss the way West stiffened at his closeness.

"And why the fuck not?" West demanded.

"Well, your father—Harrison," he corrected quickly when West's scowl deepened. "Harrison had... concerns about your personal investment in Double Arrow Ranch after... well, he said... I'm not sure I want to repeat—"

West's hand slammed on the folder Hart held onto, making the man jump.

"You say the exact words he said, and I'll put your ass in an early grave, you feel me?" he growled. *Jesus fuck.* "Learn to summarize, Charles."

"Of course." The actual relief on the man's face was surprising. I found myself real damn curious about what Harrison had said. "Your father—Harrison didn't think you'd be of sound mind and clarity upon returning to Double Arrow Ranch."

"Of course he didn't," West scoffed.

"As a result, he had his will changed."

"To what?"

"In order to benefit from the sale of Double Arrow Ranch, you have to work the ranch for no less than one year. If you don't, you forfeit the money you'd make and everything automatically goes to Jackson Myles."

CHAPTER 03

"I HAVE TO *WHAT*?" I demanded. There was no way in hell I'd heard the stupid attorney right.

"In order to benefit from the sale of Double Arrow Ranch, you have to work the ranch for no less than one year. If you don't, you forfeit the money you'd make and everything automatically goes to Jackson Myles," Charles repeated.

"The fuck I will!" I exclaimed, shooting to my feet. Just the idea of going back there made my skin fucking crawl. *Was the room warm?* It felt fucking warm. I paced the length of the table, desperate for something to do with the panic clawing at my chest.

I didn't want to go back there. I didn't need that shit.

"There sure as fuck better be a workaround," Jackson growled. From the look on his face, he didn't have a clue about Harrison's change either.

Fuck, this was just one last ditch effort by my own fucking father to screw me over.

"There isn't," Charles said. "He has to work at Double Arrow Ranch—as an employee, not an owner—"

"Fucking hell," I muttered. *Of course, I'd have to work for Jackson.* That steely look he shot me didn't bode well for any of this. He was mad. I didn't even fucking blame him. I didn't have a clue what the hell Harrison had told him—probably made me out to be some fucking villain in Jackson's mind.

After all, I had left him, too, hadn't I?

"—in order to receive the money from the sale," he finished as if I hadn't said a word.

"How much?" I found myself asking. "How much would I forfeit if I just said fuck it?"

Maybe it wouldn't be worth my time.

"To sell off the almost fifteen thousand acres, you'd be set to make almost fifty million plus what the business itself is worth—"

"We're ready to sell for forty-seven," Jackson interrupted.

"*Fuck*," I groaned. That was more money than I could dream of. I wouldn't have to scrounge for odd jobs just to put food on my table ever again. I could find some quiet fucking place off the grid and be alone for good.

"Now, hold on." Charles sat taller. "The land alone is worth forty-nine million and some change. The business—"

"He ain't getting a single penny from the fucking business," Jackson snarled. "That's my business. I've put my blood, sweat, and time into it for the better part of a decade while your client was off doing what? Getting drunk? Robbing people? He'll be fucking happy I give him what I do for that land, and then he'll walk the fuck away."

"It's his family business too—"

"I don't give a fuck about the business," I interrupted before the two of them went back and forth on shit I didn't care about. If Jackson didn't want to pay me for the business, I didn't give a fuck. I just wanted to walk away and never look back. "He can have it. The forty-seven is fine. I just don't want to work a fucking year for this asshole."

"Oh, *I'm* the asshole?" Jackson pushed away from the wall, fists clenching.

"Before we do the whole alpha male thing, boys," Maggie snapped, "you have to understand there's not a damn thing we can do to get around Harrison McNamara's will. You two need to put on your big boy panties and act like men to figure out how the hell you're going to get through the next year—*if* you're going to get through the next year."

She chastised us like children, but maybe we deserved it.

"If I do this, I want to get paid. There ain't no way I can pull off working for a year and not get paid."

"You'll be paid." Charles nodded.

"There ain't no way I'm paying him to work his own fucking ranch," Jackson cut in.

"You're paying him to work *your* ranch, Mr. Myles," she corrected. "For this next year, the ownership of the ranch as far as Mr. McNamara is concerned is tied up in a trust. You'll be the sole owner with full executive decisions—minus firing Mr. McNamara."

"Jesus fuck," he grumbled. "This is a load of fucking bullshit."

I grunted my agreement. One year at the ranch in exchange for forty-seven million? *Fuck, most of my goddamn demons stemmed from that place and from Harrison.* I wasn't sure there was enough alcohol in Oregon to help me get through.

"Fine," Jackson said. "There's no way he'll stick around long enough to make it to a fucking year anyway. No skin off my back."

"Fuck you," I shot back. The problem was that he was right, even if he didn't know it. The longest commitment I'd ever made was prison, and it wasn't like I had a goddamn choice in that.

The fucking meeting had been a disaster. I went in hoping to sell and run, but instead, I was trapped. Yanking open the door to my truck, I fished my flask out from the inside door well. I tipped it back and took a long drink, desperate for the cheap burn and the relief that followed. Jackson was wrong. I wasn't just good at leaving. I was damn good at staying drunk and functioning. I didn't give a fuck. Alcohol chased away the demons in my head. The silence it offered was far better than the alternative.

One year. *One fucking year.* I could do this. I just had to keep telling myself that.

"Let's you and me get one fucking thing straight," Jackson damn near yelled as he stormed across the parking lot. His anger set my nerves on edge. I wanted to punch him in his stupid face and run all at the same time. I also wanted to knock that goddamn hat off his head and see if what they said about a cowboy and his hat were true.

Fuck, I was a mess.

"Fire away, *boss*," I snapped as I tossed my flask across the console. I reached for a piece of gum on instinct. Gum hid the smell of alcohol. No smell, no questions. I liked no questions.

"If you're going to work my ranch, you're going to respect my fucking rules," he began, and I rolled my eyes. "Starting with that shit right there. I am your goddamn boss, and this is my fucking ranch. I say jump, you say how high. None of this rebellious fucking bullshit you got going on. I don't need some felon coming in and fucking up what I've worked my ass off for."

"You going to be my daddy too?" I demanded, crossing my arms. We squared off, and he looked ready to rip my head off. While Jackson looked tough, I'd win in a fucking heartbeat if he took a swing. I'd done a lot of shady shit in my life, which meant I knew how to survive—fist fights, team-ups, weapon fights, I was used to it all. I had the scars to prove it. "Do I have a curfew too? Got to call you to tell you everywhere I fucking go?"

"You haven't in seventeen years, so why the hell would you start now?" he snarled. *Low fucking blow.* Maybe I deserved it.

"Whatever," I muttered. Fighting him would get me nowhere, and all I wanted to do was find a bar to drown in. Ignoring anything else he said, I climbed into my truck and turned it on. The engine was too old and a little too broken to run quietly. It made for a great escape tool. Out the open window, I pointed to my ear and shouted, "Sorry, *boss*, can't hear a fucking word you're saying."

From the way those blue eyes blazed with anger, Jackson heard every word. Good. I just needed him to stay pissed off and at a distance for one year. I wanted my money, and I wanted to get the fuck out of Oregon. I didn't need Jackson Myles opening old wounds he had no business poking around in.

CHAPTER 04

JACKSON

I SLAMMED THE DOOR to my truck, taking my anger out on it. Cussing out Harrison and West McNamara while I drove only did me so much good. What I really wanted was eight seconds on the back of a beast trying to take his rage out on me to center myself, but that shit wasn't happening. It left me wound up and ready to fucking snap.

My foreman, Mickey Hughes, sat on my porch when I rolled up. Mickey began working for my family when he was eighteen years old. That was over forty years ago—not that anyone ever brought up his age to him. Old and weathered, his gray hair was thinning, his skin was wrinkled, and those brown eyes were tired, but he didn't stop. I wasn't sure he knew the meaning of slow down. *And I wasn't about to tell him to either.* I may have been the ranch owner, but everyone around here knew Mickey was in charge.

He was also the only employee allowed at my house. No one else dared to cross the creek for a visit unless the world was ending. *It hadn't so far.*

"Your truck broke, boy?" Mickey asked as I stopped on the step.

"You know it ain't broke," I snapped.

"I'm guessin' the sale didn't go real well." He took off his hat, dropping it on his knee.

"It didn't go at all. Did you know Harrison changed his fucking will?"

"Boy, I don't take a shit without tellin' you what I'm doin'," he reminded me, his tone hardening. Unfortunately, that was true. The man told me everything he did on any given day without sparing me any fucking details. I sure as fuck wished he would though. "So, don't you go actin' like I kept somethin' from you."

"I know." I sighed and dropped into the rocking chair next to him. Sighing, I scrubbed a hand over my face. "Harrison changed his fucking will so it prohibits an immediate sale. Instead, the McNamara's half of the ranch has been put in a trust for the next year. West has to be my goddamn employee for one year in order to inherit and sell."

"That sick son of a bitch," Mickey grumbled. "He sure did know how to fuckin' stick it to you in the end, didn't he?"

"Yup," I muttered. That was the understatement of the century. It was no lie Harrison McNamara and I didn't see eye to eye. It'd been rough before my dad died, but these last five years? Fuck, they'd been a nightmare. I had no clue why the man fucking hated me, but every turn of business was a goddamn fight with him. And that was before his gambling problem toppled the ranch's finances.

I wasn't thrilled when anyone died, but I sure as fuck didn't feel bad when the old man keeled over from a heart attack either.

"So, what now?"

"Now, I just need to wait him out and sell in a fucking year."

"At the rate things are goin', you ain't goin' to have the money to settle up that deal." Mickey reminded me—not that I needed it. I didn't offer forty-seven to West because I wanted to cut him out of the business—I did, but that wasn't the reason behind the number. The truth was the ranch was drowning. I couldn't do it all. Between bull riding, sponsorship duties, and the ranch, I was stretched thin to my limit.

In the last year, we had not one but two viruses sweep the herd. It killed nearly half my cows, including most of the young. The recovery was brutal and almost didn't happen. As was, buying new stock was out of the question.

It also cost me half my men. *Not that I blamed them.* They had families to feed and take care of. But that left Mickey and I working our asses off to make up for it.

My plan had been to sell off the land once West was out of the question. That money could've been funneled back into the herd to pick the ranch off its ass. I had four months to figure this shit out. I didn't want to spend it chasing around West McNamara just to protect what was mine.

"How's he lookin'?" he asked, pulling me out of my thoughts.

"Like shit," I answered all too quickly. Mickey's head tipped back in the chair as he busted out laughing—a full, body-shaking kind of laugh that I rarely saw from him. *And at my own goddamn expense.* I scowled.

"Boy, you forget I've known you since you were born," he replied. I wanted to wipe that stupid grin off his face. "You may fool most of them, but you ain't foolin' me. And quit your grumpin'. I taught you that shit."

"Fuck you," I muttered. Mickey had been the first person I came out to, though he hadn't been surprised in the least. *Really no one was.* But he was the one person around the ranch who treated my sexuality like any other part of me—interesting only when it entertained him. Changing the subject, I said, "Look, I want you to run a full background check on West. I don't want any fucking surprises where he's concerned. We can't afford surprises."

"Speaking of surprises," Mickey began slowly.

"Fuck. Cows or horses?" *Because my luck would have my mom's horses getting sick now too.*

"Lost two in herd three on the west side last night."

"*Fuck.* It wasn't Daisy, was it?" I had a favorite cow. Couldn't fucking help it. Daisy was more dog than cow at this point, but I was fond of my girl. Most of my lunches on the ranch were spent cuddling that cow—not that I had a choice. That girl was the definition of forcing cuddling on anyone.

"That heifer?" He chuckled. "Nothin's goin' to kill that girl. Nah, these two were older, but I got the boys quarantinin' that portion of the herd."

Fuck, I wasn't sure we could keep segmenting the herd. As was, we had the fields divided up way more than I was comfortable with using makeshift fences. It was the best thing I could do to try containing the virus that kept killing my goddamn cows.

"Another thing," I continued, trying to sort my thoughts. *Fuck, this whole West situation had me riled up and all over the place.* "I don't give a fuck why he's here or that half of this is his family's land, I don't want West knowing any of the inside shit you know. Or anyone else. No one fucking talks to him. If he has questions about how my fucking business is going, he can ask me. I'll set him straight on where he fucking belongs."

"And where's that?"

"Gone. That's where. He did it once, he can do it again." I knew how I sounded, but I didn't fucking care. I didn't need West popping in for a year and fucking everything up. I had enough troubles without his help.

"Now, you ain't got a clue what sent that boy packin'," Mickey said quietly.

"Oh, I know." *Me.* While Harrison had never quite come out to say it, I had a feeling he found out what happened in that field that night between West and me. And Harrison had been real upfront about West's upset state of mind—ranting about this couldn't be his life and all that shit and how he was off to find something better. *Someone better.* The implication was real fucking hard to miss.

The worst part was that I'd fallen for West's shit in the field. Hell, that night all but confirmed what I'd been thinking about for the better part of a few years: I knew I loved West, but was I gay?

On top of that mess, I hadn't expected shit from West. He could've told me it was a mistake, and I would've recovered just fine. Hurt? Sure. But I was built tough. He didn't have to run away and never say a goddamn word to me again.

And so if West wanted to find someone better and leave me then fuck him. Karma was a force of fucking nature, and it sounded like she'd handed him his ass more than a few times. *Good.*

"I want him gone, Mick," I said, making my intentions as clear as day as I stared the old man down. I didn't want there to be any confusion. "He gets nothing extra, we give nothing but the bare minimum, and I want him gone. I don't care what the fuck it takes. I don't want West McNamara making it a fucking year here."

"Now, I know you got a bunch of hurt feelin's invested—"

"I'm not fucking hurt," I scoffed. "I'm fucking pissed. This is bullshit. You know it and I know it."

"—but you're startin' to sound a lot more like Harrison McNamara than Jacob Myles," Mickey finished. His entire expression hardened at the mention of my father. *Fuck.* "Your daddy was good man, boy, and I know you got a good heart in there too. I don't give a flyin' fuck how hurt you are over the shit that went down between you and West. You're a Myles, and your daddy would be rollin' in his grave if he thought you were tryin' to set that boy up to fail. Tryin' to cheat him out of what he's earned."

"He hasn't earned shit."

"And you don't know the full fuckin' story," he snapped. "You think you knew Harrison McNamara but you didn't, boy. You think you know everythin' about West McNamara, but you don't, boy. I suggest you get that thick head of yours out of your ass before he shows up here. If he don't cause trouble, neither should you. And I ain't sayin' more than that."

He slapped his knees as he stood, groaning the whole way. My scowl couldn't have been any deeper as I watched him meander down my front porch. *What the hell did he mean by the full story?*

What the hell did Mickey know that I didn't?

CHAPTER 05

WEST

Somewhere between drowning in cheap whiskey and knowing I needed to go, I forced myself to drive to Double Arrow. It took me forever to pull up the dirt drive leading to the entry arch. The thing hadn't changed in seventeen years. Knotted branches joined together to create some stupid fucking aesthetic. And that goddamn hanging sign at the top?

Double Arrow Ranch: Where Everyone is Family.

Fuck that.

I furiously smoked my way through another cigarette while I stared at that goddamn sign. I couldn't bring myself to drive under it. I needed to but fuck. I knew what was waiting for me down that drive.

Memories. Memories of shit I didn't want to go back to. My life had been fucking hell since I ran to get away from Harrison. I'd accepted that my life was crap. I'd accepted just how fucking broken and worthless I was. I made do with working to get by, staying alone, and keeping my head down.

And never looking back. At least, trying not to look back. Sometimes, I couldn't help but wonder if my past would catch up to me.

It did, and fuck me, I'd never be ready for it. All I needed to do was keep my head down, do my fucking job, and survive the year. I could do that. Would probably take copious amounts of alcohol, but I could do it.

I hoped to hell I could do it.

The main drive beyond the ranch entrance wound through a thick patch of trees and opened up to the main fields. It split three ways. That first path on the right would've taken me right up to Myles' house. I'd leave that path alone. Considering Jackson had taken over, there was no doubt that it was his house now. I didn't need any part of pissing him off just by existing in more of his space than necessary.

The middle drive went straight back to the stables. The whole ranch branched out from there. Fields for cattle, the barn, equipment storage, employee living, and everything else. It was the most traveled path of the three.

And if I took that far left path, I'd end up straight at Harrison's house. That thought made my heart race. I wanted nothing to do with that. It could burn to the ground for all I fucking cared. There was no way I was going back there. I didn't give a fuck if my old man was dead.

To the stables with me, it was. At least I'd always felt at home around the horses.

The stables were dark when I pulled my truck along the back of the old building. The red wood was peeling and in definite need of cleaning. Even the smell was off as I got out. *Fuck, had they not been taking care of the goddamn horses?* Hard to believe Jackson would let that happen considering the horses were his mother's passion project.

I let myself in and let out a sound of frustration as I flipped the overhead light on. The herd had dwindled, and the stable was in crap condition. It needed a damn good cleaning, and the horses needed more attention than they were getting. It pissed me off. They deserved better.

I took a quiet survey as I walked down the center aisle. Most of the horses I didn't recognize, but there were a handful along the way that I did. Older horses that Mrs. Myles had let me help take care of when I was younger.

Somewhere in the middle of my inspection, I stopped and stared at the horse with her snout hanging over the stall door. My chest tightened painfully. The soft gray leopard Appaloosa watching me was fucking gorgeous. *My girl was gorgeous.*

"Hey, pretty girl," I whispered and held my hands near her snout. I wasn't sure how to approach her. *Did she even remember me?* Bailey's ears twitched as she let out a huffy breath. It took a moment but she pushed her nose into my palms. For the first time in a very long time, a genuine smile turned my lips. I ran my hands over her velvet snout as she pushed harder into me. "Oh, I missed you, sweet thing."

Emotions choked up my throat, and I stepped closer, bringing her head against my chest. The fact that Bailey was still alive surprised me. She had to be twenty years old. Sure, it wasn't uncommon, but I hadn't pictured reuniting with her.

Pulling open the stall door, I took the time to inspect her head to toe. Her coat was dusty, her mane and tail needed a good brushing, and her hooves looked in desperate need of trimming. I frowned as I smoothed my hands down her neck once more. How she leaned into me was reassuring. *At least I hadn't quite lost everything.*

"I've got you, pretty girl," I promised. "I've got all of you."

CHAPTER 06

JACKSON

Mickey's face wasn't the first thing I wanted to see in the morning. I stood in my doorway wearing a pair of sweatpants and nothing else as I waited for my coffee to brew. I scowled at my foreman's presence in my doorway, but as always, Mickey never flinched.

He did, however, spoil Tess with one too many treats as he stood there. Tess was my red border collie. She was smart as a whip, great at herding, and a big fucking baby for Mickey whenever he was around.

"What the fuck do you want this early?" I demanded.

"Mornin' to you too, you grumpy shit," he greeted with that toothy grin of his. "I got a question for you."

"What?" Without explicitly saying so, I invited him in just so I could get my coffee. He followed, removing his hat and holding it close to my chest.

"What exactly do you want my boys doin' this mornin'?"

"It's stables day," I reminded him. I fucking hated my mother's horses, but I kept them as an honor to her. All we really needed were a few horses for the men to use to get around the ranch. Keeping a fucking herd didn't interest me. It was just more work, more money, and more time wasted—things I didn't need and didn't have.

"About that," Mickey began, "West did it all already."

That sentence both gave me pause and made my blood run hot. I didn't want West doing a damn thing on my ranch without my permission, and he didn't have my permission to fuck around with my horses.

"West did *what* exactly?" I frowned. I certainly didn't give him permission to do shit. *And I didn't need that man waking up before me just to show me the fuck up.*

"Oh, he cleaned the stables, but he fuckin' cleared it all out," he explained. "Power washed that thing top to bottom. While that dried out, he's been washin' and groomin' the horses. He's takin' his time with that one to trim their hooves too."

I took a long sip of black coffee, doing my damnedest to process what he'd just said. It wasn't even six. *In the fucking morning.*

"There ain't no way in hell he did all that this morning," I snapped finally. "Not unless he did a shit poor job."

Which he probably did. As far as I knew, ranch hand wasn't on his resume of odd jobs. There was no way in hell he knew how to take care of the horses. I highly doubted he remembered all that shit from when we were kids. Sure, West had always taken to my mother's horses. He'd skip out on the lessons our dads taught us about running a ranch to go spend time with my mom and the horses. He'd lose himself in them for days on end if we let him.

"Nah, he did a damn fine one," Mickey replied. "It's lookin' better than it has in fuckin' years. "

"Give me five." I didn't wait for an answer as I stormed up the stairs. There was no way in hell West pulled off some shit like that. I refused to believe it until I saw it for myself.

It took me less than four minutes to get into clothes for the day. I found Mickey on the porch with Tess eating up every bit of attention he gave her. Snapping my fingers, I tried to get her attention, but she just gave me a judgy side-eye while Mickey laughed.

"Damn dog," I muttered and didn't mean it. Mickey just babied the hell out of her, and she lived for every second of it. "Let's go, Mick."

"You go ahead, boy," he replied. "I'm goin' to spend a few minutes with my favorite girl."

In other words: he wasn't getting off my porch any time soon. Not uncommon for Mickey these days. I gave him leeway because no one worked harder than he did. The rest of my ranch hands could stand to learn a thing or two from him about work ethic.

The fastest way to the stables was by truck—though, sometimes I did take my horse, Zeus. That just depended on the level of forethought I had the night before. My truck jostled and bounced along the dirt road. I took it slow in case a cow got out. We had broken fences that needed fixing and temporary fences that didn't do shit. As a result, my cows sometimes wandered. I didn't mind it, but I had a strict slow the fuck down rule on my ranch. The last thing I needed was for someone to hit one of my girls because they weren't paying attention.

The stables came into view, and it was a fucking mess. My ranch hands clumped together on the dirt in small groups, and all of them were watching West. I hopped out of my truck to survey the entire situation before getting involved.

We kept two stables: one for the working horses and one for my mother's horses. Both stables had been emptied out with the horses kept in a nearby area. Water soaked the dirt, spilling out of both stables in rivulets. In the space between both, West stood bent over a horse with a hoof stand between his knees. He worked efficiently with a pair of nippers to trim down the horse's hooves—and damn if that wasn't the most fucking patient I'd ever seen Beamer while undergoing a trimming.

All the while as West worked, Bailey hovered with her snout pressed into his back. It was as if she wasn't about to let him out of her sight again. It did something uncomfortable to my heart. I cursed under my breath. I didn't need *that* fucking complication in my life.

Every so often, West stopped to pull sugar cubes from his pocket. He alternated between feeding them to Beamer and Bailey.

This West was different in a way I couldn't quite put my finger on. There was a softness to him as he handled the horses, talking quietly and moving carefully. It was like a glimpse into the past—of who he used to be.

That whole thought pissed me the fuck off.

"He say anything?" I demanded as I approached three of my ranch hands, specifically talking to Jake. Jake was young, but he was damn good at working my ranch—focused and driven. If he kept it up, he was my pick to replace Mickey when the old man finally retired.

"Just one sentence. Don't touch him to get his attention," Jake said. When I glanced at him in confusion, he just shrugged. "Don't ask me, boss. I ain't got a clue what it means."

I grunted but said nothing else. Though, I did want to push the matter by doing the exact opposite of his request.

"So, uh..." Peter, a seasonal ranch hand, shifted uncomfortably. The kid had been working for me for years and still got awkward whenever he had to talk to me. I blamed poor social skills. Mickey said it was because I was a mean son of a bitch and scared the kid. "Does this mean we answer to both of you now that he's back?"

My temper flared.

"Listen up, you lazy fucks!" I shouted to get everyone's attention. It wasn't hard. I was loud. I stepped back to make sure they all saw me. "Just because West McNamara is back don't mean you work for him. It's my name on your fucking checks. You work for me, you take only my orders or Mickey's, and if you go behind my back at all to do a damn thing *he* fucking tells you, you best start looking for a new job. Do I make myself clear?"

The mumble of agreement that greeted my ears was sufficient enough. I didn't bother looking at them. I watched West for some kind of reaction, but all he did was flick his gaze in my direction for a second before going back to Beamer.

"Now, I'm paying you to work, so get to fucking work," I snapped. "There's shit to be done so go do it!"

"But our horses!" Tyler said and motioned to the paddock.

"You got feet, don't you?" I retorted. "Walk your scrawny ass to a fucking UTV and drive where you need to go, boy! And don't hit my fucking cows."

While they dutifully filed out of the area for the day, I made it my job to inspect everything West had done inside the stables. I stalked down the aisle and paused inside each stall to give it a good once over. Short of the mud I tracked in on my boots, the place was damn near spotless.

All the blankets had been tossed in the back with the washer and dryer on while a stack of clean ones were folded on a nearby table. *Fuck, he'd even done their laundry.* Buckets were clean, waterers cleaned and refilled, and the mats had been scrubbed clean. Hell, even the walls had been hosed down.

I stood with my hands on my hips, trying to find one thing wrong but couldn't. This kind of work took time. *A lot of time*

"There ain't no way in hell you did all this this morning," I said to him as I exited the stables. "That's too much work for a short fucking time."

"Don't sleep much," West muttered, never looking up.

"Did you work all fucking night?" I demanded. His silence told me all I needed to know. "Nuh-uh. We don't do that shit here. My ranch, my rules. My employees don't work overnight."

That was a whole legal can of worms I didn't need to open.

"Then don't fucking pay me for last night," he replied. More soft words came out of him as he set down Beamer's leg and rubbed the muscle. When he finally did give me the time of day, it was to glare at me. "The horses needed tending to so I fucking did it. If you've got a problem with the hours, whatever. I don't give a fuck."

With gentle hands and quiet words, he turned Beamer around and guided the horse into the paddock with the rest of them. Bailey remained practically glued to West during the whole thing. I had a feeling that horse would be attached to his hip unless he made her go away.

"You got something you want to say?" West asked after locking the gate. He pulled a small towel from his back pocket and wiped his hands.

I grunted again, passing by him to survey the second stable. Just like the first, it was damn near pristine. *Fuck.* I wanted to be mad. Hell, I was mad but not at the job he'd done. No one had done half as well in fucking years—my fault, not theirs. I just didn't have the space to care as much as I should.

"From now on, you don't do shit on my ranch to my business without fucking telling me," I clipped. "I run my business my way. I ain't about to have you come in and try to change that. One year you're mine. That means you do what I say when I fucking say it. I ain't got a fucking problem telling the lawyers I can't work you and then firing your ass."

I wasn't actually sure if I could fire his ass, but he didn't know that. *Definitely needed to ask Maggie about that one.*

"No," West said. *So fucking close.* His shoulders squared off as my eyes narrowed. "You ain't the boss of me. Not with this."

"The hell did you say?" I demanded, my temper flaring. I stepped up close and watched his entire body go rigid.

"You've done a shit job taking care of them. They're animals," he continued all too brazenly. "They deserve to be treated with respect and to be taken care of. They're your horses. You're fucking responsible for them, and until you get your head out of your goddamn ass and realize that, I ain't taking orders from you."

"You keep talking and I'll put your ass on the ground," I warned.

"Try it, and I promise you won't get back up again," West replied. There was an odd calmness to him as he chewed his stupid gum and stared me down. It was both unnerving and infuriating.

Intimidating him wouldn't work. I had to switch tactics.

"You want to take care of the fucking horses, fine. They're all yours since you're so fucking keen on everything." I gestured between the two stables. "All of this, my men ain't helping you. You think you know better, then you figure it all out."

"I will."

"Good," I told him with a smirk. He had no fucking clue what he was getting into. "Mickey's horse is Annie, Peter's horse is Checkers, and Jake's horse is Lucky Luna. The three of them are here at five every fucking morning. The horses need to be fed, brushed out, saddled, and ready to go before they get here. Not a minute later. Javi's horse is Ruby Rider, Tyler's horse is Thunderstruck, Nicky's horse is Noir, and Caleb's horse is Pippa. They get here at five-thirty. I expect the same shit with their horses. And my horse is Zeus. I leave at six."

"And I'm guessing you're about to fucking tell me I can't ask who or what to figure this shit out, is that right?" His gaze slid over the mingling herd of horses.

"You bet your ass that's right. You want to fuck around on my ranch, you'll find out I ain't playing games."

His jaw ticked as he simply nodded. I would've given anything to know what the fuck was going on in that head of his.

But I knew one thing: I wasn't letting him out of my sight. I strode back to my truck and dropped the tailgate. Making myself comfortable, I stayed silent as I watched West because I didn't trust him to not fuck everything up. Mickey could run shit for me for the day. I knew he wouldn't steer me wrong. *But West?* I didn't trust him in the least.

CHAPTER 07

WEST

Cold water never felt so fucking good in my life. I didn't care that it came from the stable hose or that I stood buck ass naked in my fucking boots. All I cared about was how damn good it felt to wash the grime and shit off my skin.

My muscles ached. I couldn't remember the last time I worked so fucking hard in my life. After fighting with Jackson, I prioritized the ranch hand horses. That took way longer than needed because I couldn't figure out who belonged to who. I damn near contemplated murder as I tried to sort the horses. Luckily, they seemed to know their stalls, and the stalls were labeled. I was fairly certain the small lot of them were tended to properly and ready to be saddled tomorrow.

I'd do the rest of the herd tomorrow. Still pissed me off that I even had to. They deserved better. They never did anything to anyone other than exist, and they weren't being cared for right.

Unfortunately, as I tried to settle down for the night, my head wouldn't stop buzzing, and my skin kept crawling. Clothes scraped uncomfortably on my skin, and every fucking noise made me jump. Horses moving, grass rustling, an engine turning over somewhere. *Everything.*

There was no way in hell I'd get any sleep until I soothed my demons. Which was why I ended up unpacking my motorcycle from the bed of my truck and driving into town after dark. I took the long way, knowing the roads like the back of my hand. It was funny how some things were just fucking muscle memory, even after seventeen years. I liked the quiet and the dark that a night ride had to offer.

Wood Springs was the big kind of small town. The population was small, but it was all ranchers and farmers. Lots of land spread out between them. The downtown was a single road. That was it. One fucking road with the essentials needed to survive. Lots of residents made the big trek up to Eugene once a month to stock up on the things they couldn't find in Wood Springs.

Thankfully, the only bar, *Lucky Lenny*, was still considered a town staple. It was small, dingy, and probably full of health code violations. *But it'd do.* That was all I fucking cared about as I walked in the door.

Of the five tables, one was occupied by two older guys talking and a party of three sat at another table. Two men also sat at the long bar, chatting with Lenny. When I walked in, all chatter stopped and eight heads turned in my direction. *Fuck.*

"They said you came back to town," Lenny commented from the bar. I knew Lenny going way back. There'd been a few too many nights I'd illegally driven out here to peel my old man off the bar floor. I would've gone to a different bar if that was even a fucking option.

"They weren't wrong. Beer, please. I don't give a fuck what," I said as I picked a lone spot at the bar that gave me a good view of the door and put no one at my back.

"Your father had a lot to say about you," he continued without moving.

"I'm sure he fucking did," I replied tightly. "Harrison McNamara always did have an opinion about everyone and everything."

A loud fucking opinion.

"He had a lot to say about the kind of man you are," Lenny snapped. "About the kinds of things you like to do and the people you do them with."

Ah, there it was. Good ol' Wood Springs, where the people are welcoming as long as you look like them, think like them, and fuck like them.

"Do you like making money, Lenny?" I demanded, refusing to acknowledge the not-so-subtle homophobia. "You're looking a little scarce in the patron department tonight. It's a handful of regulars nursing a beer or two, am I right? Now, I got money to spend and I want a beer. Am I drinking here or going down to Merrillville instead?"

The idea of going there made my skin crawl. Merrillville had a lively population with heavily trafficked tourist attractions. I'd buy cheap gas station beer before I picked a bar in Merrillville. He didn't need to know that though. He needed the money just like anyone else in Wood Springs did.

"You pay upfront," he grumbled as he poured a cheap beer. "I ain't opening no tab for the likes of you, you hear me? And I'm charging you double. Your father died with an open tab."

"Of course he did," I muttered under my breath but put down the money nonetheless. I just wanted my fucking drink, even if it meant paying off Harrison's debt in the process. Lenny set down the drink, making me reach for it as if he couldn't handle the thought of getting too close to me. *Fucking idiot.*

The beer was warm and crappy, but it did the job. By the time I reached the bottom of the glass, the demons in my head were beginning to settle down. That buzz began to fade while my skin didn't bother me as much. The ache and discomfort were there, but after a few more drinks, I wouldn't notice that either.

Without a word, I put more money down—extra to pay Harrison's fucking tab too—and Lenny handed me another drink. At least the world went on like I didn't exist, making it easy to lose myself in the comfort of my drink.

"Evening, Mickey," Lenny greeted with a genuine smile. My daze faded, and I stiffened. I had no desire to talk to Mickey. I'd managed to avoid him on the fucking ranch—not very well but still. I didn't want to talk to him while I tried to keep the demons at bay.

"Evenin', Lenny," Mickey replied, taking his hat off. "Good night?"

"Some unwanted vermin but the money pays," he said, and I scoffed into my beer.

"That ain't no way to talk about the Wilson brothers over there." He used his hat to gesture to the two men in the corner. "They got just as much right to be here as the rest of us. Their next beer is on me."

Lenny let out a disgruntled sound but let the matter go. Looking pleased with himself, Mickey walked his way to the bar and sat two stools down.

"Some folks never learn," he muttered. "You're lookin' good, West. Never did get the chance to say howdy."

I eyed him for a long moment, trying to decide just how fucking sincere he was. That sad look on his face told me everything I needed to know.

"I told you then and I'll tell you now," I began, my tone dark, "go home, Mickey."

I didn't want Mickey's help and I sure as hell didn't want his pity. He was the only one I was sure knew the shit I'd gone through after leaving the ranch. But considering how close he was with my *boss*, I had no doubt Jackson knew too. I'd rather Mickey be a grade-A asshole to me than be nice. I knew what to do with assholes. I didn't trust a nice gesture. The hit always came after and hurt so much more.

"Now, look, son, I—"

"I ain't your son," I snapped over him. "I ain't your boy, I ain't your responsibility, and I sure as hell don't want your pity, Mick. You want to pity someone? Find someone else who fucking needs it because that ain't me. I'm just fine the way I am."

"No, you ain't fine." Mickey sighed, but to his credit, he did ease back off the barstool and swiped up his hat. He paused, staring at my profile for a long minute, but I refused to turn. Instead, I focused on my drink.

Tension clawed at my chest. I didn't want to fight Mickey, but I would if it made him leave me the fuck alone. To my relief, though, he only stood there an extra minute before walking away, his boots loud in the bar.

"Another," I said quietly to Lenny after I gulped down the last of my beer.

Mickey was right about one thing: I wasn't fine. I hadn't been in seventeen years.

CHAPTER 08

JACKSON

The horses were saddled and ready to go, tied to the fence, but West was nowhere to be seen. While I usually went out at six, I'd woken up earlier to make sure he didn't fuck over my men. I walked the perimeter of the stables in an attempt to find him, considering he had a fucking job to do.

His truck sat along the back of the building with a motorcycle parked alongside it. *Was that all he brought with him?* The black Harley was well taken care of while the truck had clearly seen better days with its rust and chipped paint.

Lying in the truck bed with a jacket tossed over his chest was West, passed out. *Jesus fucking Christ.*

"Hey!" I yelled before kicking the bumper. West bolted upright in a panic, eyes wide. He battled his jacket as he tried to get it off. "What the fuck do you think you're doing?"

"What the fuck is wrong with you?" West snarled as he threw his jacket aside. He stumbled to his feet and dropped out of the truck bed, his knees practically giving out on the way down.

"This is your fucking job and you're passed out drunk—"

"Fuck off. I'm allowed to drink during off hours."

"This ain't off hours—"

"Last night, you fucking moron!" he interrupted. "Don't believe me? Go ask Lenny. He'll have all sorts of opinions to fucking share. Not sure he'll share them with the town's gay bull rider but who knows? Maybe you can fucking kick it out of him too."

I avoided *Lucky Lenny* like the plague. Dealing with Lenny's homophobic rants and bullshit made me want to put his face through the bar.

"What the hell is wrong with you?" I asked instead.

"You! You're what's wrong with me!" West ranted. From the liquor on his breath and the glassiness in his eyes, he was still drunk. *Just what I fucking needed.* "You and your stupid fucking attitude. I did the job! You wanted those goddamn horses taken care of, they are! And I did a damn good job, even with all your stupid ass rules. I figured it out, and I did a damn good job! I know you fucking know it. So why don't you get the fuck out of my face and let me sleep! Fuck!"

He kicked the wheel of his truck in anger. There was no fucking reasoning with him at this point—not that I wanted to.

"Your ass better be fucking sober when the day is done," I snapped. "It's your job to take care of the horses, and I expect you to do your goddamn job."

"Fuck off," he muttered again. He ran his hands through his hair and scrubbed them over his face.

"Fuck this up and you're done," I warned him. "I don't give a fuck what the goddamn lawyers say. I won't have you on my fucking ranch."

"I said fuck off," he repeated. "Get off your high horse, you asshole. You've proven you don't give a fuck about those horses."

Anger boiled my blood. I clenched my fist and seriously considered hitting him. *Oh, how I wanted to fucking put him on his ass.*

"Don't fuck this up," I repeated and stormed away before I did just that.

Year in and year out I poured everything I had into this place, and it only made me grumpier. Some days, I wondered why the hell I didn't just sell. *Take the money and start over.* Unfortunately, I didn't have a solid reason as to why I should—at least not one that didn't make me sound like a fucking child throwing a tantrum. Family legacy was important. My father and his father before him and all the rest had poured their blood, sweat, and time into it.

I may have been cut from the same cloth as my father, but I wasn't fucking made for this.

It made the days long—longer than they should've been—and by the time I guided Zeus into the paddock for end-of-day maintenance, I was coiled tight. My guys were in a good mood, so that was something. They chatted and made plans that I quickly turned down when they offered.

As they disappeared, I stopped at the fence alongside Mickey to watch West work. *Shirtless as he washed a horse.*

The universe hated me—was getting in a good fucking laugh—because Jesus fuck, West McNamara had filled out fine. Broad shoulders, a strong back, and a tapered waist. Those dark jeans of his showed off muscular thighs and an ass I didn't need to be noticing. Black ink covered his tanned skin in a wild array of tattoos. The most prominent was the pair of angel wings coming out of his shoulder blades, covering both arms, and ending in roses on his hands. Barbed wire spiraled down his spine while stars cascaded over his right side.

The nine rough scars etched into his left side piqued my curiosity, but I'd be damned if I'd ever ask what happened. So did the fact that he had barbells through his nipples—but again, things I didn't need to be noticing.

I hated the man, but fuck me, my dick had other thoughts. *Thoughts I tried to shove aside because I didn't need to be sporting a hard-on while staring at him.*

"You keep lookin' at him like that, boy, and I'm goin' to start questionin' if you want to fire him or fuck him," Mickey commented, ripping me out of my borderline dirty thoughts.

"Jesus fuck, Mickey," I scoffed. I turned to the old man, but he just had that shit-eating grin on his face. "What the fuck made you think that was okay to say?"

"Look on back at him and I'll take you a picture," he said. "You had that same look on your face with Eli year before last."

Fucking Eli. Eli was the dumbest thing I'd ever done. I maintained hard boundaries with my employees but Eli got under my skin. I hated the man, but I also couldn't stop my dick from intervening when I talked to him. Instead of firing him on a Friday like I meant to, I spent a weekend fucking him. That made Monday real awkward when I actually had to fire the insufferable man.

"I'm startin' to think hate fuckin' is your thing," he commented.

"Jesus fucking Christ, Mickey! Do you have a filter?"

"Around them? Sure. Around you? Nope." *Cheeky fucking man.* "Don't you worry, boy, all dicks need attention."

"Mickey!" I snapped. I didn't need to be talking about my attention-starved dick with Mickey. Admittedly, I only got laid a few times a year while on the road with the League. And I was real fucking careful when I did that. I didn't fuck around when it came to my employees, and Wood Springs was so goddamn small that I was fairly certain I was the only gay man in town—at least openly anyway.

Except for maybe West, but I didn't have a fucking clue what he was. *And I didn't want to think about it either.*

When he stopped to take a long drink from a black water bottle, I frowned. Why did I have a sinking suspicion he didn't have water in there?

"How much does he drink?" I asked. That was a matter that needed attention. I didn't need him drunk and screwing shit up.

"Boy, you don't know that's what he's got in his bottle," he replied.

"Come on, Mick, don't think me a fool," I said. "We both know Harrison was so far down the bottle that he bled whiskey."

"No reason to think that boy followed in his footsteps."

"He was drunk this morning," I told him. "And working on the horses. How drunk is another fucking question, but I can't have him showing up like that. He's going to get hurt and then it's my fault. I'll be damned if I'm paying out because he's a fucking drunk."

"Boy, we need to have a fuckin' talk," Mickey announced. He took off his hat, rubbing the brim between his weathered fingers. I leaned against the fence post as I waited for him to collect his thoughts. "I understand you got issues with that boy after him leavin' you and shit—"

"He didn't leave me," I interrupted angrily. "I don't give a fuck about him leaving."

"You always were a shit liar, Jackson," he said. "That boy left you more than he left anyone else here. Don't think me a fool. I saw the way you two were. It ain't a far leap to know you had feelin's."

"Get to your point, Mickey." I scowled, hating every fucking sentence coming out of his mouth.

"You need to learn to give people some grace—now more than ever," he said. "There are just some times in life you need to learn to shut your goddamn mouth instead of lashin' out with all that anger of yours. This right here... this is one of them moments."

I considered his words. Mickey was about the only person in the world who could get away with calling me out on my shit. I listened to him too—most of the time. This time, though... this wasn't one of them. Everything about West's presence in my space pissed me the fuck off. Without a reason why, I wasn't stopping until he was gone.

"You going to tell me why?" I asked.

"There are some things you're better off not knowin', boy, and should count yourself lucky that you don't," he replied.

"Then no, I ain't going easy on him, Mick," I told him. Without a word, I left him standing there. I needed a cold shower and something to sear the image of West shirtless out of my brain.

CHAPTER 09

JACKSON

Magnolia Myles had zero fucks to give. After my dad died, Mom changed. I had worried it'd be for the worst, but fuck, my mom was living her best life. *Life was too short and all that.*

She lived in a senior's place—the kind with a few nurses on staff, individual apartments, and more social events than anyone needed. They had parties, card nights, brunches, and more. These old fucks really did live it up. I was also fairly certain that a few too many of them were fucking around whenever they could. More props to them if their dicks were still working.

"Ladies! Who wants a picture with a real live cowboy?" Mom exclaimed when she saw me walking across the dining hall toward her. "I mean, just look at that saunter and hair. Son, you're looking like something right out of a John Wayne movie."

Her nose crinkled as she smiled at me. I bent down and kissed her cheek, overwhelmed by her floral perfume. She always did wear too much.

"Ain't sure if that's a good thing or a bad thing, Ma." I chuckled. "And stop trying to pimp your son out."

"Honey, you're a gay bull rider. I'd be stupid not to capitalize on it whenever you came to visit me," she retorted and tossed me a wink. I knew she was kidding. Mom was fiercely protective of me. We had some serious citation issues the first few weeks after she moved in because some people had choice opinions about her gay bull riding son. It was all fun and games now, but she'd gotten into a few fights over it. As I sat down, she asked, "How's my handsome boy doing? You're looking a little tired there, Jackson. Are you sleeping or are you working?"

"Can't I do both?"

"And when was the last time you did *both*?" She arched a brow and waited for me to give her an answer. Instead, I grabbed a toothpick from the condiment turntable and jammed it between my teeth. I offered her a cheeky grin, doing whatever I could to not answer. "That's what I thought. Jackson Myles wouldn't know what life balance was if it hit him square in the face."

"Depending on how big it is, I might dodge before it can hit me," I answered with a little too much sass, making her laugh. I got that shit from her.

"How are things on the ranch? Quiet, I hope. No more chaos?" Mom asked. I knew what chaos she was referring to, which had nothing to do with my current predicament. Still, I frowned. "I don't like that face, Jackson. What's going on?"

"Did you know Harrison changed his will?" I opened a deck of cards, handing them to her. Mom and I played a lot of cards while we talked. It was an easy thing for both of us to do with the latent energy we both struggled with.

"Good riddance with that man," she snapped. "What the fuck did he do now? Wasn't good enough to just die and leave us alone?"

I chuckled like I always did when Mom swore. I disliked Harrison, but Mom downright hated him. For what reason, I had no idea.

"Well," I began with a sigh, "looks like I ain't selling to West anytime soon. Harrison made it so he has to work the ranch for one year before he's given ownership of the land and can sell."

"What a load of fucking bullshit," she spat. "He knew that boy would never come back—will never come back."

"West is back at the ranch, Ma," I told her. Those words stopped her mid-shuffle. Something sad crossed her expression.

"Oh, that poor boy," she whispered.

"See, it's reactions like that that tell me I'm missing out on something here," I said. "Something fucking vital to me running my ranch."

"Just go easy on him, Jackson," Mom replied instead. "You're so stubborn and hardheaded like your Dad was. I've seen you out there. I know you're hard on those men—almost as hard as you are on yourself—but you can't be that way with West."

"And why not?" I demanded. Someone somewhere knew some shit that I wanted to know. It was ridiculous how hard it was to get Mickey and her to fucking talk about any of it.

"It's nothing you need to work your handsome little self up about, Jackson," she dismissed.

"It's my ranch, Ma," I reminded her. "I have a right to know if he's about to fuck up my ranch."

"Or maybe you just use a little bit of that empathy I worked so damn hard to teach you about." Her dark eyes caught mine, full of fire and tempting me to argue with her. *Fuck.* I was a thirty-four year old man and that look still got me. "You don't need to know what's going on in someone else's life to exercise empathy. Maybe you should try fighting less and show more compassion—scratch that. You *should* try fighting less and show more compassion. It wouldn't hurt you. I know that ranch gets to you, and I know you ain't happy there, but that don't mean you can go around taking it out on others. And at the very least, you best not be taking it out on West McNamara. Do I make myself clear?"

"Yes, ma'am," I muttered. I had no intention of listening to her. It wasn't the first time we'd had a conversation like this. Mom thought I needed to be less grumpy and smile more. That thought held no appeal to me because then people would want to fucking talk to me. I spent roughly seven months a year putting on a smoke show to make people fucking happy—the happy gay bull rider that my agent insisted I be.

There was no way in hell I would spend my good months off playing into the same facade.

"Now, are you going to listen to your mama, or am I about to start selling photo opportunities with you?" She batted her lashes playfully, but

I knew better. Magnolia Myles had no fucks to give. She would make me take pictures with every goddamn person in the place if I tested her.

CHAPTER 10

WEST

I went over the list in my head. *One time. Two times. Three times. Fifteen times.* The horses needed stuff—real things for the stables—and both buildings needed repair. How the fuck they'd let this shit go so bad was beyond me.

I would've thought Jackson cared, considering they were his mom's, but I would've thought a lot of things about him. Instead, he was just a grumpy fucking asshole putting on a show for money. And he hated me.

That singular fact meant he would make my life hell when I handed him a list of shit he had to buy. I seriously contemplated just buying everything and making him pay me back, but I couldn't afford it. I didn't have a bank account and I sure as fuck didn't have the cash for it. Hell, I even thought about asking Mickey to handle it but knew better.

Jackson fucking Myles was the damn obstacle I needed to conquer.

He was the whole reason I fussed around at the end of the day. Horses were groomed, fed, and out to pasture as the sun set. I'd get them in soon enough after I finished hauling in hay.

What the hell was taking him so long anyway?

I was ornery as fuck. Anxiety clawed at my insides, making me want to drink and vomit simultaneously. *Maybe not simultaneously but in some random fucking order.* I didn't like fighting him. I didn't like fighting anyone.

I was so fucking tired of always fighting. Stopping and breathing wasn't an option, but I sure as fuck wished it was.

A loud huff and neigh behind me drew me out of my thoughts. I turned to find Bailey hanging her head over the fence and smiled. Something about Bailey softened me. Calmed me. All the horses did.

"Feeling left out?" I asked. Dropping the bale I was lugging, I approached her while tugging off my gloves. "Now, I know you ain't useful for moving hay, so what do you need to be over here for anyway?"

She pushed her muzzle into my hands as I went to pet her. Seventeen years and this girl still fucking loved me. I touched my forehead to hers. *I didn't deserve to be loved like that.*

Wheels on the gravel made me look up. Jackson's fancy fucking truck bounced with the dips in the road as he drove up toward the stables—no doubt to check me on. He did a lot of that. Was a real wonder how the hell he got anything else done with all the unwanted attention he gave me.

"I'll be back," I whispered to Bailey, stroking her velvety nose. "I'm going to go piss off the boss."

Not a hard feat to accomplish. I always pissed off the boss. I steeled myself for the backlash.

"You and me need to talk," I told him. His boots had barely touched the ground when I made my move to speak. It was easier to come out of the gate hot and hard rather than ease into it with him. He'd stomp my ass if I waited him out.

"About what?" Jackson demanded. He slammed the door and crossed his arms.

Now or never. For the horses.

"I need supplies," I said. Reaching into my back pocket, I took out the list and handed it to him. I didn't say a fucking word as he looked it over. There was no need. Instead, I just braced for the backlash.

The man took his fucking time. *Way longer than necessary for the requests I made.* It was just another way for him to assert his fucking dominance and control. I knew men like him. They were all the same.

"Yes or no," I snapped finally when the drawn-out silence became too much to handle. I was crawling out of my skin and ready to bolt. Or fight. Or something. "It ain't that fucking hard."

"No," he replied. *Of course.*

"Fine." I snatched back the list and started to storm away. "I'll figure it out myself."

Maybe I could prioritize the purchases and spread them out. I'd never qualify for a fucking loan, but maybe I could piece it together. I could go without.

"Like hell you will." Jackson stormed after me. I didn't stop until I was in the heart of the stable. "You don't do shit to my fucking ranch without my permission."

"And *you* need to take care of your fucking horses," I countered. "The roof fucking leaks! Your stall mats are fucking shit and half the goddamn doors stick. Half the buckets out in the field are fucking leaking. The fencing is shit and needs to be fixed or replaced. The brushes are old as shit and missing a fuck ton of bristles. You have no hoof oil, detangler, conditioner, or clippers. The blankets are old as fuck—they'll do but most of them have holes in them. You have no fucking sheets—waterproof or nighttime. Fly maintenance is a joke. What the hell have you been doing? This is fucking miserable! They're animals! They deserve better than your stupid shit."

I let out a strong huff of air at the end of my rant. I hadn't meant to go off like that, but I got pissed. The horses didn't deserve the bare minimum. Working horses or not, they needed to be taken care of the right way.

Jackson didn't say a word as his gaze drifted over the stable. He walked in slow steps down the aisle, surveying each stall like it'd give him some magical fucking answer about what to do.

However, at the last stall, he stopped. *Fuck.*

Frowning, he pushed open the door. *Double fuck.*

"Are you sleeping in here?" he asked, brows furrowed together tight. I didn't need to answer. It was pretty fucking obvious from the pile of blankets in the empty stall and my few clothes. "You have a fucking house! Go live there! Stop sleeping with my goddam horses."

My stomach practically fell out at the mention of *that* house. No way in hell was I going back there.

"I don't fucking care where I sleep."

"I do! It's an insurance liability. The last thing I fucking need is your dumb ass getting trampled and you fucking suing me over your own stupid choices!"

"Make me sign a fucking waiver," I snapped. "I don't fucking care. You don't have a fucking say in what I do."

"Yeah, I do," Jackson snarled and stepped closer. *Right into my personal space.* My knees locked as I held my ground and damn near held my breath. *Fucking hell.* My heart rate spiked, pounding erratically in my ears. *Not here. Not now.* "My ranch, my rules. No more sleeping in my fucking stable."

The urge to hit him was strong. I needed him to back the fuck up. I couldn't breathe with him so fucking close. My stomach rolled violently as I counted back from ten.

"Fine," I gritted out, hoping to hell he'd back up. I needed him to back away.

He didn't. Not for another agonizing minute. When he did, I held my ground—chin up and expression empty.

"I'll get your shit this week. Don't let it fuck with your regular work," he told me as he walked out.

I managed to keep it together long enough to know he was gone before my legs gave out. Stumbling, I caught myself in a stall door and sank to the ground. Air stuck to my lungs as I desperately tried to stave off the panic.

I could do this... I could do this...

The mantra played on repeat in my head, but who the hell was I kidding? I couldn't do this. I never had before.

The spiral downward was familiar and awful. Breathing became impossible as the panic seized my entire body. I squeezed my eyes shut and waited it out. There wasn't a damn thing I could do anyway.

CHAPTER 11

JACKSON

Two weeks passed and I was wound up tighter than a fucking coil. I wanted nothing more than to lock my door, get a cold beer, and binge-watch stupid TV until Tess and I were ready for bed. Unfortunately, I had to entertain people—rather go out with them and watch while they entertained themselves.

Once a month, Mickey insisted I take the boys out to Merrillville for a few drinks. *Morale and all that shit.* To be honest, they weren't too bad. It was the rest of Merrillville. They loved themselves a local celebrity, and they fucking loved Jackson Myles, the gay bull rider.

I silently cussed out my agent for ever convincing me to take on the persona. Mickey found it fucking funny—the asshole. He liked watching me squirm as I tried to reconcile who they thought I was with the grumpy asshole I actually was.

Either way, I hauled my ass off the fucking ranch in time to meet the guys at *Bucking Bronco Tavern*. Most of the guys anyway. I fucking threatened all of them if they dared to invite West. I could only handle so much more of the man. I was on his ass for two weeks straight dealing with the changes he wanted to make and trying to wrap my head around just how drunk he was and when. The man was a fucking liability. *Even if he was doing a damn good job with the horses—better than I wanted to admit.*

But any hope I had of sitting around and not thinking about West flew straight out the fucking window the minute I walked into the bar. Stationed at the bar with a group I recognized as regulars, West tossed back another shot. *And then he fucking grinned.* A full, honest-to-God smile. And while that smile was probably fueled by too much alcohol, it was one hell of a flashback to the kid I grew up with. My chest constricted uncomfortably but that discomfort was quickly displaced into anger. *What the fuck was he doing here?*

"Well, now," Mickey said as he joined me, taking off his hat. "Ain't that a coincidence. You didn't want to see him, and yet... there he is."

"Drunks go to the bar," I reminded him, "to get fucking drunk."

"Or maybe he went out and made himself a few friends," he replied. "You know, he needs those since your sunny demeanor ain't doin' it for him."

I glared because what the fuck was I supposed to say to that. Mickey just laughed—*the fucker*—and clapped me on the back.

"There's that sunny demeanor right there." It was the last thing he said before shuffling across the bar to where my guys had a table. I stared at them, happy and loud and way too friendly with one another. *Fuck, I hated this part of the job.*

Still, I sucked it up. Ignoring West's presence, I stomped across the bar and ordered everyone another round of drinks.

Marley Valentino slept with everyone. I knew it and the whole damn town knew that one. Good on her for knowing what she wanted out of small-town life. You weren't special if Marley picked you out of a crowd, slid up on you, and took you home. So, it was no real surprise she picked West out as her conquest of the night.

What did surprise me was how fucking pissed off it made me. *Why the fuck did it bother me so much to see him dancing with her?* Three beers certainly didn't help my mood.

"Again—"

"Mickey, if you say another damn word I swear to fuck I'll suspend your dumbass," I snapped over him. It shut him up—*thank fuck.*

My gaze never left West, tracking every stupid thing he did in the bar. How the hell he was still standing was nothing short of a miracle. The amount of alcohol he consumed should've put him on his ass. *Or six feet under.* But with every advancement Marley made, he downed another shot or another beer. And the way he handled her was... odd. It was as if he didn't know how to touch her or where to let her touch him. The more he drank, the less he seemed to care but still. It was odd.

My boys moved back and forth between dancing on the floor and drinking at the table. They told jokes, talked, laughed, and had fun. *Mission accomplished.*

I just wanted to go home. Instead, I just scowled at West and hated myself a little because this sure as fuck felt like jealousy.

"Ah, crap." Mickey's words drew me out of my own head. I glanced at him, and he nodded toward the door. "Craig's here."

"Fuck," I muttered. Craig Hartley thought he was dating Marley. The man obsessed over her in a fucking unhealthy way. He was prone to starting fights and going after anyone Marley picked. *Just how many times did that fucking kid need to be arrested before it stuck?* And the two idiots who followed him around like they were a gang weren't any better. Small-town folk needed better things to do with their fucking time, and Craig with his crew was no exception.

When Craig made Marley on the dance floor with West, I tensed. *This would get ugly fast.* One part of me wanted to intervene but that voice was minimal. I knew West would get his ass kicked, but he'd made his mess.

"Nobody moves," I ordered instantly as several of my guys started to stand as if they were going to help. I tapped the table, making sure I had their attention. "He got himself into this mess, he deals with the consequences."

Craig made a beeline for West, who had his back turned. The bartender yelled something, someone else tried to stop Craig, but none of it worked. The kid was fucking determined as he grabbed West's arm.

West's reaction was downright volatile.

He whirled so fast that he knocked over Marley in the process and threw a punch that caught Craig in the jaw. It was hard enough to knock the man over—or would've been if West hadn't caught the front of his shirt.

And he just kept hitting.

Until Craig's face was a bloodied mess.

I tensed, rooted in my seat with shock. Whoever the hell that was, it wasn't West.

Craig's guys—fuck if I remembered any of their names—damn near tackled West. They locked arms around him and dragged him across the floor. West didn't make it easy on them, bucking and fighting back with everything he had.

That look on his face was pure rage.

He managed to break their hold long enough to grab a chair. *Oh, fuck.* West smashed the chair across someone's back before lunging at the other guy.

Screaming, shouting, and utter chaos. It consumed the bar as they kept going after West.

"Get your asses up!" Mickey barked. "It ain't the boss you need to be scared of. Help stop the fight—occupy the idiots. And *no one* touches West, you hear me?"

They were on their feet and rushing to do as he said. Meanwhile, the stare Mickey leveled on me was cold as hell.

"Get your ass up, boy," he growled. "Your daddy would be *real* disappointed in the man you're turnin' into over this whole damn thing. Get your ass up and help me help him."

He wasn't asking, and I knew better than to fuck with Mickey when he got started.

CHAPTER 12

WEST

THE ALCOHOL FLOATING THROUGH my system was almost enough to make her touch feel like something other than fucking razors on my skin. *Almost.* I just kept drinking because once Marley was in my space, she wasn't leaving. And I didn't know how to get mean with her.

I knew what she wanted—what she expected. I wasn't a fucking moron. Pretty girl like her could have any guy in the place. She should've stuck with that. Instead, she picked the one guy with a broken dick. It hadn't worked in years, and that wasn't changing. Not for her. Not for anyone.

All I could hope was that, at some point, she'd realize all her efforts weren't working. All her ass-grinding didn't do a damn thing to me. When that happened, I had to think she'd move on. *Either that, or she'd try even harder to convince me.*

Fuck, I hoped to hell she didn't. There wasn't enough alcohol in the world to fix my dick. I'd tried. And I didn't know how to explain that to her—nor did I want to.

When a hand grabbed my elbow, the panic spike was instant. My chest tightened fast and hard, hurting something fierce and sparking something animalistic in me. Marley yelped as I whirled on my heel and threw a punch. I didn't know who I was hitting. I didn't care. I couldn't see past the increasing fear lighting up my entire fucking body.

I grabbed a shirt and kept hitting. Hit after hit, I went after him.

Hands slapped and smacked me, shoving at my chest and shoulders. My hold tightened and my fist flew harder.

Shadows pressed in on my vision.

I was a livewire, violently charged with no direction.

More hands grabbed at me, hauling me off my feet. I screamed and fought back. Screams filled my head—memories I tried to fucking bury climbed their way to the surface. *The fucking pain.* I felt it in every part of my body.

I hit.

I broke things.

I fought like hell.

I belonged to no one, and there was no way in hell I was going back there.

No way, no how.

I'd rather be dead.

Swaying on my feet, I gasped for air.

I couldn't breathe.

I couldn't...

Voices filled my head—voices I desperately wanted to forget.

Voices that taunted me.

"Hey!" Fingers snapped in front of my hazy vision. "Look at me, boy."

I muttered... something. *Maybe.* Words were so fucking heavy in my mouth.

"Come on, West. Look at me, boy." *Mickey?* I tried to say it out loud. Maybe I did. Nothing seemed to work. "Yeah... yeah, that's right, West. Look at me. Ain't no one goin' to hurt you, you hear me? Ain't no one goin' to hurt you."

Words fell out of my mouth, incoherent babbling even to me.

"You're safe, West. You're safe," he said, soft and soothing. I wasn't safe. My heart pounding erratically in my chest was a surefire sign of that. It galloped hard enough to fall out of my fucking ribs. I couldn't breathe. *I couldn't fucking breathe.* "Say it with me, West. Tell me you're safe. Ain't no one goin' to hurt you, boy, I promise."

My gaze flitted around the swaying room, desperate for something—anything—to help. *A beer bottle on the table next to Mickey was my only option.* I grabbed the bottle and smashed it on the table. Before he could stop me, I shoved the biggest piece of glass into my palm and closed my fingers around it.

The burst of pain was mind-numbing, and I groaned. *But I squeezed harder until I felt the blood dripping between my fingers.* The buzz in the room softened and the hazy darkness seeping into my vision began to creep away.

I squeezed hard enough to make me gasp.

But it fucking worked. The pain took over the panic, erasing the violent chaos crashing through me. I clung to that stupid piece of glass as tight as I possibly could, letting it cut deep. It was the only lifeline I fucking had.

"You're safe, boy," Mickey said again. I blinked at him. *I wasn't safe. I wasn't ever safe.* I just shook my head. "You are. You're goin' to walk right out that door, you hear me? Right out the door and ain't no one goin' to stop you. Go, West. Go."

I was numb head to toe. My legs were heavy and uncomfortable. My body barely cooperated as I stiffly walked toward the door. I ignored the deafening silence and the looks. I didn't have the answers they wanted.

Hell, even I didn't know what was wrong with me.

CHAPTER 13

JACKSON

"Clean this shit up," I barked to my guys and gestured to the mess. "Everyone gets overtime and another round on me."

Fuck. Like I needed to be putting money in that direction, but it was the only way to smooth this shit over. I turned, ready to handle the bartender, but Mickey was already on it. Thank fuck. I wasn't even sure what the hell I'd say. What could I say?

What the fuck had happened?

I stared around the bar, purposefully ignoring the questioning looks shot in my direction. No one here was getting Jackson Myles the gay bull rider right now, and Amy would have a fucking field day if I started yelling at locals. My best bet was to fucking avoid them all.

Instead, I studied the entire bar and tried to make sense of it. *Blood, broken chairs, flipped-over tables, and glass shards.* Jesus fucking Christ. And that wasn't including Craig and his guys.

West had done a number on everyone. Craig would have a crooked nose for the rest of his life. There was no good way to fix that shit. His face was a pummeled mess—there had to be more broken bones on that man than just his nose. And the other two? Despite having ganged up on West, they weren't looking any better.

Jesus fuck. What the hell was wrong with him?

This wasn't a fucking bar fight over a girl—and I wasn't getting started on how scared Marley looked. Unscathed but fucking terrified. *Not that anyone blamed her.* This was fucking chaos.

This was a wild fucking animal let out of its cage. I was having a hard fucking time reconciling this animal with the West I'd grown up with. They were polar opposites. *What the hell had happened to turn him into this?*

When Mickey walked out of the bar, I stormed after him.

"What the fuck is wrong with him?" I demanded as soon as we were outside. He rounded on me fast and planted a hand on my chest. The expression on his face was unreadable. *Guilt? Anger? Worry?* I couldn't make sense of it.

"Get your ass inside, boy, and you let me worry about West," he snapped.

"Not until you tell me what the hell is going on!"

"Lower your voice!" Mickey exclaimed

"Now, Mick," I growled. "He could've killed one of them."

"He didn't."

"He could've."

"*But he didn't*," he reiterated. "Hartley and those idiots ain't nothin' more than a town nuisance. He did those boys a favor. Maybe they'll think twice now before they pull that kind of shit again."

"Did those boys a favor?" I repeated incredulously. "Are you fucking kidding me, Mickey? Do you hear yourself? They're going to the hospital! He broke a fucking chair on one of them!"

"And they started the fight—"

"You're blind to that man," I said over him. "Blind as fuck. The sun rises and sets with that fucker, don't it? He could do anything and you'll still be in his fucking corner."

"Somebody's got to," he replied.

"What the fuck does that even mean?" I snapped. Across the parking lot, I could see West pacing between cars. He beat his hand into the side of his head as he muttered furiously. Every step was staggered from alcohol and blood drops created a trail on the pavement from his hand—which he'd done to himself. "Do you see him? He's a fucking mess!"

"I know, I know!"

"Get it figured out, Mick," I snarled. "I can't be cleaning up after his mess every time he goes off the fucking rails like this! And I sure as hell won't bail him out when he gets arrested for hurting someone or worse. That man is going to end up killing someone one of these fucking days."

Something crossed Mickey's weathered face—something uncertain—as he looked away. I took a stunned step back, running a hand over my face. It was really fucking clear what he wasn't saying. *And why he had yet to get me West's background check.*

"Are you fucking kidding me?" I scoffed. "He's killed someone already, hasn't he?"

"You don't have a fuckin' clue—"

"I don't need one!" I shouted. "He killed a man! It's black and fucking white! You don't fucking do that! Jesus fuck Mickey. There were no delays with the background check, were there?"

"No."

"Were you ever going to tell me? Or were you just going to let a murderer walk my fucking ranch like it's a normal fucking thing? He don't—"

"Now, you listen here, boy," Mickey cut me off, getting in my face as he did. "I'm gettin' real fuckin' tired of your attitude. You ain't got a clue what it's like to live hard. You've had your shit handed to you on a gold fuckin' platter your whole life. West ain't had that. Livin' hard changes people. He may not be whatever the fuck you wanted him to be, but you're goin' to just have to accept that he ain't that kid you knew no more. What you see is what you get. Now, you and me, we ain't ever had a problem, but we're about to if you don't get *your* shit together and stop pushin' that button, you hear me?"

"Are you seriously standing up for him?" I demanded.

"I'm puttin' myself between you and him so you don't fuckin' break what's already broken, you hear me?" he told me, his voice deadly quiet. "I like you, Jackson. You're family. But he needs someone. Don't put me in a fuckin' way here."

Fuck. He had me and he knew it. I wanted to fight back—to show him who was the boss here—but I needed Mickey. He was the only reason my ranch stayed above afloat. I'd have to drop bull riding to train a new foreman, and no one would ever be as good as Mickey. Not really. *And he knew that.*

"Get him back and squared away," I said angrily as if he'd do anything else. "And he doesn't come to Merrillville anymore, got it? I don't need to be cleaning up his fucking messes."

Who was I fucking kidding? As long as West was on my fucking ranch, I'd be cleaning up after him just to make sure I didn't drown.

CHAPTER 14

WEST

I couldn't breathe. Even with the pain, I couldn't fucking breathe. *The screaming—incessant, painful screaming—filled my head.* More unwanted memories haunting me.

I paced the far end of the parking lot, beating the heel of my hand against my temple. Maybe I could hit it out.

Fuck, fuck, fuck.

Time didn't exist. Everything fucking hurt.

And blood... my blood? Someone else's blood?

Fuck, it was all so hazy.

I paced recklessly, attempting to piece everything together. But fuck. That hole was so fucking big.

I remembered going for a drink... and sitting with the regulars I knew.

I remembered telling myself it'd only be a few drinks... how many had I had? Couldn't remember that.

I remembered Jackson and that pissed-off look. *And drinking more so I didn't think about that pissed-off look.*

I remembered Marley... she was all hands. *Too much touching.* Even thinking about it made my skin crawl painfully. Something dark and twisted surged through my chest, sucking the air out of my lungs.

My pacing picked up as breathing became harder.

I remembered hands... hands... someone's hands.

And screaming. *So much fucking screaming.* Who was screaming?

And Mickey. I vaguely remembered Mickey.

Safe... safe... safe... the word played on repeat in my head.

My pulse pounded erratically in my ears as I gasped for air.

"West."

The voice sent me reeling. I stumbled and fell, scrambling backward across the pavement. My back hit a car, giving me nowhere to escape. The glass dislodged from my hand and sent an overwhelming spark of pain through my body. The world swayed in a way I had no control over.

"No, no!" I choked up. The panic reared an ugly face all over again, clawing at my chest. *Not like it ever really went away.*

"Hey, hey! No, look at me, boy. Right here." *Mickey.* I tried to keep his name at the forefront of the haze in my mind, but it was so fucking hard. "Ain't no one goin' to hurt you, you hear me?"

"I don't..." I shook my head rapidly. "I don't..."

What the hell was I even trying to say?

"It's all good. It's all good." Mickey came into focus as I blinked hard. He crouched in front of me, keeping a good distance between us. *Not good enough.* I scooted back. I needed more space. His voice was quiet as he said, "You're safe, West."

"I'm not." I shook my head harder while unwanted tears burned my eyes.

"You are—"

"I'm not."

"You are," he finished over me. "You are. I ain't goin' to let anythin' happen, you hear me?"

A strangled cry tore through my throat, and I bit my fist to fight the uncontrollable surge of emotions. *Panic, fear, shame.* The storm was never-ending. Violent and demanding. Overwhelming.

"I don't know what happened," I whispered. "I don't know... what'd I do, Mickey?"

"That don't matter," he replied. "What's done is done. Let me see your hand, West."

"I didn't mean to fucking hurt anyone," I continued, words just falling out of me.

"I know. Let me see your hand, boy."

"I can't remember... I can't fucking remember... I don't want to fucking remember..." Balling my fists in my hair, I hit my head against the car. A pathetic moan filled the air—*was that me?* Fuck, if I knew.

"Hey! Don't—"

The second Mickey's hand touched my wrist, I wrenched away from him and shot to my feet.

"Don't fucking touch me!" I snarled. "Don't touch me!"

"Okay, okay." He was slower getting to his feet but kept his distance. "I won't touch you, but I need to look at that hand, boy. You're bleedin' somethin' fierce."

He wanted to help... he wanted to help.

I didn't deserve the help.

"I'm sorry. I'm sorry. I just... I don't mean to... I'm sorry," I rambled.

"You don't need to apologize, West," Mickey cut me off. "Just let me see your hand. Let me help you. Please. I ain't no doctor, but it's better than haulin' you off to the hospital."

"No!" I exclaimed. Panic crashed with terror in my chest. I wasn't going there. No way in hell. "No hospitals! I'm not going to a fucking hospital. I won't!"

"I know—"

"There's no way in hell you're taking me!"

"I know," he repeated. Carefully, he took a step closer. "But I need to stop the bleedin'. Okay? You can't keep bleedin' all over the place, now can you?"

"No."

"Right," he said. Reaching into his coat, he took out a handkerchief. "Put your hand out, West."

My hand shook violently as I did what he asked. *From alcohol? Fear? Pain?* I didn't have a fucking clue. My body was on full autopilot and I was along for the unwanted ride.

"I'm just goin' to take a look at it," he told me. When he took hold of my wrist to steady me, a pathetic whine passed through me. The simple contact was fucking torture. It set my skin on fire, burning all the way down to the bone. All I wanted to do was pull away. Instead, I turned my face into the car I was practically huddled against, desperate to hide the stupid tears I couldn't control either.

He was gentle but everything still hurt. My nerves were fucking shot and in overdrive. That piece of fabric he wrapped around my hand grated against my skin—razors I had to wear to stop the bleeding.

I sucked down air, barely holding my own.

I could do this... I could do this...

"Let me drive you home, West," Mickey said quietly as he let go of me. My arm fell limp, buzzing and painful in ways I'd never be able to describe. "You can't be on your bike anyway."

I just nodded. I didn't know what the fuck to do with myself. *Too broken to fight back and too fucking tired to try.*

Mickey drove me back to the ranch. Despite his protests, I managed to get him to drop me off at the stables. *Couldn't go back to that damn house.* Wouldn't go home with him either.

Numb head to toe, I walked lock-legged toward the stables with his headlights at my back. He watched me like a fucking hawk, making sure I made my way inside.

Which I did long enough for him to pull away. I couldn't stay here. I didn't know where the fuck I was going as I grabbed my truck keys, but I just had to get the fuck out of there.

CHAPTER 15

JACKON

F*ucking phone.* I dragged my pillow over my face as my phone rang a second time. *Jesus fucking Christ.* It was two in the fucking morning. No one should fucking need me.

If it went off a third time, I'd answer.

I regretted that thought as my phone did just that. Grabbing it and not recognizing the number, I answered.

"The fuck do you want?" I snapped, not bothering to hold my temper.

"*Sorry for the late call, Jackson. I wouldn't call if it wasn't important.*"

"Keating?" I sat up, groaning as I did. Marcus Keating was the town's sheriff—had been since before I was born. The man was old, but what need did we really have for a sheriff in our town? Nothing ever fucking happened. "What can I do for you?"

"*I got Dakota McNamara sitting here—*"

"What the fuck did he do now?" I demanded.

"*Picked him up on a drunken disorderly.*" Jesus fuck. I ran a hand over my face. "*Figured I'd give you a call as a courtesy first, considering your* history. I thought you might want to pick him up instead of having him spend the night in a cell to sober up."

Fucking hell. I just wanted to go back to sleep. Mickey's words came back to me. One fucking moment of kindness. Tolerance was more like it. I could do that. Sort of.

"All right." I sighed. "Give him some fucking water and I'll come pick him up. Any chance we can let this time slide? You can arrest his ass and throw away the key if something happens again."

Keating and I had a long history, which I was hoping would work in my favor. Small-town life lent a hand to that sort of thing.

"*One time,*" he agreed. "*But I better never catch him on the road drunk, got it? Or I'm coming after your ass too, Jackson. A drunken disorderly is one thing, but he had his fucking keys on him, so I know he drove his ass out here. And he didn't drink that much at Lenny's before it closed. I'm no idiot.*"

"No, I know," I said. "I appreciate it, Keating. I'll be there as soon as I can."

"*See you soon, Jackson.*" The call went dead, and I flipped back on my pillows with another frustrated sound.

West was so damn drunk I wasn't even sure he knew what the hell was going on. It wasn't a good look on him. But he didn't want my fucking help, which was fine by me. I watched him sway with every step as he walked toward my house. *Yeah, I'd taken him home with me.*

"Why the fuck are we here?" he demanded, damn near falling over as he looked up at my house.

"Because I don't need you dying in my fucking stables," I said. "Someone needs to make sure you make it through the night. Should've taken your dumbass to the fucking hospital."

"No!" West yelled, staggering as he whirled on me. Anger and something else—something desperate—filled his expression. "No hospitals!"

"Jesus Christ," I muttered. I waited impatiently for him to get up the stairs. The whole thing took way too long as he almost slipped down them twice. "Fine. No fucking hospitals. I'll keep the coroner on speed dial for when you kill yourself."

"You don't know what you're fucking talking about."

"Yeah, sure I don't," I agreed but didn't know what the hell he was talking about. I unlocked the door and flipped lights on as I went inside. The last thing I needed was for him to kill himself by running into a table he couldn't fucking see.

"You don't know a fucking thing about me." He slammed the door, and I resisted the urge to hit him.

"Yeah, I sure as fuck don't," I agreed. That much I knew. "What the fuck happened to you?"

It was rhetorical. I didn't want to know—not that he would tell me.

"Shut the fuck up," he muttered, words slurring together. He collapsed on my couch, boots and all, and slung an arm over his head. "It ain't like you don't know. Golden boy Jackson fucking Myles has his shit together. Yippee-ki-ay and all the shit. I don't need your fucking pity just because you know shit about me."

"I don't know what the hell you think I know," I snapped. "But I can fucking guarantee I don't."

"Bullshit," West shot back, and I frowned. "You Myles never could keep shit from each other. Whole goddamn family in everyone's fucking business and always telling each other everything."

He was talking about my mom's need to gossip—that hadn't been a new development when she moved. She'd always been that way. *But what was he saying that she knew?*

I pressed my lips together and waited to see if he'd say more but all I got was a quiet snore as he passed the fuck out on me.

CHAPTER 16

WEST

My stomach violently tried to protest my waking up, but I swallowed it down and forced myself to sit up.

"Fuck," I groaned. To say I felt like crap was an understatement. The world swayed, and my head pounded. I definitely wasn't fucking sober.

And I was on a couch.

Whose couch?

I frowned, trying hard to remember how the hell I got there. I couldn't. I vaguely remembered leaving the ranch after Mickey dropped me off, but that was it.

Fuck.

Bleary-eyed, I glanced around for some kind of clue as to where the fuck I was. *Besides on a really nice fucking couch.* There was a chair to match and dark tables—one with a lamp on. I squinted at the picture on one table.

Double fuck.

It was of the Myles family. I was in Jackson's fucking house. I couldn't remember getting there, but I needed to get the hell out before he found out I was there. He'd fucking kill me.

I stood, pausing to gain my bearings as the room tipped sideways. When I was almost positive I could make it out, I did my best to stay quiet and get out. I managed not to run into anything, which was a plus, but I wasn't too sure how well I did on shutting the door quietly.

The blast of cold air was soothing. My head tipped back, eyes sliding shut, as I took a moment to breathe it in. Nothing quite compared to the open air on the ranch. I'd holed up in a lot of places, but nothing anywhere beat this.

Shoving my hands in my pockets, I stumbled down the stairs and right into the dark. Fuck if I knew where I was going. I had a general idea where the fucking stables were but probably not enough to get me there.

Life was a crapshoot anyway, wasn't it? Might as well see how I fared trekking in the dark.

I never quite made it back to the stables. Wasn't sure where I ended up either. There were cows. Lots of fucking cows. Really damn cute ones too.

They frolicked. At least one did.

I sat my ass in the grass and didn't move. I was so fucking tired. Tired of not sleeping. Of fighting. Of breathing.

I was tired of living.

And I didn't know what else to do with myself, so I sat there, staring at cows. I zoned out, losing focus and just existing. Sometimes I saw them, sometimes the world was just a blur.

The sun rose.

The day started.

I didn't fucking move.

Couldn't, even if I wanted to.

I just sat there and zoned out on everything passing me by.

"West."

I heard my name. Couldn't tell who was saying it.

More was said but my brain didn't comprehend shit. *Oh well.*

Something heavy wiggled its way into my lap and hot breath fanned across my face. I was startled right back into the world, my heart lurching violently into my chest. Eyes wide, I stared down at the thing demanding my attention.

A gorgeous long-haired collie stared right back with a giant smile on her pretty snout. *Dogs I liked.* Dogs were easier than people.

I buried my fingers in her thick scruff, and her tail beat against my calves happily.

"That's Tess," Mickey said somewhere out of view—not that I bothered looking. "She's a right sweet girl. She'll keep you company."

As I petted her, she scooted closer until she was pressed tight against my chest. The pressure was welcome—grounding in a soothing kind of way. I moved my hands from her scruff down her back, folding over her as I did and burying my face in her neck. The smell of dirt and hay filled my lungs. There was a comfort in her that I couldn't find anywhere else—except with the horses.

"Sorry," I whispered, never looking up.

"You ain't got nothin' to be sorry for, boy," Mickey replied.

That was a lie. We both knew that.

CHAPTER 17

JACKSON

"Jackson!" My mom's face lit up when she opened the door to her apartment. When I didn't return the gesture, her expression fell. *Yeah, I wasn't in the fucking mood.*

I was running on coffee and rage alone—not a great fucking combination. West was gone when I woke up. Not dead but not in my house either. No, he was spacing out in a field somewhere with Daisy and her friends not doing his damn job. I left him. Better not touch the horses while drunk anyway.

"We need to talk," I said. "And I do mean talk because I'm real tired of everyone keeping me out of the loop."

"Oh, honey—"

"Don't *oh honey* me, Ma," I interrupted. She opened the door wider to let me in. "I know you and Mickey are keeping shit from me. Shit that West seems to think I know. And you know what? I'd like to fucking know."

"Jackson—"

"*Now.*"

"Jackson—"

"He thinks I know something I don't know," I snapped. "Mickey knows shit about the chaos going down on my ranch that I don't know. And so do you. Start talking, Ma."

She sighed, her shoulders visibly rising and falling with her defeat. I crossed my arms, and she reached out, slapping them down.

"Stop that grumpy shit, son," she ordered. "Go sit at the table. I'll be there in a few minutes. The least you can do is humor an old lady. These knees ain't what they used to be."

I did as she asked and crossed my boots over one another as I waited. *And waited.* When she swore loudly, I tensed. I knew better than to rush in and help. Mom wasn't one for unsolicited help.

"You have to understand, we Myles don't get to pick our business partner," Mom said as she rejoined me with a file in hand. She eased into the chair across from me and put her hand on top of the file. "Your great-great-whatever-grandfather, he picked his partner in the McNamaras. They were good together. But all these generations later, that's who we're stuck with. If we'd had a choice, we never would've associated with the likes of Harrison McNamara."

"Don't blame you," I replied. "The man was a fucking dick."

"That's putting it mildly, yes," she agreed. She paused, her head tipping slightly as she considered me. "Are you sure you want to know, Jackson? There's no going back once you know."

"It's impacting my business, it's impacting my employees," I ticked each one off on my fingers, "and frankly, I'm real fucking tired of it being thrown around that I need to handle West with kiddie gloves but no one will tell me why. I deserve to fucking know."

"Okay." She let out a deep breath and stared out her balcony door, her fingers drumming on the file. I just sat there because what the hell else was I going to do? "Do you remember when you came out to us?"

"Vaguely," I said. *Honestly, I hadn't put much stock in the moment because my parents just let me know that they were already aware I was gay.* It made the moment pointless.

"We knew you were gay because we knew what happened between you and West the night he left," she told me. I carefully held my expression as I waited for something more. They hadn't said a damn thing about the night West left—and definitely not about knowing what we'd done in that field.

"We got a call from Sheriff Keating that following morning. West had been picked up from the bus station in Merrillville and taken to the hospital. While we were told it wasn't pretty, we weren't really sure what to expect when we got there, but we were told not to tell Harrison."

I frowned. *Why the hell not?*

She opened the folder showing off what looked like a police report—complete with pictures. *Gruesome ones.* She only handed one to me, which I was honestly grateful for.

The aged picture was of West in a hospital bed, and fuck, he was in bad shape. One eye was swollen shut and his brow was split while his lip was busted open and his nose had been broken. His entire face was a cascade of purple bruises that matched the deeply bruised band of angry flesh around his neck.

He looked like hell—a kid beaten senseless. It made me sick to my stomach.

"Harrison did this to him?" I whispered. My brows furrowed together tighter as I stared at the picture hard like it'd give me all the answers as to what the hell West had gone through. Mom nodded, and I asked, "Why?"

"Because West told him that he loved you." *He what?* My gaze snapped up to meet hers. "We knew that Harrison wasn't treating that boy right for years, but we never imagined... we never imagined Harrison would try to kill him."

"What do you mean you knew?" I demanded. "How could you know and not do anything?"

"West wouldn't talk about it," Mom told me. *I wanted to be mad, but how many times had I teased West about being clumsy?* A sprained wrist, a black eye, a busted lip. West had always laughed it off as being clumsy as fuck, and I let him. "There was nothing we could do."

I didn't buy that for shit, but I didn't say a fucking thing otherwise. To be honest, I didn't know what the hell to think.

"He was afraid to come back with us," she continued. "He didn't think we could protect him, but we were determined to try. And he wouldn't press charges against Harrison—he was too scared for that. Your dad paid for his hospital bill outright to make sure Harrison's insurance wasn't charged, and he made sure Keating never told a soul. We have the only police report made."

"Why?" I asked. I couldn't let go of that stupid picture, and I couldn't look away. "Why would you keep this?"

Why couldn't I stop staring at it? I ran my thumb over the damaged picture. How could such a simple thing blast through every wall I'd ever built around my memories and feelings for West? My chest was painfully tight at the thought of what he'd gone through. He never deserved this. *And not because of me.*

"Insurance," Mom said. "Your dad had had enough of Harrison, but it wasn't enough to end their business partnership. He wanted to keep it in case he ever figured out how to use it, and I just put it away and tried to forget it."

"What happened?"

"Your dad and I set him up in a hotel in Merrillville—one of those pay-cash kind of places. Cash only, no names, no questions asked. We figured he'd be safe there. Mickey was supposed to find an apartment or a small house for him—something we could buy for him in our name so Harrison would never find him."

"But?" I prompted. I could feel it coming. It was right there.

"But he ran away in the middle of the night without either of us knowing," she whispered. "I don't think he thought we could protect him."

"Do you blame him?" I asked. "It wasn't like you ever had."

"Jackson," she began, but I shook my head.

"He needed your help long before it ever got to this point." I dropped the picture on the table. "It never should've gotten to this point."

"He wasn't our son—"

"It doesn't fucking matter," I snapped. *Bullshit. He wasn't their son.* West had practically been theirs. "He was a hurt kid in need, and you did nothing."

"We did our best to keep him away from Harrison as much as we could without it turning into a legal battle that could've cost us the ranch," Mom said. The words made my temper spike, but I bit back my angry response.

"What happened next?" I demanded instead. "That ain't the whole story, is it?"

"No."

"Keep talking, Ma." *Maybe I was being a little too mean, but I didn't give a fuck.*

"We got a call almost a year later. West was in prison in Texas—had been for a while. He'd been arrested for armed robbery. There was a riot, and the guards lost control for almost a day. West…" Mom choked up. I ran a hand over my beard and just fucking waited with my stomach in knots. There was no way in hell this story ended well. "I didn't go, but your Dad and Mickey did. And your Dad… your Dad only cried three times in his life. The first was on our wedding day, the second was the day you were born, and the third… I sat with him on the phone as he cried outside the hospital. What those men did to him… oh, Jackson… it was so awful…"

She let out a small cry, her hand covering her mouth as she looked away. My heart lodged in my throat. I was torn between wanting to know and wanting to stay oblivious.

"No one should have done to them what those men did to West. He was just a baby. He was just trying to make it through, and they… they took him… and they… they…"

"It's okay, Ma," I cut her off as she struggled with words. I didn't need her to say a damn thing to have a real strong inkling of what they'd done to him. *And truthfully, I wasn't sure I wanted to hear the words.* The tears rolling down her cheeks killed me, and I covered her hand with mine. "I get it. I do. You don't need to say anymore."

We sat in silence as her shoulders shook. I gave her the time she needed to regain her composure before nodding, needing her to continue.

"Mickey stayed with West for a while," she said quietly. "Your dad came back, and he confronted Harrison. You probably remember that fight. I had to call Keating because I thought your dad was going to kill him."

"Yeah, I remember that." It was the one and only time I'd ever seen my dad lose his temper. "What did Harrison say to set Dad off?"

"Your dad had hoped that maybe… some part of Harrison would care about what had happened to his son. The only thing that man could say was that maybe it'd cure the—it's so horrible, baby boy," she told me, interrupting herself. "He said… maybe it'd cure the faggot in him, and that was when your dad lost it."

"That sounds about right," I muttered. Nothing about that surprised me. Harrison had always had a special way of talking about people he didn't approve of, which was pretty much everyone. I frowned as a thought occurred to me. "That was right around the time Dad taught me how to shoot and had me carrying a gun around the ranch. He said we had wolves."

"The only wolf on our ranch was Harrison McNamara," Mom replied. "Your Dad was real afraid of what he'd do to you if he ever got you alone. He didn't think Mickey needed to teach you a damn thing. You were always so attentive to what running the ranch took. He just knew that Harrison wouldn't start shit if Mickey was there with you."

And that would explain why Mickey was my assigned shadow for fucking years.

"And West?" I asked. "What happened to him?"

"We decided it was better to let the memory of West McNamara fade," she admitted. "For his sake and yours."

"Mine?" I repeated, my voice rising. "Harrison had me thinking West left because he didn't want to be around me anymore. Like I suddenly wasn't fucking good enough to be in his life. And you never said a fucking word otherwise. I spent seventeen fucking years hating him for it. *And you let me.* Harrison wasn't going to fucking leave the ranch. Who the fuck do you think you're kidding? You just wanted to bury the fucking secret. Harrison may have been a fucking monster, but you aren't much better."

"Jackson—"

"He needed you. West needed you, and the ranch came first. Didn't want to upset the fucking balance at the ranch."

"That ranch is our entire family history!" she exclaimed. "There was no good way to separate the two! Being an abusive asshole wasn't enough to break a generational contract. We would've had to sell the ranch—sell everything we had."

"Or you could've just told me," I said as I pushed to my feet. "I could've walked off the ranch at any point and found him. He could've had the chance at a real life instead of the one he got. He didn't deserve *any* of what the three of you put him through. If you'd done a single fucking thing to protect him, he wouldn't have gone through any of that."

I left, stalking straight out her door while she called after me. There were a lot of things I wanted to say to my mother and not a single one was appropriate. Not with the anger surging through my blood.

Not with the thought of what they'd let happen to him stuck in my head. Her words haunted me. *And I didn't know what the fuck to do about them.*

CHAPTER 18

JACKSON

Convincing myself to go back to the ranch was hard. What the hell was I supposed to say to West? What *could* I fucking say?

The answer: not a damn thing.

That fucking killed me.

I eased my truck to a stop outside the stables because going home felt wrong. *I felt like I owed West something.* What that was... I didn't have a goddamn clue. I just knew I couldn't go home and sit with this.

As always, West was in with the horses. The sunset settled across his shoulders like the proverbial new light I was seeing him in. He wasn't the West that left me. He was the West I'd lost. That did something to me. *Something painful.*

Those gray eyes caught mine and I swore the fucking world stopped for just a moment. Any of the anger and hatred I had for West had dissipated, replaced with a kind of sadness I couldn't describe. Even with the giant fucking rift between the two of us, I wanted to fix it. I wanted to take away all the awful things. The anger, the fear, the panic. Every single damn thing.

West broke eye contact and returned to work while I just stood there, staring and wondering. *What the hell was his life like now?* The drinking and the fighting were just the smallest of indicators. But what couldn't I see? How deep did his self-harm and self-loathing go? Was it worse than that? Did it affect his ability to keep a job? A house? Was it why he stayed as far off the grid as he could manage?

And the guy he killed... was it related to...

I couldn't bring myself to think the thought. How fucked up was that? It was his everyday reality and my stomach rolled just thinking about it. *Fuck.*

My mind was a wild mess as I tried to make sense of it all. Of all the things I expected my mom to tell me about West, this wasn't it. This was the kind of thing you didn't want anyone to go through.

"You knew," I said under my breath when Mickey joined me. "You knew and you didn't say a fucking word."

"And what the hell was I supposed to say, Jackson?" Mickey replied. He sighed heavily, draping his arms over the fence and staring out to where West traded horses. "There's just some things..."

His voice trailed off, and I glanced over at him. The haunted expression on his face did nothing to quell my anger. He didn't have a fucking right to be haunted. Not after everything he helped hide.

"You know, I ain't ever wished someone dead," he whispered, "but when I saw that boy after... I couldn't help thinkin' it. You know, they marked him. One cut for every man that..."

The nine scars on his side. Bile stung the back of my throat with that little piece of information.

"And the guy he killed?" I asked. Did I want to know? Not particularly. But I felt like I needed all the information I could get—to understand what the hell West was going through.

"You know, he had to go back in there with those animals once he was out of the hospital," Mickey told me. "Your daddy tried to convince them to send him to another prison—somewhere he'd be a bit safer—but no one fuckin' listened. Or maybe they just didn't care.

"It changed him. Not sure how it couldn't, you know? But it did. And I don't know the details—not sure I want to—but two years later, he killed one of them. Not that the fucker didn't deserve it, if you ask me. He had to go back to court and all that. Got off with self-defense. Had a damn good lawyer. She managed to get him transferred to another prison too. Your daddy and I went to watch the trial, and West... he wasn't there, you know? He's got that empty look about him right in the eyes. Still does."

I knew that look. I saw it every fucking day. *And it made sense now.*

"Sometimes, I still wonder if he would've been better off dead," he admitted, his voice cracking slightly. That fucking guilt he felt? He deserved it. "Livin' with somethin' like that... I don't think there's livin' after somethin' like that."

"Y'all should've done something, that's what should've happened," I said. While I understood where he was coming from, it was all a load of fucking bullshit. There'd been chances—a lot of them—to spare West this life. Instead, the lot of them picked a fucking plot of land over a kid.

That shit I couldn't let go.

"I'm tryin' here, boy. It's the best I got."

"You failed him," I snapped, feeling that familiar rage bubbling to the surface. "You can say and do whatever the hell you want now, but don't you think for a minute you're doing it for him. You're doing it for you because you feel bad. You should've stepped up when he fucking needed you.

"No, y'all decided to bury your fucking heads in the sand, and for what?" I gestured around me. "For some fucking land? For fucking cows? You failed him—all of you—when you decided his worth wasn't more than this stupid fucking business. Than a stupid fucking job!"

"Now, it ain't like that—"

"It is like that!" I interrupted. *How could none of them understand that?* I was sure my dad probably thought the same shit. That keeping West busy here and there was enough. It wasn't. "I would've burned the whole fucking place to the ground before I let him run away afraid for his life."

"Jackson—"

"You can say whatever the hell you want, Mick," I continued over him. I was on a roll. I didn't fucking care. "It don't change a damn thing about what y'all didn't do when he needed you. Y'all let Harrison terrorize a boy without protecting him and that's just the fucking start of it. It's no wonder he don't want to be here. Nowhere is fucking safe. This place is full of bad memories and people who didn't protect him."

I stormed away before I kept going and fired Mickey because I was real damn close to doing just that.

Every now and then I did stupid shit. Most would say bull riding was the stupidest shit I could do. But this? This right here? This was going to top it, and I didn't give a flying fuck.

I couldn't get rid of the memories that haunted West, but I sure as hell could burn the reminders to the fucking ground. Which was why I drove right to the old McNamara house in the middle of the night. I backed my truck up to the front steps, running over the old bushes with no fucking remorse.

Hopping out of the truck, I rounded the back and lowered the tailgate. I grabbed the crowbar and one of the six containers of gasoline I had in the bed of the truck.

Harrison's lawyer had locked up the house after he died, but that didn't stop me from kicking down the goddamn door. My boots echoed in the empty house as I stomped up the stairs.

I broke out windows and smashed holes in the walls.

I dumped gasoline on every fucking surface until I stormed through puddles.

Second floor.

First floor.

Basement.

Fuck, I even wrecked the goddamn porches.

Everything had to fucking go until this awful goddamn house was nothing more than smoke on the horizon and a pile of ashes.

When every inch of that godforsaken house was drenched in gasoline, I tossed the last can in the back of my truck along with the crowbar. My boots were soaked, and I reeked, but I didn't give a fuck as I took a pack of cigarettes out of my pocket. I set one between my lips while I stared up at that old house. I hadn't smoked in fucking years, but I wanted one.

"I hope you rot in hell, Harrison," I murmured, wandering close to the front steps. Rotting in hell was too good for him, but it'd have to do.

Lighting a match, I held it to my cigarette until the end ignited before dropping the match onto the porch. The gasoline burst to life and ran with the flame. It'd probably be enough, but I walked the perimeter for good measure, tossing lit matches through broken windows as I went. Flames erupted violently and raced through the house at an impressive rate.

When I was certain the house needed nothing else to burn to the ground, I returned to my truck. I leaned against the tailgate and crossed my arms. Taking a long drag from my cigarette, I watched the house burn with a wicked kind of satisfaction. Black smoke billowed into the night sky while the orange glow lit up the dark field.

Only when I was certain there was no saving the goddamn place did I put a call in to the Sheriff.

"Keating," I said when he answered.

"*What do you need, Jackson?*" the Sheriff demanded, grumpy and annoyed with me bothering him. "*This better be damn good. It's late.*"

"I need you to give Carter a call and get him out to the ranch. Tell him I have a..." I faltered briefly, staring at the fire for the right words, "controlled burn I need his help on."

The momentary silence that followed was so damn telling.

"*What the hell are you setting fire to now?*"

"The McNamara house."

"*Fuck.*" He sighed and the silence lingered. "*Fine. I'll give Carter a call. He'll want to know what happened. You know that.*"

"Tell him I slipped while carrying... what?" I glanced back at the empty containers in the bed of my truck. "Call it twelve gallons of gasoline while smoking a lit cigarette."

"*Jesus fuck, Jackson.*"

"Oops."

CHAPTER 19

WEST

THE HOUSE WAS ON fire.

Harrison's house was on fire.

The smoke and orange glow were the first things I saw from the stables. It was real damn hard to miss. I just stood there dumbfounded and wondering just how drunk I fucking was to hallucinate *that*.

But then the sirens came, blaring and cutting through the night. Several fire trucks bounced along the road as they navigated their way through the ranch.

I ran after them.

I had to see it for myself.

By the time I got there, the firefighters had set up but no one was doing a damn thing. They stood ready but no one moved, and the fire just kept on raging.

I stared at my childhood home as flames wrecked it. My chest constricted painfully. I hadn't laid eyes on this place since the night I left. *Since Harrison damn near killed me.*

There was so much shit built inside those walls—secrets I'd kept to myself. My mother's suicide. No one else knew I'd been in the room with her the night she killed herself. Harrison's drinking. No one knew just how often I picked my old man off the floor night after night. The hits I'd told myself I could take. No one knew just how bad his temper really got. The whole place was a fucking hellhole wrapped up in one bad memory after another.

And every one of them was burning right before my eyes.

I swallowed hard against the hefty rise of emotions inside me. I wouldn't break down. I wouldn't panic.

"What happened?" I asked, unable to look away from the fire as I approached the fire chief.

"Controlled burn," the fire chief snapped, and I frowned. When I glanced at him, he said, "Don't ask me. Ask him."

I followed his gaze to see Jackson. My heart kicked up harder in my chest, anxiety clawing at me. He was completely undeterred by everything with his arms crossed and a dying cigarette balanced between his lips. The expression on his face was one of odd satisfaction.

Had he done this?

But why? Was he that fucking pissed off at me that he burned the whole thing down?

"Jackson!" the fire chief yelled, anger lacing his voice. "We need to shut this thing down before it spreads to the whole goddamn ranch!"

"No one fucking moves a goddamn muscle until that house is as dead as Harrison fucking McNamara," Jackson ordered. "My ranch, my rules. I want the whole damn thing gone."

"Then hire a demolition crew!"

"It had to go," he replied. His gaze locked onto mine. The usual contempt and anger were gone—replaced with a kind of sadness. "Tonight."

It hit me right then and there. *Jackson hadn't known.* He hadn't known any of it. Not the shit with Harrison. And probably not anything else either.

I didn't know what to do with that piece of information.

And so I stood there, dumbfounded. Conflicted. Crawling out of my skin.

Why? *Why the fuck was he doing this?*

It made no sense.

Eventually, the fire chief ignored any of Jackson's protests and moved in. But at that point, there was no saving the house. Everything was charred and crumbling.

I should've been happy. I should've been fucking thrilled. *But I wasn't.* Some weird sense of dread and panic did its best to take hold of me—memories set free from a dying house. I wanted to crawl into a hole and drink until I didn't have to think or feel anything anymore.

I should've walked away. And yet, I couldn't. Some twisted part of me was convinced I had to stay and see it through—like I owed it to someone. Anyone. Jackson maybe? Harrison's memory? Myself? *Fuck, I was so fucked up in the head over all of it.* Inexplicable emotions that I didn't want to feel had complete control of me.

When Jackson rounded the side of his truck with his keys in hand, I chased after him because what the fuck?

"Jackson!"

"*No!*" he hissed as he turned on me fast. I took one long step back, his livid expression sending my heart racing. "You and me, we are going to talk, but not right now. I'm just as likely to fucking fight you as I am to talk to you, you hear me? Go away, West."

I just nodded. *What the hell was I supposed to say to that?*

CHAPTER 20

JACKSON

The northern ridge area of the ranch was largely untouched. *Our spot.* I'd gone back there in the first few weeks after West left, but eventually, I gave up on the place. I pretended it no longer existed. The place was full of nothing but painful memories.

But tonight, it was the only place I wanted to be.

I took Tess with me—letting her hang her head out the window in the night air like she liked. If I had her, I had to be responsible. I had to keep my head on. She kept me smart when all I wanted to be was stupid.

Though, I'd already burned down the McNamara house. Wasn't sure how much more stupid I could get in one night.

I didn't park my truck too close. A part of me didn't want to disturb the place. Why the hell this place still felt important was beyond me. It should've lost that significance a long time ago.

Tess bounded ahead of me when we got out, and I damn near lost her in the overgrown grass. She was nothing but a rapid tail and bouncing ears. Something about that made me envious. To be a dog in this world was something else. What I wouldn't give to feel the kind of joy she felt just running through the long grass.

As I sat against a tree, I let out a whistle. She came running and damn near barreled into me.

"Come here, girl," I said quietly, patting my chest. She settled in my lap, though that tail of hers never quit going, especially once I started scratching her behind the ears. "What the fuck am I supposed to do?"

Was I talking to my dog expecting her to have all the answers? *Yeah, I fucking was.* But at this point, Tess was as likely to have the answers as anyone else. I propped my hat on my knee and tipped my head back against the rough bark, staring up at the dark branches.

"Fuck, I'm so tired, Tess," I whispered.

I hated this goddamn ranch. I owed it to my family. Our entire history was tied to this place. Every fucking Myles for generations ran this place, but it felt like I was the only one running it into the ground. My heart wasn't in it. I didn't want to manage people or raise cattle. I wanted to ride bulls until my body couldn't take no more—which was coming up faster on me than I wanted to admit aloud. Taxes, paychecks, and business connections weren't me. *Never had been.*

I did it because I was supposed to, but I would've given anything to be elsewhere.

And then there was West. Fuck, my whole goddamn heart hurt over that situation. Everything he'd been through was so fucking unnecessary. I knew Mickey and Mom didn't see it that way. They'd done their best—at least that was how they saw it. But their best was too little too late.

Way too late.

Someone should've stepped in when he was a kid. Fuck this goddamn ranch. Fuck family history and all that shit.

All my anger and hatred was tied to a broken fucking heart. I knew that, even when I lied to everyone else about it. West had been my everything—loving him aside. We'd spent every waking moment together from the minute we both could walk. He was my best friend. He was the one I was supposed to do this whole goddamn thing called life with. I'd counted on that. When he'd disappeared, it fucking hurt.

But I had to let all that hurt go. Or at least set it aside. *For West's sake.*

I closed my eyes with a heavy sigh. The look on his face in the bar was branded into my brain. It wasn't anger. It was pure fear—an animal backed into a fucking corner. And knowing what I knew now, I got it.

Something had to give. He didn't belong here. He didn't belong trapped in a place that reminded him of all the awful shit he'd been through.

West deserved to be free.

I spent the whole fucking day dealing with legal shit. *I hated legal shit.* Correction: I hated lawyers. I hated trying to connive my way into information as I figured out the logistics of Harrison's will. There had to be a loophole somewhere. *At least, I wanted there to be.*

When it was clear that there wasn't, it left me trying to create an alternate path. One that would cost me my hide if someone found out. But I was determined to make it fucking happen. By the end of the day, I had a solid plan. There was only one last thing I needed to do before I could put the plan into play.

Which was how I ended up on Mickey's doorstep late at night. The old man stood in the doorway wearing flannel pajama pants and a Merrillville tourist tshirt. I said nothing about it, but I was more focused on the two braces the man had on his knees.

"Knees bothering you, Mickey?" I asked.

"You that bored you came all the way here to ask me about my knees, boy?" he countered, leaning against the doorframe. The TV played quietly in the background—some old Western movie, which I would've found funny on any other occasion.

"Just how guilty do you feel?" I demanded. There was no fucking point in beating around the bush. "About what you did to West. How guilty do you feel?"

"Jackson, we talked about this shit." Mickey blew out a long breath. "I did the best I fuckin' could given the goddamn circumstances."

"I know that's what you think, but I'm trying to determine just how far you're willing to go to make up for it now."

"All right, boy. Tell me what you're thinkin'."

"I need you to be willing to commit perjury for him," I said. His eyes widened slightly. *Yeah, he wasn't expecting that question.* "Invite me in, Mick. I ain't having this conversation out here."

I waited him out, watching the wheels turn in his head. I was about to ask a lot of him—something that could get him in real trouble if anyone found out—but it was the best plan I fucking had.

CHAPTER 21

WEST

Three days. It'd been three days since Jackson burned down Harrison's house. My childhood house. *My house technically.* I had no idea what the fuck to do with myself. I felt more things than I wanted to admit—more things than I thought I was capable of feeling.

Strangely enough, most of those feelings were wrapped up in Jackson. I wanted to know what he knew and why he reacted the way he did. He hated me—supposedly. Had he burned the house down because he hated me? *Or for some other reason?*

That thought was just one of a million useless things tumbling through my head. I struggled to take care of the horses. The downward spiral I was desperately trying to stave off bled into the worst possible areas of my life. The horses needed me, and I couldn't pull my shit together. *Even the alcohol didn't help.*

Mickey wasn't talking to me either, which only made me feel worse. At least he sent Peter to help. Peter was quiet and kind—asked no questions and just did his job.

When Jackson's truck stopped outside the stables, I steeled myself for whatever backlash was headed my way for not doing my damn job. He got out and beckoned me toward him. *Fuck.*

"Let's go," Jackson said as I approached slowly. He opened the passenger door to his truck. My heart lodged in my throat. No good would come from me being locked in the same goddamn truck as him.

"I ain't getting in there with you," I said, my voice tight.

"Get in the goddamn truck, West, or I swear to fuck…" He drew in a deep breath, hands falling to his hip. His mouth moved as he silently… counted? I had a feeling he was counting to ten or some shit to keep from yelling. In a slightly less irritated tone, he repeated, "Get in the truck, West, please. We need to talk, and I ain't doing it here."

Oh. That made me falter. Fuck. What was I supposed to say to that?

"I'll drive behind you," I countered.

"No. We ain't staying in town, and I want to make sure you actually get there."

Fuck me. That didn't sound any better. But I silently nodded. I could do this. I could survive being stuck in a small space with him.

And yet that little voice in the back of my head just laughed at my own stupidity.

One hour in the fucking truck and Jackson didn't say a word. I needed to know where we were going or what to expect. *I was dying.* I couldn't sit still, my skin was crawling, and my stomach rolled. I wanted to hit something and throw up at the same time. That clawing in my chest was fucking persistent, and the fear of losing control was intense.

The second he turned off his truck in a crappy fucking parking lot, I bolted. I gulped down fresh air. It didn't ease my nerves or haunting panic, but it was better than sitting in that fucking truck.

"Could've opened the window," Jackson said when he rounded the front of the truck with a thick manila envelope in hand. I glared. There was no way he'd understand.

The stop was some dinky off-the-road diner—the kind where you knew the food was crappy and greasy but it was cheap and fast. The kind of place no one gave you a second glance because they didn't fucking care. Everyone just passed on through.

"Let's go," he damn near snapped. I wanted to push the buttons—tell him no—but what the hell would I do then? I was in the middle of fucking nowhere with no way back. And I wasn't exactly hitchhiking material. *Though, I did glance at the road and consider it for a long moment.*

But eventually, I caved and followed him inside. No one gave us a second look as I trailed after him to a table in the corner. I let him take control because I sure as hell didn't know what we were doing here. He ordered himself a burger with fries and me a BLT with chips on the side. *How the hell he still remembered what I liked was beyond me.*

An awkward silence settled between us when the waitress left. He took that stupid hat off and set it on the chair next to him while keeping one hand on the manila folder. His fingers drummed on the table as we stared at one another.

How long we did so, I wasn't sure. It was enough time to notice just how blue his eyes were against the tan of his skin. And time to notice just how much muscle he'd built for himself. I knew he ran every morning, but it was obvious he worked hard on his body. *Those were things I didn't need to be noticing. Didn't want to notice.*

I fussed and fidgeted under his unrelenting stare. I wasn't good at this shit. This was uncomfortable as fuck.

"Why didn't you tell me?" Jackson asked finally. I stilled. *He was kidding, right?* Not that it showed on his face. No, he was dead serious.

"Exactly when the fuck have we been on talking terms since I got here?" I demanded.

"Not now." He shook his head. "When we were kids, why didn't you tell me what Harrison was doing to you?"

"I don't know. I could take it," I said with a shrug. I wasn't sure what the hell he wanted me to say about that. There was no changing Harrison.

"But you shouldn't have fucking had to."

"It is what it is." *Still wasn't the worst shit I'd gone through.* "It wasn't like anyone could do anything anyway. What was I going to do? Run away?"

"I would've gone with you," he replied. Under his breath, he added, "Hell, maybe I still would."

"Right," I scoffed. "We'd never get along long enough for that shit."

"No, West, that's where you're wrong." Jackson sighed and sat back in his seat. "I'm done fighting with you. It ain't doing either of us any good."

What the hell did that mean?

"And I'm giving you an out," he continued. "I tried to find a loophole to that stupid one-year thing, but there is none."

"We fucking knew that," I muttered. *This asshole better not have dragged my ass to a middle of fucking nowhere diner just to repeat what I already knew at me.*

"Here." Jackson slid the envelope across the table to me. "There's bank information in there for an account with the forty-seven million in it. My name and yours are on it. All you have to do is go in and ask them to remove me. They're ready for you when you show up, so it should be quick and painless.

"There's a contract in there as well that I need you to sign. It states that if you take the money, you agree to come back in one year and sign the ranch over to me. You also can't mention this contract to our lawyers—they'll ream me a fucking new one and probably make my life a living hell. Mickey and I will both go on the record to state you've worked the ranch for a year. If the last few weeks are any indication, I know you would've worked hard and we wouldn't have had any problems. It's the easiest way to do this."

"What?" He was saying words, but I was positive I was fucking hearing things.

"You're free to get the hell out of here," he said. "You don't have to stay for the next year, you get the money for the ranch, and next year, you'll sign the ranch over to me. As far as the lawyers are concerned, you'll have worked there per Harrison's will."

Free to leave? As in, I didn't have to stay in this fucking place and be miserable for a year just to appease Harrison's twisted demands. My heart pounded faster in my chest. There was actually a way out of here.

"Why?" *It was the only word I could think of.*

"Because you don't belong here. I get why you haven't come back in seventeen fucking years. This place is nothing but one bad memory after another, and you shouldn't be stuck here another year. So, take the money, sign the contract, and go. Just make sure you show up next year for the official sale."

"This is you taking pity on me." *Pity was the last thing I wanted.* I could fucking handle my own life. I didn't need him to rescue me.

"Jesus fucking Christ," he muttered. "No, this is me saying I fucking get it—I can't understand it. I never fucking will. But I fucking get why you hate it here, and I'm trying to do something to help."

"Oh." I stared at the envelope. Part of me wanted to push back—to figure out what the catch was. *What was it that he wanted out of me?* No one ever did shit like this for someone. Especially not with forty-seven million attached.

But the other part of me didn't want to look a gift horse in the mouth. This was a chance to start over and maybe find some peace outside of just surviving. Or at the very least would make it real fucking easy to disappear. I could go to Alaska, get a small cabin, and never see anyone again. I liked the cold.

"*Or,*" Jackson began slowly, dragging me away from my thoughts, "you could stay for the year. Work the ranch. You and me. Like we planned."

"Are you fucking nuts?" I blurted out stupidly. He couldn't possibly think that was a smart idea. Not the way we fucking argued, even if he did claim to be done fighting with me. He shrugged, trying to look casual and not pulling it off.

"There'd have to be some changes if you stayed. The horses would still be all yours, but you'd need to get sober. It's too dangerous to be drunk around them. But you're damn good with them, so they'd be yours," he told me. "And as for you and me... I'm just saying, that door is open. If you want it to be."

The what was what? *This man had to be on something.* Yeah, there'd been something between us once a long time ago. But who knew what that even was besides one night rolling around in the fucking grass.

Not to mention that was a lifetime ago. We were both very different people now—as if that shit wasn't obvious.

"You've got to be kidding me," I muttered.

"I'm not." *Yeah, he was dead serious.* "I ain't saying you have to. I'm saying we were robbed of a chance to find out, and if you ever wanted to find out... that door is open on my end."

"I'm so fucking broken, Jackson. Nothing has worked since..." I couldn't finish the sentence. The admission made me feel pathetic—less of a man. It must've shown on my face because his expression softened. *Damn it.* I didn't want him looking at me like that. "I ain't worth it."

"I ain't talking about sex here." *Fucking hell.* Folding his hands, he leaned on the table as his voice dropped in volume. "I know I'm all wrapped up in the bad memories so the likelihood you'd ever want anything to do with me is slim to none. That makes me real fucking aware of how goddamn stupid I sound right now, and you know I'm not one to do shit that makes me look like a fool."

"I know."

"So what I'm saying is... your stables, your rules," he whispered. This man was a goddamn moron. *Had a bull kicked him in the head too fucking hard?*

"You're a fucking idiot."

"Probably. But I am done fighting you."

"Fine," I grumbled. Anything else I was going to say—which was just a bunch of bullshit anyway—vanished when the waitress showed up to drop our food off. Jackson wasted no time eating, but I just stared at it. I didn't need him feeding me. I could take care of myself.

"Eat," he said around a bite of his burger.

"I'm not hungry," I replied. I didn't need his charity.

"When was the last time you ate something that wasn't fucking alcohol?" Jackson demanded. I didn't have a good answer, so I just glared at him. "Right. Eat the damn food, West. It ain't going to kill you."

No, but it would probably kill what little bit of pride I had left. That thought only made my scowl deepen.

"Fine, tell you what," he continued, "I'll get this time. You can get the next time. There. It's done. Now, eat."

Like we'd be doing this ever again.

Still, it was the best damn sandwich I'd had in a long fucking time.

CHAPTER 22

JACKSON

There was gray in his beard. That was the odd thing I noticed as we sat in silence at the diner eating. Instead of trying to start a conversation, I just studied him and how life had changed him. Somehow, I got stuck on the faded grays tucked in his beard. It was easier to focus on that than the fact that he thought I was a fucking moron for suggesting that he stay with me.

Why the fuck had I said it?

I blamed Mickey for that shit. He'd put the idea in my head when we talked—that West and I had been robbed of a chance at something together. That there was something still there under all the anger and hurt.

I hadn't planned on saying a goddamn thing, but my mouth ran away with me before I had a chance to stop myself. *And of course, West thought I was fucking nuts.* Couldn't blame him for that one. I would think I was an idiot too if I were him.

It led to a silent meal and an awkward ride back. He didn't say a fucking word, and I didn't know how the hell to bridge the gap. So I didn't. I just drove us back to the ranch. As soon as I turned the truck off, West climbed out with the envelope in hand.

"I'll look these over," he told me, his voice stiff, "and get them back to you."

"Okay." I nodded. There was an uncomfortable feeling in my chest at the idea of letting West go all over again—something I didn't know how to explain. Though, I knew it was probably the best thing for him.

"Okay," he echoed. Without another word, he started across my lawn back toward the main drive.

Fuck, he was going back to the stables. Which he'd been sleeping in. It wasn't exactly like he had a house to go back to.

"Door is open if you need a place to stay," I called gruffly over my shoulder. "Guest room is on the first floor. Tess won't bite. She will steal the bed though, if you let her."

West made a sound but said nothing. *Not that I expected him to.* He disappeared into the dark while I went inside. Tess bounced around, her tail banging on the wall as she danced in excitement. If only everyone got this damn excited when they saw me.

Her whining grew incessant while I took off my boots before giving her attention. If I started with her, I'd never leave the entryway.

She ran ahead as I followed her to the living room, bounding onto the couch. That happy smile of hers was almost enough to take away the crappy feeling settling inside me. I ran my fingers through her scruff and hit all the spots to make her wiggling increase.

"I did the right thing," I told her softly—though, I wasn't sure if I was trying to convince her or myself. Either way, it had me feeling a hell of a lot more than I wanted to.

CHAPTER 23

WEST

I WAS FREE. *To leave.* I couldn't wrap my head around that piece of information. Jackson was ready to lie to a fucking judge just so I could get the hell out of there. He gained nothing from it.

Okay, maybe he gained not having to be around me any longer, but that didn't feel like the reason either. Not really. Not considering everything he'd said.

And that fucking thing about his door being open? What the fuck was I supposed to do with that? Did he honestly think there was a shred of anything left between us?

Or was there?

I shook that question free as I arrived at the stables. There wasn't. He couldn't see it. I was too fucking broken to be with anyone—even if I did want a relationship. Who the fuck would choose to be with someone like me? I had nothing to offer him but the demons I couldn't conquer.

I was free to start over—to take the money and find somewhere remote and alone to start over.

Bailey huffed, her head popping out over her stall door. The sight of her tugged hard at my heartstrings. *Did I want to be alone for the rest of my life?*

I couldn't take her with me. There was no good way to take a horse on a road trip with no destination in mind. She deserved a hell of a lot better than that. She deserved everything she had at the ranch.

Beamer's head joined hers in the aisle with a neigh. A small smile turned the corner of my lips. Beamer was loud and nosy. It wasn't so much that he liked people. He just liked knowing what was going on and what snacks he could get out of it. He didn't like sugar nearly as much as he liked peppermint, but he'd trample a bitch for some pumpkin. *Hell, he'd almost trampled me the first time I brought it out.*

Two more heads popped out at the noise—Domino and Dolly. They were brother and sister, inseparable in the most annoying way. *Cute but annoying.* Wherever one went, the other just had to go or they became irate. It made doing everything with them all the harder—especially with the way Domino liked to chew on shirttails if he wasn't the one getting attention.

As I stood there staring down the line of stalls, I wasn't so sure I wanted to leave. Sure, living in a stable wasn't ideal, but it wasn't the worst place I'd ever slept. And I had a purpose for the first time in a long fucking time.

But was it enough to make me stay?

I didn't have a clue what I was supposed to do.

CHAPTER 24

JACKSON

Thank you for everything.

F OUR WORDS SCRATCHED ONTO a piece of torn notebook paper never hit so hard. Somewhere in the middle of the night, West had come in to drop off the signed contract. It sat on my table with that stupid note—a neon sign that he was gone.

Whatever weird tiny shred of hope I had that he'd stay shattered with it. *Not that I truly expected him to.* I couldn't blame him for getting out as quickly as possible. Hell, I would've too.

After texting Mickey to handle the morning crap out in the fields, I did the one thing I never did. I went back to bed. Or at least tried to. Tess made it damn difficult to go back to sleep. Once she was up, she was up. I managed to doze on and off for a few hours while also giving her the attention she demanded.

Somewhere around noon, I managed to crawl my ass out of bed. I pulled on whatever clothes I could find and made a cup of coffee to go. While I didn't want to, I needed to get out to the field. I left Mickey to run everything too often anyway when I was on tour. I did my best to be available when I was home.

The stables were busy—a fact that put an immediate frown on my face. My guys milled along the fence, eating lunch and talking. Their horses wandered around the corral while they did. Most of the time, my guys took their lunches in the field. It was a waste of time and ridiculous for them to come back. *Granted, with West gone, I had no idea how the morning had gone with the horses.* Fuck, I hadn't thought that one through.

Mickey peeled away from the lot of them when he saw me approach. That stupid fucking grin on his face annoyed me. It didn't feel right that he was still here while West was gone.

"All right." I sighed as I got out. "Tell me the damage, Mickey. What the hell are we dealing with?"

"Regardin' what, boy?" he asked.

"West leaving and the fact that all my guys are here," I said. "With all their goddamn horses."

"Oh, he ain't gone." That fucking grin widened.

"The hell he ain't," I shot back. "I have the goddamn contract to prove it."

"See for yourself,' Mickey replied. He nodded toward the fence. *Lord help me, my curiosity got the better of me.* I stalked toward it to see what all the fuss was about.

I didn't expect to see West in a baseball hat as he leaned out the window of his truck, watching behind him while he slowly backed a horse trailer into the corral. The look on his face was indescribable—determination and... was that pride? It certainly looked a hell of a lot like pride but over what?

"What the fuck?" I muttered, mostly to myself.

"You really should check your bank account more, boy," Mickey said as he stepped up alongside me. "He says he only took five hundred thousand. Don't need the rest. At least not the way you need it to save the ranch."

"But..." *But what?* There were a handful of thoughts combatting one another in my mind. The first being that five hundred thousand wasn't enough. He deserved a lot more money than that.

"He took that money and bought Thunder Jack."

"That fucking horse?" I demanded. Thunder Jack was notorious for his temper. A former bucking rodeo horse, the stallion was nothing but trouble since they were forced to retire him. The owners could barely touch him. "The Mathews really should've just put him down. The horse has to be miserable."

"Yeah, well, West asked me to deduct a boardin' fee for both Bailey and Thunder Jack from his paychecks."

Something warm wrapped around my heart at the idea of him taking back Bailey. *Of him taking back his horse.*

"You better not have," I snapped quickly. There was no way in hell I was docking his pay for keeping horses here.

"Already upped his pay, boy," he said. "It ain't like he don't work hard enough to have earned it anyway."

"Good," I whispered. Money couldn't remotely begin to fix the shit West had gone through, but I didn't want it to add to his struggles if I could avoid it.

I leaned against the fence, watching as West hopped out of his truck. I smiled. I couldn't fucking help it. *West stayed.* He actually fucking stayed.

I didn't give a fuck if it was the horses that convinced him to stay. He was here, and that was all that mattered.

"Do I need to remind you that I'm your head of HR?" Mickey teased. *And there went my somewhat good mood.* It grated on my nerves. I wasn't in that place with him. Not yet, maybe not ever.

"We ain't there, Mickey," I told him. Crossing my arms, I faced him and kept my voice low. Mickey braced for it—I saw it in his expression. He expected me to fire him. *Not that I blamed him.* I still wrestled with the idea. "And we may never be. What you did... rather, what you didn't do... I don't know if I can forgive that. I know you think you meant well but you should've done more."

"I—"

"I don't want to fucking hear it, Mick," I interrupted. "You've said all you need to say. You might not have hurt him but you never did a damn thing to stop it either. That's just as bad in my eyes. You had a chance to do the right thing, and you buried your head in the sand. And right now, I don't know that I can trust you."

"You know I ain't ever goin' to do a thing to hurt this ranch, boy," Mickey said.

"I know," I replied. "I don't doubt your commitment to the ranch. If anything, you've proven you'll do anything for this ranch. It's your commitment to me I doubt."

As harsh as it was, it was honest. How could I trust him?

Some kind of fierce urge to protect West had come to life inside me after everything I'd learned. Urges I intended to foster with my actions. With him staying, I wanted this to be a safe place for him—though, I had no idea what that even looked like. *Was it even possible?* I had no idea. But I was determined to try, even if that meant forcing Mickey out.

Maybe it was stupid but I didn't care. I was finding I didn't care about a lot where West was concerned as long as he was okay.

CHAPTER 25

WEST

I ALMOST LEFT TOWN—I really did. I couldn't come up with a damn good reason to stay. Horses weren't enough of one. *At least, I had myself convinced of that.* But on my way out, I drove past the old Mathew's farm and saw the cheap horse for sale sign. I should've driven right on past it, taken my five hundred thousand, and vanished.

But I couldn't. Not without asking first.

It took all of five minutes before I was signing papers to buy Thunder Jack. If they couldn't sell him, they were going to put him down. A bucking horse made to be wild and then wouldn't let them tame him didn't deserve death. He deserved freedom.

And I could give him that.

Me.

So, I bought a horse with the little bit of money I took from Jackson. Had to buy a trailer from them too just so I could get Thunder Jack back to the ranch.

Unfortunately, buying him and returning to the ranch meant I had to stay sober. I hadn't gone a single day without a drink for the better part of a fucking decade. Alcohol kept the demons at bay and without it, I could feel the darkness pressing in. It made my skin crawl and left me desperate for a distraction.

Maybe I'd buy another horse or two to help with that. *Who fucking knew?*

It was painfully clear Thunder Jack didn't know how to be around people or other horses. The Mathews had done him wrong, which meant I had to compensate to make sure all hell didn't break loose.

It meant keeping him in the trailer with the half-door open so he could see everything going on around him while I readied Jackson's horse for the afternoon—since that whole thing was still my job. The look on Jackson's face as he watched me was unnerving. *Like this meant more than it was.*

It couldn't. He had to see that my mess wasn't worth it.

By the time his horse was sufficiently groomed and saddled, my skin was crawling. The endless observation got to me. I wanted a fucking drink to calm my nerves.

"This ain't me saying yes," I said quietly and held onto Zeus's reins while Jackson mounted him. Why? I didn't fucking know. I didn't need to. He had complete control of his horse. It just gave me something to do with my hands.

"I know," Jackson replied.

"This is about the horses," I continued, running at the mouth. He leaned forward and rested on the horn of his saddle. Those blue eyes watched me closely, setting my nerves on fire. *Shit.* Why did this have to be so fucking uncomfortable?

"I know," he repeated.

"You suck at taking care of them—all of you. Someone needs to be trained or hired or something." *I was rambling.* "They don't deserve to be treated like crap."

"They won't no more," he promised. The intensity in his gaze bore right through me. *Why the fuck did it feel like he wasn't talking about horses?*

"And I ain't saying no either." The words were out of my mouth before I could stop them. *Fuck, my head was a disaster.* Why the hell had I said that? I shouldn't have said it.

"Good." He grinned—a glimpse of hope in his expression that made me want to go running. Why couldn't we go back to fighting? I could fight all fucking day long. I was used to that shit. This friendly bullshit had me on edge. "Your stables, your rules, West."

God damn it. Could my frown get any deeper? Probably.

I handed him the reins, making sure his hand never touched mine. I couldn't handle that. *Not now.*

"Come on, boy." Jackson clicked his tongue at Zeus and gently nudged him forward. "See you tonight, West."

I just grunted and walked away. *Fuck, I was in over my head.*

As it turned out, Thunder Jack was about as fucking grumpy as I was. There was no easy way to approach him. *Unfortunately for him, I didn't give up that easily.* I kept him corralled and cut off from the rest of the horses but did my work alongside him. I brought every horse next to him for grooming and maintenance, forcing a little side-by-side socialization. Whenever I gave one of them a treat, I left one on the fence post by his head—never looking. He wouldn't take a damn thing if he thought I was watching him.

He liked carrots and celery the best, refused sugar cubes and pumpkin, and didn't seem to mind bananas. *But only if I wasn't looking.* We'd get there. An unfamiliar sense of excitement weaseled its way inside me as I discovered these little things about him, especially when he grew bolder in searching for them. Maybe it was a dumb thing to get excited over—I didn't have a clue—but I was.

The afternoon passed quickly and before I knew it, the sun was setting on the horizon. The ranch hands filtered back to the stables in pairs. I bounced between stripping saddles and leaving treats for Thunder Jack just because. The increase in activity had him more on edge. But Bailey—the sweet girl that she was—hung around the fence where he was. Maybe he minded, maybe he didn't. Who knew?

I didn't talk to any of the guys. I wasn't interested, and honestly, the alcohol withdrawal made them even more intolerable. I was dying inside. The hard work and horse company helped, but with every passing minute, even that wasn't enough. I wasn't sure I was strong enough to get through this shit.

Jackson was the last to trail in with that stupid smile that broke his stupidly handsome face irritated me as he and Zeus approached.

"Good afternoon?" he asked as he pulled up alongside me. I said nothing. I wasn't in the mood for his antics. I just took Zeus's reins and went to work removing his saddle. I'd brush him down after giving him a chance to roam and eat.

I expected Jackson to leave when I didn't fucking reply, but he stayed. *Damn it.* I could barely handle being around myself. The last thing I wanted was him there too.

"Did you eat dinner?" The question sparked frustration. I didn't need him to take care of me.

"I don't need your help," I snapped and never glanced up from my work.

"I just asked if you ate dinner," Jackson said a little too calmly. It grated on my nerves. *Irrational? Maybe.*

"No," I muttered. Maybe if I answered him, he'd go the fuck away. Granted, I couldn't fucking eat anyway. The nausea threatened to take me out by the knees. This withdrawal thing was fucking brutal, and I just knew it'd get worse.

"You should eat," he told me. *Motherfucker.* I was going to kill a fucking cowboy for being irritating as all hell.

I held my tongue because I didn't trust myself if I opened my mouth. I was just as likely to bitch him out as I was to hit him. What I'd do was a fucking crapshoot was what it was with Jackson being the brunt of it no matter what.

"Good night, West," he said, but I only let out an annoyed sound in response. Over his shoulder, he called, "Door will be open if you want to use the guest room instead of the stables. Don't let Tess out or you'll be chasing her around the ranch all night long."

I scowled. *Just what fucking game was he playing at?* I didn't need his charity. The stables were just fine. I'd survived worse.

I threw myself into my work—pushing myself ten times harder to distract from the hazy thoughts weaving through my mind. But when I lay down around midnight to rest and closed my eyes, the screaming started. It echoed with unwanted memories in the back of my head.

Every muscle locked up while I tried unsuccessfully to push them down. The very clothes I wore were fucking razors slicing across my skin. That familiar panic clawed its way into my chest again—a reminder of all the shit I desperately tried to forget.

Hot tears burned down my cheeks as I squeezed my eyes shut tighter. I just wanted to sleep. I was so fucking tired.

But the harder I tried to force it, the worse it became until I was convinced I'd die just lying there. I surged to my feet and took up pacing. But pacing only made the spiral happen faster. The sadistic voices in the back of my head picked up speed, tearing me apart little by little.

With a wordless scream, I punched the stall door. *Once. Twice. Three times.* And kept going until I was bloodied and the pain in my knuckles drowned out the demons in my head. I shook violently from head to toe as I stormed out.

If I couldn't sleep, there was work to be done.

CHAPTER 26

JACKSON

"We have a... situation *down here,*" Peter said when I answered the phone, his voice hesitant as he spoke. And for damn good reason. It wasn't even five yet. I didn't like being woken up.

"What kind of situation?" I growled as I sat up.

"*I'm not real sure how to describe it, Sir,*" he told me. "*But uh... West... well, he's all worked up—muttering to himself and his hand is bleeding. Kind of looks like he got into a fight with someone you know? The horses aren't ready, but I'm pretty sure he scrubbed every saddle until the leather was spotless.*"

"Does it affect you getting the hell out of there and into the fields?" I asked. With a quiet groan, I dragged myself out of bed. My fucking bones ached. Side effects of being thrown around by bulls for over a decade. Shit, I sure as hell wasn't young anymore and I felt it more and more with every passing year.

"*Not at all,*" he replied. "*It's just...*"

"It's just what, Peter?" I demanded. I hated the hemming and hawing.

"*Hold on. I'm going to step away.*" The pause on the other end lingered, and I waited impatiently. "*Sorry, boss, I just... I don't want them to overhear.*"

"It's just what, Peter?" I didn't have time for fucking games. I just wanted to know what he had to say.

"*I had a brother, Patrick.*" Jesus fuck, it was story time. I sank down on the edge of the bed and reached out to scratch Tess behind the ears as I listened. "*He served in the Army, two tours overseas. And when he finally came home to stay, he just wasn't the same. I had a hard time with it, but I was young. My mom called it PTSD. She said you couldn't go through the horrible things he'd gone through and not be affected.*"

I drew in a deep breath, unsure of what to say, but it wasn't hard to figure out the correlation to West. It made sense when you stopped to think about it. Even before prison, he'd been living in a silent hell for years. For his whole damn childhood.

"*I'm not pretending to know what he's been through—West, that is—but it's obvious,*" he continued. "*The bar fight, the anger, the jumpiness. Not wanting to be touched and all that. You have to know it to see it.*"

"Yeah," I agreed quietly. The thing was I did see it. I just didn't know how to help.

"*PTSD is a bitch of a thing. It shreds apart all the things you knew about yourself and then keeps on taking from things you never thought it could touch.*"

What a horrible fucking way to live. I laid back on the bed to stare up at the ceiling as I let his words settle inside me. How the hell did I help someone with PTSD? Or hell, how the fuck did I help West?

"*I just think he could use your help right now, Mr. Myles. I'd feel guilty not saying anything,*" Peter said.

"All right. Just get out of there and get the day started. I'll handle it. If you need to take a UTV out there to avoid him, go ahead. Just watch out for—*"

"*The ladies,*" he interrupted with a small chuckle. "*I know. I'll make sure to protect the ladies.*"

Damn right. I wouldn't have anyone running over my girls.

"And Peter?" I stopped him before he could hang up. "How's your brother doing?"

Some part of me just needed to know that his brother was okay—that he'd been saved from it.

"*He died five years ago,*" Peter replied, his voice quiet. "*He kept saying he was fine, so we thought he was. Like I said, PTSD keeps on taking if you let it until you have nothing left. He killed himself before any of us saw the signs... acknowledged the signs. They were there. We just... we wanted him to be fine like he said he was, you know?*"

Fuck. What did I say to that?

"I'm sorry, Peter." It was about the only thing I could think of.

"*It's not your fault, Sir,*" he told me. "*I've dealt with my grief. I just... to be frank, it's obvious he means something to you—don't worry. I haven't said a word in case the others don't see it. But maybe you can do what me and my family didn't.*"

And help West, even when he said he was fine.

"Thank you, Peter," I said and sat up. "Get the day going. I'll be out there shortly."

"*Sounds good, Sir.*"

"Call me Jackson," I told him. I rarely crossed that bridge with any of my employees. But most of my employees just did their jobs, went home, and repeated the next day. Peter was going out of his way to do more—to be more—for West. That meant something.

"*Of course, Jackson.*"

If looks could kill, I'd be fucking dead. West's expression was downright volatile when he saw me get out of my truck. I ignored him while I waited for Tess to follow me out. Just because I intended to stay around the stables for the day didn't mean she needed to. She knew her way around the ranch better than anyone else here and spending the day in the fields with the cows was her favorite thing in the world.

"You find Mickey, got it?" I said as I crouched down to scratch her scruff. Fuck, I sounded like a dad sending his kid off to school. Her excited howls made me laugh. I snapped my fingers once and pointed down her usual side path. Instantly, she bolted. Mickey was waiting for her, and I knew he'd tell me when she got there.

"Go away," West growled as soon as I walked closer. I said nothing and just took inventory. He looked like shit—bags under his eyes and hair a mess of dust and dirt. Mud splattered his clothes and stained his hands. And just as Peter had said, West's knuckles were split open like he'd lost a fight with a fucking wall.

Despite his clear exhaustion, he was sober. At least he wasn't drunk. *However, I had a feeling the lack of alcohol was killing him slowly.* Granted, I had no idea how long he'd been drinking either. I could guarantee it wasn't a recent thing.

"You got something to say?" he demanded, facing me. The gruffness in his tone wasn't lost on me. I recognized the behavior. He was looking for someone to fight—somewhere to put whatever crappiness he was going through. Well, I wouldn't take the bait.

"You were right. I haven't been taking care of the horses, and I need to learn how. You're going to teach me," I told him.

"The hell I am," he snapped. "If you haven't figured it out by now, there's no way in hell I'm fucking teaching you."

"This is still my ranch and you're still my employee," I replied. I was chancing a hit by going down this road and pulling authority. "So, yeah, you're going to teach me how to take care of them the right way."

I knew how to take care of the damn horses. My mom had made it her job day and night to make sure I could take care of her horses before she moved off the ranch. Too much on my plate had been the cause for me letting their care slip—not a great reason but an honest one.

"Oh, fuck you!" West let out a sound of frustration. "You don't give a fuck about the horses. You're just over here because you think I need you to babysit me. I don't, so you can go fuck off with that bullshit."

"I ain't going to fight you, West," I said softly. I watched the way his temper flared across his expression, doing something severe to his handsome face. *Just how much anger did he bottle up?* Not that he hadn't earned the right to be angry, but just how deep did it run?

"Afraid you can't take me?" he snarled.

"I know I can't take you," I scoffed. *The problem was that I wouldn't hit him.* When he took a step toward me, I squared off my shoulders and readied for whatever the fuck came next. "We ain't doing this shit, West. If you want to beat the crap out of someone, find someone else. I ain't playing this game with you. And I ain't asking you to show me how. I'm telling you to."

If keeping him close meant pissing him off in the process, I'd fucking do it.

CHAPTER 27

WEST

To his credit, Jackson shut the fuck up and took whatever the hell I gave him—which was a lot. I was beyond exhausted. *Hurting, nauseous, stuck in my head.* Working kept me from spiraling, but Jackson's entire presence pushed me closer and closer to the ledge. I was ready to tip over it and spiral into a dangerous place.

The cowboy may have been a pain in my ass but he was fucking useful. *Mostly.* I knew he knew what the hell was going on with all his horses but was trying to keep me occupied. That piece of information pissed me off. I didn't need his pity, but I couldn't get him to leave me alone either.

Around four, he left. When that truck pulled away, I felt like I could breathe again. *For all of five fucking minutes.* And then the jitters kicked back up, making it awful all over again.

Fuck detoxing.
Fuck Jackson.
Fuck all of this.

I focused on the horses— had to focus on the horses. I gave up working and gave Thunder Jack whatever I had. It took everything in me to do just that. More treats and just existing around him while giving Bailey some well-needed attention. *Well, in her mind, she always needed attention.* There was a reason she followed me around like a puppy.

None of that changed when Jackson returned. I couldn't pull my ass off the ground to save my life, even when that frown of his struck a chord with me. It set my already screaming nerves on fire. That familiar tightness in my chest began to return, and I sucked in a sharp breath to try to bury it.

He strode across the dusty paddock toward me with a wrapped-up sandwich in hand. *Fucking hell.* I didn't need him taking care of me.

"Just turn the fuck around," I mumbled to myself. Any shred of hope I had that he'd turn around and leave me the fuck alone was dashed as he crouched in front of me.

"Eat," Jackson ordered and held out the sandwich. *Always with the fucking orders.* It grated against my nerves.

"I ain't hungry," I said. I couldn't imagine putting anything in my stomach. It'd probably revolt.

"Your hands are shaking," he pointed out. He wasn't wrong. I pulled my hands into my lap, making fists to hide it—not that it would make a difference at this point.

"I'm fine."

"Never said you weren't, but everyone needs to eat."

"Fuck off," I growled. I glared at him, but the man was undeterred. He never wavered as he continued to hold out the stupid sandwich. "I don't need your fucking charity, *cowboy*."

I said that last word with as much malice as I could, trying to piss him off. It was a small dig at how shit used to be—a poke at how many times I'd made fun of him for that stupid hat he still wore. I wanted him angry at me. Fuck this nice shit. I couldn't handle it.

His gaze narrowed as he considered me.

"Fine." Jackson dropped the sandwich between my bent knees before standing. "I'll dock your fucking pay. Now, eat."

"I don't need you taking care of me!" I called after him. I didn't need him in all his cowboy valor storming into my life trying to fucking save me. There wasn't a damn thing worth saving anyway.

"Never said you did," Jackson commented over his shoulder. "Eat the fucking food before you get back to work. Don't need you passing out."

"And I don't need you telling me what the fuck to do." *Why wouldn't he just fucking fight me?* That shit I wanted. It was the only thing I could handle.

"Stay sober, West."

"I fucking hate you," I snapped.

"Good to know," he replied. "Have a good night. Eat the fucking sandwich."

I let out a frustrated sound as he disappeared. *Stupid fucking man.* And like the idiot I was, I opened the sandwich and picked at the bread. Maybe that would help settle my stomach.

Head between my knees, I sat outside next to my truck. It was well after midnight—maybe. I couldn't tell. It was dark as shit and I was shaking so badly I couldn't walk. My breath stuttered in my chest with every unsteady inhale. My fingers tightened in my hair while the dry heaving threatened to choke me. Each wild breath made it harder to breathe until I was practically sobbing as I leaned into the tire for support.

Withdrawal and panic collided violently inside me. I had no fucking control of my body. It did whatever the hell it wanted, and I was stuck for the ride.

Squeezing my eyes shut, I begged anyone who might listen to a lowlife like me to make it end. It didn't matter how. I just wanted it to end.

I couldn't take much more.

CHAPTER 28

JACKSON

West looked like utter shit—in the kind of way that had me genuinely worried. With nothing else to do, I'd spent time researching alcohol withdrawal, and West checked off every symptom. *But those were just the ones I could see.* The ones I knew about. Just based on what I'd learned, I'd made a dangerous fucking mistake by telling him to just quit drinking. There was a whole laundry list of medical terms tied to what could happen during withdrawal, and none of them were pretty.

It left me a little more than desperate to keep him close. *It also left me wondering if I'd bitten off more than I could chew.* Maybe I couldn't help West the way he needed it. I had myself convinced that with the right help, he'd be okay, but what if he wouldn't? What if he didn't want it and I was just wasting my time? What the hell was I supposed to do then?

What if I only ended up hurting him in the process? I couldn't live with that.

All I could do was focus on the here and now and try to get him through the next fucking day. I had a plan, which involved focusing on something he cared about. *Hopefully, that'd help.* Or at least I'd be there when shit hit the fan.

"Come on," I said when I approached him by the stables. He glanced at me—glaring like all get up—before going back to buffing saddles. "You can come back to that later."

"I don't want to fucking go anywhere with you," West snapped.

"I ain't asking."

"I ain't going."

"You want to fix up the stables and fencing or not?" I demanded. He paused, and I knew I had him. When he finally straightened to stare at me, I added, "You know better than me what the hell you need."

"I gave you a list," he growled.

"I lost the fucking list." *I hadn't lost the list.* It was just a damn good excuse to keep him close while I ran out to go get shit. Everyone else was in the fields, and I sure as hell wasn't calling Mickey back just to keep an eye on him. I didn't trust Mickey with anything where West was concerned. "Now, I put in an order for some of the shit but not everything."

"Jesus fucking Christ," West muttered and ran a hand over his face. "You can't do jack shit, can you? Do you know how much fucking work I put into making that goddamn list for you? That was hours of my fucking time!"

"Yeah, I know." I nodded. "And that's why you're coming into town with me. We'll pick up the wood for the stables and fencing, but I don't have a fucking clue what you need from the *Farm and Feed.*"

"Jesus fucking Christ," he repeated and threw his rag down with the rest of his supplies. I watched as he stormed into the stables. I debated whether I should go after him or not, but I settled on waiting. I wanted to know what he was going to do first. He came out a minute later, shrugging into a black flannel jacket and burying his hands in his pockets. He griped, "No wonder your fucking business is going under. You can't even keep track of a goddamn list."

Drawing in a deep breath, I counted to ten. Three fucking times. I'd set myself up to be his goddamn punching bag this time, but I didn't have to like it. I just wouldn't comment on it.

"Just get in the fucking truck," I snapped and stormed away.

A's Hardware was as much a social spot as it was a hardware store. The Anderson family had run it for years, and they were notorious gossips. Did that make me feel any better about bringing West with me? No, it didn't. I hated the thought of putting him in the crosshairs of fucking anyone right now, but I had to keep him close.

"Just in and out," I assured him quietly when I caught him hesitating out front.

"Fuck you," West snarled and followed me inside.

Henry Anderson was the town's worst gossip. Pushing eighty, he rarely worked at the store—leaving his son and grandson to do all the work. Today, I just wasn't that fucking lucky because he sat on a tall stool at one of the registers. And to make it worse, Burt Harper stood with him—the town's second-worst gossip.

Seriously, the old ladies in this fucking town had nothing on these two. It was as if they didn't have anything better to do with their time.

"Well, if it isn't little Dakota McNamara!" Burt exclaimed. *Ah, fuck.* West tensed beside me, jaw ticking under his thick beard.

"Morning, Burt," I interjected with the hope of staving off chaos. "Henry. Didn't think I'd catch you here this morning."

"Oh, I'm just an old man needing some entertainment today," Henry replied.

"You're looking a little rough there, boy," Burt continued. He eyed West up and down real slow as if sizing him up. Maybe the man was a fucking idiot or he couldn't see how West was coiled up tight, the anger building in his face. "You know, Harrison said you went to jail for something... what was it..."

"None of your fucking business," West growled.

"Murder!" he exclaimed loudly. "That's right! Said you upped and murdered someone."

Jesus fucking Christ. Was there no end to Harrisons's reign of terror in West's life? It didn't help that we weren't the only ones in the store or that Burt was drawing attention. *Unwanted attention.*

"Burt," I warned.

"You got that look about you," Burt continued stupidly, not realizing how close he was to being decked. "Don't he have that look about him, Henry?"

"Quiet now," I snapped, interrupting him. I took three long steps to close the distance between us. I wanted to make sure he heard me when I threatened him. My height had me towering over him. "Listen real close, Burt, because you got two choices here. On one hand, you nod your head, you say goodbye, and you get the hell on with your day. On the other hand, you tell Henry here to call the Sheriff because West won't be the one to hit you. I will. And I promise I'll make it fucking hurt. So, what'll it be, Burt? Are you and me going to have a problem today?"

"No, Sir," he let out. *Good. Maybe he wasn't all that stupid after all.*

"Good," I said. "Now, say goodbye and run along, Burt."

"Have a good day, Henry." He nodded once to Henry before hurrying out of the store.

"Now, why do you have to go scare away my customers, Jackson?" Henry asked after the bell dinged.

"First off, Henry, we both know I'm your best damn customer." I leaned against the counter. "Second off, when was the last time Burt bought a damn thing in here?"

That part had Henry laughing, which was a good thing. It broke enough of the tension to let me relax.

"Tell me one of the boys is here," I continued. "There ain't no way I'm letting you carry out my order."

"Nah." He groaned loudly as he got off the stool. "I haven't lifted a damn thing in years—I could, but it's more fun to watch them run around like idiots to make sure I don't. I'll get Casey upfront to get you all squared away."

"Thanks, Henry."

"You boys behave, you hear me?" he called over his shoulder to me and West as he meandered down an aisle. "I remember the kind of trouble you two used to get into."

"You got your wires crossed, Henry," I replied loudly. "We were goddamn angels."

"So was Lucifer." His loud laughter carried through the store as he disappeared. I chuckled. *He wasn't wrong.* West and I had been a pair of hellions when we were kids.

"I don't need you to protect me," West snarled. His fingers drummed anxiously on the countertop.

"Yeah, I gathered that," I retorted. "But if someone's going to hit Burt, it'll be me. I ain't a felon. You are."

"Fuck off," he muttered, but I ignored him.

"And let's face it, Burt deserves a good hit every once in a while," I said under my breath. *Wasn't that the fucking truth.* Glancing at West, I caught the way the corner of his mouth quirked with the tiniest of smiles. It vanished almost as quickly, but I'd still caught it.

And I'd take it. It was better than him scowling at me.

Henry took forever getting Casey to come help me, and Casey took even longer getting my order together. Even with all the shit I bought, it shouldn't have taken so goddamn long. I'd blame it on an off week for them because usually, they were damn good about it. Still didn't improve my mood as I slammed the tailgate to my truck though.

Stepping onto the sidewalk nearby, West paused, his gaze lingering on *Lenny's* across the street. His jaw clenched as he drew in a deep breath. I wanted to poke and see just how bad the withdrawal was—how hard was it for him to stand there and not go in?

"Have you gone to a meeting?" I asked.

"No," he muttered.

"Merrillville has one tonight," I told him. *Yeah, I had a whole list of AA meetings on my phone in case he needed it.*

"Fuck off, Jackson," West snapped. "I don't need you to fix me."

"Not trying to fix you. Just trying to help."

"Yeah, well, you can fuck off with that too."

CHAPTER 29

WEST

I WENT TO THE Merrillville AA meeting like Jackson suggested—not that I gave him the fucking satisfaction of knowing. I just needed... something. What that was, I didn't have a fucking clue. Everything was razors against my skin. Withdrawal was a bitch. I was fucking dying. The only thing I could think of was going to a meeting. Maybe that would help.

But I couldn't bring myself to go inside the small community building. I leaned against my tailgate, arms crossed, as I stared at the building. My anxiety was at an all-time high, clawing and weaseling its way through my chest. My knees locked up, and I was rooted in my spot. The idea of being closed inside a small room with a group of strangers was nauseating.

And so I just watched like an idiot as people milled around the front of the building, wandering in and out. They chatted with one another and were all so friendly and comfortable with one another. I didn't understand it. *I didn't know how to be like that with anyone.*

Just before the turn of the hour, an older guy showed up in the doorway. He ushered people inside, briefly greeting everyone as they passed. He caught sight of me across the parking lot and offered a friendly smile—at least, I knew he was trying to be fucking friendly. It didn't feel that way as my stomach turned violently. He gestured inside in a silent invitation. Pressing my lips together tightly, I declined with a quick shake of my head. He waited just a moment longer before closing the door.

I couldn't go inside. *I wasn't worth it.*

I went to three more meetings but never made it inside. Hell, I couldn't bring myself to walk to the fucking door. And I sure as hell didn't know why I kept coming back. At least when I was in the parking lot staring at the building, I wasn't in the stables losing my goddamn mind.

As I watched cars start to roll in, the door opened as usual and the same man stood there. He was older with graying hair and a love for polos. *So many fucking polos.* He knew everyone and spent his time talking to each person before the meeting.

Except today.

No, today, he smiled as he walked right past everyone and toward me.

Fuck.

"Coffee?" He offered me a to-go cup of what I expected was crappy fucking coffee. I took it. I wasn't sure I could stomach it, but I still took it. "Mind if I join you?"

I nodded, and he leaned against the tailgate of my truck next to me.

"You know," he began quietly, "we have coffee and donuts inside. The coffee is pretty average, but the donuts are fantastic. They're the actual bakery kind."

"I don't think I could eat a donut right now," I muttered. Just the thought of it made my stomach clench.

"The withdrawal is hard, but once you get through it, it gets better," he said. I didn't ask how he knew. "I'm Bobby."

"West."

"I'm proud of you, West."

"Why?" I demanded. *I hadn't done a damn thing to deserve that shit.*

"Well, you've made it to four meetings," Bobby replied as if it was as simple as that. "Even if you haven't come in yet, that's still progress."

"Not really," I muttered.

"It is," Bobby insisted. "It's okay to be scared to ask for help, West. It makes you human."

"I'm not..." I faltered. *Yeah, I was fucking terrified.* There were too many people, I didn't know what to expect, and I didn't want to have to talk in front of everyone. Every wild scenario I ran in my head never ended well. I didn't want to lose my fucking shit in front of everyone, but that was where it always ended. Under my breath, I admitted, "I don't want to fucking talk to people."

"That's okay," Bobby said. "No one is here to make you talk. Some people don't talk for weeks or even months. It's about having a group of people to help each other, learn from each other, and just get through life. Addiction at any stage is difficult, and people don't understand it the way we do."

I just nodded. I didn't have a clue what I was supposed to say.

"We don't do circle style here," he continued. "It's just rows of chairs, so you could sit right at the back away from everyone as you get a feel for it. I'll even walk you in, so you don't have to do it alone. What do you say?"

Taking a slow sip of coffee to buy myself time, I considered his question. I really wanted to just get in my truck and drive away with my fucking tail between my legs. That was the safe option. *But also the stupid one.*

I was fucking struggling—hard. I couldn't do this on my own. But I refused to ask Jackson for help. The man was already up my ass and driving me insane.

"Okay," I whispered.

"Okay," Bobby echoed with a nod. He stepped back as I closed up the tailgate. I held onto that stupid cup of coffee like my goddamn life depended on it, and my legs were lead as we crossed the parking lot. To his credit, Bobby didn't say a word. He just walked alongside me at my pace.

True to his word, he pointed out a seat in the very back row. Most of the back was empty with everyone sitting in small groups toward the front. I picked a seat in a far corner, close to the door and able to see everyone. I didn't want any surprises.

"It's a great first step, West," Bobby told me softly, giving me another smile as he patted me on the shoulder. The simple contact was fucking torture, but I held back a flinch. I just nodded, and he walked away.

That crawling-out-of-my-skin sensation had settled in, and the walls felt too close. The room was hot and loud, making my chest tighten something awful. I was stuck in my seat, unable to move, even if I wanted to. *He could say whatever the hell he wanted but it sure as fuck didn't feel great.*

CHAPTER 30

JACKSON

Working the stables was a nice change of pace from moving cows around the fields, lawn maintenance, perimeter inspections, and every other mundane task I was used to doing. I still wasn't a fan of the horses, but I was gaining a newfound appreciation for them. And while I trusted Mickey to make sure everything out there went off how it was supposed to, this meant I didn't have to deal with him face to face nearly as much—a fact I liked.

The only one upset with this new arrangement was Daisy. Usually, my girl followed me around the fields every day in the off-season, but I wasn't there. That didn't stop her from an eventual jailbreak to find where I was at. *Which was exactly how I ended up manhandling a moody cow while trying to fix corral fencing.*

"I know you're there," I said once more when she headbutted me in the hip hard enough to knock me off balance. I grabbed the fence to keep from toppling. "You're making this shit hard, little lady."

Daisy mooed. I wasn't winning this goddamn fight with her. Shoving the hammer into my tool belt, I faced her, my hands dropping to my hips.

"You have no shame," I told her. When she pushed her head against my chest, I gave in and gave her the pets she demanded.

I wanted to be mad—I really fucking did—but it was real hard to be grumpy with a twelve hundred pound grass puppy. *Especially one that liked as much attention as she did.*

Typically, I had a no-attachment rule with the cows. Sure, they were cute, but I sold cows for slaughter. It'd be bad for business to get attached. Daisy, though... she'd been something different from the start. I was fairly certain she gained all her behavior traits as a calf from watching Tess and me. So, now I had myself a dog and a grass puppy. Thankfully, only one came inside.

The longer I gave her affection, the harder she leaned into me until I could barely stand. Guiding her to the ground wasn't hard, but it did mean that I'd be stuck cuddling a cow for a while, which didn't seem so bad with her big body wrapped around mine and her head in my lap. *When was the last time I'd slowed down to just enjoy sitting with my cow?* Or anything for that matter. I couldn't remember.

As I sat there stroking the wide space between her eyes—her favorite spot—I glanced across the corral to where West was working with Thunder Jack. I had to admit, he was doing good work with that horse. Little by little, the horse was warming up to West. Granted, they were still in the barely lukewarm phase of getting used to each other, but West was able to get Thunder Jack to eat out of his hand in small amounts.

Watching West with the horses was slowly becoming a favorite pastime of mine. I'd steal glances where I could or just cave and stare at him. He was different with the horses—calm and focused. That same intensity of his came out, but he streamlined it all into their care. The herd never looked better than it did under West's care.

But if I was being honest, it wasn't just his way with horses that held my attention. I found myself caught up on the way he always ended up shirtless, even with the cool weather. My gaze snagged on the stark lines of his tattoos. *The way they curved and outlined his strong arms drove me fucking nuts.* I'd never been a tattoo guy, but I liked them on him.

Did I belong staring at him like that? Probably not. But I just couldn't help it.

Under my hand, Daisy let out a long moo as if echoing the thoughts in my head.

"Yeah, I get that," I muttered, glancing down at her. "I probably shouldn't be looking at him that way, should I?"

Did Daisy care? Absolutely not. But I found talking to animals about this kind of shit—or any hard shit—sure as hell beat talking to humans.

When I looked up again, West was on his way over. *Still shirtless.* And as I watched him, I realized I wanted to ask him why the hell he pierced his nipples of all things. I didn't see the appeal.

Okay, maybe on him I could see the appeal, but again, there were things I shouldn't focus on.

"I..." West faltered as he stopped on the other side of the fence. He stood there awkwardly, his gaze dropping to the rag he wiped his hands on. I waited. *Sometimes just waiting him out seemed to be the best way to get him to say anything.* I was slowly figuring him the fuck out—at least I felt like I was. That didn't stop him from throwing me a curveball every few hours. "Do you always cuddle a fucking cow?"

"You treat Daisy with respect," I retorted and gave her an affectionate rub between the eyes.

"You named her?" he asked. "Isn't she going to be someone's dinner someday?"

"I will personally fucking kill anyone who tries to eat my damn cow," I snapped. His lips quirked at the corner, but he said nothing. That tiny as fuck smile was all the reassurance I needed. "What do you need, West?"

"What's the policy on adjusting my work hours?" *That wasn't the question I was expecting.*

"I don't have one," I said. "Typically, I just deal with shit as it comes up for everyone. Why?"

He nodded slowly, lips pressed together tightly.

"Tuesdays and Thursdays I need to be in Merrillville at six," West continued. It clicked immediately. Merrillville had AA meetings on Tuesdays, Wednesdays, and Thursdays. There was no way in hell I wouldn't do my damnedest to make sure he could get to his meetings. "But I know that's right in the middle of the evening wrap-up. I wouldn't be here to take care of the horses until after, but I don't know if that's okay. And I don't exactly know when I'd be back."

As much as I was ready to let West skip all of his duties in order to go to his meetings, I was also aware of his need to pull his own weight. The man wouldn't accept help from anyone over anything.

"Okay," I replied after pretending to think about it. "I'll unsaddle and get them situated with feed after the day wraps up. Just make sure their stalls are clean before you leave if you can and brush them down when you get back."

"I can do that." The weight lifting off him was visible. Resting his forearms on the wood, he leaned against the fence. He still fussed with the rag, but at least he seemed calmer. "Thank you."

"Any time."

"It's a meeting," he told me quietly. *Holy hell, he was sharing something with me.* "Two... two of them. That's why I need to leave."

"I'll make sure it works," I promised. "You just worry about taking care of you. That's all that matters."

He just nodded, that expression on his face telling me he wasn't convinced. I knew there wasn't a damn thing I could do to make sure he knew it. That was just something he had to figure out for himself.

CHAPTER 31

WEST

THE ONLY THING I got out of AA meetings was the fact that I wasn't the only one going through this shit. *The alcohol part, not everything else.* I didn't talk and wasn't sure I ever wanted to. Bobby gave me *the Big Book*, which I was supposed to read, but every time I tried, I had a panic attack. I never made it past the first page or two.

All of this was too much change too fucking quickly. I struggled to stay afloat, which felt like the complete opposite of what this fucking program was supposed to do.

To my credit, I didn't drink. I fucking wanted to, but I didn't. So maybe that was something.

Bobby was far nicer than I deserved. Every meeting he was there greeting me beforehand and checking in afterward. He talked. I listened. It worked for us—at least I thought it did. Eventually, I'd probably have to do some kind of talking, but I wasn't there yet. The idea of it made me want to run. Or hit something. It depended on the day.

Instead of a quick conversation at the back door, Bobby invited me out to dinner. While I wasn't hungry, I wasn't ready to return to the ranch yet, so I followed him down the road to a small diner.

"How are you doing?" Bobby asked when the waiter left. I started to shrug but stopped myself. Shrugging never got me fucking anywhere with him. It wasn't that he was pushy in any way, but he had this tendency to just wait me out until I was so uncomfortable that I started talking. It was a horrible fucking gift that he used to his advantage.

"I'm okay enough," I said. "Don't feel as crappy."

"But still not hungry?" he replied. I didn't blame him, considering I hadn't ordered food. But I didn't know how to explain that I'd gone years without eating much, so I just never ate much. Food had always been scarce. I was good at one meal a day or a few snacks because I was used to it.

"Not really," I muttered. "But that's nothing new."

"It'll catch up to you," he told me knowingly. "The first few weeks or so can really knock you on your ass."

"Yeah." *That was the understatement of the fucking century.* I couldn't count the number of times I was tempted to go right back to drinking just so I'd feel better. At least when I was drunk, I didn't feel like I was fucking dying nearly as much as I did lately.

"Have you thought about who you want as a sponsor?" he continued, and I frowned. *What the hell were he and I doing if not exactly that?* Fuck, did I have to talk to someone else?

"Can't you just be my sponsor?" I replied. The thought of getting to know another fucking person wasn't appealing. Not that Bobby and I knew each other either, but it was better than nothing. "Is that a fucking option? I don't know how this shit works."

"I can be if that's what you want," Bobby said. "But I will be honest and say that I have some reservations about doing so."

Fuck.

"I'd like to revisit the idea of ninety meetings in ninety days with you," he replied. I resisted rolling my eyes. I couldn't do ninety days straight of this shit. I didn't have it in me. *The people.* The people fucking drove me to the brink of panic.

"I can't with my job," I said, using the same excuse I did the first time. It wasn't a total lie. I had a hard time believing that Jackson would let me run my schedule wild for ninety days of meetings, even if he was overly helpful.

"Those first ninety days are crucial, West. Newcomers often find that they need the most support in the first ninety days. I know you're at two meetings a week right now, but I think it'd be smart to add in at least another meeting or two a week to keep you going."

"I just can't get it in with my job," I reiterated. He nodded slowly, and I could tell he didn't approve of my choice.

"So, let me ask you something," Bobby began slowly, "and know that this comes from a place of observation. There is no judgment here."

I made a sound, already hating whatever the hell he was going to say.

"Do you live out of your truck?" he asked. "I ask because I've worked with a lot of people in different living situations, and there are signs—"

"I have a fucking place to stay," I snapped. "Sort of."

"Can I ask what *sort of* means?"

"I live with the horses I work with."

"So, you live in a barn."

"A stable," I corrected. *Like that was any better to most people.*

"Okay." He paused as the waiter dropped off his food as well as another glass of water for me. When we were alone, he said, "This comes from a place of understanding because I've been there, West, but stability is the key to you working this program successfully. Wanting it is important but stability is everything if you want to make real progress. Without it, relapse is a lot closer than you might realize."

Nothing about that surprised me. I wouldn't know stability if it hit me in the fucking face. I was used to laying low, panicking with every change, and just dealing with all the crap life threw at me. Hell, life on the ranch was probably the closest thing to stable I'd had since prison. I may have been sleeping with the goddamn horses, but at least I had a routine to follow. That part felt good—or at least as close to feeling good as I could get.

"Yeah," I whispered, not knowing what else to say.

"I know some programs that are great for helping people get back on their feet if you need help."

"I don't need help." *I was so tired of everyone thinking I did.*

"Learning to accept help takes quite a bit of courage," Bobby said. "It makes us stronger."

"Are you a walking motivational poster?" I demanded. We were navigating a little too close to shit I didn't want to talk about or deal with.

"I have a whole collection of them." He grinned, undeterred by my attitude. "Let's get you through your first ninety days and I'll give you a motivational poster."

"I don't want one," I replied. *And where the hell would I hang one anyway?* The horses wouldn't give a fuck about some goddamn motivational poster. Neither did I. "Does that mean you'll be my fucking sponsor?"

"Yeah, we're going to get you through this, West," he told me. "One day at a time."

"One day at a time," I repeated under my breath. *One miserable fucking day at a time.*

CHAPTER 32

JACKSON

"You trust him," I commented, watching the way Thunder Jack wandered openly in a corral with Bailey. I sat on a fence with West as we kept an eye on the two. I'd known that Thunder Jack was big, but I hadn't realized just how huge the horse was. He made Bailey look small as fuck.

"He ain't going to hurt anyone," West said around a mouthful of food. I glanced at him and noted how half his sandwich was already gone. While he still didn't eat a lot of food, I did notice the way he readily ate whenever we did meals together. *That had to be a good sign, right?*

"You're doing good with him." That much was true. I was the first to admit that Thunder Jack was a lost cause—at least, he had been. But with West's guidance, the horse was taking a positive turn. There was still a lot of life left in him, which I hadn't been able to see.

"He just needed to feel like he was safe, that's all," he dismissed. "Animals are simpler than people think. They need to be cared for, have their needs met, and know they're safe. Do that and you'll see a whole new side of them."

"That's true," I agreed softly. His gaze tracked how Thunder Jack moved around the corral while Bailey just wandered about doing her own thing. She couldn't be bothered with his existence, not that he seemed to mind. "You always did have a way with horses."

Well, not just horses. West had a way with all animals. There was just something about him that had animals flocking to him when we were kids. I couldn't begin to count the number of neighborhood dogs that went missing only to be found hanging out with West in the fields. And when my mom started bringing home horses? They may have been her horses, but they responded better to West than anyone else.

"Horses are easy," West said around another big bite. "It's people that suck, and the horses know it."

"Why the hell haven't you gotten on any of them?" I asked. The fact that West had yet to ride any of the horses—especially Bailey—surprised me. At first, I'd thought it was a drunk-sober thing, but I wasn't convinced. His withdrawal symptoms were waning, which meant he'd be fine on the back of any horse. Considering how he'd practically lived on the back of a horse growing up, I was curious why he hadn't yet.

"Just haven't figured it out yet." He shrugged.

"Oh, come on. That's bullshit and you know it."

"It's not. I haven't fucking figured it out yet."

"You know how to ride a goddamn horse."

"Jackson—"

"It's muscle memory at this point. Even if you haven't been on one in the past seventeen years, it's not that hard to get back on—"

"My dick is pierced," West interrupted loudly.

His dick was... what? I choked on my sandwich, coughing hard. I slid off the fence as I sputtered and tried to regain my composure. My brain struggled to wrap around the words he'd just said. Maybe I'd heard him wrong?

That had to be it.

"I'm sorry, what?" I rasped when I had just enough of a voice to say something.

"My dick is pierced," he repeated. The way he said it was as if it was the most casual information to give. "I want to get on a horse, but I'd like to keep my dick where it is. I'm still figuring out the risk of ripping out a barbell."

Jesus fucking Christ.

"Well." I cleared my throat, nodding slowly because thinking about barbells in his dick wasn't something I needed to be doing. "That makes sense."

That made sense? What the fuck was wrong with me?

West's expression was unwavering as he stared down at me. Just fucking waiting. For what I had no idea. The corner of his lips quirked—a habit I was starting to realize meant he was more than likely about to say some stupid shit.

"I have six barbells," he continued. *Oh.* "You know, in case you were going to ask."

"I wasn't," I said tightly. *Nope, I definitely was not. Could not. Would not.* I refused to think about what the hell his dick looked like pierced.

"I could've done eight," he told me. *This motherfucker.*

"That's just... yeah, I could see why you'd be more careful while riding." I changed the subject. Lord fucking help me, I changed the goddamn subject, but that image kept trying to weasel its way back into the forefront of my brain. "I'm going to fucking... check in with Mickey and see how... things are going."

"Enjoy, cowboy," West called after me as I stormed away. *Enjoy what?* The demanding thought of what West's dick looked like pierced? Because I refused to enjoy that.

No, no, I would not. I was better than that.

I absolutely wasn't fucking better than that. West's pierced dick was the only thing I could think about all day long—right up until I ended up in a cool shower at the end of the day.

Was he fucking with me?

Why the fuck would he tell me about his piercing? What did he think that would accomplish? There was no need for it. He could've made up some shit about fucking anything instead of telling me that.

Fuck me.

And what the fuck was that cowboy shit? Why had he called me that? The last time he said it, it was out of malice, but this time it came out as light-hearted and almost playful. It did things to my dick.

Which I probably should've felt guilty about.

Except I didn't.

Instead, I leaned against the tile wall in my shower with my cock in my hand. I was so goddamn hard and ready to lose my fucking mind. All I could think about was West and his pierced dick as I stroked myself.

But imaginings of West's piercings quickly turned into the things I'd like to do with those piercings. What sound would he make if I ran my tongue over them? Was he quiet? Loud?

The little wondering built with the heat wrapping around my spine as I fucked my fist, my pace picking up. I had no clue what the hell I was doing with West, but at that moment, I sure as hell liked the idea of making him come undone with just my mouth.

My breath came faster, and my head tipped back against the wall.

I wanted to taste him. I wanted to feel those goddamn barbells running over my tongue. How quickly could I make him lose control? How fast would his cum coat my throat?

That thought did me in.

"*Fuck*," I groaned while my balls seized. I came hard, drenching my fist in hot cum as I stroked my way through the intensity. I kept going until I had nothing left in me.

Letting water run over my hand, I closed my eyes as I caught my breath and reality slowly sunk in. They were just fantasies—things that could never happen. *Would never.*

I had a real strong feeling West would forever keep me at a distance. It was a safety thing for him. I understood it—respected it even—but I hated it.

CHAPTER 33

JACKSON

AND ANOTHER ONE BACKED *out*. Fuck.

Sighing, I sat back in my chair. I ran my hands over my face, needing something to distract me from the all-too-polite email on my computer. *I hated the polite emails.* I'd rather have a customer cuss me the fuck out than politely let me know they were going with a different supplier.

Fuck. I couldn't even blame them. Who wanted to butcher cows coming from a dying herd? The liabilities alone were a business nightmare.

A low whine next to me made me drop my hands. Tess scooted closer, her head resting in my lap while those big brown eyes watched me closely.

"Do the math for me, girl?" I asked. Inching back in my chair, I tapped my chest. In an instant, she was up in my lap and laying her head on my shoulder. Teaching her to give hugs had been a silly thing to do, but I liked it. I liked the comfort I found in her. "Tell me how many more customers I can lose before I tank this whole goddamn ranch?"

The answer was a lot less than I wanted to admit out loud. My numbers were more and more in the red every month, and I didn't know how to get myself out of it.

A knock on the front door sent Tess scrambling. I barely managed to toss her off me without getting hurt. *Who the fuck was at my goddamn door?* It was eleven-thirty at night. No one should've been knocking on my fucking door.

I checked my phone just in case I missed something from Mickey but nothing. *What the fuck?*

Another knock had me damn near scowling. The only thing I could think of was West had gotten himself into shit and the Sheriff was here. *Which was a whole goddamn mess I didn't need.*

"Fuck, I'm coming," I yelled after a third, more incessant attempt to get my attention. I snapped my fingers and pointed to the couch. "Tess, back."

She listened, though her entire body shook with excitement. At least one of us was looking forward to figuring this shit out.

But when I answered the door, seeing West was the last thing I expected. He stood there with his hands in his pockets, looking awkward. He still wore the same clothes and there was dust in his hair like he'd come straight from the stables, which only made me worry.

"Did something happen with the horses?" I demanded. *Fuck, that was the last thing I needed.*

"What?" His brows came together tight. "No. They're fine."

"Don't tell me something happened with the cows."

"No, they're fine. At least, I think they're fine. I don't fucking know." *Then what the fuck did he want?*

"Okay," I replied slowly. "What do you need? It's late."

"Is that... is your... *fuck*," he said softly. He shifted uncomfortably and stood a little taller, shoulders squaring off. *Please, for the love of God, tonight wasn't the night for a fucking fight.* "Is your offer to stay here still available?"

I stared at him. *Had I heard him wrong?* Was he actually willing to move out of my stables? I honestly never thought I'd see the day that happened. He was so adamant about avoiding any help I offered.

His tension and anxiety visibly increased. *Right.* I had to put the man out of his misery.

"Yeah, it is," I told him. Nodding to the small duffel at his feet, I asked, "Is that all you have?"

"I got my truck and my bike," he said. "But I don't think you want those in your fucking house."

"No, I don't," I agreed. Still, I couldn't help myself from glancing down at his bag. He couldn't have had much in there. A few changes of clothes at most. It would explain the rotating four shirts he had. That thought saddened me. No one deserved to be living out of a bag. And not one that small.

"Don't start pitying me because I don't have a house full of shit," West snapped as if reading my thoughts. "I'm fine the way I am."

"I never said you weren't." *But I was planning on buying him more clothes, even if I had to throw them in his room when he wasn't looking.*

"I don't have guests often," I admitted as I switched out the sheets. *Fuck, I was pretty sure the last person who stayed in my house was my mom.* And that was over five years ago.

West stood in the doorway with his hands in his pockets and his bag at his feet. He looked as wildly uncomfortable as I felt inside. This whole dynamic was unexpected.

"Tess listens well," I rambled, feeling a weird need to fill the silence. "If you let her, she'll sleep with you, but she's a bed hog. Snores too."

"I can sleep on the fucking couch if that's easier," West offered.

"It's fine," I said as I struggled with the fitted sheet. *Why the fuck were they even a goddamn thing when they were so difficult to get on?* "It's not much, but it'll do."

The guest bedroom was simple with a bed, a side table, a dresser, and a chair. Thanks to my mom there were about half a dozen yellow throw pillows tossed around the room. Why? I didn't have a clue. Who the fuck used throw pillows? *What* was a throw pillow?

"There's extra blankets in the hall closet," I continued. "The bathroom is just outside the door. I think you'll have to grab towels from the closet too. Maybe? I don't fucking know. I don't use it."

"It's fine," he whispered. Could he look any more uncomfortable?

"I get up at five-thirty, but I usually sleep heavy, so just do what you need to in the morning. Help yourself to whatever's in the kitchen. The coffee is on a timer—"

"I said I'm fine," West snapped. "Just the room is fine."

"Okay." I sighed and ran a hand through my hair. "Well, help yourself. I'll be upstairs if you need me."

"I won't."

"I know. Good night, West."

"Night," he mumbled so softly I barely heard him as he let me pass.

I was halfway down the hall with Tess on my heels when the door shut quietly. I paused to stare at it, some part of me still in disbelief that West had taken me up on my offer. It took everything I had to not walk right back, knock, and ask. If he wanted me to know, he would've said something.

Tess whined, and I glanced down at her. Ears back and big-eyed, she looked as confused as I felt.

"Don't look at me," I whispered to my girl. "I'm as surprised as you are."

CHAPTER 34

WEST

The idea of leaving the stables and living with Jackson didn't sit well with me, but I understood why I needed to fucking do it. *Didn't make it suck any less.*

It took me all of three minutes to shove my shit into my bag but it took me a good hour to say goodbye to the horses—mostly Bailey. I spent a little extra time settling Thunder Jack in his new stall away from the others. He was on edge, which was almost enough to make me say fuck it and stay. This whole trying to do better thing was exhausting and difficult.

The lights were still on at Jackson's house when I showed up. That made me feel a little better. At least I wasn't about to wake him the fuck up. The last thing I needed was to piss him off by doing that.

I knocked and nothing. *I couldn't blame him for that.* Who answered their door this late at night? Fuck, I should've done this earlier or said something to him.

But I kept knocking until the door flew open to Jackson wearing nothing but a pair of gray sweatpants. *Fuck.* Something pulled in my chest at the sight of him like this—something uncomfortable and familiar. Sure,

I'd know he was in shape, but it was different seeing the miles of toned muscle right in front of me.

Thankfully, the expression on his face was more than enough to distract me from whatever weird fucking thoughts were trying to form in my head. He looked confused. *Then annoyed.* I couldn't blame him. I'd be fucking annoyed if he showed up on my doorstep unannounced.

"Did something happen to the horses?" Jackson demanded.

"What?" I frowned. "No. They're fine."

"Don't tell me something happened with the cows."

"No, they're fine." *What the hell did I know about his cows?* Besides the fact that he liked cuddling the one. "At least, I think they're fine. I don't fucking know."

"Okay," he said, slow and pointed. "What do you need? It's late."

His annoyance set my already frayed nerves on edge.

"Is that... is your... *fuck.*" This shit fucking sucked. It felt like admitting I couldn't do this without him. *Maybe I couldn't.* That stung even more than the fact that he wanted to help. "Is your offer to stay here still available?"

And there it was... the thing that felt like a low moment. I needed his fucking help, and now he knew that I knew that I needed it. And that endless blue stare was nauseating. My pulse threatened to explode from my neck as I waited for him to say something.

Fucking anything.

Shit. Just put me out of my goddamn misery if that was what he planned to do. The waiting was torture.

"Yeah, it is," he said finally. He nodded down at my small duffel bag. "Is that all you have?"

"I got my truck and my bike, but I don't think you want those in your fucking house." He made me fucking grumpy.

"No, I don't," Jackson agreed, but that didn't stop the pitiful look he gave me as he weighed my words. Jesus fucking Christ. I didn't need his pity on top of his help.

"Don't start pitying me because I don't have a house full of shit," I growled. I wouldn't know what to do with all that shit anyway. "I'm fine the way I am."

"I never said you weren't." He stepped aside and held the door open for me. "Tess, stay."

One step. I could do this.

I grabbed my bag and went inside, my legs heavy like lead. This was a good thing. *This was supposed to be a good thing.*

Stability. I just needed stability.

This was better than buying a house in a fucking town I wanted out of, and it wasn't like rental properties were a thing around here. The town was too small for that shit.

"Come on." Jackson snapped his fingers and Tess hurried after him as he walked across the house. He waved lazily for direction like maybe I wouldn't remember the house he grew up in. *Truthfully, I didn't remember much.* "Kitchen, living room, back door. You can figure it out. Your room is on the first floor this way."

I welcomed his silence as I followed him through the house. Tess trotted happily between us, stopping at least twice and almost tripping me in the process. I gently nudged her along to keep the process going. I didn't feel like being fucking stuck in a hallway with Jackson and his dog.

"Fuck," he muttered as he opened the door. He pointed to the floor, ordering, "Stay."

So, I stayed. In reality, I knew he wasn't talking to me, but I didn't know what to do with myself. I dropped my bag to the ground and just stood in the doorway with Tess at my feet while Jackson flipped on a side lamp. I lost sight of him as he moved around the room.

Yellow.

So much fucking yellow.

The color made my pulse jump anxiously. I couldn't handle yellow, and it was fucking everywhere. Pillows, bedding, and three stupid sunflower paintings on the wall.

Fucking everywhere.

"I don't have guests often," Jackson said, his voice foggy in my ears. I tried to focus on him, but it was hard to do so when the walls were fucking vibrating. *Were they vibrating?* Or was I imagining it? "Tess listens well. If you let her, she'll sleep with you, but she's a bed hog. Snores too."

Dog bed? Had I taken his dog's bed? Fuck. That was pathetic.

"I can sleep on the fucking couch if that's easier," I said under my breath. I blinked hard, doing whatever I could to focus on how he struggled to put on a new sheet.

"It's fine. It's not much, but it'll do," he replied. Something painful clawed at my chest, and I sucked in a sharp breath.

I would not panic.

I would not panic.

I would not fucking panic.

Not in front of Jackson.

"There's extra blankets in the hall closet." Jackson just kept on talking while I suffered in fucking silence. "The bathroom is just outside the door. I think you'll have to grab towels from the closet too. Maybe? I don't fucking know. I don't use it."

"It's fine," I managed to say. I dug my nails into my palm in a desperate attempt to ground myself. Pain helped. Sometimes.

"I get up at five-thirty, but I usually sleep heavy, so just do what you need to in the morning." *Right, I had to be at the stables before him.* Maybe I should've stayed there. There was no yellow in the stables. "Help yourself to whatever's in the kitchen. The coffee is on a timer—"

"I said I'm fine," I snapped. "Just the room is fine."

I didn't need his handouts on top of letting me stay with him.

"Okay." The sigh he let out grated on my nerves. So did the way he ran his hand through his hair like he was trying to find a reason to stay in the room. *I needed him to leave the fucking room.* "Well, help yourself. I'll be upstairs if you need me."

"I won't." The only thing I needed from him was to walk out the fucking door.

"I know," he said. When he started for the door, I skirted out of the way, shrinking into myself to avoid being touched. I couldn't handle it. "Good night, West."

"Night," I muttered and watched him walk out. When he was gone, I shut the door, leaving me alone in the awful yellow fucking room. I let out a shuddering breath as I stared at the walls. *Was the room smaller?* The room felt smaller. Too small. "I can do this..."

The sheets and blankets were white with yellow flowers.

Fuck, it was too much. How was I supposed to sleep on that? I couldn't.

With shaking hands, I tore everything off the bed and shoved them in a corner. It wasn't far enough, but it was all I could do. *All I could fucking manage.*

I sank to the ground at the foot of the bed and buried my head in my hands as the familiar demons in my chest tore their way to the surface. Another shattering breath escaped me, hot tears leaking out as I squeezed my eyes shut.

I hated the fucking color yellow so goddamn much.

CHAPTER 35

JACKSON

MY KITCHEN WAS SPOTLESS. My kitchen was never spotless. Granted, I rarely used my kitchen. I was a pop-it-in-the-microwave kind of guy—which wasn't how my mother raised me, so I never told her that shit. She'd move her ass right back into my house and teach me how to cook if she knew that.

Top to bottom, it practically shined. Counters, sink, windows. Hell, even the floor looked scrubbed clean. And sitting on the counter were two covered plates of food—one labeled with Tess's name and the other with mine. I took a peek at my plate, wondering what the hell West could've made. Scrambled eggs, bacon, and toast. *Did I even have eggs and bacon in the house?* Shit. Did West know my kitchen better than I did?

And what the hell had he made Tess? I looked. It was some kind of cooked-up meat and vegetables thing—did I even have any of these things in the house? I had to believe West wouldn't make shit that Tess couldn't eat. He liked animals too much.

My gaze drifted around the kitchen. He'd done a fuck ton of work. *Which begged the question as to when the fuck did West sleep?* If his track record held steady, I had a feeling he hadn't.

Curiosity got the better of me. I walked down the hall toward his room. The door to his room was cracked open, and I peeked inside, frowning.

The bedding had been stripped off and thrown into a corner. *Fucking rude.* I put work into that. Tess lay on the bed, sprawled out and happy. Her tail thumped against the mattress when she saw me but that was it.

There was no sign of West at all in the room except for his duffel bag on the floor.

"You're really going to make me say it, aren't you?" I asked my girl. Her ears twitched but that was it. "Come on, now. You've got breakfast to eat and work to do."

It never ceased to amaze me how quickly that dog could move. She bolted from the bed and sprinted down the hall before I had a decent chance to turn and follow.

Closing the door, I filed away talking to West as something to do later. Sure, he had free reign of the house to do whatever the hell he wanted to do, but that sure as hell wouldn't make me worry any less.

"I'm coming, I'm coming," I grumped as Tess howled in the kitchen. I never did move fast enough for her.

CHAPTER 36

WEST

I TEMPTED FATE. *Not that I fucking cared.* Thunder Jack needed his hooves taken care of—desperately—but he and I weren't at that point of comfort with one another. Not yet anyway.

After leaving him and Bailey in a water-soaked section of the corral, I separated him from her—much to her dismay. She'd grown fond of him in the few days I put them together. As I guided him back to his secluded section, she trailed after us. When I closed the gate, she hung out on the other side and just waited for him. I liked their relationship. It was good for her, and she was good for Thunder Jack. Something about her presence calmed him.

It worked in my favor as I balanced his front hoof between my thighs, thankful for the non-slip fabric of my chaps. I steadied myself and waited. I wasn't about to put anything fucking sharp near either of us until I was sure he could handle the contact between us. One minute turned into two and quickly became three, four, five, and nothing. *Thank fuck.* He seemed comfortable enough with being there, which was good enough for me.

I was fast and efficient, working my way through removing the unnecessary horseshoe on him, trimming, and then balancing the hoof. It was still hard work. Clearly, no one had put in the fucking effort to maintain them. I would've been fucking grumpy too if I was him.

"I'll get you feeling fucking better," I grunted as I worked.

When I was satisfied with the way his hoof looked, I lowered his leg and rubbed down the muscle for both reassurance and comfort. Thunder Jack shifted and chuffed in reply. His demeanor was wildly calm compared to what I'd expected.

"Yeah, you ain't so bad, are you?" I said softly while moving around his front, brushing a hand over his soft snout. He huffed and pushed into my palm. I took a moment to give him the affection he'd let me before moving on to the next hoof.

As I worked, I didn't have to look up to know he was fucking there. *Just standing and watching.* Jackson did that a lot, wearing that stupid cowboy hat and an expression I couldn't read. I hated it. It made me anxious. I wanted him to say whatever the fuck was on his mind and get it over with instead of staring at me.

This time, I had a feeling it had to do with his kitchen and the breakfast I'd made them. Admittedly, it was probably a stupid fucking thing to do. I should've just come back to the stables and cleaned shit here that he wouldn't notice. But no, I made myself stay in his house. *Stability and all that bullshit.*

That didn't stop the demons from trying to take over, and I had to do something to stem the chaos. Keeping my hands busy was always the best option, which left me cleaning his kitchen. But when that was done, I still had time on my hands, so I made him and Tess breakfast before cleaning up everything a second time.

It was stupid, but it was all I fucking had. And now I fucking regretted it because I had no idea how Jackson would react to the whole thing. I wasn't in the mood to deal with his pity or annoyance.

I chanced a quick glance at him. His expression was clear as day under that stupid cowboy hat.

Pity.

Yeah, I was going to avoid him as long as I fucking could.

I ran out of things to do to keep me busy and out of Jackson's house. The fucking urge to hide in the stables was at an all-time high. I'd done everything in my power to avoid talking to Jackson, but I couldn't do so forever. *I wanted to, but I couldn't.* Mostly, I just didn't want to know what the hell he had to say about his kitchen.

Dragging my feet, I made my way up the steps to his house well after the sun had set. Every fucking light was on, ruining any hope I had of avoiding a conversation with him. I sucked it up as I let myself in. I had to. There was no avoiding whatever came next.

"Son of a fucking bitch!" Jackson exclaimed. Something loud hissed in the kitchen followed by a slam heavy enough to make me freeze, my heart surging in my chest. "Fucking hell!"

Taking slow steps, I went toward the kitchen. Jackson stood in front of the sink, waving a towel over a smoking pan as he ran water into it. The scowl on his face and the burning smell in the air made it real easy to figure out he'd fucked up cooking. *Maybe cooking wasn't his strong suit.*

Tess sat at his feet—correction, on his feet. Her whole body pressed against his leg as if trying to comfort him.

"I hope you like frozen pizza," he muttered when he saw me. "Because this shit ain't edible."

"I can take care of myself," I said. "You don't have to fucking feed me."

"And you didn't have to make my goddamn breakfast," he shot back. I forced myself to stay still as the anger on his face sent my pulse skyrocketing.

"Fine," I said. *I didn't have to eat anything he gave me.* "I'm going to take a fucking shower."

I didn't wait for a response as I stalked down the hall toward the bathroom. The idea of a real, decent shower was a nice one. I hadn't had one of those in years. Truck stop showers and cheap motels could only offer so much.

As I shut the door to the bathroom and flipped on the light, I froze. *Yellow.* Everything was fucking yellow. Walls, shower curtain, towels, stupid accessories on the countertop. Fuck, even the garbage can was yellow.

I swallowed hard against the lump in my throat. This was my fucking reality until I was out of this damn house. It wasn't Jackson's issue. It was mine. I had to learn to deal with it.

Stiff-legged, I made myself turn on the shower, turning it to full blast. *I could do this.* Quick in and out. I could do this.

But the room was insufferably hot long before the shower temperature spiked. My chest was unbearably tight and breathing was a fucking chore, every breath scraping painfully against my lungs. I grabbed the towel rack for support as the panic clawed its way violently through my chest. The room swayed, and I squeezed my eyes shut.

Screaming echoed in my ears while everything around me tipped, my knees giving out. I sank to the ground.

There was no stopping it.

CHAPTER 37

JACKSON

The pizza sat cold on the stove while I scowled at the clock. West had been in the shower a long fucking time for a guy who was just going to shower quickly before dinner. Yeah, I'd fucked up dinner but at least I tried to make it up to him. He didn't have to hide in the bathroom for damn near an hour to avoid me.

Fuck that.

I stormed down the hall and stopped outside the bathroom door. The light was on as was the shower, but I didn't hear a goddamn thing otherwise. No moving or anything. It didn't sit right with me. Why I tried the doorknob was beyond me. It was an invasion of his privacy, but my gut was also telling me that something was wrong.

"West?" I said again as I opened the door. Anything else I planned to say was lost when I saw West sitting on the floor, fully clothed and unshowered. His head was buried in his hands while ragged breaths shook his entire body.

Fuck.

"West, what happened?"

He let out a pathetic sound, visibly shrinking into himself.

I reached beyond him to turn off the water before cramming in the small space by the cabinet. I did my best not to touch him, which was fucking hard. There wasn't enough room.

"How can I help?" I asked, though I didn't expect an answer. He let out another quiet and painful sound. I didn't know what to do—how to help him—so I just sat there. His panicked, uneven breathing filled the quiet. I felt each one in the pit of my stomach.

My brain ran rampant as I watched him. Was this what panic attacks were like? Did they get worse? Did he get them often? What did it feel like because it sure as hell didn't look good? I knew panic attacks were a thing, but I'd never seen someone go through one. This was fucking awful. My heart ached for him as I sat there uselessly.

"The walls were yellow," West rasped, his voice barely audible. "In the… when they…"

Oh.

"Fuck," I said under my breath, glancing up at the walls. I reached up and shut off the light, letting the darkness blanket us. It wasn't much, but hopefully it'd help a little. At least he wouldn't have to see the yellow.

My mom loved the color yellow. She said it was a happy color, and so she went overboard when decorating the house. The bedrooms had all been yellow, and every other room had been covered in yellow accents—pillows, paintings, dumb knick-knacks. When she gave me the house, I'd gotten rid of most shit and repainted most of the rooms. With my lack of guests, I hadn't bothered touching the guest room and bathroom.

I fucking regretted it.

West needed out of there. Sitting on the floor immersed in it wouldn't do him any good.

"Come on," I whispered, holding out a hand to him as I stood. I wouldn't touch him if he didn't want me to, but I also had a strong feeling he wouldn't be able to stand enough on his own. The least I could do was get him up.

To my surprise, he accepted the help. I could feel the tremble in his hand as I pulled him to his feet. He swayed, and I resisted the urge to grab hold of him. It probably would've made everything worse. I kept my hold on his hand until he was ready to let go.

Except, instead of doing just that, his hand tightened around mine. Desperately tight. Like I was his lifeline. If he needed that, there was no way in hell I was letting go.

Taking my time, I led him out of the bathroom and through the house. I kept silent, focusing on his rampant breathing behind me as we went up the stairs. There wasn't a damn thing I could do about his bathroom, but I could set him up in mine.

I left him sitting on the toilet, gently removing his hand from mine—though, it killed me a little to do so. He was letting me help him. Comfort him. Be there for him. Granted, I didn't know what the fuck I was doing, but I wanted to be that person.

I turned on the lights, picking the lowest setting possible to keep it dim for him. I had to imagine lights that were too bright would be too much. Maybe? Who knew? I was winging it.

"There's a built-in bench," I rambled pointlessly, needing to fill the silence with something as I started the shower. "I've hurt myself a few too many fucking times to not have one. Use whatever you need. There's..."

There was no yellow. Everything was blues and browns. That part I didn't add. It didn't feel right.

"If you need anything, I'll be right downstairs," I said as I started for the door.

"I'm sorry," West let out so softly I almost missed it. I paused to look at him, but he didn't make eye contact. His gaze was glued to the floor in front of him. I would've given anything to know what he was thinking just so I could fix it—make him feel better.

"You don't have to be sorry," I assured him and shut the door.

"Answer the damn phone, Mick," I snapped as I rushed down the stairs two at a time. The phone rang several times, each one pissing me off further. *The one fucking time I needed him to answer.* Right before it sent me to voicemail, he answered. "Jesus fuck, it took you long enough."

"*My world don't revolve around you, boy,*" Mickey retorted. "*I—*"

"Yeah, yeah," I dismissed him. I didn't have time for any back and forth with him. "I need you to run everything tomorrow."

"*Any particular reason?*" he asked.

I stopped in West's room, staring at the room. The rolled-up bedding in the corner suddenly made a lot of sense. And I would've bet everything I had that West hadn't slept in here. The amount of yellow was glaring.

It needed to go.

"None that you need to worry about," I said. "I just need you to take care of everything."

"*Okay.*"

"And do me a favor? Call Peter and tell him I need him to meet me at my house instead of the stables. He's working with me tomorrow." I couldn't do everything on my own. I needed help, but I also needed someone who would understand. Peter was all I had.

"*You got it, boss,*" Mickey replied.

"Thanks, Mick." The words were barely out of my mouth before I hung up. I had too much shit to do.

I took down the sunflower paintings and stashed them in the basement. I'd donate them later. Mom sure as hell wasn't missing them. I threw the sheets in the laundry and put on the spare white ones—no yellow flowers. The pillows were tossed in the trash outside because I had no need for them anyway.

There wasn't a damn thing I could do about the bathroom besides close it up. *Out of sight, out of mind.* At least for now. It was the best I could do on short notice.

But by the time I got back upstairs to check on West, the shower was off and he was passed out in my bed with nothing but a towel wrapped around his waist. He had to be fucking exhausted. I moved quietly, covering him with a blanket and turning off the light. The last thing I did before I left the room was set the alarm for him. Working with the horses was a good thing for West, and I'd be damned if I took that from him right now. He needed them as much as they needed him.

CHAPTER 38

JACKSON

"The key is under the mat," I repeated grumpily into the phone. It was eight in the morning, I'd driven an hour and a half out of town for one of those has-everything stores, and I was fucking annoyed to shit. I had so much crap to do and dealing with stupid questions wasn't what I wanted to do.

"*That's a terrible place to put a key, boss,*" Peter replied. "*Don't you think anyone trying to break into a house is going to look under the mat first?*"

"I'd like to see someone try to break into my fucking house. They might do it, but they aren't living to fucking talk about," I snapped just as an older woman walked by. She gaped at me—probably at the audacity of my mouth. I tipped my hat in her direction and smiled. "Ma'am."

"*Are you scaring old ladies again?*"

"What the fuck do you mean again?"

"*You have this reputation—*"

"I don't have a fucking reputation!" I cut him off. *Jesus fuck,* Peter was brazen when he wanted to be. "We're getting off-topic here. I have a job for you."

"*I have successfully broken into your house,*" he told me. "*You have a nice house.*"

"Fuck with my house, Peter, and you'll never see the light of day again," I growled.

"*You should get coffee while you're out,*" he said instead. "*You're grumpy without your coffee.*"

"I'm not..." I stopped in front of the cart corral to draw in a deep breath. He was right. I hadn't had time to make my fucking coffee. "Fine, yes. I'm fucking grumpy without my coffee, but I have a lot of fucking shit to do today. *We* have a lot of shit to do. I don't need the goddamn peanut gallery making this shit harder."

"*Just tell me what you need me to do, boss, and I'll do it.*" Oh, thank fuck. Granted, Peter wasn't really pushing his luck. I just hadn't slept well. After West fell asleep in my bed, I tried to spend the night on the couch without much luck. I couldn't turn my brain off. The night's events kept playing in my head on repeat. I never wanted to see West go through that again—though, deep down, I knew that wasn't possible. It just didn't work like that.

"There are tarps on the kitchen table," I said while taking a cart out. "Down the hall on the first floor is the guest room. I need you to pull all the furniture out from the walls and tarp it."

"*You got it.*"

"And then I need you to go into the bathroom. Take all the little shit off the counters and floor and just toss them in a fucking garbage bag. You'll find them under the kitchen sink. Take the shower curtain down too. Just toss everything."

"*Okay.*"

"I need you to tape up all the trim and shit in the bathroom for me to paint. Do the same in the bedroom too. And then I need you to paint the bedroom," I told him. I waited for him to protest, but when he said nothing, I just continued as if this wasn't the weirdest shit I'd ever asked an employee to do for me. "There's gray paint on the table with all the supplies you need. Just start in the bedroom. I have to pick some shit up and then I'll be back to help."

Thankfully, the hardware store opened early enough in town that I'd been able to go in and grab paint. I couldn't take away what yellow meant to West, but I could get rid of it in my house to make him feel safer.

"*You got it, boss,*" Peter replied.

"Call me Jackson," I corrected. "You're painting my goddamn house for Christ's sake."

"*You got it, Jackson.*"

I hung up the phone as he laughed and pulled up the list I'd made in my notes app. Before doing anything, I ran through it one more time. *Bedding, bathroom shit, shower curtain, shirts and jeans for West, doorknobs.* Maybe I was doing too much, but I didn't care. It was the only way I knew how to help.

Loud rock music filled my house as I trudged back and forth carrying bags in. I'd probably bought West too much shit—enough to make him pitch a fucking fit—but I didn't care. This was what I did. I fixed shit. I couldn't fix how his mind worked against him, but I could fix the circumstances around him to the best of my ability.

Kicking off my boots, I went to check on Peter. I glanced in the bathroom as I passed by. Everything was out and taped up like I'd asked. *Good.* To my surprise, the bedroom was half-painted already.

"Oh, hey," Peter greeted when he saw me, hurrying across the room to stop the music on his phone. "I didn't hear you come in."

"Not a surprise," I muttered. Minding the plastic, I wandered into the heart of the room to inspect his work. The dark gray color covered the yellow walls smoothly. "It's looking good."

"Yeah? Good." He ran a hand through his short hair as he surveyed his work. "So, what exactly are we doing here?"

That dreaded question. It was the entire reason I asked Peter to help me. He was the only one who'd get why I needed to do this.

"Let's just say," I began with a sigh, "that PTSD stole the color yellow."

"Ah." He nodded with more understanding than I wished on anyone. After a long moment, he added, "You know, I never liked the color yellow. It's an ugly color."

I fucking appreciated this man.

"It is."

"When do we need to be done?"

"The end of the workday," I said. While his track record suggested otherwise, I couldn't guarantee that West would stay at the stables any longer than necessary. It gave us a very short window to paint and redo everything.

"Well, all right then. Let's get this shit done."

Without waiting, he went right back at it. I followed suit, heading for the bathroom as my brain began another run-thru on my plan for the day.

"You're doing a good thing," Peter called after me. I paused at the door. "I know you're probably questioning it, but you're doing a good thing for him. He probably won't see it right away, but he will."

"I sure as fuck hope so," I whispered. Truth was, I didn't have a clue how West would react. He was so averse to being helped that I could see this blowing up in my face.

CHAPTER 39

WEST

After waking up naked and in a towel in Jackson's bed, I couldn't go back to the house. I'd managed to sneak past him in the morning, and with him being gone all day, I hadn't seen him. I did every extra little fucking task I could think of just to avoid going back to his house. Maybe I could sneak in and try to sleep for a few hours on the couch without him knowing I was there.

Having Jackson take care of me while I lost my fucking shit was embarrassing. *Even if some part of me was comforted by it.* I didn't want him to see me like that. And I didn't know how to face him after that.

Well after midnight, I trudged my way into his house. The only light on was the one above the kitchen table. Two sets of keys and a note sat on the keys but that was it. Jackson wasn't in sight and neither was Tess.

Morbid curiosity got the better of me, and I peeked at the paper. I wasn't even sure it was meant for me, but I couldn't help myself.

> West,
> Check the bedroom, check the bathroom. Both sets of keys are yours. You have the only copy.
> Jackson

What the hell did that mean? I toyed with the keys, wondering what the fuck I was supposed to do with them. The idea of going back to either of those places made my anxiety spike. A lump formed in my throat, and I swallowed hard. I had to look because he'd gone ahead and done something.

I swept up the keys and forced myself down the hall. The bathroom was first, but my hand faltered on the doorknob. *A new doorknob.* I ran my thumb over it. Why was there a new doorknob on the bathroom door? I pushed it open, and the smell of paint was an overwhelming blast to the face making me flip on the light.

The yellow was gone.

In its place were deep grey walls, a black shower curtain, and matching accessories placed around the bathroom. Even the garbage can was black.

My chest tightened painfully. *Jackson had taken away all the yellow.* And he put in a new lock that only I had the keys to.

Why?

With my heart doing something wildly uncomfortable in my chest, I made my way down the hall to the guest bedroom. *Grey walls, black bedding, and an old framed painting of horses hanging on the wall.* It was a completely different room.

He'd gotten rid of all the yellow. That singular thought stuttered around my brain, breaking off little pieces of me in a way I couldn't describe. No one had ever done anything like this for me.

I sank down to the bed, unsure of what to do about everything he'd done. *And why?* It made no sense.

CHAPTER 40

JACKSON

A LOUD BANG STARTLED me out of my sleep, and I sat upright, bleary-eyed and disoriented. *What the fuck?* Was someone trying to break in? Tess, on the other hand, couldn't be fucking bothered as she snored away at the foot of my bed.

"Some fucking guard dog," I grumped to the girl who wouldn't hear me anyway. Tossing off the blanket, I grabbed a shirt off the dresser and struggled into it as I stormed down the hall to the stairs. Whatever the fuck was going on, it had to fucking stop. I needed sleep. *I wanted my fucking sleep.*

Any fight I had disappeared when I rounded into the kitchen and saw West furiously scrubbing a pot. Every fucking pan I owned lined the counters along with all my mugs and glasses, piled on dish towels and bath towels after being scrubbed clean. Except I knew they hadn't been used. Not a single one of them.

Which meant that West had cleaned out my cabinets to clean everything. *Anxiously clean them.*

Fuck.

I ran a hand through my hair as I watched him spiral. His entire body was rigid, tension wracking his muscles. *What the hell had incited this?* Was this because I painted and redid everything for him?

Whatever it was, I knew I couldn't leave him like this.

"I'm turning off the water, West," I announced as I came up behind him, careful not to scare the hell out of him and get my ass kicked.

"I'm fine," West snapped, his voice cracking.

"I know. I'm going to take the sponge now, West." My hand covered his. It took a moment but he relented, letting me set it down in the sink. "We're going to go sit down in the living room now."

"I'm fine," he reiterated. The rising tension in his voice suggested otherwise, but I wasn't about to argue with him. If he needed to feel like he was, then I'd let him.

"I know," I repeated. And then I warned, "Hands on the shoulders, West."

I gave him a chance for the words to register before I took him by the shoulders. I felt him flinch, but he didn't pull away.

"I need to clean all that shit up," West said while I guided him from the room.

"Yeah, and you will," I told him. He stalled for a second, and I ushered him to the couch. "But it's one in the morning. I'm tired and you're tired, so we're going to sit in the living room for a while."

"But—"

"Just for a little while," I interrupted. "We'll clean everything up later, okay?"

"Okay," he muttered. He didn't fight me as I sat him down on the couch. Nor did he fight me as I grabbed the nearest blanket and covered him with it. I'd read that people with anxiety found blankets comforting and relaxing. I didn't have a clue if that was true for him, but it couldn't hurt to try. *Fuck, I'd try anything at this point if it'd bring him a few moments of comfort or peace.*

"Reality TV is my guilty pleasure," I admitted, telling him something I didn't fucking tell anyone. That was shit I didn't need getting out. While he wrapped himself up in the blanket, I sat next to him and propped my feet up on the L of the couch. "I like watching other people do stupid shit."

He made a quiet sound but said nothing as I turned on the TV. I mindlessly scrolled through my options until I settled on a stupid mass dating show. It was always messy and ridiculous, but I found it entertaining nonetheless. And hopefully, it'd distract West long enough to let him relax.

My tired brain zoned out on the screen, barely catching a word said. I was determined to stay up with him, but fuck, it was hard. All I wanted to do was go back to sleep. Somewhere in the middle of it all, a slight bump and pressure on my shoulder made me freeze. I glanced down to see West had fallen asleep. *Good.* Minding my movements, I lowered his head into my lap and waited with the expectation that it'd wake him up. It didn't.

Pressing my luck, I brushed his hair away from his forehead. Instead of pulling away or waking up, he sighed—the sound quiet and content. I adjusted the blanket around his shoulders and just stared at him as I ran my fingers through his hair for comfort. *His or mine, I didn't know.* It was just oddly nice sitting there with his head in my lap. He looked peaceful. More peaceful than he had in a long time.

I whistled just loud enough for Tess to hear me from upstairs. She bounded down the stairs, tail wagging with excitement. I shook my head. *Some guard dog.* Good thing no one had actually tried to break in. Coming around the side of the couch, she sat.

"Gentle," I ordered in a hush. Her ears perked up as she waited patiently. I pointed to the far end of the couch and said, "Up."

She hopped up on the far end, nearly landing on West's feet.

"Crawl," I told her. Laying down, she inched across the couch, lining up along West's chest. She nudged her way under his arm. He shifted slightly, his body curling around hers and his fingers burying in her fur as he held her closer. I whispered, "Good girl."

With my fingers brushing through West's hair, I closed my eyes and rested my head against the back of the couch. Was it the most comfortable way to sleep? No. But honestly? It was nice.

CHAPTER 41

WEST

I WAS SO FAR inside my head that I quit working. I couldn't fucking focus on anything and damn near screwed up everything I touched. Instead, I sat on the far side of the horse corral and just watched the horses do their thing. *All the while, I thought about Jackson.*

I could barely remember a fucking thing about panic cleaning the kitchen. Finding the rooms painted had triggered another stupid episode. I didn't know how to handle Jackson's kindness—his attempts to take care of me. No one had ever done shit like that for me.

And what did he get out of it? What was I supposed to give him in return? That question fucked with my head. I didn't have a damn thing I could offer him.

It almost fucked with me as much as when I woke up with my head in Jackson's lap. His hand had rested around my shoulder as he slept, and it felt almost nice. Almost nice enough for me to close my eyes and pretend to sleep some fucking more. But I couldn't—not with the weird buzzing coursing through my body.

Hell, I had pretended to sleep, even when he woke up. Instead of moving me, he just sat there with his fingers running through my hair. *It was almost nice.* It set my nerves on fire but it was almost nice. No one has even touched me like that.

And at the end of it all, Jackson got up and left for work as if nothing had happened between us. *Which was for the better because I didn't know what the hell to say or do.* Fuck, I didn't know what to make of it all.

It left me confused and anxious. I didn't know how to act around Jackson, so I avoided him. *That was what I did best: run away from my problems.* I didn't know what I was supposed to do. What did normal people do when they woke up cuddling their former best friend turned boss turned whatever weird fucking thing we were now?

The sight of Jackson walking across the corral pulled me from my thoughts. *Fuck.* If I was being honest with myself, Jackson was attractive—not that I'd tell him that. The problem was I didn't know if I was attracted to him. *Honestly, I didn't know what it felt like to be attracted to anyone.* The whole concept was foreign to me. While I'd tried many times to force the experience—to prove I could be like everyone else—it never happened. I never felt a fucking thing.

But with Jackson?

Things with Jackson were different lately. There was something. I didn't have a fucking clue what that thing was but there was something. Was this what it was like to be attracted to someone? To Jackson? Fuck, I'd been attracted to him when we were young but that was so goddamn long ago. I couldn't remember what that felt like.

He stopped in front of me, hands bracketing his hips. I just stared at him—maybe I glared at him. I didn't have a fucking clue. I wasn't in control of my face at this point.

"You want to talk about it?" Jackson asked quietly. *Fuck.* I should've known this shit was coming. He always wanted to talk.

"No."

"Okay," he relented real damn fast. *Thank fuck.* I couldn't handle more of his pushing and prodding today. "Can I sit with you?"

"It's your fucking fence," I snapped. His nostrils flared as he took in a deep breath, clearly holding his composure. I immediately felt bad. He didn't deserve my anger. I scooted slightly on the rail to make room for him and whispered, "Yeah."

He climbed up on the fence next to me. I waited for him to start talking like he always did, but he kept the silence and just sat there watching horses with me.

The violent clap of thunder overhead came out of nowhere as did the heavy downpour that followed. The horses panicked, and we were left scrambling to collect them. It was a fucking mess of a situation with horses scattering, Jackson swearing, and me trying not to get trampled.

By the time the horses were sorted out in their stables, Jackson and I were both soaked and out of breath. I ran a hand through my wet hair as I stared out the open barn doors. Jackson settled on the other side, leaning against the frame with a scowl on his face.

"I checked the fucking weather," he grumbled. I didn't hear the rest of whatever he said. My brain went right back to the train of thought about Jackson. I was obsessively stuck on everything.

"Why'd you do it?" I interrupted whatever the fuck he was saying. He let out a small sound of confusion. *Yeah, that was my fault.* I elaborated, "The paint... the locks... why'd you do it?"

"Because." He shrugged as if that was enough of an answer. *It wasn't.*

"Why do you care so damn much about what happens to me?" I asked. That was the one thing I couldn't wrap my head around. *And I wanted it to make sense.* I needed to know why.

"I'd rather go through hell with you, West, than watch it destroy you."

He'd... what?

What did that mean?

I didn't know what the fuck to do with that, but something hot flared in my chest. It wrapped around my heart and did something inexplicable to me. Closing the distance between us, I grabbed his shirt and kissed him. *Was that really what I was doing?* I didn't have a clue. I felt as awkward as I did the first fucking time. Sure, I'd kissed a handful of people, but none that I wanted to. None that mattered.

Jackson mattered.

His hands cradled my head as he stepped closer. My body stiffened in reaction. *Why was this so fucking difficult?* I kissed him again and again in an attempt to silence the demons in my head telling me this was all wrong.

In the end, the voices won.

"I'm not worth it," I whispered breathlessly against his mouth.

"You just let me keep believing that for the both of us," Jackson said, quiet and full of conviction. He kissed me again. When his tongue touched the seam of my lips, I opened.

Everything about his kiss was soft and gentle, but I felt it with every fiber of my being. The sensations rolling through me were overwhelming. My world tipped and the spiral from his touch was intense.

"West," he began as he broke the kiss, "I can feel you shaking. Do you want to stop?"

Shaking? Was I shaking? I didn't have a fucking clue. I didn't know what I was feeling. It was... something.

Good?

Bad?

I couldn't tell.

But I wanted to find out.

I had to find out—had to figure out if I liked kissing Jackson.

Wordlessly, I shook my head, unable to clear the fog in my head, and kissed him again.

CHAPTER 42

WEST

Palms against the wall, I closed my eyes as scorching water burned down my body. No matter how hot it got, it didn't chase away the chill in my bones. *And it had nothing to do with the weather.*

I spiraled. Everything was out of control. I didn't know what to do with myself. I'd kissed Jackson, and it felt... nice. Good? Maybe?

I felt something—something I hadn't felt in practically a lifetime. Something I hadn't anticipated feeling ever again.

Arousal surged through my body in uncomfortable waves that set my nerves on fire. Good or bad, I couldn't tell. I was too overwhelmed by it all. Just the water rolling over my skin was torturous.

My dick was painfully hard—standing at full attention like it wanted something from me. I had no control over it. No chance of making it go down.

I couldn't remember the last time it fucking worked.

And I didn't know what to do with it. With the guilt. The shame.

Why the fuck did I even feel this way? I was in over my head. My body wasn't mine to control, and I hated it.

Kissing Jackson had been one thing but this? I didn't want this. I wasn't even sure I wanted that kiss—my brain was all fucked up—but I didn't want this.

This was normal. It was supposed to be normal.

I tried to push that thought to the front of my mind—to justify that this was okay—but the dark thoughts kept taking over everything. It clawed through my head. The familiar edge of panic dug its way into my chest, and I drew in a sharp breath.

I just wanted it to go away. To not be a thing.

I just wanted to be okay.

CHAPTER 43

WEST

"Now, listen here," I whispered as I stroked Thunder Jack's soft snout. He pushed further into my hand—something he'd started doing every time I pet him. The frequency was incredible.

I wasn't sure what fucking possessed me to do it, but I saddled him up. It took me a good three hours to walk him through the process, but he let me do it. *Did I need to take that long?* Probably not. But I wanted to make him feel comfortable after everything he'd been through. After what he'd been put through. He deserved that at least.

He let me brush him head to toe without flinching or wandering away. If he had, I would've quit. Instead, he stayed put and relaxed. I expected him to bolt when I laid the saddle blanket over his back. I wouldn't have fucking blamed him, all things considered. But he trusted me and remained in his spot, his head turned and tracking me.

And when I fitted him with a saddle? Not a damn thing. I was impressed.

The last big test would be if he threw me or not if I got on. *When.* When I got on.

"Now, look," I said as I continued to give him some much-needed attention. "I'm going to need you to work with me here. I like my dick where it is, and I want to keep it that way, got it?"

I waited like he actually gave a fuck about what I said. Did I expect him to respond? Who knew? I just hoped to fuck he didn't fucking throw me.

"Don't throw me," I reiterated one more time before rounding his left side. Grabbing the pommel and stepping into the stirrup, I pulled myself up on his back and settled in the saddle.

I tensed, every muscle in my body locking up.

Beneath me, Thunder Jack shifted. The slight movement rolled through my body, and my instincts told me to jump off while I still fucking could. I fought the urge to do just that.

I had to give him the chance.

"You're doing good," I praised as I rubbed a hand along the side of his neck. "You're doing real good, boy."

He relaxed slightly, and I felt the smallest of smiles tug at the corner of my lips.

"This ain't so bad, is it?" I continued, practically speaking for both of us. There were no words to describe what it felt like to be back in the saddle. Seventeen years and it still felt like home. Any worry I had about tearing out a barbell seemed to vanish as I got comfortable. "Should we try to move a bit?"

He let out a quiet neigh, tossing his head and stomping in place.

Keeping my movements gentle, I nudged him forward, but he didn't move.

"Not yet?" I asked. I offered another long rub along the side of his neck. "It's all good. We have all day."

And so we stayed like that: me rubbing his neck and him in full control of whatever the hell we were going to do. Throw me? Run for it? Sit there all day? It was a fucking crapshoot. *Oddly, I didn't mind.*

Who knew how long it took—I wasn't counting—but when Thunder Jack took his first step forward, my heart lurched into my throat.

"That's it," I whispered and gripped the reins tighter. "Good boy. You've got this."

His first steps were unsteady as if he wasn't too sure about me being on his back. I didn't blame him after everything he'd been put through.

"C'mon now." I gave him a reassuring pat. "We got this."

Despite my hold on the reins, I let Thunder Jack take the lead. I was at his mercy as he slowly wandered around the corral. I kept up a quiet stream of praises while he did, doing my best to keep him at ease.

As his steps grew steadier, I took over in slow increments—a pull of the reins here, a nudge on his side there. I gauged his responsiveness. Surprisingly, he let me take over.

"That's a good boy," I murmured while I turned him around toward the gate and the open field that waited for us. "Should we see what you can do?"

CHAPTER 44

JACKSON

A MY PORTER, MY AGENT, was single-handedly the most irritating person in my life—and that was fucking saying something. While the woman was partially responsible for my fame and name as a bull rider, she was also the one who'd cultivated the image of me when I refused to pretend I wasn't gay just because a bunch of men weren't comfortable with me. But the older I got, the more fucking angry I got about the whole damn thing.

She also had this habit of endless phone calls and text messages. Considering everything else going on in my life, I was ignoring the woman. *Was it smart to ignore my agent as the season approached?* Probably not but it kept me sane.

Until she fucking started emailing. I stared at one of her many emails as I sat bored on my horse in the field.

Jackson,

Since you won't answer any of my phone calls, I'm stuck with sending this email instead. You know how I hate emails. It's an impossible way to communicate when dealing with time-sensitive matters.

Lexington Farms would like to have a conversation with you when the season starts. I've secured them as your sponsor. They are looking forward to the upcoming season with you.

No arguing!

Call me.

Amy

The fuck? Lexington Farms was a major competitor of Double Arrow. The downfall of my ranch was giving them a fuck ton of business—something Rex Lexington had been overly nice and sympathetic about in a way that sat wrong with me. This felt underhanded.

I typed out a quick message because fuck that.

No.

The answer is no.

Not a fucking chance.

And if I have to spell this shit out for you: I'm not taking a handout from the people benefiting from my business failing.

I didn't bother signing it before sending it. She knew who I was.

My scowl was practically permanent at this point when dealing with Amy. The mood carried over as I pressed a button on my radio.

"How we looking out there, boys?" I asked, doing a random check-in. I needed something to do and micromanaging them was as good a task as any.

"*It ain't too—*" Peter's response was cut off with static.

"Fuck," I grumbled. Overall, the radios were a good idea, but sometimes, they were just a pain in the ass depending on cloud coverage. *I was too grumpy for all this crap.* I pressed the button again. "Peter?"

The sound of whooping and laughter mixed with the static.

"What the fuck is going on over there?" I demanded.

"*Ooh-wee! Look at 'em go!*"

"Who?" I snapped. *What the fuck were they doing over there?* I didn't like not knowing what was going on with my ranch.

"*Just you wait! They're coming your way!*" Peter laughed.

"Who the fuck is coming..." My words trailed off as I caught sight of what had my men riled up.

It was West.

West was riding Thunder Jack.

West was back on a horse.

And damn did he look good.

I stared for all of a few seconds, taking in his wind-blown hair and relaxed stature. There was a flash of familiarity—a little glimpse of the West I grew up with. He'd never looked more comfortable in his skin than when he was on the back of a horse.

And from the look of it, some things never changed.

I urged my horse Zeus forward, and he broke into a run. We galloped across the field, following after West. For as fast as Zeus was, he had nothing on Thunder Jack.

But I was used to chasing after West. Growing up, we'd always been like this. On a horse, he was fast and reckless. *Free and unrestrained.* His pick in horses always reflected that part of him.

And me? I never minded chasing him down. *Hell, I still didn't.* There was an exhilaration in pushing myself to keep up with him. A thrill in the challenge.

I'd chase West anywhere.

The North Elm River bordered the edge of the ranch. The region was largely untouched. I couldn't remember the last time I'd come out this far.

And even as they neared the bank, Zeus slowed. They crashed into it with a massive splash while I pulled up on the bank. I leaned on the pommel, watching with utter fascination as Thunder Jack trampled through the water. *But it wasn't the horse that held my rapt attention.*

It was the giant smile on West's face. The utter joy in his expression was a sight to take in—one that tugged at my heart in a way I hadn't known possible.

"Afraid of getting that hat wet, cowboy?" West teased, that grin never wavering. *Hell, if he kept on smiling, I'd let him make fun of my hat all he wanted.*

"Yup," I drawled and tipped my hat in his direction. His smile widened, and damn if I didn't love it. "I see you finally got back on a horse."

"Yeah." He ran a hand through his dark hair, pushing wet strands away from his face.

"Feel good?"

"Feels good." *That made me stupidly happy.* Not that I told him that.

"Good," I said.

"I'll race you back," he said, and I made a face. We both knew he'd win. "What? You afraid the hat's going to weigh you down, cowboy?"

Yeah, I fucking liked it when he called me that. I liked the smirk he wore and the depth of his voice when he said it. I felt it in every nerve in my body.

"You're on," I shot back, feigning my annoyance.

I had the window to gain a lead as he nudged Thunder Jack forward, prompting the horse to climb up the angled bank. But for the life of me, I got caught up in his smile.

That moment cost me the win, but fuck, I didn't care.

CHAPTER 45

JACKSON

WEST WAS MORE RELAXED than he'd been... *well, ever.* It was like riding a horse again unlocked something inside of him. He went on and on about the horses and what he was doing with them as we sat on the corral fence. I didn't have much to add to the conversation, but I could listen to him talk all afternoon. *And I did.*

Eventually, evening rolled around and my guys wandered in. I didn't bother getting off the fence. I'd kept track of their work on the radio—not that there was much going on anyway. Instead, I just tipped my hat in their direction as they corralled their horses and stayed right where I was.

The last one to come in was Mickey, and I stiffened as he started in our direction. I had no fucking desire to talk to Mickey. There wasn't a damn thing I needed to be updated on, so there wasn't a damn reason he needed to talk to me.

"Boss." Mickey tipped his hat in a pleasant greeting that I didn't return.

"Night, Mickey." The words came out short, but they were all I had in me. West glanced in my direction, but I purposefully ignored him.

"West," Mickey continued. "You're lookin' mighty good on the back of that horse today. You did good work with him."

"He did most of the work," West corrected. Mickey shifted his weight as he considered West's words. I didn't want him to consider anything. I wanted him to continue on his fucking way.

"Night, Mickey," I repeated, my tone sharper this time. His tired gaze met mine, but I was unwavering.

"Night, boss." He tipped his hat one more time before shuffling away.

"Why the hell are you so mad at him?" West asked when he was out of earshot. "For weeks you've been giving him the cold shoulder or snapping at him. What the fuck is wrong with you?"

"You're fucking kidding me, aren't you?" I demanded, but West just shrugged. "After everything he did—rather didn't do when it came to Harrison."

"What the hell are you talking about?"

"Mickey, my mom, my dad... they should've done more about Harrison. They knew what the hell he was fucking doing and they did nothing. He never should've been allowed to treat you how he did. You deserved better, and they should've fucking done something about Harrison back then."

His brows furrowed together as he thought about what I'd said, his hand running over his beard. His silence felt damning.

"Look," he began with a sigh, "I know you're mad at them, but they did protect me, you know? They did their fucking best. Your mom bought the horses because I liked them, not because she did. The more horses she had, the more work I needed to help her with. It kept me away from him. Your mom doesn't like horses all that much if we're being honest. Most of her herd were horses I picked out when she took me to auctions to help her with shit."

I hadn't known that. Mom had always made it seem like the horses were her thing.

"And Mickey... Mickey used to lie for me whenever I was late or not where I was supposed to be," West continued. "And your dad... well, your dad kept Harrison busy. If Harrison had shit to do, then he was too busy to beat on me. I don't blame them. They did what they could."

"It wasn't enough," I said. "They should've done—"

"It was enough," he interrupted. "This ranch... this is their legacy. It's their whole family history. I ain't that important, Jackson. Never was, never will be."

"West—"

"Some people are born great, some people are born worthless, and everyone else is somewhere in between," he told me "I know where I stand on that scale."

Knowing what I knew, he believed himself to be on the worthless end of that scale.

"You can't really fucking think that." *I hated when he talked like this.* It killed a little part of me. I understood where it came from but fuck. A part of me wanted to grab him by the fucking shoulders and shake him until it made sense.

He made a small sound and half-heartedly lifted a shoulder.

How the hell could I make him see otherwise?

"Look." West slid off the fence and rubbed his hands on his thighs. "I ain't mad at them. You're wasting your fucking energy fighting with Mickey and ignoring your mom."

"How the fuck do you know I'm ignoring her?"

"She leaves a lot of messages on your answering machine," he replied. "You also have to be the only motherfucker I know who still has a goddamn landline."

"Don't make fun of my fucking phone," I snapped.

"Let it go, Jackson," West said. "I ain't worth all that shit."

Yeah, he fucking was.

"We're going to come back to that," I warned him, knowing that if I tried now, he'd walk away. I hopped off the fence and followed him while he approached the horses. "I should probably visit her, shouldn't I?"

"Yeah."

"You could come with. I know she'd lose her shit to see you again." I suggested with no belief that he'd take me up on it, but to my surprise, he nodded slowly.

"Sure, why the hell not," he muttered. "Now, get the hell out of here, so I can get my work done. You're a goddamn distraction."

I grinned, liking that idea. However, I liked the idea of him coming home faster instead of delaying that more.

"All right." I took off my hat and fussed with the brim of it. *What was the protocol with him?* If he were any other guy, I'd kiss him before I left—it wasn't like any of my employees had stuck around. But with West? With the way he didn't like being touched? How the hell did I approach him?

"What're you looking at, cowboy?" West asked when I did nothing but stare at him.

"If I wanted to..." My voice trailed off, and I shut my mouth. It was a dumb fucking question to ask. *If I wanted to kiss you, could I?*

"It's your goddamn ranch. You can do whatever the hell you want."

"It's your stables, your rules," I quipped back. That made him falter, his back going rigid. *Fuck.* His shoulders squared off as those gray eyes held mine. He was bracing for whatever shit I threw at him. That was the last thing I wanted to make him feel.

"Just ask your question, Jackson."

"*If I wanted to kiss you before I left, could I?*" *God, it felt stupid asking that out loud.* Boundaries. I had to keep reminding myself about the boundaries. And the look on his face didn't help the situation. It was as if he was debating the right way to respond—as if he didn't know the right way to approach the situation either.

"I guess," West whispered. "I mean... yeah. That's fine."

But did he mean it?

I couldn't tell.

I didn't want to question it either. It was his choice, and he was giving me permission. Who was I to second guess that?

With several long strides, I closed the distance between us and kissed him—the kind of kiss where my lips barely touched his. His chin tilted slightly as he kissed me back, but it was... awkward as hell.

For both of us.

I pulled away and drew in a deep breath, trying to gain some semblance of understanding. That kiss in the barn had been intense and emotional. It meant something. It felt like something. And for the life of me, I assumed it would lead to more. I just didn't know how—especially not now with both of us just standing there and staring at one another.

"This was awkward, wasn't it?" I muttered.

"Yup," he agreed all too quickly, nodding.

"Fantastic." I dropped my hat back on my head. "See you at home, West."

"Yeah," he replied, but I barely heard him as I made a quick exit, feeling all too uncomfortable with everything that had happened. I didn't know how to be around West. *Not like this.*

CHAPTER 46

JACKSON

West furiously smoking had me reconsidering taking him to see my mom. He insisted he was fine, but his visible anxiety said otherwise. I leaned against my truck as I watched him. There was no reason he had to struggle this much.

"We can go back to the ranch," I told him.

"No." He shook his head as he puffed out a cloud of smoke. "No, I'm fine."

I wasn't wholly convinced. But I also wasn't winning in telling him what to do. Sure, I could try to toss his ass in my truck and drive away but then I'd just be stuck for an hour with a feral West pissed off at me. No one wanted that shit, so I just waited him out as he chain-smoked his way through his anxiety.

"I'm fine," he repeated.

"I know," I said. I had a lot more I wanted to say, but I kept silent. It was easier to let him work through it than insert myself. Arms crossed, I leaned against the side of my truck as he paced.

"I couldn't sleep," West whispered as he joined me. I simply nodded slowly. His quiet admissions were something I appreciated and would wait forever for. I recognized them as his attempt to build a broken bridge across the gap between us—the one where he was fighting something I would never be able to understand. His gaze was a million miles away as he added, "And I've got a headache. It won't go away."

"I've got something that might help with that." I left him to rummage around my glove compartment until I found an old pill bottle that I always kept on hand. Naproxen had been my friend for a long fucking time—keeping me functioning through an injury that almost put my ass out of business.

"Why the fuck do you have painkillers in your truck?" he asked when I dropped two pills in his hand.

"Three years ago a bull fucking tossed me. Usually, it's a tuck, roll, and get back on your feet kind of situation," I explained, "but this fucker threw my ass right into the fencing. You ever been thrown into a metal fence?"

"No, but I was thrown through a bar door once," he replied. "It was one of those kitschy old-fashioned saloon-style ones."

Jesus fuck, West.

"That'd hurt too," I said. "I fucked up my back. For a while, I was on naproxen to help with the pain. Occasionally, my back still fucking hurts, so my doctor has me keep it around."

"Makes sense." He tossed back the pills without hesitation or a need for water. *I'd probably regret giving an addict prescription painkillers, but there was no reason he should suffer either.* If it became an issue, I'd toss the pills later.

Hopefully, it wouldn't become an issue.

Fuck. Was this a bad idea? Had I screwed this up for him?

"I can take painkillers, Jackson," West told me as if reading my mind. He let his cigarette fall to the ground and stepped on it. "Drugs don't fucking do it for me. Not for a lack of trying."

I stared after him as he started for the front door. *Not for a lack of trying?* What the hell did that mean?

"Are you coming, cowboy?" he called over his shoulder.

"Fuck!" I chased after him, knowing full well that Glinda—the front desk nurse—would eat his tattooed ass alive if I let him go in alone. *Steamroll him, marry him, and spit him right back out.*

Sandy Oaks Retirement Facility took the sandy part of its name way too fucking seriously. Everything was beach-themed from the fake flowers to the tropical paintings on the walls to the obscene amount of Hawaiian vacation shirts everywhere. *Was this retirement?* Was I destined to become a pot-bellied old man wearing overly bright flowered shirts?

"Sorry about that," I whispered to West as we strolled through one of the halls. My mom was very likely hanging out in the social center. She usually hustled the hell out of people until lunchtime. "I know we haven't... defined shit with us, but Glinda would eat you alive if I didn't say something."

I'd stupidly told Glinda that West and I were dating while she eyed him like a piece of meat—not that I blamed her for that part. He'd pulled himself together for today. Dark jeans hugged his ass in a way I purposely avoided looking at and a blue Henley brought out the color in his eyes. His hair was shaggy as ever but his beard was trimmed. Hell, he looked better than I did. I hadn't even bothered to shower. I just shoved a backwards hat over my hair and called it a morning.

"I don't know." His lips quirked at the corner. "Watching you damn near fight an old lady over me was kind of fun. Maybe I'll see how many other women I can get you to fight."

"Don't you fucking dare."

"We'll see how the day goes."

"I hate you."

"Good." *This fucking man.* He drove me a little bit crazy. And yet, I craved every second of his annoying antics.

We rounded our way into the social center and sure enough, there was my mom at the center of some fucking card game. She was surrounded by a group of men. To most people, they'd assume Mom was caught in some kind of love circle shit with all of them. *Especially with how they looked at her.* But I knew better. She was back to hustling them for their money.

"You better not get your ass kicked out of here for hustling, Ma," I said loudly as I started across the room. West hung back, which I understood why, considering the last time they'd seen each other. "I ain't taking you back in."

"Get your singles ready, ladies!" Mom matched my enthusiasm with her smile as if nothing had happened between us. "The League's only gay bull rider is back in the house. And look at that! He lost his hat. The flannel and hat are a good look on you, honey."

"Stop pimping me out, you crazy old lady," I retorted.

"Oh, where's the fun in that?" she demanded. Anything else she was going to say was lost when she caught sight of West behind me. Her gasp was damn near audible from across the room. "*West...*"

She dropped her cards and got to her feet, ignoring anything anyone said to her as she hurried toward us.

"West McNamara is that you?" she asked when she was close enough to be heard without shouting.

"Hey, Mom," West whispered. Something about hearing him call her that again made my chest tighten.

"Oh, my sweet boy..." A small sob tore through Mom as she dragged him close, hugging him fiercely. I took a few steps back to give them privacy. It hit me as I watched that West really did believe what he said—that my parents and Mickey had tried their best. Harrison had just been a fucking force of nature that none of them could handle. I hated that.

And I hated how blind I'd been to all of it.

Mom spoke quietly with West as she stared up at him. She rubbed his arms, touched his face, ruffled his hair, and more. She didn't notice how he stiffened at the contact nor did it faze her when he tried to move back. *But I sure as fuck did.* West would never tell her to back off. Lucky for him, I didn't have a problem asserting myself where necessary.

"Come on now, Ma," I interrupted. I wrapped an arm around her shoulders and casually put myself between her and West to give him the space he needed. He took a step back, and I winked at him before giving my mom my attention. "Did you forget about your own damn son? What the hell am I? Chopped liver?"

"Oh, please," she scoffed but leaned into my side. "I see you all the time."

"And you pimp me out all the time to your ladies," I retorted. "I think I deserve a decent hello for the shit you put me through."

"*That I put you through?*" Her voice rose dramatically. "Please. You love the limelight, baby boy. Don't even pretend."

"Some limelight," I corrected.

"You can say that all you want, but I've been in Hester's room. She has six framed pictures with you, and I know for a fact that she only paid for two."

"I don't know what the fuck you're talking about." *Yes, I did, but Hester was adorable.* I steered Mom toward the elevators. "Keep up, West."

"It's good to see you, baby boy," Mom said quietly as she hugged my side. Squeezing tight, I kissed the top of her head. "I missed you."

"I missed you too."

We made our way across the building. The entire way, Mom kept a constant stream of conversation going with West—rather, she talked at him while he made small sounds of agreement. I was still figuring out most of West's tells to understand him, but I would've bet anything that he was overwhelmed, itching to smoke, and needing a minute alone.

What he needed was a mini-escape plan. I was damn good for one of those. *How many nights had I strategically escaped all rodeo media just to hook up with some straight-swearing cowboy?*

"Stairs are down that way, West," I told him loudly when the elevator door opened. West stopped just outside of it and looked at me like I was a fucking moron.

"What?" Mom demanded, her brows coming together as she frowned. "Jackson—"

"Fifth floor," I continued over her. I nodded down the hall while I ushered Mom into the elevator. "There's not enough room in the elevator."

"Right," West began slowly, "fifth floor. Take the stairs, got it. See you upstairs."

He took his leave without hesitation. *Mission accomplished.* At least, I hoped he got it. If not, he probably thought I was a fucking asshole.

"Jackson!" she exclaimed. "There's more than enough room for him in the elevator. You didn't have to be rude."

"Ma." I hit the fifth floor button as the doors closed. While I crossed my arms, Mom squared off her shoulders. *Yeah, I got my fire from her.* "You have to stop touching West."

"What does that mean?"

"He doesn't like to be touched, so you have to keep your damn hands to yourself. I don't want to fight you, but I will fight you if you don't stop touching him."

"You'll fight me?" She laughed, and something about the way her face lit up was frustrating.

"What?" I asked. "What are you laughing at?"

"I forgot how cute you were when you got all protective of West," Mom said.

"I'm a grown-ass man! You can't call me cute!"

"Oh, baby boy." Reaching up, she pinched my cheek. I scowled. The woman dared to pinch my goddamn cheeks. She hadn't done so since I was a fucking kid.

"Ma!"

"You're my son. I can call you cute all I want," she retorted. The elevator dinged, and the doors opened. Stepping out, she waved down the hall and ordered, "I'll keep my hands to myself. Wait out here for West since you so rudely made him walk up five flights of stairs."

"It wasn't rude." *It wasn't rude.* I was trying to make this experience less miserable for West. "It wasn't rude…"

But she didn't hear me. She was already down the hall and in her apartment. *Damn woman.*

I paced up and down the hall as I waited for West to make an appearance. It took way too damn long, all things considered. What the hell was he doing? Meandering? But I worked hard to curb my impatience. I didn't understand what he was going through, which meant I couldn't understand the length of time anything took him.

"Was there a reason you kicked me out of the fucking elevator?" West huffed out after finally making an appearance.

"Figured you wouldn't be a big fan of enclosed spaces." I shrugged. There was no way in hell I was telling him what I said to my mom. It'd piss him off. He made a small sound, nodding slowly as if he was judging my lie.

"You ever watch those action movies where they go up and out of an elevator and into the elevator shaft?" West asked. "You think it'd be hard to do?"

"You watch action movies?" I replied instead of answering his question.

"From time to time. Better than watching reality dating shows."

"Don't you make fun of my shows. My bunnies got me started on those."

"Your bun—do you have buckle bunnies?" he demanded, his frown deep when he faced me.

"As the only out gay man on the circuit, I'm in with all the buckle bunnies," I told him. "And I have a say in when all the straight men get laid."

"That's evil."

"That's fucking funny. You ever watch a pent-up cowboy try to get laid when every available woman tells him no? It's the best fucking revenge." It really was. I didn't use that power often, but if one of the other riders was being a particular pain in my ass, I had no problem exercising it. Sometimes I got petty. *And then I got payback.* My girls never had a problem rallying. Softly, I asked, "You doing good?"

"Yeah, I'm fine," he said. "Let's just... go in there."

I hated seeing him struggle. Stepping closer, I reached for him but let my hands hover on either side of his face without touching.

"May I?" *No touching unless he said so.* He nodded without a word. My hands framed his face as I tilted his head down slightly, just enough to kiss his forehead in a tiny gesture to comfort him. There was no awkwardness, and he didn't pull away. *Win, win.* "Talk about horses. Lord knows she may have bought those damn things for you, but she does love them. And fuck, she loves talking about them."

"Okay," West replied.

What I didn't tell him was that I intended to keep the conversation on track. I couldn't make him feel less of any one way— I didn't have that kind of power—but I could make things easier. Less triggering, less difficult.

That shit I could do all day for him and I would.

CHAPTER 47

WEST

I DID MY BEST not to fidget, but I was fucking dying inside. My skin crawled uncomfortably as I sat in Mrs. Myles's small-as-fuck kitchen. Even with an open patio door and a light breeze on my back, I was dying.

Jackson sat next to me, watching me like a goddamn hawk. I wasn't sure what was worse: my anxiety or the way he looked at me. *Like he was waiting for me to break.* I fucking hated that look.

I couldn't handle it.

Any of it.

But I was stuck. Mrs. Myles was wonderful. She wasn't the problem. *I was.* The room was too small, my skin was crawling, and breathing was a fucking experience.

"It's so good to see you two together again," Mrs. Myles said all over again. I'd lost track of how many times she'd said that exact thing. Granted, she'd done a lot of repeating herself. So much so that I wondered if that wasn't part of the reason why she was in a retirement home, to begin with.

We talked about how I was, about the horses, about me, about where I'd been—Jackson helped me skirt around that one several times over—about the horses, about how I was, and it kept going around and around. The constant roundabout was overwhelming and frustrating.

"The whole damn town seems to think so," Jackson commented with a cheeky grin.

"Oh, I doubt that," she retorted. "You two were hellions then, and I doubt that's changed."

"We're fucking angels, Ma. We were back then, still are now."

I scoffed, shaking my head. *That was so far from the fucking truth.*

"And the horses?" she asked again. "I'm sure it's nice being back with the horses. Well... unless, you had horses where you were at..."

"Ma, stop asking already," Jackson cut in. "It doesn't matter where he was."

"I just worry!"

"I know," he said, "but you're getting annoying—"

A knock at the door interrupted our conversation. *Thank fuck.*

"Oh, who the hell could that be? Hold on, boys, I'll be right back," she told us as she hurried toward the door. When she was gone, I blew out a long breath and sank back into the uncomfortable chair.

"May I?" Jackson's hand hovered over mine. I did my best to bite back my frown. Damn it. I hated that he did this. It made me feel even more broken than I already knew I was. He just sat there with that stupidly calm look on his face. *Just waiting for permission to touch me like he did every fucking time we made contact.* There was no way in hell he did this with anyone else.

Fucking hell.

"Yeah," I muttered. He lowered his hand, fingers curling around mine. I tried to keep from tensing—from going rigid at the simple contact. Every place his hand touched mine was on fire. *Burning across every fucking nerve.*

I wanted this. Wasn't that why I kissed him? My head was all sorts of fucked up over this shit—way more than I probably should've been.

"You good?" Jackson asked. *I fucking hated that goddamn question.*

"Yeah," I repeated. "She just keeps talking about the same shit."

"I know." He sighed, rubbing at his beard slightly. "She gets like that. Overall, she's doing good, you know? But sometimes, her age shows. That's all. You just have to..."

"Deal with it?" I finished for him, and he nodded. *Just deal with it.* I was used to that life philosophy.

"Pretty much."

I didn't envy him. Watching her decline sounded fucking miserable. I had nothing to offer him that could help, but I did manage to squeeze his hand once in a feeble attempt to comfort him. It seemed to work as he smiled. *That smile did something uncomfortable to my heart.*

"Jackson!" Mrs. Myles called from the door. "Come out here, handsome. Some of the ladies want to see you!"

"That's my cue," Jackson announced and got to his feet, groaning as he went. It was all a little too dramatic to come across as real.

"You like this shit, don't you?" I asked, my eyes narrowing.

"Me? Never," he scoffed. But he winked before turning away. *Fucker.* He really did enjoy this limelight shit.

"Jesus fuck, you're an old lady magnet," I said as we walked across the parking lot to his truck. Two hours. For two hours, this fucker took pictures and flirted with old ladies. He could say whatever the fuck he wanted, but that man enjoyed the attention. It was the tiniest insight into understanding that Jackson enjoyed being a professional bull rider more than he ever enjoyed running the ranch. "I can't believe your mom fucking makes them pay for pictures with you."

"She puts the money in the weekly poker pot." He laughed. "Besides, my old ladies love me."

"Old ladies, buckle bunnies, screwing over straight men... sounds like you like the whole bull riding thing."

"It has its moments," Jackson replied, clearly trying to be nonchalant about the whole thing. I had a feeling he was holding back on me, but I wasn't about to push the matter. *Not right now.* I was a little too irritable for that shit. Something—maybe everything—about the whole trip had rubbed me raw. Mrs. Myles, Jackson, all the questions. I was so far in my head questioning all of it that I was frustrated as fuck with myself.

Instead of going to the driver's side, he moved to my door and opened it. I stopped dead in my tracks.

"Why the fuck are you opening my door?" I demanded.

"Because I wanted to."

"You don't have to fucking do that," I told him. "I can open my own damn door."

"I know you can, but I still wanted to." He held out a hand to me. "May I?"

Something inside me broke.

"I need you to stop!" I exclaimed, my temper flaring. "Just stop asking all the goddamn questions!"

"Okay." His casual response irritated me even more.

"You have no idea how... fucking horrible it feels!" I continued. I couldn't stop. "I'm here, ain't I? I'm doing this whole fucking thing with you, ain't I? Isn't that enough? Do you need to put me under a goddamn microscope every time anything comes up? You want to hold my hand, then hold my goddamn hand! You want to touch me, fine! Just do it! Do it and... and... and..."

I stumbled over my words, my brain glitching as I struggled to say what I wanted to say. I shoved my hand through my hair, frustrated and overwhelmed by it all.

"Just what?" Jackson prompted quietly.

"Just..." I felt myself deflating until my voice was barely a whisper. "Just... stop if I ask you to stop."

The look on his face was unreadable. *I fucking hated it.* I wanted to know what he was thinking—needed to know.

I hated not knowing.

I just... *fuck.*

He crossed the short distance between us and took hold of my face, stepping close. His warm breath fanned across my face as his forehead pressed to mine.

"You don't ask, you hear me?" he said softly. My brows came together in confusion. "You just tell me, okay? That ain't the kind of thing you ask for. Just tell me to stop, West, and I'll stop."

A pathetic sound passed through me as I tried to make the words make sense. I wanted to trust it. *I wanted to trust him.* But that little voice in the back of my head picked at it. What if he was just saying it to say it? What if he didn't mean it? How could I trust the words?

"Just tell me, okay?" he repeated. Words stuck in my throat, and I wasn't sure how to say the little things bubbling up inside me, so I just nodded. Tipping my head down slightly, he pressed a lingering kiss to my forehead. *Why was it so oddly comfortable when he did that?* It confused me. "Come on. I've got somewhere I want to take you."

I bit back a frustrated groan. I didn't fucking want to go anywhere.

"You'll like it," Jackson assured me. "I promise."

CHAPTER 48

JACKSON

The Kent Farm was half an hour from ours, straight down the road and through the woods. More than once, West and I had taken our horses on the old beaten paths to Kent Farms—mostly because we liked to pick fights with his son, Matt. *Maybe we really were shitheads as kids.*

"So, what the hell are we doing here?" West asked as he stepped out of my truck.

"You remember Matt?" I replied.

"Didn't we dump his ass in the creek one year?" He leaned against the hood, his brows furrowing slightly.

"Yeah." I chuckled. *Fuck, we were assholes.* "Anyway, Matt up and moved to Canada a few years back."

"Why the fuck is he in Canada?" he demanded.

"Who fucking knows. All I know is that Warren is selling everything to retire down to Florida or someplace old people go," I told him. Warren Kent, Matt's dad, was pushing eighty. Running a full farm was too much for him. It was easier for him to let everything go rather than to preserve a legacy of sorts. *I wondered what the hell that felt like.*

"Maybe he'll go hang out with your mom."

"You shut your mouth," I snapped. We were not talking about my mother that way. "Besides, Ma would eat him alive."

"That's why it'd be fucking funny." West's lips quirked slightly at the corners, making me smile. That tiny gesture meant more than he'd ever know. I liked being the reason he relaxed a little. "What the hell are you looking to buy from him? I'm assuming we're here to buy farm shit."

"Horses," I said and started up the gravel drive.

"Wait!" West called after me. I heard his boots on the drive as he rushed to catch up. "Horses?"

"Warren is getting rid of everything—selling it off—including the animals," I explained. "The cattle are spoken for and so are his chickens, but his horses are still available."

"Are we buying horses?"

"Maybe." I shrugged. We rounded the back of the old farmhouse, bringing Kent's horses into view. At least three dozen horses grazed in a massive corral. I watched as West stopped dead in his tracks, stuck on the sight of them. "Don't hurt to look, does it?"

"Well, look what the cat dragged in!" Warren exclaimed with a crooked grin from his spot on the porch. "You boys back together means trouble is back in town."

"Why does everyone keep fucking saying that?" I asked, feigning annoyance.

"Because you two were little shits back then and I guarantee you're just big shits now," he retorted.

I caught West's gaze. He pretended to mull it over before nodding slightly, making me smile.

"You're looking good, Dakota," Warren said. The grimace on West's face had me biting my cheek to not laugh at him. I couldn't remember a single time in his life when anyone called him Dakota. He hated his first name.

"It's just West," he replied. "And thank you."

"You two can start on over to look at the herd. I'll make my way over when my knees catch up," he told us and jerked his chin in the direction of the fences. "Let me know if you have any questions."

"Are we really here looking at horses?" West demanded under his breath as we approached the fence line.

"Are you really complaining about looking at horses?" I shot back.

"No, it's just—"

"Just look at the horses, West." I interrupted. "If you decide you want a horse, we'll go from there."

"There's at least... three dozen horses here."

"And?"

"That's a lot of horses."

"*One* horse, West." *Jesus fuck, I had to clarify.* I should've seen that coming. He'd take home the whole damn lot of them if he could. I didn't have the room for that many horses.

"Two horses?" West countered. *And fuck me, the faint smile on his mouth did me in.* I had no hope of telling him no.

"Fine." I sighed. Crossing my arms, I leaned on the fence and just waited. I didn't give two fucks about the horses. I just wanted to pick up his mood. It wasn't hard to see how the trip to my mom's wore him down. And when in doubt, the answer was horses. Always horses.

Did I exactly have it in the budget to buy him a horse? *Just barely.* But I wanted to do something for him—something that would mean something, and horses were it.

I stayed put while West wandered along the fence to look at the herd. He was completely lost in the way he looked at them and I was lost in watching him. How he studied them was damn near reverent. *What I wouldn't have given to know what he was thinking.*

"They're a good-looking lot, aren't they?" Warren said, finally joining us. He shoved his hands in his pockets and laid into a fence post for support.

"What about that one back there?" West asked. He moved further down the fence line. I followed his gaze to where a single horse was corralled separately from the rest of the herd.

"Oh, that's just Betty," he replied. "She's set to be put down next week."

"Why?" His frown was deep, and I could already see the wheels turning in his head. "She looks just fine from here."

"She's blind and has a mean attitude," he told us. "I've tried to put in some work with her, but I'm just one man. My guys don't have the time to deal with her."

West let out a small sound but said nothing. And then he hopped the fence.

Yeah, I saw that one coming.

"What does he think he's doing?" Warren glanced at me.

"It's best just to let West do his thing when it comes to horses," I said.

Even from where I stood, it was clear Betty was wary of West's presence when he entered the corral with her. Her hooves beat against the ground while he talked to her. My heart lurched into my throat when her display grew more irate.

"He's going to get himself hurt," Warren warned.

"I trust him," I replied. *That didn't make it any easier to watch.*

Within minutes, West had her calm and nuzzling against his hand. He tested her responsiveness, moving around and snapping his fingers to see how well she followed him. She chased after him eagerly, even when he pushed her to a trot. I was fairly certain that mare would do any damn thing he wanted her to.

His way with horses was nothing short of captivating.

"So, he went away and came back a horse whisperer?" Warren asked.

"Nah, he's always had a way with horses," I said.

When West tried to leave the corral, Betty was at his back with her snout over his shoulder. That smile on his face did wild things to me, and I'd do whatever I could to keep it.

"Well, I guess we're buying Betty," I announced. There was no way in hell we were leaving here without her—not that West would let us. *I was pretty sure he'd come back and steal the goddamn horse if we didn't.* "How much do you want for her?"

"For Betty?" Warren scratched at his scruff, making a face as if I'd asked him a tough question. "I mean, you sure you don't want one of the others? One that don't got so many issues?"

"How much do you want for her?" I reiterated. At his continued hesitance, I said, "Either we're leaving with that horse or West will be sleeping in your stables tonight."

He laughed like I said something funny, but he had no clue just how serious I was.

CHAPTER 49

WEST

He bought me a goddamn horse. I still couldn't believe it. Even when I told him that I could buy Betty on my own, Jackson insisted. By the time she was comfortably put away for the night, he had me feeling some kind of way that I couldn't explain.

Fuck, if that didn't describe my entire relationship with Jackson.

I followed him up the steps at the end of the night. It'd taken him three attempts to get me out of the stables before damn near threatening me. Betty was fine. She was more than fine. She was content and almost happy with her new setup. Not that I blamed her. Our stables were better than the Kents any day.

"She'll be fine, West," Jackson said for the umpteenth time.

"Maybe I should've stayed out there," I replied, closing the door

"West." The slight uptick of annoyance in his voice wasn't lost on me. *Fuck.*

"Sorry, I just—"

"West," he repeated, turning. He closed the distance between us, his arm wrapping around my waist as he dragged me to him. His mouth brushed against mine in a slow kiss. My eyes slid shut as I gave in.

I met him kiss for kiss, feeling each one down to my very core. My heart pounded violently in my chest. I grabbed onto his shirt to keep my knees from giving out.

When his tongue swept along the seam of my lips, I opened. The taste of him flooded my mouth—something soft and spicy that I wanted more of. I knocked his hat off and curled my fingers in his hair, kissing him harder. Needing more. *Of what exactly? That was a damn good question.*

His warmth, his strength, his intensity. I liked the way he felt pressed against my body. I was painfully aware of just how much I liked it as my cock thickened in my jeans. The foreign feeling was unsettling, but I tried to push that thought out of my head. *This was normal.*

I could do normal.

Strong hands anchored on my hips as he dragged me across the room with him. When his knees hit the couch, we toppled over. His hands tightened, and I landed on top of him. *Hard.* I adjusted quickly to alleviate the way my weight pinned him to the couch, and my hips settled between his.

"I'm too old for this shit," Jackson half-groaned, half-laughed. In the dark, I couldn't see his face but I could hear the smile in his voice. I shut him up with another kiss. His laughter faded completely, and I swallowed the moan he let out.

His hips thrust upwards against mine. The thickness of his dick rolled across my own, sending a shockwave of sensations through my body. *Good? Bad? I couldn't tell.*

I was a fucking livewire—a bomb ready to detonate. Every touch did wildly unpredictable things to my body. Things I hadn't known possible. *But they were things I couldn't identify as good or not.* My skin crawled and tingled, making my brain glitch.

I kept going. *I wanted this.* I wanted normalcy with him. And some part of me had to want more. I wouldn't be a fucking stone pillar if I didn't. *Right?*

Fuck, my head was swimming—intoxicated by him and drowning in confusion.

My lips drifted along his jaw, my teeth scraping against his scruff. His head tipped back as I ran my tongue down the line of his neck. Fingers danced along the waist of my pants, sending my heart lurching into my throat.

When his palm grazed over my hard-on, I grabbed his wrist.

"Don't," I rasped against his skin. He stilled as I froze. *Where the fuck did we go from here?* What if he asked me to explain? I didn't know how to.

He slowly pulled his hand back, even as I clung to him.

"We can stop, West," Jackson whispered. We could, but I wasn't sure I wanted that.

But him touching me?

I couldn't handle that.

"No," I said, shaking my head. My lips skated slowly up his neck.

"Hey." He tried to turn, but I nuzzled closer. I didn't want any attempt to make eye contact in the dark. "West—"

"Don't fucking do that."

"We don't have to do anything you don't want to."

"But what if I want to?"

"West..." The doubt in his voice irritated me.

"It's not like I haven't done shit in the last seventeen years," I told him, my tone sharp. I nipped at his earlobe and liked the quick breath he pulled in. "I have. With both men and women. I just... don't like being touched."

That was a lie. I didn't have a clue if I did. Nothing had ever worked down there. I just figured my dick was broken for good.

And I never trusted anyone enough to let them touch me anyway. *What if they...*

Jackson changed shit. From the way my fucking dick strained against my jeans uncomfortably to the way I actually wanted more with him.

But that little voice in the back of my head shattered everything. What if he didn't care? What if he did hurt me? What if all he wanted was to use me?

The list was endless.

It kept my walls high in place.

"Are you really going to fucking complain about my mouth on your cock?" I asked. I gently set his hand on the couch and out of the way.

"No, but..." His voice trailed off as I ran my palm over his dick, pressing hard enough to be felt through his jeans. I continued to stroke him as I kissed my way back up his neck. I reveled in the slight roll of his hips in demand for more and the breathy sounds he let out. Still, he continued, "You're sure?"

"Just relax and let me suck your dick, cowboy," I said and dragged my teeth over his earlobe. I didn't wait for his response as I undid his buckle and opened his jeans. As I reached into his pants, he lifted his hips enough to shove them down.

The thickness of his long dick pressed against my abdomen as I worked my way down his neck. I pushed his shirt up, letting my hand wander over his sculpted muscles. The man was fucking gorgeous. There was no denying that.

But getting my hands on him was a whole different way to appreciate the body he'd built for himself. I took my time tracing the dips and curves of his muscles with both my hands and my lips. The experience was oddly grounding in a way that touch in any form usually wasn't for me.

Jackson shifted underneath me, making himself comfortable on the couch, while I stroked him slowly—my hand skating up and down his long cock. I flicked my tongue over his slit, licking up the pre-cum gathering there. Something about doing so stalled me in my head. He wasn't the first guy I'd done this with, but he was the first one that mattered—the first one where any real feelings were involved. I wanted to get this right. *For him.*

What if I fucked this up?

I needed to get out of my head. Focus on Jackson.

I ran the flat of my tongue along the length of his shaft and slowly circled the crown of his cock. Repeating the action, I enjoyed his drawn-out moan. I took an inch of him in my mouth, teasing him.

"Fuck, baby, just like that," he rasped, his hips flexing. His cock glided over my tongue as I took him deeper in my mouth. My pace was unrushed as I moved up and down his length. I paid attention to the way he reacted and let it guide everything I did. Salty pre-cum smeared along my tongue, the taste intoxicating.

His taste, his sounds, his scent. All of it was so damn intoxicating.

When he hit the back of my throat, I breathed through my nose and took him as deep as I could. I swallowed, my throat constricting around the head of his cock.

"Jesus fuck," Jackson let out, his voice tense. His fingers weaved through my hair, gripping lightly. A bolt of panic lanced through me, and I grabbed his wrist to stop him. Yanking him away, I pinned his wrist to the couch. *That was a fucking no.*

I licked, sucked, and stroked him into a frenzy. His hips thrust upward with every pass. His cock pulsed along my tongue, and his body tensed under me.

"I'm going to come," he warned, his voice thick as gravel. I hummed but kept going. I pushed him until he lost control completely. With two quick thrusts deep into my mouth, he came. Spurts of hot cum coated my tongue and my throat. I swallowed until he was spent, his movements slowing. I sucked and licked until he practically melted into the fucking couch.

His quiet pants filled the deafening silence in the room as I leaned back. Something seized in my chest, wrapping tight around my heart. My stomach rolled as the temperature in the room skyrocketed.

"I'll be right back," I said gruffly. I didn't wait for him to say a thing as I headed down the hall. In the bathroom, I clung to the sink for support. The weight in my chest was unbearable as I struggled to pull in a breath.

I wanted this.

I wanted this.

I kept reminding myself of that single thing to stave off the pending panic. Every ragged breath burned in my lungs, and I blinked back tears.

I wanted this.

I'd initiated it. I chose to do it. So why the fuck was I spiraling over it?

I didn't go back to Jackson. Instead, I slipped out the back door before he could notice. A shitty thing to do? Yeah, but I couldn't break down in front of him.

CHAPTER 50

WEST

I RAN. LIKE A fucking coward, I ran. My head was so fucked up that I couldn't think straight—let alone face Jackson. *What a fucking asshole I was.* I left the house without a goddamn word. I left the whole fucking ranch without even telling him.

What I wanted to do was drink. And drink. And keep on fucking drinking until the voices in my head stopped taunting me. *Fuck, what kind of man couldn't handle giving a goddamn blowjob without panicking?* I was so fucking broken it was damn near funny at this point.

I was fucking laughable.

But I didn't drink.

Almost but not quite. I walked inside two different bars and barely managed to drag myself out without drinking something. I was doing so damn good about not breaking down and drinking to drown out everything. This wouldn't be the thing that sent me off the ledge again.

But my resolve was fraying and fast. I couldn't do it much longer.

Which was how I ended up two towns over waiting for Bobby outside a diner as I chain-smoked my way through a pack of cigarettes to keep from doing more stupid shit. *To keep me from completely falling apart.* I was barely hanging on.

I was on my fifth cigarette by the time he finally showed up, stepping out of his car in navy dress pants and a firefighter shirt. He looked exhausted but still smiled nonetheless when he saw me. I couldn't return the gesture.

"Sorry about the outfit," he said. "I finished my shift and ran."

"You're a firefighter?"

"The captain actually," he told me proudly.

"Captain Bobby," I murmured. "Never would've guessed."

"I think there's a lot about ourselves we keep out of our meets," Bobby replied. "Granted, we don't know too much about each other, so everything is a surprise right now."

I made a small sound of agreement as I dropped my cigarette and stepped on it. I didn't know a whole lot about him other than he was persistent as fuck and drove a car that very well might've been older than me—in a classic car kind of way.

"I work with horses," I managed to tell him, my throat constricting as another wave of emotions hit me. The horses were the whole damn reason I wasn't halfway down a bottle. I knew there was no way in hell Jackson would let me work with them if I relapsed.

Had I told him this already? Maybe I had. I couldn't remember. My head was all sorts of fucked up.

"I know very little about horses." He opened the door to the diner, holding it for me to go through. "But when I was five, a horse ripped out a chunk of hair on my head. I swear that's why my hair is thinning back there."

Fucking Bobby. I didn't have it in me to respond to that. I let him do the talking with the woman who greeted us and let him figure out a table for us. Thankfully, he picked something in the back—somewhere I could easily put my back in a corner and keep track of everything in the restaurant. No one could sneak up on me that way.

He ordered a slice of pie and a Diet Coke while I couldn't fathom the idea of even drinking water. I just shook my head at his offer to buy me something.

"Would you like to talk about it?" Bobby asked, his tone gentle. The request still hit me hard. *How the hell did I explain any of this to him?*

My leg bounced erratically under the table as I tried my best to come up with something to say—something that would make sense to a guy like him. How the fuck did I explain that I was spiraling after giving my something-other-or-what a fucking blowjob because of... of...

My eyes watered, and my nose burned. I stared hard out the window, trying to hold back tears. *Fuck, I couldn't even think about it.* I pinched the bridge of my nose as I tried to get ahold of myself.

To his credit, Bobby was silent while I struggled. When the waitress brought over his order, he waved her off quickly. Maybe to give me peace, maybe because she was fucking annoying. I couldn't tell.

And so we sat there in the quiet with him eating pie and me doing my damnedest to find my voice—to say something, to do something other than fall apart.

"Can you..." I whispered finally, my voice breaking. It was such a pathetic thing to ask. I didn't know what I needed. I didn't know how anyone could help me. *Fuck, I didn't know how to help myself.* "Can you just... sit with me?"

"You know what always caught my attention about this place?" Bobby said casually around a bite of pie. "They have seventeen flavors of pie. I keep telling myself I'm going to try them all, but I never do it. I always get the coconut cream. I think I'm going to try them all."

What the fuck was he talking about?

"You know what?" he continued. "I'm going to do just that. We'll be here a while. That's a lot of pie."

Oh.

"Hold on. I'll be right back," Bobby told me. I just nodded as he left, confused as to why he was doing this.

I'd never understand why people did things like this for me. I wasn't worth the hassle. *Why couldn't he see that?*

CHAPTER 51

WEST

Avoiding Jackson was easy. I buried myself in my work. Figuring out Betty and all her little behaviors took up a lot of time. She had no social skills with other horses and didn't know what to do with them. It turned her snippy, and while she wasn't outright aggressive, I knew better than to put her around the other horses until she was completely relaxed.

I relied on Bailey all over again to be the comfort point. Bailey was just fine being a social buddy. Granted, Bailey liked anything that involved following me around, and she was damn good with the other horses.

It was easy to lose myself in my work. The consistency and constant flow of tasks kept my brain from spiraling—at least more than it already was as it teetered on the edge of fucking chaos. The horses made me feel better, and anytime anyone else showed up, I made myself scarce. I didn't want to deal with people.

Which was all well and good until Jackson tracked my ass down two days later while I hid out in the stables. He'd traded the cowboy hat for a backwards baseball hat and his work shirt for blue flannel. It struck me that the man looked good no matter what he was fucking wearing, which bothered me more than it probably should've. It'd be easy to be mad at him and keep my distance if I wasn't so wrapped up in him.

So I focused hard on sweeping stalls and fucking ignored him.

"You know," Jackson began as he strode down the center aisle, "you can only avoid me for so long, considering I'm your boss."

"I'm not fucking avoiding you," I snapped. Why? Who the hell knew? It wasn't like we both didn't know I was lying my ass off.

"Right." He nodded slowly. "Look, I think you and I need to talk about a few things."

"Fuck," I muttered. *The last thing I wanted to do was fucking talk.* I tried to leave but he stepped in my path. "I don't want to fucking fight you right now."

"I don't want to fight either," he promised. "But I do want to go for a ride."

We took Zeus and Thunder Jack out for a ride. I let Jackson take the lead. A little over halfway there, I realized where we were going. *The northern ridge.* Fuck, I hadn't been out this way since the night I left Double Arrow. My chest tightened uncomfortably with the meaning of this place. A million fucking memories were tied up with the simple plot of land.

I followed his lead as he tied up Zeus to an old tree branch and dropped to the ground, sprawling out in the long grass with a sigh. I laid down next to him. Every inch of my body was tense as I waited for him to say whatever he had on his mind.

"I think you and I need to talk about what's going on," Jackson began, and the bottom of my stomach dropped out. I didn't know how to talk about any of this shit. *How the fuck did I explain how goddamn broken I was?*

How did I tell him anything without making him run in the other direction?

"I don't need details," he continued. "I ain't about to pretend that I understand a thing about what you're going through... what you've been through. But I think we'd both be idiots if we didn't acknowledge that it's affecting things between us."

"Sorry," I muttered. Any other relationship he had would be normal. I couldn't give him that. *Maybe scaring him away was the better option. For his sake.* "I told you I'm not fucking worth it."

"I'll keep believing you are for the both of us." He said the words with such conviction that I wanted to believe him. I wanted to so fucking badly that it hurt. "I've got all day, West, so take your time. I just want to know what happened the other night. You left without saying a word. I tried calling you but you didn't answer. I didn't have a clue if you..."

"I didn't fucking drink," I snapped. *Yeah, my defenses were a little too high, all things considered, but I also had no idea how to fucking lower them.* It was the only way I knew how to survive. "I didn't."

"I believe you."

"I wanted to."

"I had a feeling."

"But I didn't."

"That's good," Jackson told me. "That's real good, West, but where did you go?"

"I went to drink," I admitted. My gaze was pointedly fixed on the moody sky overhead. I couldn't look at him. Maybe I was too ashamed of my own faults or maybe I just couldn't handle the kindness I knew I'd find in his expression. I didn't deserve the way he treated me no matter how much he thought I did. "Almost did but I called my sponsor instead."

"That's progress. I'm a little confused about why you left. I'm trying not to draw conclusions here. I'm trying not to push you into talking about things you don't want to talk about—I get why you don't want to talk about them—but I don't know how to be in a relationship with you if I'm kept in the dark about everything."

"Then don't," I cut him off. *It was probably easier for him that way anyway.*

"That ain't what I want and you know that," he retorted. "I meant what I said: your stables, your rules. But I need a heads up on the rules or a heads up on what's going on. It ain't just you anymore, West. I'm right here."

My chest constricted painfully tight at the sentiment. I was very used to being alone—to handling everything alone. I was just fine alone. I didn't know how to let people in. I didn't know how to talk to people or any of that shit.

But he was right. He didn't deserve me running out on him all the time because I couldn't handle my own shit either.

Fuck, this shit was hard.

"When I say that nothing has worked, I mean nothing has worked… down there," I said quietly. "It's not a stupid medical thing… it's just… I'm just broken. They…"

My voice caught in my throat just saying it. My eyes burned, and I blinked hard.

"They broke me," I managed to whisper.

"You're not broken, West," he said.

"Nah, I'm fucking broken," I repeated. *There was no denying that shit.* "I have been for years. Still am. I just…"

I blew out a shaky breath. I didn't know what the fuck I was trying to say. In the silence, Jackson's hand found mine. His fingers wove through mine, and he held on tight.

Something about the gesture made me braver—just a tiny bit.

"I like you," I rasped, sounding pathetic as fuck. "I just… can't get the logical part of my brain to match the part of my fucking brain that can't tell if you're going to hurt me or not."

"I won't."

I knew he meant it, but my brain struggled with that. *With believing him.*

"I don't let people touch me… I've never let people touch me. Not since…"

Not since they broke me.

"I don't know how," I admitted. Silent tears burned down my temples and I let them. There was no point in fighting it as my chest seized horribly. I wasn't in control all over again. I fucking hated it.

"Tell me how to help, baby," Jackson whispered as he squeezed my hand for reassurance. The weight of his stare was heavy—fucking unbearable. I resisted the urge to wipe away the tears. That'd only make it worse. *Would only draw attention to how ridiculous I was.*

"I don't know," I said.

"It's okay," he replied. His voice was so fucking gentle that it hurt. "We'll figure it out. Together."

Together. What a foreign concept. I'd been doing this thing alone for so damn long that I didn't know how to let anyone help me.

CHAPTER 52

WEST

Jackson's inability to cook should've been more legendary than his goddamn feats as a bull rider. This man burned everything he touched. It was no wonder he fucking survived on freezer meals alone. But not me. Those things were absolute crap. I'd rather eat takeout than a fucking freezer meal.

As it happened, I actually did know how to cook—not a lot but enough. Which was exactly how we ended up grocery shopping together.

I trailed after him while we walked down the meat aisle with him chatting casually about dinner plans. In the week since our talk, we'd fallen into an almost comfortable routine of work, dinner, relaxing, and then bed with him in his room and me in mine. He was consistent in a quick kiss good morning and one good night along with holding my hand when I could handle the contact, but that was it.

A little part of me looked forward to those moments.

"How much meat do you fucking eat?" I demanded when he put another package in the cart. He already had at least twenty different containers of meat in there.

"How much can you cook?" Jackson countered with a grin. *Fuck, that grin did things to me.*

"Where did your Mom go wrong with you?"

"I'm good at a lot of things. Cooking ain't it," he told me. "You didn't answer my question."

"Just put it in the fucking cart," I said. *We both knew I'd cook him whatever he wanted.* I might complain the whole way but I'd still do it. It was the least I could do, considering everything else he was doing for me. "And get a fucking vegetable or two. Jesus Christ. You can't live on meat alone."

"I fucking could if I wanted to," he retorted. I groaned as he grabbed three more packages and dumped them in the cart.

"Do you have a second freezer?" I asked. "There ain't no way in hell this shit will fit in the kitchen."

"I have a deep freezer in the garage," he replied. He made a face. "I think I have like twenty pounds of venison in there."

"Jesus Christ."

"I ain't got a clue how to cook that either."

"Yeah, I fucking figured," I muttered. *This goddamn man.* I didn't get a chance to say anything else because I realized a woman was staring at us. I did my best not to glare. She wasn't the first and she certainly wouldn't be the last. But she kept staring at us in a way that had me thinking I should've known who the fuck she was.

"Well, look at you, West McNamara!" she exclaimed and started toward me. *Ah, fuck.* I hated this part. I hated the fucking nosy people in this goddamn town. A guy disappeared for seventeen years and they all suddenly thought they had a right to know all my business.

Before she could get too close, Jackson pushed the cart in front of me and damn near ran over my toes. He leaned over the handlebar, arms crossed and a cheeky fucking grin on his face.

"Hello, Mrs. Harris," he greeted and tipped his hat in her direction. *That stupid fucking cowboy hat seemed to do it for people.*

MaryAnn Harris. That was about all I remembered. Her first name. I didn't remember most people in this goddamn town.

"Jackson Myles, didn't your mother teach you to eat more than just meat?" Mrs. Harris chastised.

"I like meat!" he protested. "And it ain't like I know how to cook vegetables."

He didn't know how to cook meat either.

"I do," I said.

"See!" She gestured to me. "At least he knows how to cook vegetables."

"I don't know how to cook at all," Jackson told her.

"He doesn't," I agreed. "He burns the shit out of everything."

"Remember when I burned down one of the ranch houses?" he asked, chucking.

"Jesus fuck." My lips twitched slightly with the memory. "Weren't you making s'mores or some shit?"

"Popcorn," he corrected. "At least I was trying to. Sprayed the cooking oil right into the pan—"

"Which was sitting on an open fire, right… you're a fucking idiot, you know that?"

"Was."

"Still are."

"How in the world are you two boys still alive at this point?" Mrs. Harris asked.

"Well, a bull ain't killed me yet—"

"Oh, don't you even say that!" she interrupted. "What an unsavory thing to say. Now, come on. I'm going to teach you a thing or two about side dishes."

She grabbed the corner of his cart and used it to drag Jackson along with her.

"You too, West!" she called over her shoulder. "Someone has to make sure he eats some real food every once in a while. Your mama would be so disappointed in you, Jackson! Eating like that. Maybe I should give Magnolia a call."

"No!" Jackson exclaimed. "Don't you dare tell on me to my mama. That's just rude."

I trailed after them, hands in my pockets, as Jackson took the brunt of her attention so I didn't have to. He'd never understand just how much I appreciated that. I couldn't put that shit into words.

I had to make six steaks for dinner. Why? Because Jackson did have twenty fucking pounds of venison in his freezer. We ran out of room. I had to cook extra shit and make some for the dog to get rid of it.

Not that we ate all six steaks—though, it was disturbing just how much food this man could put away. Some of it got packed away for later. He was never allowed to just wander a fucking grocery store again. We'd end up with more shit than I knew what to do with.

Dinner led to hanging out on his porch talking while he tossed a ball for Tess. We talked about stupid shit—the dumb things we'd done growing up, ridiculous town gossip I'd missed out on, and the four marriage proposals he'd gotten from the same woman in town over the years.

I let him do the talking as much as possible. I liked listening to him, but I also had nothing real positive to say. It was blatantly obvious that we'd lived wildly different lives. His life had been full of adventures. Mine had been filled with a whole lot of bad.

As always, at the end of the night, he kissed me. Only this time, it didn't feel like a simple good night kiss. His tongue slipped past my lips and he gently walked me backward until I hit a wall. The weight of his body was heavy against mine, and I was all too aware of how his hips pressed into me.

My dick was too. It thickened until it was strained against the zipper of my jeans. Every kiss and every touch shot straight to my cock. *And when his hips rolled against mine—the ridges of his dick pressing into mine?*

Fuck, I liked that too.

"Do you trust me?" Jackson asked, his breath warm against my face. I nodded as the words caught in my throat. "I need to hear you say it, baby. Do you trust me?"

"Yeah," I rasped.

"Do you trust me to stop if you tell me to?" he continued. I swallowed hard as my mind fought my anxiety.

Jackson would never hurt me.

"Yeah," I repeated. He kissed me again, his lips gentle against mine. As he did, he ran his palm over the front of my jeans. The explosion of sensations was an onslaught to my senses. He did it again, and I groaned, my knees damn near giving out. His mouth skated along my jaw, and his teeth scraped against my scruff while my head tipped back against the wall.

My whole body tensed when he tugged open my jeans.

"Breathe, baby," he whispered into my neck. "Just tell me to stop if you need me to. Your stables, your rules, West."

That kind of power was foreign.

But I trusted him. I trusted him to listen.

I didn't have the words to say that, but I did and just nodded to let him know how aware I was.

His fingers hooked into my jeans and boxer briefs, pushing them down until my cock was free between us. A shiver ran through my body, and I forced myself to stay grounded in the moment. *The musk of his cologne, the softness of his mouth on my skin, the warmth of his body against mine.*

Those were good things.

Jackson was a good thing.

He ran his thumb down the length of my shaft, rolling over each small barbell. I moaned. *Why did something so simple feel so fucking good?*

"It's wild how fucking sexy these things are on you," Jackson whispered in my ear. He repeated the action, drawing out a louder moan from me. "Does that feel good, baby?"

"Yeah," I breathed out. He took the admission as motivation to wrap his hand around my dick. His fist skated up and down my hard length, slow and steady. The slight pressure was fucking euphoric.

Was this what this was supposed to be like?

I shoved that fucking thought from my head. I didn't want to think about it. I didn't want to spiral on the bad things.

"*Jesus fuck.*" I gripped his forearm as he reached under and gave my balls a light squeeze. My heart pounded erratically in my chest as liquid heat built in my core.

"You're doing so damn good, baby," Jackson praised. My breathing kicked up as he combined the two—his hand working up and down my cock before squeezing my balls enough to make me gasp. As he kept going, he said, "I'm dying to taste you, baby, so I'm going to get down on my knees and I'm going to suck your dick until you come in my mouth, do you understand?"

He what?

My brain struggled to understand the words he'd just said. Enough so that he leaned back, those blue eyes leveling on mine.

"Are you okay?" he asked.

"I think so," I admitted a little pathetically. This was the shit that made me feel less than I was. How many people needed to be talked through this kind of thing? Needed to practically have their hand held just to get off?

"You're doing real damn good, West." Jackson's lips brushed over mine. "Can I keep going?"

My eyes practically rolled back as he squeezed my balls one more time. *Did I want to do more? Could I handle it?*

I shut down those thoughts. My body was fine. His hands on me felt good. From the way my cock throbbed in his hand with pre-cum leaking from my slit, I couldn't deny that I liked what he was doing. Hell, the urge to rock into his hand—to feel more—was overwhelming.

"Yeah," I whispered.

"Keep going?" he reiterated one more time.

"Keep going, cowboy," I told him, barely recognizing the strain in my own voice. His hand never left my cock as he lowered himself onto his knees and my gaze followed him.

"Hand in my hair, West," he ordered. I brushed my fingers through his hair as he instructed. "Faster, slower, deeper... you're in control, got it. Whatever the fuck makes you feel good."

Him.

He made me feel good.

Jackson was meticulous and focused as his tongue traced each one of my barbells. That slight pressure and the warmth of his tongue had me moaning. His tongue ran over my slit, lapping up my pre-cum with a small sound of appreciation.

There was something undeniably sexy about the way he did that.

His tongue circled the crown of my dick and pressed into that sensitive spot right underneath it. *Fuck me.* My fingers tightened in his hair, inciting him to do it a second time.

"Fuck," I rasped, my head falling back against the wall.

His mouth covered my crown, and he sucked hard once before popping off. The action had my hips thrusting forward on their own. I was desperate for more of whatever the hell he was doing.

Every nerve in my body was on fire—and not in a particularly bad way. I was hot and panting as he took me in his mouth again, lowering a little further down my length. With each pass, he took me deeper in his mouth.

Jesus fuck, his mouth felt so goddamn good wrapped around my cock.

Even when I hit the back of his throat, he went further until he'd taken my entire length. The feel of his muscles swallowing around me threatened to take me out by the knees. And when he pulled off slowly, his tongue pressed into my piercings.

Whatever the hell all of that was, it was fucking magic. There was no hope I'd last at all if he kept doing that.

Jackson alternated his pace—working me up by stroking me with his hand and his mouth around the crown of my dick before taking all of me all over again. I was fucking flying. Nothing had ever felt so goddamn good. My cock pulsated against his tongue as every muscle in my body trembled. The heat in my core was intense—unlike anything I'd ever experienced before. It built and built until I was ready to combust.

"*Fuck*," I managed to get out. "I..."

I never got the rest of the words out as I came, my balls seizing up violently and my breath catching in my throat. His head continued to bob along the length of my cock, drawing out the orgasm until I was damn near shaking head to toe. My fingers anchored hard into his hair as I desperately clung to him for dear life.

He kept going until there was nothing left in me—until my dick began to soften. His tongue ran over my barbells one more time before standing. One arm wrapped around my waist as he stepped close.

"You with me, baby?" Jackson asked, his gaze searching my face. I nodded slowly. I was breathing too damn hard to hold a fucking conversation. Every inch of my body was buzzing, but it wasn't bad. "Are you going to run away from me again?"

"No." *I meant that.* Curling my hand around the back of his neck and closing the distance between us, kissing him deeply. There wasn't a single part of me that felt the need to run. Maybe I could do this whole thing with him.

Maybe.

CHAPTER 53

JACKSON

"Aᴌᴌ ʀɪɢʜᴛ, ʟɪsᴛᴇɴ ᴜᴘ!" I snapped, annoyed beyond belief. My guys stood in front of me, fidgeting and silent—as they should've been. "I don't give a fuck whose goddamn fault it is. What I give a fuck about is that the fucking boundaries got moved. My cows don't belong hanging out with my horses!"

As if I needed to, I glared pointedly at the forty-some cows currently mingling with the horses as if it was the most natural thing in the goddamn world. Maybe it was but not on my ranch. Not with everything we had going on.

"We have the fucking boundaries up for a reason," I continued. We'd lost too many damn cows for them to be fucking up my system. How the hell was I supposed to keep more of them from dying if the quarantine boundaries were breached? "Do I need to go over why the hell we have boundaries again?"

I waited. And waited. And kept on fucking waiting with the expectation that one of them said something. There was no goddamn reason for my cows to be so far in.

"You're going to get your asses back out there and get my fucking boundaries set back up. I want my fucking cows back where they belong!" I damn near shouted to make my point.

"Watch out, boys," West said, his voice startling me. I hadn't seen him all morning. Even the horses were ready by the time I got up and out here. A part of me worried that we were back to him avoiding me. But no. He leaned against the fence on his forearms, looking at ease as he joined us. "All this hootin' is goin' to lead to a hollerin' if you ain't careful."

The men laughed while I scowled.

"Is the peanut gallery done?" I demanded. His lips turned up in a small smile—more than I was used to seeing from him. *And damn if I didn't love that fucking smile.* Not that I'd say that in front of my employees, and he knew that.

"Simmer down, cowboy," he replied. I glared at him, but he was completely undeterred.

"Now," I went back to yelling at my employees for their fuck up, "if you don't get it right this time—"

"You'll have yee'd your last haw," West interrupted once more, eliciting more laughter.

"What the fuck is wrong with you?" I asked. Turning, I put my back to everyone else because so help me, if this fucking man made me smile in front of them, I'd lose my credibility as a hard ass.

"Woke up in a good mood today." He shrugged as if it was that simple. *Maybe it was.* What did I know? This whole thing was new to me.

And despite the joking way he poked at me in front of my guys, I was so goddamn thrilled to hear it. I wasn't an idiot. I knew how big a deal last night was for him. It was the entire reason I'd been up all night overthinking things. Had I been wrong for pushing him just a little bit? Was it too much? Was he going to run away from me again? Or avoid me completely?

The truth was that I didn't know what I was doing where West was concerned. *And that scared me.* I'd let down a few too many walls all too easily with him. The potential to get hurt grew with every day.

But he was worth it—more than he'd ever understand.

"All right, you goddamn morons!" I yelled, turning fast on my heel. "I want those boundaries back in place asap! And I want my fucking cows to stop hanging out with my goddamn horses. Got it?"

A murmur of agreement rolled through them. They didn't need more direction than that as they dispersed. Only Mickey remained, watching me closely as he fussed with the brim of his hat.

"Mick, a word?" I jerked my head slightly, gesturing for the old man to follow me. Even though West had been clear about not being mad at Mickey, I still hadn't worked through my shit. I needed to though. If West wasn't mad at him, I wasn't sure I had a right to be either. I wanted to believe there was more that they could've done to protect West, but everyone kept telling me it wasn't as simple as that.

"What can I do for you, boss?" he asked when we were a good distance away from everyone else.

"Your knee okay?" I replied, glancing down at the knee brace he wore. Mickey rarely wore them out in the field.

"Just old." He chuckled.

"Okay," I said. "I need to go into town for the day. Why don't you take Tess and pop her in a UTV with you for the day? I need my cows back where they belong as soon as possible. We've been doing damn good with them but until the vet comes and clears every single one of them, I can't have the whole goddamn herd together. I can't afford for shit to happen. The ranch won't survive it."

"You got it, boss."

"Jackson," I corrected.

"Is it now?" He cocked a brow, and I sighed. *Of course, he wasn't going to make this easy on me.*

"Look," I crossed my arms, "I ain't going to pretend that I think anything y'all did was right. I think you should've done more for West while he was here. I think Harrison should've had an accident early on that no one would've fucking questioned out in one of our fields. I have a lot of fucking thoughts on what should've happened to Harrison. But West ain't mad. He's fucking grateful for what the lot of you did for him. And if he ain't mad, then I need to learn to let it go."

Mickey made a small sound, a slow smile spreading across his face as he nodded.

"Spit it out, Mick. Whatever the fuck you're going to say, just say it."

"Do we need to revisit the HR rules?" he teased.

"Get the fuck out of here, old man," I snapped but grinned nonetheless. As he began to limp away, I called after him, "And, Mick?"

"Yeah, boss?"

"Find out who the fuck screwed up my boundaries. Someone's getting fired over this shit," I told him. His mouth pressed into a tight line, but he said nothing. Mickey liked all the guys that worked for me—hell, I did too. But I couldn't let this pass without repercussions. Not something this big.

"You got it, Jackson," he said.

"Take it easy, Mickey. Make my girl do all the hard work." I wandered back to where West stood waiting for me as I watched everyone head out.

"You're a mean boss," West commented when I reclined back against the fence next to him.

"I'm a damn good boss," I retorted.

"Just another grumpy fucking cowboy giving people shit," he continued.

"Fuck off."

"Nah, I don't feel like it." *Good.* "Besides, it's fun watching you squirm in front of them."

When we were completely alone, I turned to face him. Before I could say a damn word, he leaned over the fence and kissed me, taking me by surprise. The kiss was brief but fuck me, it sent my pulse through the roof.

"You still look stupid in that fucking hat," he murmured against my lips. I frowned and pulled back.

"What the hell do you have against my hat?" I demanded but that smirk on his face said it all. "You fucker."

I kissed him again, letting it linger briefly.

"Where'd you go this morning?" I asked.

"I wanted to check on Betty before getting all the horses ready," West said. *That tracked.* Honestly, I probably should've assumed he was with the horses instead of avoiding me. Granted, he had a history of using the horses to avoid me so the thought wasn't completely unfounded. "Turns out Betty likes cows more than she likes horses."

"Because why the hell would we have one normal fucking animal on this farm," I muttered.

"And the cows seem to like her."

"Not surprised."

"They aren't the only ones who seemed to like her." His lips quirked, and I had a sinking feeling I wouldn't like what he said next.

"What the fuck happened?"

"How do we feel about Zeus doing his thing with Betty?" West asked.

"Jesus fucking Christ." I ran a hand over my face. I knew we were heading into breeding season with the horses, but usually, I didn't have to worry about anything. Most of the horses were mares, and the few stallions I did have didn't seem to give a fuck. "And you didn't fucking separate them?"

"The next time that beast fucking mounts a mare, I'll let you come in and tackle him off her," he retorted dryly. "No, I wasn't about to fucking interrupt that shit. I like all my body parts where they are, thank you very much."

"Fuck." I sighed. "Fine, I'll let the vet know to take a look at her too. Jesus fuck. New rule, keep Zeus away from Betty. And all of Betty's friends."

"Betty's friends are cows. Are we worried about him fucking cows now too?" West teased. "Lock up your heifers now, cowboy."

"Don't you fucking start with that shit." Somehow, with my luck on this goddamn ranch, Zeus would do exactly that. I'd end up on the front of some science fucking magazine with cow-horse babies. I didn't need that bullshit. "Come on. We got shit to do."

Fishing my keys out of my pocket, I headed toward my truck.

"Where are we going?"

"The sperm bank," I called over my shoulder.

"The *what*?" he exclaimed. I just laughed but didn't stop, forcing him to run after me.

CHAPTER 54

"You could've said it was for bull sperm," I said.

"It ain't my fault you assumed something else," Jackson replied, that shit-eating grin on his face widening. I walked alongside him down a sidewalk in Eugene. I couldn't remember the last time I'd been to this city. Sure, it was the biggest city near Double Arrow, but we rarely visited it.

And yet, the city wasn't the weirdest part about the whole damn thing. It was the fact that the container Jackson carried had several vials of bull sperm in them.

"You could've fucking said something sooner," I retorted.

"I could've, but it was funnier this way." *Jackass.* "I figured after we meet up with Beau, we could go get lunch or whatever. We've got the whole day. Mickey's taking over everything for me. I didn't feel like rushing back if I didn't have to."

Beau Abernathy was a businessman through and through. The exact nature of his business always eluded me. When asked, his answer had always been the same: he did a little bit of this and a little bit of that. Anyone in the ranch business knew who he was, though I wasn't sure anyone actually knew what Beau did. It just came down to what did you need from Beau or what did Beau need from you.

In this case, apparently, he needed bull sperm from Jackson.

"How the hell did you get hooked up with Beau Abernathy anyhow?" I asked.

"About fifteen years ago, my dad ended our bull breeding program," he explained. "Harrison wasn't holding up his weight where the bulls were concerned, and my dad couldn't keep doing it all. But, he didn't stop collecting samples—though, he kept that from Harrison. After my dad died, I found out he had an account at the bank here in Eugene. It was more meant for backup income if needed. I have all the certifications for each vial. Every now and then I sell a handful off to keep the ranch going."

"How often are you selling them off?"

"More so recently than I used to," Jackson told me, his answer vague as fuck. I frowned. Again, I found myself wondering how bad off the ranch was. I wasn't blind to some of the shit going on, but I also knew Jackson. He was proud—sometimes to a fault. He always had been. There was a good chance things were much worse than he was letting on. "Anyway, Beau's decided to get into the bull riding business. He's opening a top-of-the-line training facility up on the Washington border. I've seen it. It's fucking incredible. I would've killed to learn at a place like that when I was younger."

I made a small sound, not sure what I could add to the conversation.

"He asked if I'd be willing to teach after I retire," he continued. That was the first I'd heard anything about him retiring.

"Are you planning on retiring?"

"I've got maybe a few more seasons left in me at best," he admitted quietly. "It's just an age thing. I don't bounce back the way I used to. My agent wanted me to retire after this upcoming season, especially with my current sponsoring issues. People don't want a thirty-four-year-old gay bull rider when they can get some fresh twenty-year-old that fits their fucking values and draws in more attention."

"That's bullshit," I said. Older or not, Jackson was still one of the best.

"That's the business. I want to go two or three more years if I can, but I don't know. I haven't decided shit yet."

"Will you take Beau up on his offer to teach?" I asked. It sounded like a good alternative to keep his career going.

"I can't. I have the ranch to run." There was a hint of sadness in his voice—something fleeting and curious. But I didn't get the chance to dwell on it as we stopped in front of a bustling bar. My heart dropped. I wasn't ready to sit around in a bar. Jackson must've sensed my hesitation because he whispered, "Don't worry. We ain't staying. Beau knows that. Just stick close. I've got you."

I trusted him. I just didn't trust myself.

This was business. I kept that thought in the forefront of my mind as I followed him inside. For mid-day, the bar was active. There was food, drinks, and sports news on random TVs. The smell of greasy food and alcohol filled my lungs, making my stomach turn and my throat ache. My gaze trailed after a waitress and her tray of beer with more longing than I ever wanted to admit out loud.

"Is there anything weirder than walking through a fucking bar carrying bull sperm?" I muttered under my breath. Jackson chuckled but said nothing.

We headed straight out the back door onto the empty patio. I sucked in a breath of fresh air, thankful for the lack of alcohol out here.

"Well, now. Myles and McNamara!" A booming laugh greeted us. "When I heard y'all were back together, I didn't believe it."

Beau sat alone at a table with a spread of food and drinks in front of him. He looked every bit of the stereotypical southern businessman that he was from his big belt buckle to his gray cowboy hat that matched his suit. A huge smile took over his face as he stared at us.

"How many fucking people are out there talking about us?" Jackson demanded with a grin. He set the container on the table and crossed his arms.

"The trouble you two shits caused was damn near as legendary as your career," Beau said. "I got to tell you, boys, it's impressive you two haven't landed your asses in jail yet."

One of us hadn't. I kept that piece of information to myself.

"Please," Jackson scoffed. "Y'all are so damn dramatic. We weren't that bad."

"You keep tellin' yourself that," he replied. His stare leveled on me, and I shoved my hands in my pockets, squaring off my shoulders as he sized me up. "And you? How you doin', West?"

"I'm doing all right." I kept it short and simple.

"The last time I saw you, you were a scrawny thing," he commented. *Was I?* When the fuck had I met him? I could recall my dad talking about him but nothing else. "You're lookin' good. Still got a thing for those horses?"

"Yes, Sir," I said with a slight nod.

"You were always real damn good with those horses," Beau continued. There was a gleam in his eye that made me uncomfortable. "People used to say you had the magic touch."

"Oh, come on now, Beau," Jackson interrupted. "You can't capitalize on everything and everyone."

"But I can try." He chuckled. Grabbing his napkin, he wiped his hands as he leaned forward in his seat. "You decide to take me up on that offer yet, Myles? The bull riders you could turn out would be legendary. Your name on my school would draw in the best of the upcomin' best. Boys would be linin' up to be trained by Jackson fuckin' Myles."

Jackson snorted as if he didn't believe a word Beau had to say.

"You'll do just fine without me, Abernathy," he said. "That right there's all you need from me."

"I'll convince you one day," Beau replied instead. "Maybe I'll convince West over here to come train me some prime racin' horses while I'm at it."

"Nah, I'm good where I'm at," I told him. I had no interest in being a part of something like that.

"One day." He said the words like a promise—like he didn't believe a damn thing either of us said. "You boys have a good day now. We'll be in touch, Myles. Our business ain't done yet. I'll be watchin' you this season."

"I'll be sure to put on a show just for you, Beau," he said. "Just let me know if you need more."

With that, he strode right over to the half fence wrapping around the patio and swung one long leg over it.

"Where the fuck are you going?" I demanded.

"Please," Jackson scoffed, swinging his other leg over the low fence. "I'm a grown-ass man. I can jump a goddamn fence any time I want."

"It's a wonder your ass hasn't been arrested yet," I retorted, shaking my head. Nonetheless, I jumped over the fence after him, grateful to avoid the bar—a fact I had a feeling he was all too aware of.

We found a restaurant across town to stop for lunch. The place was tropical-themed with so many fucking colors it should've been illegal, but they had a quiet rooftop section. We sat under a ridiculous pink pineapple umbrella with two plates of burgers and fries.

"So, how bad is it?" I finally gained the courage to ask.

"The burger ain't bad." Jackson shrugged. "Fries are a little dry though."

"You know I ain't asking about the food," I said as I pinned him with a glare. He sighed, wiping his hands and sinking back in his chair. "How bad is the ranch doing? Really."

"When I offered up the forty-seven million for the ranch, that was pretty much everything I have and then some," he admitted quietly. "I took out a hefty loan to be able to pay you that. The truth is, I don't know if I'll be able to make it to the end of the year without going bankrupt."

"What the hell happened?" I asked.

"Well, it started when Harrison made a few poor fucking choices with our business money," he told me. "He never recovered the money and didn't have the money to put back into the ranch. That left me covering up for his mistakes. But he kept making stupid ass decisions and left me doing nothing but bailing his ass out so the business didn't tank.

"Then the virus hit the herd and that just continued the spiral. Between vet bills, canceled contracts, employees I couldn't pay... I've been floundering for a while. When Harrison died, I had fucking hoped to pay you off and then downsize the ranch. If I sell off three-fourths of the land, I can recoup my losses enough to at least break even on everything I owe everyone. Without that... well, I'm not moving cattle, the animals all cost money, the employees all cost money, the ranch costs fucking money, and my mom's retirement facility costs money. I'm bleeding through my savings from bull riding to cover the differences on everything right now."

Jesus fucking Christ.

"How much did Harrison fucking lose?"

"Harrison gambled away everything he had and kept taking out of business money to pay off loan sharks."

My chest burned hot, and my temper spiked. *Fucking Harrison.* He couldn't get by without screwing anyone over, could he?

"How much is the ranch worth right now?" I sat back in my seat, suddenly not very hungry.

"Nothing," Jackson said, crossing his arms. "No one wants the cattle—not after the virus shit, which I can't blame them. The horses aren't worth shit. Sorry, but they're more pets than anything else at this point. The only valuable thing I got is the land, but it's all tied up until the next nine months of Harrison's trust terms are over. I even asked if I could sell off what I have, but the division of land is tricky. It's collective land tied up between both our families, which means I need your approval—"

"Tell me where to fucking sign and I'll sign," I interrupted.

"—and that can't happen until the whole situation with the trust is done," he finished over me. "So, I can't do shit until everything is officially signed over to me. The sale with Beau should hold me over long enough until bull riding season is over and I'm back in town. After that... I don't fucking know."

"Fucking hell," I muttered. "How much did Harrison gamble away?" *Maybe there was some way I could get him the money back.*

"Don't go down that road, West," he replied. "There's no way in hell you or me will ever recoup those losses. Once the next nine months are over, I'll take the money you didn't want and pay off the loan I took out. And then I'll move fast on selling the land. Between that and letting a few people go, I'll be good. I just have to start over."

"Pay the loan off now instead of eating the fucking interest," I said. *That much seemed like common sense.* He didn't need the extra debt.

"And what if you decide you want the money you're owed for the sale?" he countered.

"I already signed the paperwork that says I don't."

"I know, but that's a lot of fucking money. If you change your mind, I don't have that kind of money sitting around and I don't know that I could get another loan to cover paying you off."

"I don't want the money, Jackson." *I wouldn't know what to do with that kind of money.* Not really. In theory, the thought of it had been nice but actually having it? I couldn't fathom it.

"And I like to have my bases covered where I can—"

"Pay the fucking loan off."

"I won't—"

"I ain't taking the fucking money. There's no point in—"

"Are you staying?" Jackson demanded, cutting me off. The question shut me the fuck up, taking me by surprise. He repeated, "When the year is up, are you staying at Double Arrow?"

"I don't..." I faltered. I didn't have an answer—didn't know how to answer. On one hand, I was getting used to what Jackson and I had going on. I also had Bailey, Thunder Jack, Betty, and the other horses to think about.

But that little voice in the back of my head wasn't so sure I'd last there. I didn't know how to make peace with all the shit that had come out of Double Arrow. I wasn't sure I ever could.

And honestly, I barely knew what I was doing on any given day let alone what came after this whole ranch trust was taken care of.

"That's what I thought," he whispered. "It's fine. I don't blame you. But we made a deal... you get the money for the ranch and the freedom to go whenever. No one would blame you if you changed your mind and wanted that money. I wouldn't. But I can't bank on you not changing your mind."

"You don't trust me," I said. Something about that stung worse than anything else he'd said.

"West," he rested his arms on the table and leaned closer, "I do trust you. I walked into this thing with you knowing full well that at the end of this year together, you're going to break my heart. I just know that if anyone deserves every opportunity to start over, it's you. And that's why the money will be there for you if you fucking want it. If you change your mind, it ain't because you're trying to screw me over. It's because—and I fucking hope for this—you'll finally see just how much you fucking deserve the chance at a good life outside of the God-forsaken ranch."

I swallowed hard, unable to find the words to say a single damn thing. *How the hell was I supposed to respond to that?*

CHAPTER 55

JACKSON

I couldn't read West's mood, and it was killing me.

After lunch, he followed me around as I ran a few errands—stupid shit to fill my time. I picked up things that my mom had been asking for and even took the time to drop them off. I didn't need to, but I was avoiding going home with him. And honestly, she loved seeing West again. They sat outside talking about Betty for the better part of an hour while I didn't say a damn word.

On the drive home, West didn't say a fucking thing. He hadn't said much at all to me since we left lunch. I replayed every moment at the restaurant in my head, trying to figure out where I'd lost him—where I'd scared him away. Was it the state of the ranch? Was it the fact that I called him out about his time here? Was it telling him all of the shit Harrison had gotten involved in?

Who fucking knew? It could've been any of them. Hell, it could've been all of them. I would've given anything to know.

Either way, by the time we walked into the house, I was restless and grumpy. Tess wasn't around, which told me that Mickey probably took her home—not an uncommon thing for the two of them. There were no wild messages about the stupid shit going on with my ranch, which was a good thing.

All of it just left me with time to fill.

Kicking off my boots, I left the door open for him and started across the house.

"Good night," I called over my shoulder. It was too early to go to bed but going upstairs to my office seemed like a better option than sitting around in silence with him.

I was halfway across the house when he grabbed my arm, turning me fast. I didn't get a chance to say a single fucking word as his mouth crashed into mine in a deep kiss, his tongue driving past my lips. The sudden invasion of him was intoxicating. Every kiss was more intense than the first.

Pulling away slightly, his forehead pressed against mine. My panting mirrored his as we both caught our breath.

"Don't..." he began quietly, "don't... don't give me the power to break your heart. I'm not fucking worth that."

This man. *This fucking man.* He just didn't get it, did he?

"It's too late for that," I whispered. Taking his face in my hands, I kissed him once. Twice. Three times. Each kiss lingered longer than the last. "I loved you back then just like I love you now."

The admission hit me like a fucking truck. I'd never said those words to anyone besides my parents. The truth was I had loved West back when we were kids—even before our first kiss—and I never got over him. I never stopped loving him.

His crashing back into my life only brought all those feelings rushing right back to me. And every little moment we had together solidified them and molded them into something I couldn't deny.

West's arm wrapped tight around my waist, and he walked me backward until I hit a wall. His body pressed into mine as he kissed me again. Something moved through him like a desperate need to express things he couldn't say out loud—things I hoped one day I'd hear from him.

But this? I'd take this weird and confusing thing we had going on over nothing.

His hips rolled against mine, drawing a moan out of both of us with the friction building between our bodies.

Jesus fuck. I was so goddamn wound up by this man. No one had ever made everything so simple like making out and practically dry humping against a wall feel so damn good.

His teeth nipped along my jaw, scraping against my beard, as he worked his way to my neck. The sweep of his tongue had me groaning as he hit the right spot.

"Jackson," West whispered against my skin. I made a small sound, doing my best to pay attention. "What if I want more?"

That slammed me right back to reality. I grabbed the front of his shirt, pushing him back slightly so I could see his face. His expression was unreadable as I searched his face for more information. *Was he saying what I thought he was? Or was I thinking too much?*

"I don't expect anything," I told him quietly.

"I know."

"We're good where we're at. There's no need to rush anything, baby. I'm not... I don't expect more."

"I know *you* don't," he said. "But what if *I* want to? I've never... but just... what if I want to try?"

Try...

Christ, this man was going to be the death of me. He didn't deserve any of the shit he'd been through. He didn't deserve to feel the way he did.

"If that's what you want," I replied softly. My lips brushed against his briefly, some small gesture of reassurance.

"I can't..." His head shook slightly as he struggled to finish the sentence. "There's just... certain things... I don't know... I can't..."

There was no way in hell he could handle being topped, which didn't surprise me. Not with everything I knew. I was typically very strict about my role when it came to sex, but for West, I'd be whatever the hell he needed. I'd relish in any little bit of himself he was willing to share with me.

"Your stables, your rules, West," I reiterated because I felt he needed to hear it. "I ain't rushing you into a damn thing. However you want to do this thing. You take the lead, baby."

CHAPTER 56

WEST

Shirts off. Pants kicked aside. Boxer briefs who the hell knew where. Socks too.

Hands. Tongues. Teeth.

He was anywhere and everywhere—his hands roaming over every inch of my body that he could touch. I wasn't nearly as bold. My confidence was fading fast as I realized just how inexperienced I was compared to him.

We collapsed into Jackson's bed. I settled between his hips, my cock rolling against his as I made myself comfortable over him. The sensation made me moan into his mouth, and I repeated the action. His fingers dug into my ass, guiding me to do it a third time. The room swayed as the temperature skyrocketed.

My body was on fucking autopilot as I thrust against his cock. He met each one with equal enthusiasm. Pre-cum painted my stomach and his, mingling with sweat. His breath was my breath and vice versa as we panted, both worked up into a frenzy of need.

"Lights off," I told him quickly when he reached for the lamp.

"Whatever you want," he said. I heard the drawer slide open and close quickly, and he dropped something on the bed. *Lube.* That much I knew we'd need, especially with my piercings.

Fuck, what if I hurt him?

I shoved that thought aside and focused on the man underneath. On Jackson. On making him feel good.

Trailing my tongue along the strong line of his neck, I nipped his earlobe before moving my way down his body. I took my time exploring him all over again with slow kisses and hesitant touches. It gave my body the chance to level out as I made my way to his cock.

I didn't know a hell of a lot about what the fuck I was doing, but I wasn't an idiot either. I knew I couldn't just dive dick first without some prep work—without making sure he was ready.

I grabbed the bottle of lube and covered my fingers, using the excess to swipe over his hole. I swept my tongue over his slit, lapping up the pre-cum gathering there. His legs opened wider as he moaned. I dragged my tongue up the length of his cock a second time. As I did, I slowly pressed one finger inside him. That moan of his grew louder.

I swirled my tongue around the crown of his cock and lowered onto him. I took my time working one finger in and out of his ass with ease while sucking on his dick. Whatever the hell I was doing, I was doing it right. It had him worked up more than ever. His hands fisted in the sheets while his hips rocked up against my mouth.

I added a second finger, stretching him and quickly adding a third. The amount had him writhing underneath me. My head bobbed up and down his pulsing cock in tandem with the pace my fingers set. His breaths came faster, and his hand wrapped around my forearm, gripping impossibly hard.

"You keep doing that and I'm going to come before you ever fuck me, West," Jackson rasped. I took that as a compliment—at least I could do some part of this right—but still backed off.

My hands trembled slightly as I grabbed the lube bottle a second time. I coated my cock, working myself from root to tip and making sure my piercings were slick. The cool liquid was an uncomfortable shock to my system. I tried to shake off the disorienting feeling while situating myself over him.

Jackson propped himself up on one elbow, and I was all too aware of how he tracked my movements. I lined the crown of my dick with his hole and faltered as it hit me. *I was really doing this.* My fingers rolled over my piercings as I stroked myself once before slowly thrusting forward just enough to push past that ring of tight muscles.

The onslaught of sensations was instantaneous and overwhelming.

"*Holy fuck...*" I gasped. Jackson's hand ran through my hair as his lips brushed along my neck. A shudder surged through my body, rolling like lightning over my nerves.

"Are you okay?" he said, his forehead touching mine. I nodded slightly, though I didn't have a fucking clue. "Let me hear you say it, West. I need to hear you say it, baby."

I swallowed hard against the lump in my throat and did my best to find the words to describe what the hell I was feeling. *Fuck, I didn't know.*

"Yeah," was all I managed to say.

"Okay." His mouth brushed over my cheek, gentle and reassuring. I eased in and out of him, daring to push a little deeper each time. The pressure was wildly intense as his body adjusted to mine—his muscles wrapped tight around my cock and hugged my piercings.

It was too much.

"That's it, baby," Jackson whispered. His mouth found mine, tongue driving through my lips as he kissed me hard. *The heat of his body, the quickness of his breath, the roughness on his hands.*

I felt every bit of him everywhere all at once. I was damn near shaking head to toe, and I wasn't sure why. My whole body screamed at me. Good? Bad? I couldn't fucking tell.

I couldn't fucking tell up from down as I practically vibrated right out of my own skin.

I tried to focus on him as I picked up a slow pace thrusting in and out of him—on the way his body moved under mine, on the sounds he made, on the way he touched me—but I felt myself slipping. The ledge was right there, dragging me under in a way I couldn't stop no matter how hard I scrambled away from it.

I slammed my eyes shut and forced myself to keep going. That familiar panic clawed its way through my chest.

I could do this.

I had to do this.

I didn't want to let Jackson down. Not like this. Not now.

Desperate for a distraction from my own demons, I wrapped my fist around his dick. My hand kept pace with my hips. I honed in on his panting and moaning, using the sounds as an anchor—whatever would keep me from falling apart.

Not here.

Not now.

"That's it, baby," Jackson praised, the words barely audible amidst my spiral.

I was only vaguely aware of the way his legs moved higher up my side or how he asked for more. *Faster. Harder.*

I obliged, doing whatever the hell it took to get him there—to get myself there. That foreign feeling built in my core, painfully hot this time and rubbing against my every raw nerve.

It was too much.

Too much.

But not for Jackson.

His hand covered mine as he took over jerking himself up, his pace faster than what I was doing. In seconds, he came—hot cum spilling between the two of us.

And, as if waiting for permission, my body followed his. My balls seized up, and I lost all fucking sense of self-control. With a deep moan, I buried myself inside him, my cock jerking as I came. His fingers dug into my hips as he held me as close as possible.

I couldn't pull out fast enough but did my best to be normal about the whole thing. *What counted as normal?* Was I supposed to stay there? Cuddle?

I didn't know what the fuck to do.

I settled on a faint kiss before I collapsed on the bed next to him, blinking back hot tears and thankful for the dark. Something painful burned its way through my chest—something I could barely hold back.

What the fuck was wrong with me?

"Are you okay?" Jackson asked softly. His fingers wove through mine and squeezed gently. His touch fucking hurt. It took everything I had to not flinch or pull away. *I couldn't do that to him.*

"Yeah," I lied, breathless and dying a little inside.

CHAPTER 57

WEST

I nhale...
    Exhale...
Thump... thump thump... thump...
Inhale...
Exhale...
Thump thump... thump... thump thump...
    My heart galloped wildly in my chest as I attempted to breathe. I couldn't catch my breath. The weight sitting on my lungs was too much. The shadows pulsated around me while the room swayed unsteadily.
    I sat on the floor at the end of the bed, a tangled mess in the sheet. It was as far as I managed to get before my legs gave out.
    Panic clawed its way violently through my chest. I just wanted to get the fuck out of there. I squeezed my eyes shut and tried to pretend I was somewhere else—anywhere else.
    Open fields.
    Horses.

Clouds.
Dark clouds.
Darkness.
Screaming.
So much screaming...
I couldn't stop the screaming...
I lost control completely, succumbing to endless screaming in my head.

CHAPTER 58

JACKSON

R AGGED BREATHING PULLED ME out of my sleep. Groggily, I sat upright and tried to gain my bearings. *Fuck, deep sleep never did me any good.* I reached over to check on West only to discover he was gone. I flipped on the light fast and saw him sitting on the floor at the end of the bed in a mess of sheets—unmoving.

Fuck, fuck, fuck. My heart lurched into my throat, a feeling of dread settling in my chest. I refused to jump to conclusions, but it was hard to avoid when I'd been worried about this, to begin with.

I slid off the bed and rounded it fast. As I crouched next to West, I did my best to assess the situation. His chest heaved with uneven breaths while tears stained his cheeks. The sheet was a mess around him as if he'd been unable to untangle from it stumbling out of bed.

And that glazed-over look in his eyes... *fuck, I wasn't sure if he was here with me or a million memories away.*

"West?" I said. Reaching out, I ran my palm down his arm to get his attention. His reaction was immediate—his hand lashing out and latching painfully hard around my wrist.

"Don't touch me," he snapped, never once looking at me. That anger fizzled fast as he whispered, "*Please...* don't touch me."

His grip on me loosened, and I pulled away.

"Okay," I replied. "What happened?"

I could hazard a guess what happened, but I wanted to hear it from him.

Nothing.

His gaze remained fixated on something I couldn't see, and his knuckles were stark white as they gripped the sheet. I didn't know how to help him like this, especially when he wouldn't talk to me. *Maybe he couldn't talk to me?*

Well, I couldn't help him. Not me personally anyway.

Giving him space, I picked up his pants and pulled out one of my sweatshirts. I set them out on the bed before grabbing my clothes. I didn't get dressed in front of him. The last thing I wanted was to trigger anything else.

"Get dressed and meet me downstairs," I ordered gently from the doorway. "West?"

It took a hot minute but his gaze finally flicked in my direction to acknowledge me—though, I wasn't sure if he was looking at me or right through me. It was hard to tell with that empty expression of his.

"Get dressed and meet me downstairs," I repeated. "I've got you, okay?"

I drove us across the ranch to the stables. I didn't know what the hell I was doing or if I was out of my goddamn mind, but it was the only thing I could think of.

If not me then maybe the horses.

West followed me out of the truck, silent and vacant. My fucking heart broke. He looked so goddamn small as he buried his hands inside my sweatshirt, his shoulders slumping.

"Wait here," I told him gently. I didn't bother waiting for an answer and went inside. The horses stirred as I strode down the center aisle to Thunder Jack's stall. The massive stallion loomed over the ledge of the door, eyeing me warily. I paused. We stared at one another while I debated how to best approach him.

"Now, listen here," I began as I opened his door. "Don't be a dick, got it? I'm trying to fucking help him, and I don't feel like fighting you tonight. Got it?"

Like the horse understood a damn thing I said.

Thunder Jack took several steps out of his stall, and I braced for chaos. The horse tolerated no one but West. I was probably going to have my ass handed to me by a thousand-pound stallion wearing nothing but flannel pants and a baseball tee.

I waited with bated breath. The stallion did nothing but judge me with enough intensity to rival my mother. *Thank fuck.* I could handle that shit.

With a focus on efficiency, I saddled Thunder Jack in the quickest way possible. I skipped steps like brushing him out. Any other time, I would've, but I couldn't just leave West standing with the truck.

I grabbed a set of night boots and a headlight harness. Getting that fucking close to his hooves didn't sound like a great plan to me, but I worried about making West visible out there. Any time someone was out late with one of the horses, I required night boots. Was it overkill with the headlight harness? Probably. But visibility was important. We were still surrounded by woods.

With the harness light switched to a blue color for less abrasiveness, I led Thunder Jack out of the stable. The horse followed my lead—*thank fuck*. Though, maybe he could tell something was wrong.

West stood exactly where I left him, staring off into the darkness.

"Go," I said softly as I guided Thunder Jack to a stop in front of West. The blue lighting illuminated his pale eyes in a haunting way—one that amplified the pain residing there. It fucking killed me to let him go. I wanted nothing more than to wrap him up in my arms and hold him until he felt better, but I wasn't it. I could never be that for him.

His horses, however, could.

He hesitated.

"Just go," I reiterated and handed him the reins, careful to never let our fingers touch. The less contact, the better. "I'll be around when you're ready."

That earned me the slightest of nods. *I'd take it.*

I'd take whatever the hell West would give me because I knew just how painful it was for him to share himself.

I stepped back as he pulled himself up into the saddle, settling quickly. With a slight nudge of his boots, he urged Thunder Jack forward. Drawing in a deep breath, I crossed my arms as he started down one of the paths at a slow trot.

I watched the blue lights fade into the shadows until West was completely gone. A heavy sadness settled in my chest, wrapping around my heart as I let him go. What I would've given to be out there with him. To be what he needed.

CHAPTER 59

JACKSON

H OLY FUCK, I WAS too goddamn old to be sleeping in the front seat of my truck. Old injuries made themselves known as I sat up. *Yeah, I'd spent the night in my truck.* I was honestly surprised I'd managed to fall asleep at all with how wound up I'd been.

I barely remembered two in the morning rolling around, which meant I'd waited for three hours for West to return. Filling that time had been awful. Not knowing if he was okay was fucking torture.

And somehow, I'd passed out in the middle of it all.

Had West come back and just ignored me completely? Or was he still out there? If he was, I was grabbing my fucking horse and chasing him down.

My body ached as I climbed out of my truck and went straight to the stables. Thunder Jack was right back in his stall, munching on hay as if nothing had happened. His saddle and tack were neatly hung up as were the boots and harness. *All of which meant I'd missed West coming back.* I wandered down to the last stall just in case—just on the off fucking chance he hadn't gone back to the house.

And sure enough, he hadn't. West was curled up in the corner of the stall, hands shoved in the sweatshirt pocket with the hood pulled low over his face.

I ran my hands over my face, biting back a sound of frustration. I didn't know what to do. Should I wake him? Leave him? What was the right thing here? What was the best way to help him?

In the end, I left him. If he'd wanted to go back to the house, he would've. If he'd wanted me to know he was back, he would've told me. Both of those things told me he needed space.

It also left me with horses to tend to. I left and crossed to the working stable, determined to do West's job before my guys showed up. Unfortunately, wrangling horses wasn't my thing. Even before West showed up, I never did it.

Still, I put my everything into it—doing my best to emanate West's level of care and attention. I wasn't half as good as him but at least I got the job done.

I was halfway through my fourth horse when the first truck pulled up. Any shred of dignity I had went straight out the window. I didn't know how to explain this to anyone.

"Hey, boss," Peter said as he got out. *At least it was only Peter.* He stopped along the fence next to me. "You okay? You're... you're not..."

"Dressed to fucking work?" I finished for him. I'd worn a lot of shit around my ranch but wearing flannel pajamas to saddle the horses was a new one. I didn't like it. "I know."

"Rough night?" he asked softly. I paused, drawing in a deep breath as I stared out at the readied horses.

"I fucking hate PTSD," I admitted quietly. I could've lied, but I didn't want to. I was grumpy and mad and stewing over shit that wasn't even something I could fix. The man I loved was falling apart in ways I couldn't begin to fathom—tortured by memories and trauma I didn't understand. Could never understand. It fucking killed me. "I fucking hate it."

"I hear you," Peter said. *Of course, he did.* "Why don't I finish the horses for you? You go shower and take the day off."

"I can't do that to you."

"Yeah, you can," he insisted. "Besides, you'll break your toes if that horse stomps on your slippers."

I ignored the slippers comment, fully aware of how dumb I fucking was for wearing them instead of going back for my boots. There hadn't been time.

"Are you sure?" I ran a hand through my hair as I stalled. I was so fucking tired, and from the expression on his face, I probably looked it.

"You need to take care of you too, Jackson," he told me. "You can't just take care of him. You're no good to him if you're drowning too."

"He's asleep in the stables."

"I'll keep everyone away, and I'll let Mickey know when he gets here. Promise."

"Can you text me when he's up?" I asked, and Peter nodded.

"You got it, boss." He smiled in that easy way that was just him. I liked Peter. I liked having someone who understood a little bit of what I was feeling—someone who helped me make it make a little more sense.

"Thanks, Peter. I mean that."

I didn't go home and shower. Instead, I made a pot of coffee and sat down at my laptop. I bypassed all my work emails and bullshit to do some research on sexual assault survivors, PTSD, and every little thing I could think of in between.

I was so fucking lost as to how to help West. I hated watching him struggle, but I wasn't sure what the hell I could even do to help.

CHAPTER 60

WEST

I DIDN'T HAVE A fucking clue what time it was when I finally came to. I was numb from head to toe and it had nothing to do with sleeping on the stable floor. Sitting there with my eyes shut, I tried my best to bury memories of last night—of falling apart after having sex with Jackson. *Fuck, I had sex with Jackson.*

I had sex.

My brain struggled to wrap around those words. Around that concept.

That familiar tightness built in my chest as I struggled to push away the memories. I should've said something... should've stopped... should've done something.

Except I did do something.

I kept doing what I thought Jackson wanted me to do at my own expense.

I groaned, dragging the hood of his sweatshirt down over my face and letting my head thud off the stable wall. *How fucking pathetic was I?* I was fucking lucky if Jackson wanted anything to do with me after this. He had to see there were better people to date out there—normal fucking people who could do things like have sex without panicking.

A grumpy-sounding neigh ripped me from my own thoughts. I frowned as I leaned forward, turning my head to listen closely.

"Shush now, sassy thing." *Peter?* What the fuck was Peter doing in my goddamn stables? "Hey, don't you dare. I like my fingers where they are! Shush! Oh, come on now. Don't do that. No, no. Uh-uh. Come here, sassy thing."

Jesus fuck, he was trying to move Betty. Only one horse in my stable was stubborn enough to make a man beg.

The kid was going to get himself bit while trying to manhandle her.

I stumbled to my feet, shoved off my hood, and hurried out of the stall to rescue him. Peter stood arguing with Betty while she pulled back from him slowly. I clicked my tongue twice and her ears perked right up. Her head jerked hard to pull away from him.

"Easy, girl," I rasped, my voice rough and my throat uncomfortably dry. I smoothed a hand over her back. She stilled, her head swinging in my direction. "No one's taking you anywhere."

"I just figured—"

"They're my responsibility," I told him gruffly. "My horses."

"Okay." Peter nodded slowly. He took a few steps back to give us space. It wasn't his fault that I was grumpy. Hell, the kid was just trying to help. I didn't have a clue what fucking time it was, but if Betty was getting cared for, I'd missed all my fucking duties for the morning.

"I..." I faltered as I ran a hand through my hair. "Thanks for taking care of them."

"My pleasure," he replied with a smile that was all too easy.

"Have you seen Jackson?" I called after him as he went to leave.

"I told him to take the day off," he said. *He what?* No one told Jackson to do jack shit, especially one of his employees. "Figured he could use it after I found him saddling the horses wearing his slippers this morning."

His fucking what?

Fuck. He covered for my stupid ass being passed out.

Jackson had been asleep in his truck when I finally came back in. I should've woken him up. That would've been the right thing to do. Because of me, his whole day was fucked up.

All of this was my fault.

"Thank you," I replied quietly. "For helping him."

"Anytime." That smile got wider for a brief moment before he disappeared, leaving me alone with my guilt and my horses.

I worked my ass off all afternoon and evening. I had to do something considering I'd skirted doing all my fucking work in the morning. The guilt was fucking awful. In less than twelve hours, I'd managed to fuck up so much of Jackson's day. The least I could do was make sure the rest of my duties were done perfectly.

Somewhere after ten, I managed to drag myself into the house. I was exhausted, sore, and miserable. I knew the smart thing to do was eat and go to bed, but as I stood in the hallway, I realized I didn't want any of that.

All I wanted was Jackson.

But did he want anything to do with me?

I stared up the dark stairs wondering if he was even awake. Probably not. I should've just left well enough alone, but I didn't. Instead, I made my way upstairs and snuck into his room while he slept with my side of the bed clear.

"While I'm good with you coming to bed," Jackson mumbled sleepily, "if you try to crawl into my bed wearing the same clothes you had sleeping on the floor of the stables, I'm going to beat your ass."

A small smile tugged at the corner of my mouth. Just the sound of his voice was comforting in ways I didn't know I needed.

"Fair enough," I replied. I stripped down to my boxer briefs and dug through his drawers until I found a shirt of his to wear. The old material scratched uncomfortably against my skin, but I forced myself to put it on. I didn't feel like going downstairs just to find my own clothes.

Carefully, I crawled into bed, keeping to the edge and away from him. I hugged one of the spare pillows to my chest and curled around it for comfort.

"Missed you today," he let out.

"Missed you too." *I meant that.*

"You can move closer," Jackson told me. I wasn't sure that I trusted myself to get any closer to him. And the idea of touching him? Just the idea made my skin crawl. After a long heartbeat, he added, "If you want."

"I'm good here," I said. *And I was.* Next to him was good—felt good. I was okay with this. I wanted this.

"West?" he began, and I made a small sound. "You smell like a goddamn horse."

"Sorry," I muttered.

"Don't. But you are changing my sheets tomorrow," Jackson whispered. A quiet chuckle passed through me. *Sounded about right.* But there were worse things than doing Jackson's laundry. "Night, West."

"Good night, cowboy."

CHAPTER 61

JACKSON

THAT SLEEPY SMILE OF his was dangerous when he woke up. So was the way the stray beams of morning sunlight washed over his face. Half-asleep and completely relaxed like this, West was so goddamn beautiful that he took my breath away. Staring might've been creepy but I just couldn't look away.

"What time is it?" he asked.

"I don't fucking know," I admitted. "I forgot to set my alarm last night."

"You keep taking mornings off and people are going to start thinking you'd rather be here in bed with me, cowboy," he teased. And I knew it was just teasing but damn if I didn't love the idea of doing just that.

"Or that I'm just a crappy fucking boss," I deflected.

"That's my grumpy cowboy." *His cowboy.* I liked the fucking sound of that. A lot. More than I wanted to admit out loud.

He shifted and inched closer, his hand crossing the space between us. Instead of taking mine, however, two fingers brushed over the inside of my wrist.

"Are you feeling my pulse?" I asked, frowning slightly.

"Yeah..." He let out a small sigh. "It was a thing my mom used to do when she couldn't hold my hand because she had things to do and when she wasn't allowed to cuddle me anymore in case my dad saw."

My chest tightened painfully. *Jesus Christ.* He wasn't even allowed to cuddle his mom because of Harrison.

"I can stop," he said. "It's fucking weird, isn't it?"

"No," I interjected quickly as he started to pull away. "No. I like it."

I liked him finding comfort in me, no matter what that looked like. As if to prove my point, I moved my arm closer to make it easier for him. I rolled onto my side, facing him.

"Do you remember her?" I asked quietly. He never talked about his mom, even when we were kids after she died. It was as if she just suddenly didn't exist anymore in his life.

"She liked music—old music," West told me. His eyes slid shut as he spoke, and his fingers tightened slightly on my wrist. "*Hall & Oates* was her favorite. She liked action movies and hated cooking, but she taught me how to cook—said it was important for me to learn."

And that would be why he knew how to cook.

"She taught me how to take a hit," he continued. The sadness in his voice broke my heart. "Harrison... when he drank, he got mean. He was always an asshole, you know? But it got bad when he was drunk. He'd take it out on her. *Just a hit or two and he'll cool off*. That's what she always said... how she got us through it. Stay quiet, don't fight back, I can take it."

"West..." *Jesus fucking Christ.*

"After she died, I followed her advice. It worked most of the time. He usually cooled the fuck off after a few hits. It sucked but fighting back always made it worse."

I didn't know what to say. *What the hell did you say to that?* Good job, you learned how to survive your abusive dick of a dad? There was no good thing to say.

While I felt bad for his mother and everything she'd been put through, she failed him too. West never should've been taught how to take a hit. He should've been taken away from Harrison. Protected and loved.

"He blamed me for her death," West said, his voice barely audible.

"Why?" I asked.

"Because I was in the bathroom the night she killed herself," he told me so softly I wasn't sure I heard him right at first.

My heart damn near fell out of my chest. *What?*

"I thought she died in a car accident."

"Harrison didn't want anyone knowing what she did... how she died. I wasn't allowed to talk about it. He blamed me... said if I loved her, I would've saved her."

"Jesus fuck, West." My temper soared, burning hot in the pit of my stomach. "You were seven. What the hell could you have done?"

"I don't know." His voice broke. "I did love her... I just... I didn't know how to save her."

It took everything I had not to drag him to my chest and hold him until the pain went away. No one deserved to be told shit like that—to live through something like that—let alone a child. And growing up, I never had a clue. We spent every moment we could together and I didn't know a damn thing about the dark shit going on in West's life. *That single fact killed me.*

"It wasn't your job to save her, West," I settled on saying instead. "And it doesn't mean you didn't love her."

"I know. He still hated me for it," he replied. "Made sure I knew just how worthless I was... how he wished I had died with her. I don't know... sometimes, I wonder if I was supposed to."

"Baby, no..." The admission was a punch to the gut. *But honestly? Could I blame him?* He'd spent his whole life fighting and hearing horrible things about himself. His entire worldview was shaped by the way Harrison talked to him and treated him.

"I'm fine. I promise," West said. *He wasn't.* It didn't take a genius to figure that out. "I won't fucking do anything."

I wasn't even thinking about *that* until he said something.

"Have you?" I dared to ask. "Tried... that?"

I couldn't bring myself to say the words out loud. I didn't even want to think about him like that. But I also realized just how little I knew about West's life. My life was pretty standard. My career was publicized while the rest of my life was at the ranch. But what about West? What the hell had he done over the last seventeen years?

That question burned a fucking hole in my mind.

"Once," he admitted. Pulling away from me, he rolled onto his back and stared at the ceiling. That spot on my inner wrist felt obscenely naked without the pressure of his fingers. "Almost anyway. I couldn't go through with it."

"I'm glad you didn't." *What a ridiculously pathetic thing to say.* There had to be a better way to phrase that, but for the life of me, I couldn't think of one.

"Yeah." He sat up, getting out of bed before I could say anything else. "We should get up. The ranch ain't going to take care of itself."

And there he went shutting down on me again. I fucking hated when he did that. But how the hell did I fix that? How did I get him to open up to me more?

"I know," I whispered. But I didn't follow him right away. Instead, I propped myself up on one elbow and watched him leave with a million little thoughts running through my head. All I wanted to do was drag him right back into bed with me and stay there all day—like it'd help him feel better.

CHAPTER 62

WEST

J ACKSON WAS THE SHADOW I didn't want. I had a feeling admitting my one failed suicide attempt had him fucking spooked in light of everything. I couldn't blame him for that one, especially after telling him my mother had done it. I was already an alcoholic asshole like my father. Was it hard to believe that I'd follow in my mother's footsteps too?

Not that I blamed her. It was the only way out for her. I adjusted the leather band on my wrist, running my thumb over the old thing as I thought about her. It was all I had left to remember her by.

"Four weeks," Jackson was saying into the phone. I did my best to ignore him, but I was also curious. It wasn't my fucking fault he was having his conversations this goddamn close to me. While I dealt with hooves and horseshoes, he dealt with Amy the pain-in-the-ass agent—his words, not mine. "You have four weeks to find a new goddamn sponsor. Oh, come on! It can't be that fucking hard."

He paced up and down the fence line while she said something.

"I'm a goddamn ray of fucking sunshine," he snapped. I barked out a laugh, unable to stop myself. Jackson paused pacing to glare at me, but I just shrugged. "I'm not old, Amy—I'm not *that* fucking old."

I made a sound like I disagreed with him, only prompting his scowl to deepen. Honestly, I didn't have a fucking clue what was going on, but I liked fucking with him.

'*You're not helping,*' Jackson mouthed, and I shrugged. I wasn't trying.

"There ain't no fucking way I'm letting Lexington Farms sponsor me," he snapped. *That caught my interest.* I knew Lexington Farms. They'd been our biggest competitors since before Jackson and I were fucking born. "Well, you can tell him I said to go suck a—don't you call me by full name, woman!"

I made a face. I did not want to be her.

"No, I ain't got time for a fucking meeting tonight. I have a goddamn date," he said. I cocked a brow, and he gestured between us suggestively. *Eh, why the hell not?* I nodded. "That's right. I have a fucking date, and no, I ain't telling you shit about it. Some things I can keep to myself, Amy."

"I think he just needs to fucking fire Amy," I whispered to Bailey as I rubbed my hands down her snout. She let out a huff. "Yeah, you too?"

"There ain't no way in hell I'm letting Lexington Farms be my goddamn sponsor," Jackson damn near shouted at me as he hung up the call. The rise in his voice set me on edge, but I kept that shit to myself. He had enough problems on his plate. "Who the hell does Rex think he is anyhow? He's taken most of my fucking business at this point and now this? Do I look fucking stupid to you?"

"No—"

"No, I fucking don't," he raged over me. *Yeah, was just going to keep my mouth shut until he was done.* "I have four fucking weeks—four fucking weeks, West—before the goddamn season starts. I ain't got the time to deal with his bullshit. It's the twenty-second! Is this the next fucking thing he's going to do to me? Get inside my head and fuck with my career? Was my ranch not enough?"

Panic lanced through me. I heard him wrong. That was all. I'd heard him wrong. *There was no way it was the twenty-second.*

"It's what?" I stared at him, breathing hard. I had to have heard the date wrong. "What's the date?"

"May," he repeated as if annoyed that I even asked, "twenty-second."
Oh...
He kept ranting about something or some bullshit, but I couldn't hear him. All the blood rushed to my head as my chest tightened painfully.
I'd forgotten the date...
How the fuck had I forgotten the date?

By the time I walked into *Lenny's* that night, I was completely numb. I couldn't feel a fucking thing—physically or emotionally. I could hear the fucking screaming though. Over and over inside my head as my demons clawed their way through me.

I'd fucking forgotten the date.

That was a good thing—it should've been a good thing. I was so fucking settled into my situation at the ranch that I'd fucking forgotten. But somehow it wasn't a good thing. All it did was trigger something deep inside me all that much harder.

I was fucking dying. I barely managed to drag my ass through my daily routine, and I sure as hell didn't do a good job at any of it. The world swam around me—slow as fuck and painfully loud. My skin crawled, and I couldn't focus for the life of me.

And the fucking screaming. Every time I closed my eyes it was right there, ripping me apart little by little.

I just wanted to drown.

To forget it all.

To just float away.

I grabbed the stool farthest from Lenny as he glared at me. *Yeah, I was back, motherfucker.* I threw cash on the bar with hopes that it'd be enough to keep Lenny quiet.

It was.

He swiped up the cash and left a cold beer in its place. It worked in my favor that he fucking hated me. There wasn't a damn person in the world I wanted to talk to right now.

I just wanted to silence the demons in my head.

A. WINCHESTER

That first sip hit the back of my throat, bringing a flood of relief. Any tiny part of me that would've felt guilty about breaking my sobriety washed away with it.

I downed that fucking glass—chasing something I couldn't explain.

Cash.
Beer.
Drink.
Cash.
Beer.
Drink.

Each glass went down faster than the others until my demons were drowning alongside me.

CHAPTER 63

JACKSON

It was one thing to be ditched for a date, it was something entirely different to get a call at one in the morning that West was fucking drunk. To say I was livid was an understatement. But I dragged my ass out of bed anyway because I wasn't about to let a drunken West end up in a ditch or worse.

By the time I found him, he was staggering his way out of town—presumably heading toward the ranch. I eased off the brake until I was practically crawling alongside him. I kept enough of a distance to make sure he didn't stumble in front of my truck and get his ass run over.

"Go away," West snapped when I rolled down my window.

"Get in the truck, West," I ordered.

"Go the fuck away."

"Get your fucking ass in the truck." *Fuck his attitude.* I was fucking tired and wanted to go home. I didn't want to be driving alongside his dumbass.

He ignored me, shoving his hands in his pockets. *Yeah, I wasn't having that bullshit.*

"What the hell were you thinking?" I demanded loudly.

"I don't want to fucking think!" West exploded. His words slurred together as his breathing turned heavy with anger. "I don't want to fucking think! I don't want to fucking feel a goddamn thing! I don't want to fucking remember! Today of *all fucking days* I don't want to remember a fucking thing!"

Without another word, he continued storming down the street. I slowed to a stop and watched him in my headlights. *Today? What the fuck happened today?* We'd had a goddamn normal day on the ranch besides me dealing with Amy, but that had nothing to do with him.

Horses.

Cows.

Fencing.

All of it was normal shit.

So, what the hell was today? I replayed his ranting in my head. It wasn't his birthday. His mother died around Thanksgiving. He'd run away in June when we were kids.

All that was left was... *fuck.*

The realization of what the date had to be for him punched the breath right out of my lungs. There was only one fucking day that I could imagine would make him deteriorate like a landslide.

"Fuck," I muttered. I parked on the side of the road and hopped out, chasing after him. Rolling around in my truck and yelling at him wouldn't help a damn thing.

"Get the fuck out of here," West snarled as I fell in step beside him. The smell of alcohol was overwhelming. What the hell had he done? Drink the whole damn bar?

"No," I said.

"I don't fucking want you here."

"I know."

"So, go the fuck away!"

"I am going away," I retorted. "*This way.* Which just so happens to be the same way you're going."

"Jesus fuck," he growled. "You don't know when to give up, do you?"

"My mama always told me I was stubborn to a fault," I told him.

"I don't fucking want you here!" he continued to rage. I let it roll off my back, knowing full well he didn't mean it. "Jesus fucking Christ, you're dense."

He stumbled, and I resisted the urge to catch him as he tried to right himself. It took everything I had to keep my hands to myself, but there was a damn good chance he'd hit me if I touched him. *And I hated that.*

"You're going home, and I'm—"

"You don't have a fucking clue where I'm going," he interrupted roughly. I pressed my lips together and counted back from ten to keep from saying something stupid. Even with everything I knew, his pushback was getting under my skin.

"Where else do you have to go, West?" I asked.

"Fuck you."

"I know, I know." It was a low blow. He had nowhere to go if he didn't come home to the ranch. "Now, we're both going to the ranch. Either we can walk the whole way there, or you can get in my truck and let me take you home."

"Fuck you. I don't need your stupid fucking help."

I held my tongue. *Yeah, we fucking established that.* There was no point in fighting him. It'd get me nowhere except further away from my fucking truck.

"I know."

"I don't need your goddamn pity."

"I don't pity you, West," I told him quietly. But my heart did break for him. There was so much pain built up inside him that I couldn't begin to touch or take away for him. It killed me. I wanted nothing more than to help him and I couldn't.

"Fine," he relented. He stumbled as he turned, and I clenched my fists to keep from reaching out. *Fuck, I hated this.*

I kept my distance as we walked back to my truck—close enough to intervene if I absolutely had to, far enough to remind myself where my hands belonged.

West disappeared when we got back to the house. I probably should've checked on exactly where he'd gone, but at least he was in the house. I knew he was safe, which was about the best I was going to get.

But that didn't put my mind at ease. There was no way in hell I was going back to sleep. And so I stood in my kitchen doing the dishes I'd avoided doing earlier in the evening when I went to bed. I didn't even use the goddamn dishwasher. I just let the hot water sting my hands and angrily scrubbed every single one.

I didn't hear West join me, but I stilled as his arms wrapped around my waist from behind. I felt how he pressed his forehead to the back of my neck, his hot breath washing over my skin. *How the hell did I respond?*

Hug him back? Tell him to get off? Every instinct told me to turn around and hold him, but I wasn't sure I could. Maybe he could hug me and it didn't bother him, but maybe I couldn't hug him back.

Fuck, this touch thing was stressful. I didn't want to set him off, but I didn't know how to comfort him either. I didn't have a fucking clue what to do, so I just stood there with my hands resting on the sink.

"Please, don't hate me," West whispered, the words slurring together.

"I couldn't hate you."

"You should."

"I never will." *That was a promise.* Sure, I'd hated him before he came back, but I hadn't known everything about why he'd left. Back then, I couldn't see all the puzzle pieces that made up West's life. Hell, I still didn't. And every little piece he did share with me only gave me a clearer image of what his life had been like and how it affected him. *Broken him.* I could never hate him for that.

"It just hurts," he admitted, his voice breaking. "Everything fucking... hurts..."

A sob ate up anything else he was going to say.

I turned slowly, maneuvering him until he was wrapped up in my arms with his head buried in the crook of my neck. He broke down completely, and I held on tighter than I'd ever held anyone in my life.

And he let me. I bore the brunt of his weight as he gave in. There wasn't a damn thing I could say, but I wasn't going anywhere. We could stand against the kitchen sink until the sun rose for all I fucking cared. I wasn't letting go until he wanted me to.

CHAPTER 64

WEST

I FELT LIKE FUCKING crap. Maybe it was the alcohol, maybe it was the all-night breakdown until I passed out laying on Jackson. Either way, I just wanted to crawl into a fucking hole and never come back out.

My emotions were so all over the place. *Guilt. Shame. Fear.* I was drowning in memories I didn't want and I realized I was actually afraid of the future—afraid of what would happen with Jackson. With my horses. With my fucking life.

I couldn't eat. I couldn't sleep. I couldn't do my damn job, but mostly that was because Jackson wouldn't let me near the horses until I called Bobby and went to a meeting. I resented him for that shit.

Admitting I drank again to Bobby only made me feel even more like crap. Instead of being mad or disappointed, he was empathetic and understanding. The man fucking invited me to dinner.

I borderline hated his kindness. Anger I could handle. I knew what to do with that. I didn't know what to do with the man eating soup across from me.

"You know, this program gave me my life back," Bobby began, "but this program isn't the end all. Everyone who goes to AA, we all drink for different reasons. For me, it was social. I started drinking when I was fifteen. My friends and I would sneak out to drink all night long. I was an addict before I even knew what the word meant."

"That's young," I commented mostly because I knew I was supposed to say something but what was beyond me.

"It is," he agreed. "My question for you is—and it might be a hard one—why do you drink, West?"

That wasn't a hard question at all.

"I don't know how to survive without it," I admitted quietly. I'd relied on it for years to silence the demons in my head.

"Do you have other coping mechanisms?" he asked. My gaze flicked in his direction. "When I first got sober, I didn't know how to be the guy who didn't drink when we went out. It was my whole personality. At first, I just tried to fake it—pretend my drink was alcoholic and still act like an idiot. It wasn't until I relapsed that I realized this wouldn't work unless I was honest with myself and with others. Did I lose some friends along the way? Yes, but they weren't friends to begin with. What I did gain was the confidence to stand up for myself and a support group outside of this program—friends who were more than happy to help stave off the temptation. We picked up golf. Do you know how much someone has to love you to take on a four-hour sport that requires that much walking?"

A faint smile turned the corner of my mouth but that was it.

"My point is, you can't just work the program and think the rest of your life will change as a result. You have to change your life, West."

"I don't know how," I replied.

"I don't know what you've been through," he told me. My breath hitched in my throat. I didn't want to talk about that with him. "And you don't have to tell me—I'm not asking you to—but if it's the root of why you drink, you need to find a way to work through it."

"I don't know how," I repeated.

"Have you considered therapy?"

"No." I didn't want to consider therapy. I could barely handle AA. The idea of sitting down and telling someone all my crap? That shit would be the end of me. *And for what?* It wouldn't fix me. Nothing could.

"I have some great resources if you want them," Bobby said. *What was the nice way to say thanks but I wasn't about to do a tell-all with some fucking stranger?* "I know the idea of it is daunting, but therapy can be extremely beneficial."

I said nothing because I didn't have a clue what to say. I was beyond anyone's help.

CHAPTER 65

JACKSON

I took his horses away, which I knew made me an asshole. While I understood his need to drink—especially on a day like that—I had to stick to my guns about the fucking consequences. He needed to be sober when dealing with the horses. It was the safe thing to do.

But all of that didn't make me feel any less like a complete dick for taking away the one thing that brought him peace of mind.

"Don't you get huffy with me," I grumped as Thunder Jack stomped in the dirt. I stood outside the stable with Zeus and Thunder Jack both saddled and ready to leave whenever West came back from his meeting. The fact that he was an hour late and wasn't answering his phone put me on edge. I didn't want to think the worst, but I also didn't know what to think.

I heard the crunch of West's truck over the gravel and dirt long before he ever came into view. Hands in my pockets, I slowly wandered in his direction as his truck rolled along the back of the one stable where he always parked. Even with him living in my house, he still kept his truck here. I tried not to dwell on it too much, hoping that one day he'd feel comfortable enough to move all his shit over to my house.

"Is there a reason you have my horse saddled?" he asked.

"Thought you and I could go for a ride before dinner," I told him.

"Oh." West blew out a slow breath of air, looking uncomfortable as all hell.

"It's fine. We don't have—"

"I ate dinner already with Bobby," he said over me. *Who the fuck was Bobby?* And why the hell was West having dinner with someone else? I didn't like the spike of jealousy. "My sponsor. I had dinner after my meeting with my sponsor."

Leave it to me to be jealous of his sponsor.

"Oh. Your sponsor." I nodded like I already knew that shit. Truth be told, West hadn't told me a damn thing about his meetings let alone anything about his sponsor. And I wasn't entirely sure if it was my place to ask or not. "That's good. That's good. I'm glad to hear that."

"Yeah. I could probably be fucking convinced to go for a ride with you though," he replied. I couldn't help but laugh.

"When the hell would you ever say no to going for a ride?"

"See?" His lips quirked ever so slightly. "I could be convinced."

There were moments when he was on the back of a horse that West looked free. Free of his demons. Free of his insecurities. Free of his pain. With his head tipped back, with the wind in his hair, with his body completely at ease.

Those moments were ones I clung to even as they wrapped around my heart like barbed wire. I knew they were fleeting. I would've given anything to bottle that feeling up and keep it for him.

"I'm sorry," West said softly, pulling me from my thoughts. We wandered around the ranch on our horses, lazy and pointless.

"You ain't got a damn thing to be sorry for, West," I replied. "You—"

"No, I do," he cut me off. "And I need you to stop letting me off the fucking hook just because you feel sorry for me."

"I'm pretty fucking sure I'm the asshole who took your job away until you went to a goddamn meeting," I shot back. "I wouldn't qualify that as letting you off the fucking hook. Your actions have consequences, even if they come from a crappy place. I'll hold your ass accountable—especially where the horses are concerned—but I ain't about to be pissed at you and fight with you over a bad moment."

"I don't want you to feel sorry for me."

"Well, lucky you," I drawled, "because I don't. I don't feel sorry for you, West. I'm pissed about what happened to you, I'm pissed about what people didn't do to protect you when we were kids, and honestly, I'm a little fucking pissed I didn't know about all of what was happening to you until now. And before you get upset about those things, if roles were reversed, you'd be pissed too."

"I would," West admitted. I glanced at him as he fell silent. His lips were pressed together in a tight line and his brows furrowed as he focused pointedly on the horizon. "Do you remember growing up and thinking we'd live and die by this ranch?"

"Yeah." I nodded. "Ain't that the Myles and McNamara way?"

"I never wanted it," he told me. *That wasn't a surprise.* West never did like the ranch. The horses, yes. But the rest of it? It never interested him. "Did you?"

"I was raised to run this place."

"I know that. We both fucking were. But did you *want* it?" West repeated. "Or are you just doing it because we're supposed to?"

Well, that was a fucking question, wasn't it? Our entire lives were woven into the ranch—our ancestry and our legacy. But when I let myself entertain the thought of an ideal future, it never involved this ranch. Duty outweighed desire every time. In the end, I'd die on this ranch, and I knew that.

But for the sake of honesty, I didn't tell him that.

"Bull riding," I said. "It was always bull riding that I wanted to do. If I had my way, that'd be all I do, even after I retire."

"What's that like?" West asked. I made a questioning sound, not following his line of thinking. Honestly, the whole conversation felt completely off-topic compared to where it started. But sometimes, talking to West was like that. He'd get that far-off look in his eyes and come back with some question that made no sense compared to everything else going on. I just kind of rolled with it to see where we ended up. "Knowing what you want from life I mean. What's that like?"

"Oh." *Well, fuck.* That I didn't know how to answer. Not easily anyway. "It's... comforting and devastating. When I'm able to do it, it feels right. It's... where I belong, you know? But when I can't? I don't know. I don't feel like me."

"I don't know what that's like." His voice was so damn quiet I could barely hear him over the breeze around us. I nudged Zeus a little closer. "I've never wanted anything for my life."

"Not even when you were a kid?"

"I just wanted to feel safe as a kid." The barbed wire he kept weaving around my heart dug in a little deeper with those words.

"And now?" I dared to ask, mostly because I wanted to know—for both him and me. "Do you feel safe now, West?"

He gave half a shrug.

"Most days I don't feel a whole lot of anything," West said. He fell silent, which was probably a good thing because I didn't know how to talk to him like this. How did I comfort him? How did I make him feel better?

How the hell did I help him?

CHAPTER 66

JACKSON

Hot water soothed the perpetual ache in my muscles as I stood under the shower. It did nothing, however, to calm the chaos in my mind. And it wasn't so much chaos as it was uncertainty and sadness—feelings that were becoming synonymous with West. The more he divulged about himself, about his life, and about the little ways he felt, the more out of my depth I felt.

I had no idea what I was doing. And what little I was doing, was it enough? Was loving him through this enough? It hadn't been for Peter's brother. I didn't want to lose West because I didn't do enough.

The glass door slid open, and I turned just as West stepped in—completely naked, of course. My heart stuttered at the sight of him. Working the ranch had given him more muscle and tanned his skin. He was sinfully hot with his tattoos and piercings.

I shut down that line of thinking real fucking fast.

"What the hell are you doing?" I asked. It wasn't that my shower didn't have room for the two of us—it did—but I was a little confused as to why he was joining me. After everything, I didn't have a clue where he and I stood in the physical department of things.

I moved aside, his body brushing against mine as he stepped under the water. The audible little sigh he let out was sexy as hell, and it shouldn't have been.

"There's no hot water downstairs."

"That's bullshit."

"It is. But you're not down there." *Yeah, that was hard to argue with.* The idea that he wanted to be around me was a nice one. "Why the hell do you have so many soap containers?"

"Let me guess, you have one bottle for everything?" I retorted. "Actually, I don't want the answer to that."

"It's a bar, not a bottle," West told me. There was something akin to amusement in his voice, and I couldn't tell if he was fucking with me or not. I decided he had to be. No self-respecting man would use a bar of fucking soap for everything. *At least, I fucking hoped not.* "May I?"

He reached around me to grab the shampoo bottle. His body slid across mine in more places than I could acknowledge. All I knew was it set my nerves on fire, awakening everything all at once, and I tried real damn hard to get my dick in control. I thought of the stupidest shit I could come up with out of respect. I could handle one shower with West without my dick running rampant. *Maybe.*

"Turn around, cowboy," he ordered. I scrutinized him for a hot minute before relenting. What I didn't expect was the way he massaged shampoo into my hair. It was hard to be on edge when his fingers worked magic over my scalp. "Why'd you cut the long hair?"

"What?" I frowned.

"Your hair," he repeated. "It used to be long. Why'd you cut it?"

My hair had been long once–like down to my shoulder blades—but that had been years ago.

"How'd you know about that?" I replied instead.

"I kept up with you over the years," West admitted. *He what?* "Just your career. Shit the public knew. The tabloids were fun there for a while. They liked you. The League's only openly gay cowboy with his long golden hair."

I knew those articles, but I was a little too stunned for words. I'd just assumed he'd up and left—forgotten everything like I tried to forget him. It never occurred to me that he kept up with me that much.

"That," I cleared my throat, "stupid commentary was why I cut it. Someone said I looked like a wannabe country singer."

"They clearly haven't heard you sing," he muttered. I couldn't even be offended with that one. I couldn't sing if my life depended on it. "Head back."

I complied easily, shutting my eyes while he rinsed out the soap. There was something undeniably comforting about how he ran his fingers through my hair—taking careful mind to the way he handled me. This kind of intimacy was foreign to me. *Wonderful but foreign.*

"Are you one of those weird people who fucking conditions their hair?" West asked when he was done.

"I'm going to pretend you didn't just ask that," I retorted. Apparently, I had to teach him a thing or two about proper hair care.

"Do they make it in a bar?" The amusement in his voice was unmistakable. I turned to chastise him, but he cut me off by kissing me. His tongue stroked mine as he took advantage of my surprise. Fingers wove through my hair as his body pushed flush to mine. The weight of his cock and the smoothness of his barbells pressed hard against my hip.

And there went any hope I had of controlling my dick.

But I had to focus.

"West..." I began. I wasn't sure what the fuck to do. My dick had its own ideas from how it stood hard at attention between us—his too—but was this okay? I didn't want to pick him up off the floor again and send him into the wild because something we did together sent him spiraling. I'd rather take care of myself so to speak if it meant protecting his headspace.

"It's not your job to fix me," he whispered.

"I ain't trying to—"

"I want normal, Jackson," West said over me. The desperate edge in his voice tugged at my heart. "How are we supposed to be normal if I don't fucking try? I don't know what the fuck I'm doing, but I'm here and I'm fucking trying. That's something, isn't it?"

It was fucking hard to argue with his logic. I wanted him to feel safe—to feel like we could be whatever he needed. His stables, his rules. How was

I supposed to argue with him wanting to try when I kept pushing the control in his hands?

"You tell me to stop if you need me to, you understand?" I replied. When he opened his mouth to protest, I shook my head. "I mean it. Don't push yourself if you don't want it, West—even if that changes somewhere in the middle. I don't care. You're more important than anything we do together."

I hated that I even felt the need to say it, but I did. *Fuck, if I had to reiterate that every time, I would.*

"Okay," West whispered.

CHAPTER 67

WEST

Hıs warmth, the spice of his soap, the rough calluses in his touch. I was fucking sky high, my nerves ablaze and misfiring all over the place. His fingers skated up my sides as I walked him across the room, dripping wet and not caring. My teeth scraped over his lower lip, and I drank up the moan he let out.

We collapsed on the bed. As I settled between his thighs, Jackson ran his hands up my side. The simple gesture sent a myriad of sensations rolling through my body. When his fingers skated over the scars on my ribs, pain laced the pleasure. I went rigid, instinctively grabbing his wrist to stop him.

"It's okay," Jackson whispered. "Do you want to stop, West?"

"Just..." I shook my head, struggling to find the words. *How did I make it make sense to him?* I couldn't explain them—the reminder of them. "Not there... just... don't touch them..."

"Okay." He lifted off the pillow and kissed me, slow and reassuring, while moving his hand to my lower back. I flexed my hips against his and groaned at the friction it created. My nerves lit up violently in a way that I couldn't control. Couldn't predict. My chest tightened.

Focus.
I could do this. I wanted this.
I wanted a normal relationship with Jackson. He deserved it.
I could fucking do that for him.
Dragging my tongue up the length of his neck, I used the taste of water and sweat to ground myself. When I sank my teeth lightly into his neck, the sound he made only helped. *Who knew Jackson could make such sexy goddamn sounds?*

His hand wrapped around my cock and his, stroking both of us slowly. The feel of his hand, the way his dick moved against mine, the pounding of my own heart... it was all so overwhelming.

Good? Bad? I couldn't tell.
It was too much.

That familiar clawing built in my chest—tearing me apart little by little. I desperately tried to drag myself back from the edge, but I couldn't. I wasn't strong enough.

I couldn't focus enough to stay grounded in the moment. Breathing was a fucking chore. I was suffocating in my own skin—dying without certainty.

"I can't... I can't..." I let out pathetically, whimpering as I rolled away from him. I damn near scrambled to the other side of the bed to put as much space between him and me as possible.

"Okay. It's okay," Jackson said. The bed shifted as he hurried to get up, moving across the room.

I slung an arm over my face as hot tears burned a trail down my face. I couldn't look at him. I couldn't handle the idea of him looking at me. The blinding need to run away clawed through me, but I promised I wouldn't. It took everything I had to stay rooted in place.

"I put pants and a shirt on the bed for you," he told me softly. "Get dressed. My eyes are shut, but I ain't going nowhere, okay? I'm right here, West."

The shirt was too much. Just the thought of it on my skin was awful. Hell, the way the sheet rubbed against my skin was fucking torture. I managed to pull on the athletic pants while Jackson sat down on his side of the bed, eyes closed like he promised he would. The small gesture was appreciated—somehow giving me back a little bit of control over my body.

But when I was dressed, I just stood there like an idiot. How the hell did we move past this? *How did I make him not hate me after this?*

"I don't know what to do," I admitted, feeling ridiculous and embarrassed all at once. I wanted to run. I wanted to hide and avoid him all over again.

"Just lay down," he replied. "Stay, West."

He wanted me to stay? *Why the fuck would he want me to stay?* I struggled to understand that. Why didn't he see what I was?

Pathetic and broken.

I wasn't fucking worth it.

"Lay down, West," Jackson repeated. The gentleness in his voice killed me. *I'd never deserve someone like him.*

But I made myself lay down again. I put as much distance between us as I could, hugging the edge of the bed. The idea of any contact with him kept me there. My skin crawled painfully and everything fucking hurt.

Closing the distance between us, Jackson carefully took my hand. I tensed at the contact—his fingers like razors across my skin. Instead of holding my hand, he placed my fingers over his pulse before letting go of me completely.

Steady and strong.

The feel of his heartbeat under my fingers was soothing—a needed comfort. The simple gesture shattered something in my chest. A sob I had no hope of controlling tore through me, the quiet sound filling the silence. I buried my face in my elbow to hide from him as I lost the fight to stop them.

"It's okay, West," Jackson said. "This right here is more than enough."

I wanted to believe him so fucking bad, but I just didn't see what he did.

CHAPTER 68

WEST

"Jackson..." I whispered into the dark. He didn't move in his spot next to me, so I tried again. "Jackson."

He let out a low groan but didn't move.

"Jackson."

"What?" he mumbled, the word coming out jumbled and damn near incomprehensible.

"I can't sleep," I admitted and felt fucking pathetic for doing so.

"Okay." He blew out a breath of air followed by another groan. "I'm up. I'm up."

He shifted and the dim light on his side flipped on. He ran his hands over his face, blinking hard against the light. *Fuck, why the hell had I woken him up?* I promised him I would stay, but even exhausted, I couldn't shut my brain off. It just kept running through things over and over without any hope of fucking stopping.

I desperately wanted to bolt—to hide somewhere until my brain shut the fuck up—but I'd promised him I would stay.

I didn't know what the fuck to do.

"What's wrong?" he asked.

"I can't fucking sleep," I repeated. *What a stupid fucking answer.* Any idiot could see that I couldn't sleep. "I can't... get my brain to turn off. I just..."

"Okay." Those sleepy blue eyes found mine and he smiled. It did something to my heart—something I couldn't explain. I remained silent as he made himself comfortable beside me, rolling on his side and pulling a pillow to his chest. *God, he was fucking adorable.* "So... what have you been up to for the past seventeen years?"

I barked out a harsh laugh, making him shrug. It was a ridiculously stupid question.

"Best I've got on short notice, baby," he murmured. "I'll make a list of late-night conversation topics later."

That sentiment sobered my amusement because he would. I knew he would. After everything he'd done for me, I knew he'd do just that for the next time this happened.

"How about you tell me what you've been doing for work for the last seventeen years," he continued.

"A little bit of everything," I said, facing him. I dragged the blanket over me, using it more for comfort than warmth. The softness did something for me that I couldn't explain. *Why the fuck hadn't I kept blankets around more in the past?* "I did housing construction for a while, but then I got fired for drinking. Worked in a bar for a while. Got fired for punching a guy. At least I didn't get arrested again."

"That's a good thing," Jackson agreed.

"Found a job working plumbing, got fired for drinking. Had a couple of odds and ends kind of jobs in there. mostly got fired for drinking." I made a face. *There was a fucking theme here that sober me had blatantly ignored for most of my life.* "I was a tow truck driver when I got the call about the ranch."

"How?" He frowned. "Don't you need a special license to do that? Being a felon, I would think you can't get it."

"I mean I can drive all the equipment, we just don't ask about the license," I told him. Technically, I hadn't even tried to get my license. "And when your boss is a cheap asshole, questions like that don't get asked."

"Makes sense."

"Yeah."

"Why'd you keep up with my career, West?" he asked.

Oh. That. I flopped onto my back and pointedly stared up at the ceiling as I tried to think about how to best answer that question.

"Do you remember when you told me you were getting lessons on bull riding?" I replied, and he made a sound. "And I told you I'd be there to watch you fall flat on your face?"

"Yeah." He chuckled.

"I wanted... I wanted to be there, you know? I just didn't... I know I left, but it was because of Harrison."

"I know."

"If I stayed... " *He would've fucking killed me.*

"I know what he did, West," Jackson cut in gently. My gaze flicked in his direction. "My mom showed me the police report... pictures and all."

Oh. I nodded slowly, my chest tightening painfully. I didn't know she had that shit, and I sure as hell didn't know that she'd shown him.

"I didn't want to leave you," I rasped. My voice broke slightly. "I just... he would've fucking killed me if I stayed."

"I know."

"And I didn't know what else to fucking do," I continued, rambling a little. The pressure in my chest built, and I sucked in a sharp breath.

"I know, West." Jackson's fingers laced through mine as he took my hand, squeezing for reassurance. "Where'd you go? After you left here?"

"South," I answered. I was more than grateful to not talk about that shit. I wasn't sure I could handle it. Harrison and everything he'd done still haunted me. I wasn't sure I'd ever be free of him. "Figured I'd put as much fucking distance between me and him as I could. Took a bus down to Texas and disappeared. For a while anyway, until the money ran out, and I didn't have a place to go or anything to eat."

"Is that why you robbed that place?" *How much did Jackson know about why the fuck I ended up in jail?* Considering our start, it wouldn't have surprised me if he did a background check or some shit on me.

"It wasn't loaded," I admitted. I closed my eyes, feeling Jackson's calm as it spread through me. "It wasn't even a real gun. At least not the one I had."

"You weren't alone?" he asked.

"No. I was just the one who didn't run. The other kid I was with shot the clerk," I whispered. "I couldn't just... I couldn't let him die."

I could still picture his face as he bled out on the floor, and when things were particularly rough, I could still feel the warmth of his blood on my hands.

"Did he..." Jackson's voice trailed off.

"Yeah, he lived." He'd been kind enough to speak in my favor at my hearing, which helped get me a lesser sentence. His kindness had been more than I deserved. Jackson's silence was unnerving. *What the hell did he fucking think of me now?* Probably nothing good. "Do you regret asking?"

"No," he replied. "If you weren't there, he would've died."

"You give me way more credit than I fucking deserve."

"Why'd you follow my career?" Jackson asked again. *Yeah, I hadn't really answered that question, had I?*

"It was the best I could do about being there," I admitted. "It wasn't perfect, but it was the best I could do."

I didn't admit that somewhere over the years I grew jealous of the life he had. Of the assuredness and happiness in his life. The direction. I wanted that. *And I didn't have a fucking clue how to find that.* Instead, I just settled on watching his life.

"I always thought about showing up one day." I kept talking, letting the random thoughts take me wherever. My body felt heavy—not entirely relaxed, but just heavy. Weirdly comfortably heavy. "At the rodeo."

"I probably would've hit you," he said. My lips tipped upward slightly. *Yeah, that wouldn't have surprised me.* "Did you see my first ride?"

"I did," I told him. The memory made me smile slightly. "I did some stupid shit to make sure I could see it, and then you went ahead and fucking disappointed everyone."

I'd broken into someone's house just so I could see Jackson's first ride. It was stupid as fuck to do, but I'd gotten away with it. Probably not a thing to be proud of, but I just couldn't imagine breaking that fucking promise.

"Hey!" He chuckled. "It ain't my fault they gave me the toughest bull there."

"Excuses, excuses," I teased. To be honest, I didn't have a clue what any of it meant when I watched it. All I knew was watching him get thrown had scared the shit out of me. But Jackson had bounced right back with that stupid cowboy grin on his handsome face.

"Do you feel better, West?" Jackson asked. He gave my hand a small squeeze. I let out a small sound. Maybe I nodded. Who knew? The exhaustion weighed heavy on my body. "Get some sleep, baby."

CHAPTER 69

WEST

WHEN I MADE BREAKFAST, I expected Jackson to join. He'd told me he would, but he never showed up. It irritated me. I knew he was in his office dealing with sponsor shit, but he'd told me he'd be down.

Was I being unreasonable? I couldn't tell. Maybe I was just grumpy after a rough night or maybe I had a right to be annoyed. Either way, I stomped up the stairs and right into his office.

"Why do you hate me, Amy?" Jackson was demanding as I opened the door. The scowl on his face stopped me short. His expression softened when his gaze met mine. Only for a minute anyway. Whatever Amy said on the other side pissed him off. "No, you do fucking hate me. I'm no one's fucking monkey. And I sure as hell ain't doing milk ads for Lexington."

I shoved my hands in my pockets as I meandered into the room. Jackson clicked a button on the phone as he met me halfway.

"I'm sorry, baby, but I swear to fuck if I have to do a goddamn milk ad, I might need pointers from you about how to survive jail," he said. He slipped an arm around my waist, pulling me close. His lips brushed against mine in a slow kiss—warm and soft.

Any comments about jail and murder slipped in one ear and out the other when his tongue slipped across mine.

"What're you doing?" I asked gruffly. Even still, I couldn't peel my mouth from his and kissed him again.

"I thought that part was obvious," Jackson teased with a grin. His nose bumped against mine in an almost sweet gesture. "Not everything needs to be hot and heavy, and I aim to prove that to you. This... this right here is nice."

My face felt uncomfortably warm. *Was I fucking blushing?* From the amused expression on his face, I had to be.

"You're still on the fucking phone," I muttered to pull the attention away from me.

"She's on mute."

"But—"

"Amy's long-winded," he replied. "It'll be a good ten minutes before she realizes I ain't listening."

He kissed me again, and I liked it. An obnoxiously shrill noise on the other end of the phone interrupted us, and Jackson groaned.

"Woman, I ain't ignoring you!" he snapped into the phone as he walked away. He rolled his eyes at me. "I've just heard you say it all before."

Listening to him argue with his agent was a lot like watching an old married couple go at it. While they went back and forth, I kept myself busy by poking around his desk. Maybe I shouldn't have been, but I was bored. Waiting around wasn't something I was good at. *And when I saw my name on a file?* Curiosity got the better of me and I flipped the file open.

My heart jammed instantly in my throat at the picture staring back at me.

Michael Miller.

That name and his face on the report made my blood run cold.

Breathing became a fucking chore as I zoned out on the image. The words in the report floated around on the page, but I didn't need to see them to know what they said.

"I asked Mickey to look into your past when you first got here," Jackson was quick to say. I couldn't look at him—couldn't take my eyes off the goddamn picture.

"I don't remember killing him," I told him softly. I touched the picture. I remembered very little about that day. My voice sounded distant to even me as I spoke, "They said... they said I blacked out. I didn't know I killed him until... fuck, it was the next morning. I just kind of... snapped out of it. Came to? I don't fucking know..."

I didn't remember a whole lot about the days after that. It was all a blur—a lot of moving and questions and things I didn't know how to answer.

The only thing I truly could remember was what Miller said to me before the world went dark.

"How about we add another notch on your side?"

My stomach rolled with the words floating in my head. I fucking hated Miller. I hated him. I hated what he'd done to me—how he'd killed a part of me.

"West?" Jackson's voice pulled me from my thoughts. I blinked at him.

"What?" I whispered.

"You just stopped talking," he said. The phone was gone. *When had he ended the phone call?* I couldn't remember.

When he took a step toward me, I backed away. The temperature in the room kept rising, the walls pulsing around me.

I couldn't be here.

"I've got to go," I replied. "Horses..."

I didn't wait for him to answer. Locked-legged, I walked my way out of the house with a desperate need to get the fuck out of there. To get away from that goddamn file.

CHAPTER 70

JACKSON

Something was off with West and I couldn't put my fucking finger on it. I wanted to say it had something to do with the file I had on him, but he insisted he was fine—everything was fine. *And fuck me, I wanted to believe him.*

But his mood made it hard to trust his words. He was withdrawn and snappy. Angry and confrontational. After he almost hit one of my guys, I quarantined him away from everyone else by putting him with the animals. At least with them, he was careful.

Unfortunately, he wasn't that careful with himself.

The radio call about him getting hurt on some piece of equipment sent my heart galloping damn near as fast as I urged Zeus across the field. I hoped for the best but prepared for the worst.

West sat on a stool in the stables with a towel pressed over his forearm. Blood dripped off his fingers and soaked through the towel, but he didn't bother to change it.

"I'm fine," West snapped the instant he saw me.

"No, you're not," I retorted, not in the mood for his fucking attitude. *Not when his blood was all over the ground.* I dropped my hat on a bale of hale and crouched in front of him. When I reached for his hand, he jerked away. "Let me see your hand."

"I said I'm fine."

"I don't give a fuck. Let me see your hand."

"No."

"Give me your fucking hand, West!"

"I don't need you to baby me—"

"Give me your goddamn hand," I demanded over him. "I ain't asking as your anything. I'm telling you to do it as your goddamn boss. My ranch, my rules, my fucking liability."

If looks could fucking kill. I didn't give a damn. I needed to look at his arm, and if that meant I had to pull rank as his goddamn boss, I would.

There was a moment where I thought he was legitimately going to fight me—that we'd see this thing all the way through with his pissed-off attitude. And I didn't have it in me to truly fight him. I knew that, and he knew that. It'd only end in an ugly blowout.

I held back a sigh of relief when he relented. It wasn't lost on me the way he tensed up when I took hold of his arm. How much of it was pain from getting hurt and how much was it something else? I still didn't quite understand his whole aversion to touch—if it was something more than just not liking it.

The gash in his forearm was deep but not enough for me to throw him in the truck and take him to the hospital. *Thank fuck.* There was no way in hell I'd get him there.

"How the hell did this happen?" I asked as I grabbed another towel to stem the bleeding.

"Hoof knife," West muttered.

"You need to be more careful."

"I don't need your fucking help," he snapped before I could say more. He knocked away my hand and took over applying pressure. "And I'm not a fucking liability."

He stormed away, stomping out the door without ever giving me a chance to respond. Shutting my eyes, I pinched the bridge of my nose as I took a moment for myself. Took a moment to process. The back-and-forth whiplash was killing me. The hot and cold was killing me. I didn't know what to anticipate or when to anticipate it. I felt like I was failing him for lack of knowing what the hell to expect.

CHAPTER 71

WEST

Everything grated on my last fucking nerve. I was irritable, overwhelmed, and desperate to drink. I didn't, but I fucking wanted to. Picking fights with Jackson got me nowhere. Short of his frustration when I got hurt, he was quiet and just waited me out. Jackson deserved a fucking award for his patience with me, but I hated that shit.

I didn't deserve it. Why couldn't he see that?

I was drowning—barely holding my own. That fucking picture messed with my head. The lack of memories messed with my fucking head, and the things I could remember were worse.

All of it had me fucked up and suffocating.

By the time I dragged myself into his house at the end of the day, I was numb from head to toe. My body was sluggish and labored, making everything more difficult. Every inch of my skin hurt. Even my clothes felt like fucking razors tearing into me. I was fucking dying. I could feel the crash and spiral coming with no hope of staving it off. All I wanted to do was crawl into a hole until it passed.

But no. Here I was entertaining the idea of doing dinner with Jackson because I felt guilty for all the shit I put him through. I said I wanted a normal relationship with him, but I couldn't even be normal for one fucking day.

I did leave Jackson to do the fucking cooking—God help us both. Who knew how it'd turn out, but he wasn't letting me near the stove, and I didn't want to either. Instead, I stood in the living room as I listened to him drone on and on about something.

Truthfully, my brain couldn't process a damn thing he said. The words were a garbled mess in my ears. Everything felt fuzzy and hazy while I did my damnedest to fight a losing battle to pay attention to him. I just kept zoning out on the floor, watching the wood dance around like it had a life of its own.

But when something touched my arm, I lost the fight as the darkness dragged me under.

CHAPTER 72

JACKSON

The first hit came out of nowhere, taking me by surprise and knocking me on my ass. I saw fucking stars, and I tasted blood as my lip split on contact. The blow took it out of me for a hot minute as my brain struggled to catch up.

I was on my feet just as my side table was thrown across the room. The lamp shattered on the floor, sending glass everywhere.

West raged, eyes wide and glassy. *Fuck, I never should've touched his arm.* This was West in the bar all over again—crazed and completely out of control. A feral animal unable to rein himself in.

He came at me hard and fast, and it took everything I had to end up behind him. I did the only thing I could think of to keep him from tearing through me and my house: I grabbed him.

The frenzy it sent him in was explosive. I barely managed to maintain my hold on him as we crashed to the ground. I dragged his back to my chest and locked my arms over his. His screaming was unintelligible as I wrestled to keep him down. The only clear thing I could make out was the continuous no. From how hard he fought me and the screaming, I didn't want to know what memory had dragged him under.

"C'mon, West," I grunted. *Shit, I rode bulls for a living but holding onto him was harder.* "C'mon, baby, I need you to come back to me."

Nothing.

Not a damn response.

He bucked in my arms, completely unhinged. He was fighting for his life. His heart pounded wildly against my hand on his chest while his choppy breaths threatened to break my hold.

Fuck, he was stronger than I gave him credit for.

"West!" I snapped through grit teeth. I squeezed harder and clung to some shred of hope that I could break through his craze. My back hit a wall. I groaned with the impact as he pushed back harder. "Please, baby... I need you to hear me."

I pleaded and begged, but everything fell on deaf ears. It left me stuck wrangling him in with a desperate hope that he'd come around.

Eventually, his fight weakened. I didn't let up, even as his screaming subsided completely. He pushed against my arms, but I held on tighter, unsure of what the fuck was happening. *How bad would it get if I did let go?*

West shoved against my arms harder until my hold broke. He rushed to his feet, falling over himself as he put as much distance between me and him as the room would allow. I sagged against the wall as I worked to catch my breath.

His wide-eyed gaze trailed over the room. The heaving of his chest increased as he took in the damage, and that crazed expression dissolved into something of guilt and despair.

"I'm... I'm..." A pathetic whine escaped him. His hands tugged at his hair as his words turned to senseless mumbling. He stumbled his way through the kitchen, knocking over shit as he went, and rushed straight out the back door.

"Fuck!" I exclaimed and scrambled after him. *To do what? Who the fuck knew?* I just... had to do something. I couldn't just leave him on the lawn.

"It hurts! It hurts!" West gasped. He struggled out of his shirt and threw it aside. I took the stairs two at a time and joined him on the grass but maintained my distance. I didn't have a clue what the fuck to do.

"West, come on, baby, look at me," I said.

His rambling was all over the place as he continued stripping—kicking off his shoes and almost falling over, wrestling off his pants and socks. All the while, the pain in his voice amplified with every passing moment.

I was completely helpless—frozen in my spot. I didn't know what to do. How to help him.

His knees gave out, and he collapsed in the grass. Screaming filled the night as his fingers tugged on his hair. He curled into himself, his body wracked with painful sobs as something tore him to pieces from the inside out.

I fell to my knees in front of him, utterly lost. I couldn't touch him. I couldn't fix it. I couldn't do a damn thing but watch the man I love completely fall apart.

CHAPTER 73

JACKSON

I CALLED MICKEY FOR help when Peter didn't answer the phone. I didn't know what else to do—who else to call. By the time his truck pulled into my drive, West's screaming had stopped. He was completely unmoving in the grass, curled up on his side. Every now and then he let out a small whimper of pain but that was it.

I didn't dare touch him. I was terrified I'd kickstart his panic all over again. But I paced. I paced my lawn as my mind ran rampant with a million unfinished thoughts.

"Tell me what happened, boy," Mickey said as he hobbled over.

"I don't... I don't fucking know," I rambled. I ran a hand through my hair, my brain struggling to catch up. "One minute I'm talking to him and the next minute, he's just... he would've fucking killed me, Mick—he wouldn't have meant it! He wouldn't have fucking meant it. He just wasn't... he wasn't here, you know?"

"Breathe, Jackson," he ordered. *Was I panicking?* Was this what panicking was like? Fuck, my heart was beating so damn hard against my ribcage. When Mickey's hand touched my cheek, I pulled away.

"I'm fine! I'm fucking fine, okay?" I snapped. "But I just... I don't know how to help him. I don't know what I'm doing! I don't know how to get him off my fucking lawn!"

"Did he hit you?" Mickey asked.

"He didn't mean it," I replied all too quickly.

"I didn't ask if the boy wanted to hit you," he said. "I'm askin' if that's where the split lip came from."

Right. I brushed my thumb over my bottom lip and winced at the twinge of pain. I'd forgotten about that.

"He didn't mean to."

"I know."

"He was just... I don't know what fucking happened, Mickey. It was like the bar all over again," I told him. He made a small sound but said nothing else. "What do I do, Mickey? How do I help him? How do I fix this?"

"Just leave him, Jackson," Mickey told me. "The boy is used to sleepin' anywhere anyways. You go inside and you take care of you. That's all you can do."

"There's got to be more that I can do," I said. *I needed there to be more.* I needed to know I could fix this for West—take away whatever pain made him like this.

"You know you can't do that," he replied as if reading my mind. "That boy has to bear the weight of his demons. You can't take that from him no matter how hard you love him."

My gaze flicked in his direction quick enough to make him chuckle.

"I ain't no idiot, boy. I see what's between you two." *I should've seen that coming.* "But you need to know, West's demons are his own. There ain't a damn thing you can do but love him."

"What if it's not enough?" I asked quietly.

"It ain't goin' to be," Mickey answered a little too honestly. "You're goin' to love him hard, but it ain't goin' to be enough to win this fight for him. It's somethin' he's got to do for himself. All on his own."

"I hate that."

"I know, Jackson. Me too."

A shred of anger flared inside me, and I bit back a mean comment. All I wanted to do was yell at him for not doing more when West was a kid—for not saving him from this future. If someone—*anyone*—had done more, he could've been spared this hell.

"Good night, Mickey," I managed to say instead. If I said more, I'd rip him a fucking new one.

"Want me to handle everythin' in the mornin'?"

"Please," I whispered.

"You just keep me updated on how he's doin', okay? Leave everythin' else to me," he said, and I nodded. "And you take care of you too, Jackson, you hear me?"

Again, I just nodded. I didn't have it in me to say anything more. I waited until the lights on Mickey's truck were gone and down the road before I moved. I didn't give a fuck what Mickey said. I wasn't leaving West out there alone. Grabbing a pillow for me and a blanket for West, I stormed right back outside. Fuck everything else.

Chancing more chaos, I gently spread the blanket over West. He flinched and curled into himself further but that was it. Knowing full well I'd need to be peeled off the fucking ground in the morning, I settled down next to him—close enough to be there if he needed me, far enough not to invade his space.

And somewhere in the middle of the night, his fingers found their way across that distance and found their home over my pulse.

CHAPTER 74

WEST

Nine horses.
    Nine hay bales.
Nine cows.
Nine buckets.
Nine fence posts.
Nine.
Nine.
Fucking nine.
The list of nines went on and fucking on. I kept seeing the number nine everywhere. It fucking taunted me—a constant reminder of things I didn't want to think about.
Things that wouldn't leave the forefront of my mind.
This place had fucking broken me. There was no other explanation for it. I was falling apart in every goddamn way possible.
Waking up disoriented and damn near naked on Jackson's lawn with him sleeping next to me felt like a last straw. I couldn't remember a fucking

thing about how I ended up there. Jackson's split lip and black eye gave me a pretty good idea about what the fuck I'd done—of how I'd hurt him.

For days, I avoided Jackson or maybe he avoided me. I saw him once or twice when he picked up and dropped off Zeus on schedule. No words were exchanged. I could barely make eye contact let alone handle a fucking conversation. I didn't go back to his house at night. Instead, I drank until I passed out in the stable.

I was good though. I watched my drinking enough to make sure I could fucking handle the horses without incident. *Just enough to chase away the demons.* Hiding away in the stables didn't help, but it was all I had. Truthfully, there wasn't a damn thing that would help anymore. Not while Double Arrow had its claws in me.

I tipped back the flask, letting the burn of whiskey help soothe the guilt and silence the screaming. Both were particularly loud after an anxious day. I was restless, exhausted, and crawling out of my skin.

Another drink, another hope for relief.

Another disappointment.

Betty's head popped over the edge of her stall, and I staggered down the aisle to visit with her. Horses were good fucking company. No judgment. No harsh words. No hits.

Just fucking silence and comfort.

I leaned on her stall door, taking another long drink.

"You don't hate me, do you, pretty girl?" I asked Betty, running a hand down her soft snout. She merely chuffed, and I pulled her closer, pressing my forehead to hers. "Yeah, well... that makes one of us."

I managed to make it a whole damn week before Jackson quit. Turned out, he was letting me avoid him. Thankfully, I was just sober enough when he strode into my stables with an unreadable look on his face.

That made my fucking heart rate spike. I hated not knowing what he was thinking. It set me on edge, and I stood a little taller. At this point, it was a survival instinct to be ready for whatever the hell came my way.

"So, how long are you planning on avoiding me?" Jackson asked.

Fuck, I didn't want to answer that question.

"I'm not fucking avoiding you." Lies. We both knew I was fucking lying.

"We both know that's a load of bullshit, West," he said. He sighed as he stopped a short distance from me, leaning against a stall door. His busted lip had healed, but there was still faint evidence of the black eye. *That shit was my fault.*

"You know why," I muttered.

"I told you it was okay." *Yeah, he'd said that.* He'd said that as he groaned picking himself up off the goddamn lawn where he'd slept with me all night.

"It's not okay." I shook my head. *How fucking dumb was he that he thought this was okay?*

Instead of saying a word, Jackson's fingers slid through my hair as he closed the distance between us and kissed me. It was languid and sweet—full of something he didn't belong giving to me. I clung to his shirt and desperately tried not to spiral. His arm slid down to wrap around my waist as he walked me right into a stall, kicking the door shut for privacy.

When my back hit the wall, he broke the kiss. His forehead tipped against mine, and I refused to open my eyes. I couldn't look at him. The surge of emotions was too much. *Guilt. Shame. Pain.* They clashed together violently inside me.

"I don't deserve you," I told him, my voice trembling.

"You do."

"No, I don't."

"Yeah, you do."

"You don't deserve me," I insisted. "You deserve someone better."

"I dare you to find someone better," Jackson said.

"Go fucking anywhere," I scoffed. "You'll be surrounded by them."

Anyone was better for him than me.

"I don't see you for what's going on in here." His finger gently tapped my temple before he pressed his palm to my chest. "I see you for the man in here. The man who loves animals more than anyone I know. Who brings home the broken ones and shows them what it means to be loved. The man who makes me and my dog breakfast and even cleans up the damn kitchen after. Who challenges me and ain't afraid to hand me my ass when I need it. I see a damn good man with the best fucking heart I've ever known."

Something painful and hot clawed at my chest, building with every word he said.

"I'm not that man," I let out. *He needed to see that.* In the end, I'd just end up disappointing him. I couldn't be what he wanted me to be.

"You are," he replied. His nose brushed gently against mine. "That's the man I keep around. What's going on inside your head... I can't fix that shit, West. I wish I could. You don't got a clue how badly I wish I could take it all away. But that don't change a damn thing for me. I want all of you."

"Why?" I managed to ask.

"Because I love you," Jackson whispered. My chest seized with something inexplicable—something like panic and fear. He couldn't love me. He kept saying the words, but he fucking couldn't. Not really. I wasn't worth that. I shook my head, unable to say the words. "I love you, baby. And I know you don't see all those things, but I'm going to keep telling you because I don't care if it's tomorrow or fifty years from now, one day you'll see it."

My heart lodged in my throat. *Fifty years?* He couldn't possibly see a future with me. Not like this.

"You didn't do a damn thing wrong, West," Jackson reiterated once more. "I know you think you did, but I need you to believe me, okay? If I had a fucking problem with what happened, I'd tell you."

I wanted to believe that he would, but I knew Jackson. I knew how fucking hard he was trying to take care of me. It wasn't impossible to imagine him lying too if it meant making me feel better.

Fuck, my head was all screwed up.

I breathed him in deep, trying to cling to something that would keep the panic at bay. I wouldn't spiral again—not around him.

"Come back home, West." As I started to shake my head, he added, "Either you come back home, or I'm coming here to sleep in that damn stall with you, but you better believe you'll be peeling my ass off the fucking floor every morning if we go that route."

"I just..." *Just what?* Just wanted to drink every night away until I didn't have to feel a damn thing? Just wanted to feel something good for once? Feel something normal?

I didn't say any of those things, but I did nod slightly. It was pointless fighting with him anyway. I knew he'd follow through one way or another.

CHAPTER 75

JACKSON

My last few weeks at home were quiet and uneventful thankfully. West wasn't himself, but if I was being honest, I wasn't sure who West was at his core. I wasn't sure he knew either.

I just stayed ever-present and ever-vigilant. I didn't push boundaries or push for more. Fingers on my pulse and late-night conversations became our norm. I had a feeling we'd done too much too fast, even if West would never admit that out loud.

I didn't need him to either. Backing off and letting him come to me was easier. The only thing I kept consistent was a simple kiss when we woke up and when we went to sleep.

I also wasn't blind to him drinking again, but that was a battle I couldn't fight. Instead, I stuck close to him and used leaving him in three weeks as an excuse as to why I didn't intervene. I wasn't an idiot. There was no way in hell that West was joining me on the circuit. He struggled with a small-town atmosphere and the tiny ranch aspect. The wild nature of the rodeo would be too much for him.

Besides, his jumps and jitters had returned in the last week, and I saw him making an effort to go to meetings. He found his way there, which was all that mattered. He had to want it. I couldn't do that for him.

"All right, as always Mickey is in charge," I was saying. I leaned against the fence with my arms crossed and my hat dropped on a post. It was my last day on the ranch before I left for the season. The last day was always the most nerve-wracking. I had a good team, even if they were a pain in my ass sometimes. Leaving my business with the lot of them always hit hard, especially with how close I was to losing everything. "He's got my number—so do you—if shit hits the fan. This year is crucial, which I know puts a lot of pressure on all of you. I wish I could say I'll pay you more, but right now I can't. Once I can sell off land in eight months, I'll make sure everyone is squared away and then some."

Even if it meant my debt wasn't covered. For as much as I bitched at them, the guys I hired were good. They'd done a lot of extra shit to make sure I didn't go under sooner. They weren't privy to just how bad shit was, but they weren't ignorant to it either. They deserved a lot more than I could give them and I felt bad about that as their boss.

"I mean, you could do us all a favor and win this year," Peter commented with a cocky grin. He earned a few laughs from the other guys while I scowled.

"Get your asses back to work," I snapped. As they made their leave, I called after them, "Remember, if you have any issues with the horses, you go to West. He'll be good to handle that shit."

"You got it, boss!"

"You'll be good to handle that shit, right?" I turned to West, who was standing behind me twirling an unlit cigarette between his fingers.

"My stables, my horses, my rules," West murmured. "How long are you gone again?"

"Until fall. If I do well enough, it could be longer than that."

He made a sound but said nothing else. I would've given fucking anything to know what he was thinking. We weren't talking about me leaving. He always shut down on me. The not knowing how he felt or what would happen with us was fucking awful.

Not knowing if he'd be here when I got back was worse.

"You're with me this afternoon," I told West, changing the topic to something I wanted to talk about.

"What the hell did I do now?" he demanded.

"Nothing," I said. "I'm taking you on a date."

"Are these your fucking dress shoes?" West hollered from his bedroom. I grinned to myself. I had a plan—or a loose plan in case it didn't go over well with West—but ranch clothes weren't going to cut it, and I knew West didn't have anything else. All of that led me to buy him dress clothes and leave them in his room.

"Yeah, figured you wouldn't want me buying you a pair," I said loud enough to be heard as I put together Tess's dinner so Mickey wouldn't have to worry about it.

"You know, when I used to fucking call you Bigfoot, I thought it was a joke. I didn't know you had feet this goddamn big," he told me.

"You were the one with the big fucking feet," I retorted. Anything else I had to say was lost as he walked into the room. *Fuck me sideways, West cleaned up real well.* He ditched the dress pants for a pair of clean jeans that hugged his strong thighs and I could guarantee made his ass look good. A black dress shirt looked tailored for his muscular form, stretching across his broad shoulders and hugging his tapered waist. He'd trimmed down his wild beard and brushed back his hair—though, I was a fan of how it curled around his ears. And in true West fashion, he wore his boots.

"I ain't wearing the clown shoes," he said as he finished rolling up his sleeves.

I cleared my throat to regain my bearings.

"Yeah, that works," I replied. *Yeah, that worked real fucking well.* I took a long moment to think depressing thoughts. Dress pants would not hide my rising hard-on and that wasn't how I wanted the night to go. It wasn't the impression I wanted to give West.

"You good there, cowboy?" His lips quirked slightly.

"I'm good. But if you're not wearing dress pants, neither am I." There was no way in hell I was lasting in these goddamn dress pants. Not with him over there looking like walking temptation.

CHAPTER 76

WEST

Our date was an early dinner at a nice restaurant—the kind where waiters had uniforms and there was a lot of shit in French on the menu. Thankfully, the few things that were in English were things I'd eat. *And fuck, the food was goddamn good.*

Jackson being Jackson thought everything out, including finding another restaurant in Eugene that offered rooftop dining. No enclosed spaces and no people chaos. It made it easier to enjoy the date with him.

And as long as we didn't talk about how long he would be gone, things were okay. I wasn't sure what to think about Jackson leaving for a few months. There was something uncomfortable in my chest—something I didn't have the fucking words for. It bothered me daily. *More than I was ready to admit.* I wasn't used to wanting people around, but I wanted Jackson around.

I didn't know what to do with that piece of information.

I did my best not to focus on it. Ignoring it during dinner was easy. After we ate, we grabbed blankets from the back of his truck. Why the fuck we needed blankets was beyond me, and he didn't give me a goddamn answer. Instead, Jackson just smiled.

"Come on, it'll be fun," he told me. *I wanted to believe him—I fucking did.* The anxiety of not knowing made it difficult. I didn't tell him that, though. I didn't want to sound ungrateful for all the work he'd put into planning this for us.

For me.

We ended up on another rooftop—one with a giant movie screen, mood lighting, and couples scattered across the ground on their own personal mounds of blankets and pillows.

"Rooftop movie?" I asked.

"Yeah," Jackson replied. I followed him as he weaved his way through a row of people until we were at the very back of it all. "I even convinced them to keep the very back open for us."

Away from people. *Fuck. Did he think of everything?*

"Now," he began as he tossed blankets on the ground, "it ain't no elevator shaft action film, but it is supposed to be funny, so we'll see."

The movie turned out to be some ridiculous Western comedy with horses, cowboys, and a fuck ton of shenanigans. I didn't have a clue what was happening. My attention kept getting drawn back to Jackson and the understanding this was it for a while.

Or maybe for good. Who knew what would happen when he got back to the ranch? Would I still be there? Hell, I still couldn't figure out what my plan was for fucking anything.

"Are you nervous?" I asked in a hush. He cocked a brow curiously. "About the rodeo."

"Usually," he said. "Not enough to make me quit. It's that big event kind of nervous. The first ride is always a big deal. It sets the expectations, you know? There's a good number of fresh blood joining this year."

"And you're old." I poked the bear a little, finding satisfaction in his grumpy scowl.

"I fucking hate when people call me old," he muttered. "I know I'm old—right on the edge of retirement—I get it. I just fucking hate it when everyone reminds me of it. I like what I do. I don't want to fucking think about the rest of it."

I didn't know what that was like.

"I could punch them," I offered, enjoying the laugh it pulled out of him. The people in front of us didn't much appreciate it from the fucking glares they sent our direction. Jackson sank down on the rolled-up blanket, biting back his laughter. "Want me to punch them too?"

"I ain't got the fucking money to bail you out," Jackson whispered. "You hit someone, I'll come see you during visiting hours."

"Throw food at them, got it," I retorted. He snorted as he tried to hold back his laughter.

"You're trouble, West McNamara," he said. "Always was."

"I'm sorry, who the fuck came up with all the plans for all the shit we did?" I asked. His smile only widened. I liked being the one to put it there.

"Will you still do shit with the rodeo when you no longer ride?"

"Maybe. Haven't really thought about it."

"Are rodeo clowns still a thing?"

"Shut the fuck up."

"You'd make a damn good rodeo clown," I teased. "You got the fucking face for it and everything."

"I will beat your ass," he snapped.

Someone in front of us shushed us, and I resisted the urge to flip them off. Jackson, however, mean mugged them into turning right back around.

"Damn, cowboy. You're a tough one, ain't you?" I whispered. "I think you scared a couple of high school girls."

"I can't fucking take you anywhere," he said under his breath.

"You can take me anywhere." *Okay, almost everywhere.* But the fucking sentiment was there.

Feeling compelled to do so, I reached over and slipped my hand in his. The way his fingers wove through mine was natural. It felt nice. Being with Jackson felt nice. And when my head wasn't a fucked up mess, I liked how he made me feel.

I wanted more of that—even if it was just one more time.

"Hey, cowboy," I began quietly. I gave his hand a small tug until he looked at me. *Again with that sexy look on his face.* "I want to go home."

"The movie ain't even that bad," he scoffed. "You ain't getting out of it."

"If I do what I'm thinking about doing here... we're both getting arrested," I told him. His brows came together slightly as he searched my face for some kind of tell-all—something to make him doubt my words. Only

I wasn't doubtful. I knew what I wanted and was just hoping to hell the rest of me would keep up later on. "Let's go home, cowboy."

CHAPTER 77

WEST

THE MINUTE WE WALKED through the door, I curled a hand in his hair and dragged his mouth to mine. Jackson responded in kind—matching my burst of enthusiasm. An arm snaked around my waist and he pushed me back against the door. A flash of panic shot through me. I forced myself to breathe, inhaling the spice of his cologne and letting it fill me.

This was Jackson.

Jackson was good.

Jackson wouldn't hurt me.

I was okay.

"You still with me, West?" Jackson whispered against my lips. *Fuck, I didn't realize I'd locked up.*

I nodded and kissed him again, welcoming the taste of his tongue across mine. His hands wandered my body as we kissed against the door, practically burning a hole through my clothes. I was drowning in him. *His taste, his scent, his touch.* My head spun, and my heart hammered against my ribcage.

Jackson's teeth scraped along my jaw and his mouth drifted down my neck in soft kisses. My head tipped back against the wall.

"May I?" His fingers skated up the buttons of my shirt.

"Jackson," I growled, "if you keep asking me shit like that, I'm going to lose my temper. I wouldn't be doing this if I didn't fucking want to."

Though I understood why he did too. Fuck, it was all a fucking mess.

"Okay." He kissed me, harder and more demanding. I moaned at the way his hips rolled against mine—the sensation driving me insane. My cock ached behind the zipper of my jeans. And with every button on my shirt he undid, my frenzied need only grew.

When his fingers grazed over the scars on my side, the twinge of pain yanked me out of the moment. I grabbed his wrist to stop him. My mouth hovered over his as I tried to catch my breath—tried to ground myself. *I was okay.*

"Do they hurt?" Jackson asked softly.

"Sometimes," I admitted, ashamed to even say it out loud. I hated them. Hated what they constantly reminded me of. "I don't know if it's real or not but yeah."

"Okay. I won't touch them." He said the words so fucking simply that it did something to me. I damn near lurched forward to kiss him again, desperate to kiss him and silently tell him all the things I couldn't get my brain to let me say. Wrapping an arm around his waist, I pulled his body flush to mine. His warmth and hard edges were welcome.

"Upstairs, cowboy," I whispered breathlessly as I broke the kiss.

How the hell we managed to make our way up the stairs and to his room was beyond me. It was a stumbling dance of tearing off clothes, quiet swearing, and one broken lamp. With every kiss, every touch, Jackson grew more intense and confident. I let him take the lead—needing some kind of direction. The brief conversation about my scars had my brain retreating. I didn't want to go where it was going and did my best to stay grounded.

When he turned away from me, I dragged his back to my chest. I kissed the line of his neck and nipped at his ear. His fingers curled in my hair while my hand skated down the strong lines of his abs. Wrapping my hand around his cock, I stroked him steadily to rile him up more.

"*Fuck*," Jackson breathed out. His body pushed back against mine. I ran the pad of my thumb over his slit, gathering the pre-cum there and bringing it to my mouth. The salty taste of him was grounding, giving me something to cling to—to keep me here with him instead of floating away. He groaned, "Jesus fuck, baby."

"On your stomach, cowboy," I ordered gruffly and walked him toward the edge of the bed. He dropped, and I went with him.

I crawled over his body, kissing my way up his spine. The little shudder that ran through him wasn't lost on me. I took my time pressing kisses up and down his spine a second time, liking the little things I could do to him. I still didn't know what the fuck I was doing. Every time we ended up in this position I felt equally lost.

But making Jackson feel good? That I was determined to figure out. It was the only thing I didn't want to fuck up.

I smiled slightly against the curve of his shoulder as he floundered to grab the lube, missing twice when I nipped at a spot guaranteed to drive him wild.

"I know what the fuck you're doing," he grumbled, and my smirk widened.

"I don't have a fucking clue what you're talking about." I sank my teeth in his favorite spot at the base of his neck, and he almost dropped the bottle to the floor. As I grabbed it from him, I teased, "Careful, cowboy."

He made a sound that dissolved into a groan as I swiped lube over his asshole and slid one finger inside him. I didn't have the patience to prep him the way I probably should've, but from the way he pushed back against me, he didn't either.

Instead, I coated my dick and slowly pressed the crown past that tight ring of muscles.

"*Fuck*," Jackson let out with a loud moan, his forehead falling to the bed. My fingers dug into his hip as I took my time working my cock in and out of him, venturing a little deeper each time.

The intensity and pressure knocked the air out of my lungs. I paused, trying to gain my bearings. He was so goddamn tight and hot around my cock. Jackson's hand found mine, his fingers weaving through mine as if for reassurance. *Or maybe he just needed it as much as I did.*

Kissing the side of his neck, I thrust into him until I was buried to the hilt inside him. His moan echoed mine, and I focused on making him feel good. My pace picked up, and his body moved under mine, matching every drive of my hips.

Sweat cooled my skin, my breaths grew ragged, and my heart pounded violently in my ears. Jackson grew louder and more demanding underneath me. From the sounds he made, he was getting there without me ever touching him.

But I struggled to keep up with him. Every thrust did nothing for me—no matter how hard I focused. I couldn't get my head in the moment. Couldn't get my body to cooperate. It felt good but it didn't at the same time. More than anything, I felt trapped. But I kept going—kept trying—until my dick quit on me, softening slowly.

"Fuck..." I let out pathetically. My head fell between his shoulder blades as I pulled out. "I'm sorry."

"Don't be—"

"I am," I reiterated a little too quickly.

"West." Jackson shifted underneath me, rolling so he could see me. He pulled my mouth to his, cradling my face with more gentleness than I deserved.

"But you didn't—"

"I don't care," he interrupted once more and kissed the tip of my nose. *How was he not the most sexually frustrated man on the planet with a broken guy like me as his partner?* I was so fucking broken and useless. I kept telling myself I could do these things, but I couldn't. And it fucking killed me. "I care about you, West. Your comfort. Your safety. Your happiness."

"Jackson..."

"You're my priority, baby, above anything else."

My heart cracked wide open with those words—such simple fucking words that probably didn't mean much to anyone else. At that moment I knew: I still loved him. I had never stopped loving him. I'd just buried the feelings somewhere deep inside me where I never had to face them again.

But I couldn't bring myself to say the words out loud. *What the fuck was wrong with me?*

I settled on his chest, pressing my ear over his heart. The sound of his heartbeat was comforting in ways I didn't know how to explain. I was painfully aware of how hard his dick was as it pressed against my torso and did my best not to focus on it—a fucking miserable task.

Jackson's palms rubbed along my upper arms and back. The sensation was painful along my skin, prickling along my every nerve.

"Don't rub," I whispered. His hands stilled, and the fucking guilt for even bringing it up was immediate. Under my breath, I added, "Sorry."

"Does it hurt?"

"Sometimes," I admitted. "Sometimes it just makes my skin… uncomfortable."

It felt weird talking about it. I never talked about it. I didn't understand it and didn't expect other people to either. All I knew was that I was a fucking mess. That was no one's problem but mine.

"What does it feel like?" Jackson asked softly. "When you're touched."

My chest tightened. No one had ever cared to ask that question. I swallowed hard as I tried to think of a way to describe so he could understand.

"Most of the time it's just uncomfortable. Like pins and needles uncomfortable," I attempted to explain, feeling ridiculously pathetic even as the words fell out of me. "When it's bad… it feels like taking fucking razors to my skin. Just… cutting into my nerves over and over. My clothes hurt. The air hurts. Everything fucking hurts, and I'm just… stuck with it until it goes away."

"That sounds horrible." *That was the understatement of the fucking century.* I hated how out of control just the existence of my own skin was. "Does this hurt right now?"

"Not really," I said. My skin was uncomfortable—hot and sticky from sweat, tingling and feeling off, but it wasn't horrible. I'd gone through worse.

"West."

"I don't want to fucking move," I told him gruffly. For as uncomfortable as my skin was, I liked listening to Jackson's heartbeat more. That made up for everything.

"Okay," he replied. "How can I touch you?"

"I don't know." I didn't have a fucking answer for that. I'd always been so adamant about not being touched—not letting people get close to me. Jackson was an anomaly. An experiment. He was something I never expected. "No rubbing."

"No rubbing, got it," Jackson confirmed. His arms wrapped around my shoulders, holding me tight to him. "Is this okay?"

The continuous questions grated against my nerves, but I said nothing. I knew why he wanted to know—why it was important to him. I just hated how fucking pathetic I had to sound out loud. It was like the man needed a goddamn instruction manual just to touch me.

He could be with any other guy and not have to deal with this shit. I struggled to understand why *this* was what he wanted. Why he wanted me.

"Yeah, I like that," I whispered because it was the truth. I liked the warmth and tightness of his arms. I liked the little good things with Jackson, and I wasn't sure how the hell I was supposed to do months without him.

Or the rest of my fucking life for that matter.

CHAPTER 78

JACKSON

For the first time in my life, I had reservations about leaving Double Arrow for the rodeo. All my reservations were wrapped up in the man I left in my bed. I didn't have the heart to wake up West before I left. Sure, I left him a note, but looking back, I should've woken him up. I should've said goodbye. I didn't have a clue when I'd see him again. I knew he'd be watching, but I would've given anything to have him with me.

Those reservations only increased in intensity when Amy informed me that the first thing I had to do upon arriving in Nevada was meet with Rex Lexington for lunch. *And unfortunately, I couldn't skip the goddamn meeting.* I was stuck with the fucking man as my sponsor.

However, Rex wasn't the one sitting at the table when I arrived at the steakhouse for our meeting. His son, Colter, was. *And I despised Colter Lexington.* Mid-twenties with an attitude like he owned the goddamn place, the kid was a self-proclaimed alpha male who looked down on everyone. I knew he'd been working alongside his father to take over the business, but I hadn't anticipated that change any time soon. Him sitting at that fucking table was telling.

That giant ass grin on his face as I approached the table pissed me off.

"Well, I'll be damned," he drawled, sounding straight out of Texas. "I was beginning to think you weren't going to show."

"What the fuck are you doing here?" I asked as a way of greeting.

"I think it's high time you and me had a conversation, Jackson." He gestured to the chair across from him. "Sit, please. Order something. Anything you want."

"Isn't it enough that you get my goddamn business?" I demanded when I sat down. I dropped my hat on my knee and crossed my arms. When the waitress asked for my drink, I told her, "I won't be staying long enough for anything, darlin'. You can go now."

"My father said your grumpy attitude was legendary. I didn't believe him."

"You should've," I snapped. "Why the fuck am I here?"

"I want to buy Double Arrow Ranch," Colter said. Silence stretched between us as my brain processed those fucking words. He was fucking with me. He had to be. There was no fucking way this kid actually thought he'd buy my ranch.

"What the fuck makes you think I'd sell you my goddamn ranch?"

"Because I know you're inches shy of going bankrupt," he replied. My scowl deepened. *How the fuck did he have that fucking information?* "I did my research into your ranch. It's not hard to figure out that you're bleeding money right now, Jackson. And you know what, it happens. One bad year got you, that's all. Ain't nothing to be ashamed of."

The audacity of this fucking kid. He'd be lucky if I didn't reach across this goddamn table and fucking kill him. It was real clear that he didn't give two shits about sponsoring me. There was just no way he'd get me in a sit down with him otherwise.

"You've got some balls, you know that," I snarled. "Conning your way into this fucking meeting only to insult my business and insult me. Why the fuck would you want my ranch?"

"Because you are the biggest threat to my business," Colter said. That took me by surprise. Taking a sip of his whiskey, he sat back in his seat. "Do you know what every single one of your customers said to me when they switched to my business?"

"Do I want to fucking know?" *This felt like it was about to be a slap in the face.*

"*It's only until Jackson Myles gets back on his feet,*" he told me. "Every single one of them. For as fucking grumpy as you are, you sure as hell have a way with your customers. They don't want me. They don't want Lexington Farms. Not in the long run. They just need an interim supplier, and you know what that is? Bad for my business. *You* are bad for my business, Jackson Myles."

I couldn't help the grin on my face. I liked being a pain in his fucking ass.

"If you pick yourself up off the ground and come back, I'm screwed," he continued. "All your old customers will go running back to you. And if you run your business like you ride, you'll come back stronger than ever next season. I can't have that—especially not in my first year running the family business. That won't go over so well for me. So, I'm offering to buy Double Arrow Ranch at the price of its peak value. That's way more than it's worth right now and you know that."

My jaw ticked. He had me there, and he knew it. That kind of money would launch my ass out of the fucking hole I was in. But the cost would be my entire family's legacy. Unfortunately, at the rate things were going, there was a good chance I was going to lose my entire family legacy anyway. I fucking hated that thought.

But I hated the thought of letting Colter Lexington get his hands on my business just to save his. I'd rather go toe to toe with him and let the cards fall where they would.

"You can go fuck yourself, Colter," I told him. The fucker didn't even have the decency to look fazed. For good measure, I added, "And I won't be doing your goddamn milk ads."

"I didn't ask for you to do milk ads," he replied. *Of course, it'd been Amy's idea.* Why didn't that fucking surprise me? Colter grinned, and I instantly regretted bringing it up. This kid was the kind who would do exactly that to fuck with me. "Though, I might now."

Two could play that goddamn game.

"If you want to ruin your business, then go ahead and try to make me do that."

"I'm your sponsor, remember?" He said the words like I needed reminding. No matter how this goddamn meeting went, I was stuck with Colter and Lexington Farms for the rest of the season. There was a damn good chance I was firing Amy over this bullshit. "I pay the money that lets you ride."

"You want to hand an openly gay man a glass of white liquid on national television?" I cocked a brow, smirking. Yup. From the look on his little rich boy face, he hadn't thought that plan through. I let that thought hang in the air between us as I stood. "See you around, Colter."

Sponsor or not, I had no fucking intention of seeing that kid ever again if I could avoid it. He could take his business offer and go shove it.

I was just fine.

CHAPTER 79

WEST

JACKSON: Fuck Colter Lexington

JACKSON: And what a stupid fucking name.

JACKSON: This asshole doesn't just want to fucking sponsor me. He wants to buy out Double Arrow. It ain't enough this fucker is taking my goddamn business, but he has the fucking audacity to tell me that I'm a threat to his business.

JACKSON: Fuck, I'm pissed.

JACKSON: Sorry for unloading. I hope you're doing okay. Can I call you tonight?

I LEFT HIM ON read—not that he could see. *Could he?* I didn't know how this whole flip-phone-to-smartphone conversion thing went. Tech wasn't my thing. Besides, I had other shit I needed to focus on.

"Thanks, Mick," I said as I slid out of the old man's truck and slung my bag over my shoulder.

"Anytime, boy," Mickey replied. Leaning on the door, I faced him.

"You going to be okay?" I asked. "If it's going to be too much work—"

"Boy, you left a goddamn binder on how to care for those horses of yours," he interrupted with a laugh. "We'll be just fine without you."

I nodded slowly, still uneasy about the whole thing. Doubt had snuck its way in on the ride away from the ranch.

"Peter's got your number," Mickey reassured me. "And he's goin' to be blowin' you up with all the updates."

"Promise?"

"I promise."

"Okay," I murmured. I drew in a sharp breath and adjusted my bag on my shoulder. "Thanks again, Mick."

"I'll be seein' you, boy." He tipped his hat, and I shut the door. I tapped the hood of his truck as he backed out, leaving me alone.

I could fucking do this. There was a good chance I was going to piss off Jackson in the process, considering the responsibilities he'd left me with. It felt shitty to hand them off to someone else.

I swallowed the guilt and forced myself to follow the dirt drive around the side of an old farmhouse to where the stables sat out back. A semi-truck blocked the view, and I stopped to watch as another horse was loaded into the back.

"When Mickey told me he knew just the guy for the job, I never in a million years would've guessed that he'd be dropping West McNamara on my farm." Rich Matteson stepped out from the truck. He wiped his hands on his thighs while I forced an acceptable smile. "You're looking good, kid."

"Thanks," I said.

"How have you been?" he asked.

Fuck, I hated that question. It was just another way for nosy small-town folk to gossip. While Rich and his farm weren't technically in Wood Springs, all the small towns in the area were entwined. Rich ran the only equestrian farm in the area. Jackson's mom had bought quite a few horses from him over the years. I had no doubt he knew more about me than he was letting on.

"You know," I replied vaguely. I tossed my bag on the front seat of the truck and went about inspecting the inside of the trailer. Seven horses were comfortably loaded in their own stalls with water and hay at the ready.

"Are you good to handle a job like this?" Rich continued, thankfully not pushing my lack of an answer. "Hauling horses is a big deal. I used to do it, but my back just isn't what it used to be anymore. It's just easier for me to fly these days."

"It's a little over eight hours to Reno from here," I told him to show I'd done my fucking research. "I'll have to stop about every three hours to take care of the horses. Depending on where we stop, I'll try to get each one out to move around even just a little. I'd say it'll take no less than ten hours to get out there. With the late start, I'm looking at getting in around midnight. Maybe later."

"My flight doesn't land until seven tomorrow," he said.

"I won't leave the horses," I replied. "But they shouldn't stay in the trailer that long."

"The coordinators will have places for you to unload the animals. They've got people arriving all day and night, today and tomorrow," he assured me. "All you've got to do is stay with them until I get there."

"And keep you updated along the way."

"And keep me updated along the way."

"Sounds good," I said. In silence, I helped him close everything up. Even though I knew what I was doing, I let him show me how everything worked anyway. It was more for him than me. Only when he was certain that I was good to go, did I start toward the cab.

"West," Rich called after me, "I'm real glad you left when you did."

I stopped, his words striking something deep. With a frown, I faced him.

"What the hell are you talking about?" I asked.

"You didn't deserve Harrison, kid." The sadness in his expression was a slap to the face.

"Are you telling me you knew what Harrison was doing?"

"The whole lot of us had a good understanding of the kind of man your father was," he answered quietly. *The whole lot of them? Who the fuck was the whole lot of them?* "I think that's why so many of us let you two get away with so much shit back in the day. Better that than telling him what you were up to when we didn't know what he'd do, you know?"

My jaw clenched tight as I nodded slowly. *What the fuck was wrong with all of them?* Something inside me frayed further apart. I was so fucking over their bullshit. I was real tired of hearing how everyone had known what Harrison was up to. And yet, no one fucking cared. I kept telling myself there was nothing no one could've done—that it was pointless to get mad—but the longer I dealt with this shit, the harder it was to hang onto that train of thought.

"Yeah, well maybe you should've done something. *The whole lot of you,*" I snapped without remorse. "The only fucking reason I left this goddamn place was because Harrison tried to kill me. But yeah, letting me get away with shit was real fucking helpful, so give yourself a goddamn pat on the back for that, why don't you?"

Rich looked fucking uncomfortable with the admission. *Good.* He fucking deserved it. They all did.

"I'm hitting the road, Rich," I said, unable to give him any more of me. "I'll update you at the first stop."

Not giving him a chance to say a damn thing, I climbed into the truck and got situated. The drive to Reno was a long one, and I didn't want to waste another minute with Rich and the bullshit he dredged up.

CHAPTER 80

JACKSON

Not hearing from West was fucking killing me. Not only had he ignored my texts but he also sent all my calls to voicemail. I spent the night worrying. Was he okay? Has he relapsed? Was he just done with me? Fuck, I even contemplated texting Mickey, but that was a desperate move. *I wasn't a desperate man. Yet anyway.*

I pushed thoughts of West out of my head as I approached the restaurant where I planned to meet my girls. It wasn't my first time in Reno, and we had a brunch place. They had a pre-game plan, I just had a plan to sit back and make sure none of them did anything too fucking stupid.

Were the buckle bunnies my first choice of tour partners? No. But most of the girls were young—practically babies enjoying the country spirit of things. They were also gullible as shit, and while most of the riders were good men, they were still men. I hated watching the girls get taken advantage of, used and discarded, or treated like shit.

It was a hell of a lot harder to come at a six-foot-two cowboy with that alpha male bullshit than it was a buckle bunny. They were good girls who deserved respect. I was just there to make sure they got it.

"Jackson!" My name was about all the warning I got before a five-foot-one tank barreled into me, throwing her arms around my waist. For something so fucking tiny, Darla Wilson had a hell of a tight grip. *And a hell of a right hook but that was a story for a different time.*

"Woman!" I exclaimed. "I can't fucking breathe when you squeeze me like that."

She stepped back, beaming up at me for all of two seconds before punching me in the shoulder.

"Ow!" I snapped. I didn't have to pretend as I rubbed my shoulder. "That fucking hurt. What the hell is wrong with you?"

"Why the hell didn't you swing on by last night to say hi?" Her accent was as heavy as the judgment on her pretty face. I did my best to glare at her—make her uncomfortable—but after almost five years of friendship, I had little effect on her.

"I was seeing you today! Right now!" I said, gesturing to all of me as if she needed the reminder.

"We got a few new girls, cowboy." She crossed her arms as I scowled. While her presumption was that it was my response to her statement, I was frowning at the nickname. It suddenly didn't sound right unless West was saying it.

"All right, pretty girl." I matched her stance. "Tell me who we got."

This was routine for Darla and I. Darla had made being a buckle bunny her thing—God bless her. She'd shown up when she was eighteen years old and just kept showing up every year. Where a lot of other girls came and went, she stayed.

But Darla wasn't just a buckle bunny. She was also a barrel racer and a damn good one. She just never talked about it. Why was beyond me.

"So, Opie, Sutton, Willa, and Wren are back this year." *That didn't surprise me.* The four of them were consistent faces around the rodeo—college girls on summer vacation. While they didn't go to every event, they went to as many as they could. "But they also brought a friend of theirs with them this year. *Birdie.*"

"Oh?" I cocked a brow. The way Darla said her name piqued my interest. "Do we not like Birdie?"

Would I raise a little hell because my favorite girl didn't like someone? Absolutely.

"Birdie uses more hair product in one day than I use in a whole damn year," she retorted, making me laugh. "It don't move! Tell me why her hair don't move, Jackson! Who in their right mind wants that?"

But all I could think about was the fact that West used the same bar of soap on his hair as he did his body.

Fuck. I had to focus.

"I don't know, pretty girl," I said. I draped an arm around her shoulders and turned her toward the door. "Why don't you and me go on in there, get something to eat, and judge the hell out of her hair?"

"Are we bad people, cowboy?"

"Damn straight we are."

Birdie's hair didn't fucking move. Not a single fucking strand. It had to be the eighth wonder of the world considering her hair went down to her ass. *How the fuck was that comfortable?*

"I wonder what would happen if someone lit a candle next to her head," Darla whispered next to me, hiding behind the guise of biting into a biscuit.

"I don't have the money to bail your dumbass out of jail, pretty girl," I muttered under my breath. *Why was this a common theme among the people I spent my time with?* Between her and West, I needed a goddamn bail fund.

And there was West again, nudging his way from the back of my mind. Jesus fuck, I couldn't *not* think about him. Every little thing sent me reeling back to West. It drove me a little crazy. Usually, I enjoyed hanging out with my girls, but right now, all I wanted was to talk to him.

"So, how does this work?" Birdie's voice broke through my thoughts. *Yeah, I was going to blame my lack of enjoyment on Birdie.* Unfair? Probably. Was I still going to fucking do it? Fuck yes. "Cowboys are hot, and you're—"

"Very fucking gay," I interrupted. "It ain't an act, honey."

"Willa said you help us pick guys—"

"No." I shook my head. "Not a fucking chance."

"Jackson just makes sure we don't get treated like crap," Wren chimed in. Much like Birdie, she was all prim and proper but at least her hair moved.

"Rule number one of the rodeo," I began, "don't trust the fucking cowboys."

"But you're a cowboy," Birdie said.

"Jackson is the exception," Darla told her. "Trust me, when some two-bit nobody is gettin' too handsy for his own damn good, you want Jackson there to put 'im in his place."

"Sounds hot." Birdie's gaze swept me head to toe, and I recognized that damn look on her face. There was always one of them—one fucking woman who thought maybe she could make me less gay. Why? Who fucking knew? Maybe it was a challenge thing.

"Still gay, honey," I reminded her. "And there ain't a damn thing you've got that I want."

"Are the live auction guys on the table?" Birdie asked, changing the conversation. "Because I was over there earlier—"

"Why were you over there?" Sutton demanded.

"I went shopping," she smiled wide, "and there was this one guy... a real tall, dark, and toss me around daddy type."

I snorted into my drink. *Yeah, this was exactly why I hung around.* This girl was going to find herself a goddamn serial killer if she kept using that criteria to find men.

"The auction guys don't stick around," I said. "The first event is always the biggest turnout—short of the finals. It's a whole ordeal. The animal sales and the live auction are included as a part of the whole fair."

The first rodeo was always a big event. People brought animals to be sold as well as auctioned off. Hell, my dad and Harrison used to sell bulls at the first rodeo auction. There was barrel riding, calf wrangling, bull riding, and more.

"That's a bummer." She pouted—actually pouted. This girl was so goddamn surreal. "I'm going to go for it. The day's still early."

"You do you, honey," I told her. The conversation moved on without me. My heart wasn't in it. No, my heart was a few hundred miles away with a man who wasn't answering the damn phone.

What the hell was he doing to me? How had I let myself become so wrapped up in him that I couldn't fucking stand the idea of being ignored for a whole day?

"You okay, grumpy boy?" Darla nudged me in the side with her elbow. I gave her a well-practiced smile—one she saw right through. "Don't you go lyin' to me now."

"Just got someone on my mind," I told her, keeping my voice down. I rarely shared my dating life with anyone. Darla knew a handful of things, but that was it. I was always cautious about what I shared. I didn't want to clean up a fucking mess publicly.

"Jackson Ford Myles!" She gasped, slapping a hand to her chest playfully. "Are you tellin' me you have a special—"

"Oh!" Birdie exclaimed, lighting up. "Well, Mr. Tall, Dark, and Toss Me Around Daddy just made this easy."

While they chattered about her conversation strategy, I decided to take a look at Mr. Tall, Dark, and Toss Me Around Daddy—ready to take notes in case I had to kick someone's ass. But I never got that far. My heart lurched into my throat as I watched West wander up to the bar. He looked ready to fall asleep on his feet. His clothes were dusty, and his hair was shoved under a backwards hat.

What the hell was he doing here?

He drummed his fingers on the bar as he waited for the bartender, and I leaned forward, silently hoping he didn't order a drink.

He did, but it was water. *Thank fuck.*

After exchanging a handful of words with the bartender and tossing down some cash, West wandered to a corner booth and damn near collapsed in the seat. He dragged his hat over his face as he leaned back.

What the hell had happened to him?

"Sorry, honey, that one's taken," I interjected over their planning. Not saying anything else, I left the table to join West. When I dropped onto the bench across from him, he pulled the hat off his face. I asked, "What the hell are you doing here?"

"I told you I'd be there for your first ride. I just never said at what rodeo," West said. The corner of his mouth tipped up in a crooked, tired smile. Something inexplicable and overwhelming weaseled its way around my heart. When I didn't reply, he continued, "I took a job for Rich Matteson hauling horses to the live auction. He's too old to drive or some shit—took a plane. That's why I didn't answer you. Got in at like fucking midnight last night and had to stay with the horses. I figured I'd sleep in the truck, but one of the horses was too damn restless. I stayed up to keep him calm, so I haven't slept yet. And then Rich's plane was fucking delayed, which left me being a goddamn salesman."

I just stared at him. There was no fucking way the man in front of me was qualified to sell anything. He was more likely to scare them all away.

"Don't give me that goddamn look, cowboy," he retorted as if reading my mind. "I sold all seven of his horses before his plane fucking landed this morning."

Shifting uncomfortably, he pulled his wallet out of his front pocket and tossed a check on the table.

"That's for you," he told me. I frowned as I took the check and unfolded it. The number stopped me in my tracks. *So did my name on it.*

"What the hell is this?" I demanded.

"Well, I am an employee of Double Arrow, which makes you my boss," West explained. "I contracted with him as a service offered by the ranch, and I put his quote together by the horse for the whole thing, not by mileage. Figured you could use it for the ranch."

"West," I faltered. The gesture was unexpected. "I can't take this. You earned this."

"Nope." He lazily popped the 'p' as he said it. "Mickey drew up a contract for overtime hours, so you still have to pay me my normal rate for yesterday and today. And I need somewhere to sleep."

"I think I can arrange that." *There was no way in hell he was sleeping anywhere that wasn't with me.* Folding the check again, I lifted it a slight bit as I said, "Thank you for this."

"Anytime, cowboy." West dropped his hat over his face again and slouched down in the seat. "Wake me when my food shows up."

CHAPTER 81

JACKSON

Sneaking West into my room proved to be more of a fucking feat than I wanted. In the end, I gave him my only key and told the main desk I'd locked myself out. I hated it, but it was easier to avoid people that way.

The last thing I needed was for some misconstrued gossip article to end up on the internet about me and West. Amy would kill me, and I had no idea how West would handle it. We hadn't talked about that part of my life. While I wasn't some famous celebrity, the circuit was popular. I did interviews, ads, and dealt with our version of paparazzi—also known as the idiots who had too much time on their hands and followed us around looking for a story. I wasn't an idiot. Five minutes on the internet and they'd dig up shit on West that would cause the kind of issue that'd have Amy banging down my door.

"Should I bring a fucking pizza next time?" West teased as he let himself into my room. "Pretend I'm the goddamn delivery boy."

"I think me hooking up with the delivery boy would piss Amy off," I commented. *I'd gotten caught doing that shit when I was nineteen.* I still had yet to live down the pizza boy fiasco. Hell, half the time I ordered pizza and sent her a picture when I was mad just to fuck with her.

I took his face in my hands and kissed him, overwhelmingly grateful that he was there. West moaned as my tongue swept through his mouth. He inched closer, wrapping his arms around my waist.

"Hey, cowboy," he whispered, his forehead tipping against mine.

"Hey, baby." *Fuck, I couldn't believe he was here.* "I'm glad you showed up."

He just nodded, eyes still shut. I hugged him tight and felt the exhaustion as he leaned into me. This was more than just not having slept. West didn't like dealing with the occasional random person—I knew it made him anxious, even if he never told me out loud. Dealing with the chaos of the animal sales area had probably been too much for him.

"All right," I pulled away, "to bed with you."

I took him by the shoulders and steered him to the bed. He didn't sit. No, he straight up just dropped back on the bed. There was no effort to get comfortable as he let out a heavy sigh and just lay there.

Clearly, I had to intervene. Crouching, I untied his boots and slipped them off. I expected him to move, but he didn't.

"You know you can use the whole bed," I said. When he didn't move, I went around the side and stared down at him. Bracing on the mattress, I brushed his hair away from his forehead.

"If I kiss you, are you going to wake up?" I wondered aloud.

"I'm not a fucking Disney princess," he mumbled.

"Your way with animals is pretty fucking magical," I hummed.

"Fuck off." That sleepy, lopsided smile he gave me didn't back up the threat.

"Get your sexy ass on that pillow, baby," I ordered and gave his shoulder a nudge. "You need to sleep."

"I need a power nap." He groaned as he rolled, just barely making it to the pillow. I smiled, watching the way he dragged the pillow and blanket to his chest. The action had become something of a comfort behavior for him. *I adored it.*

"You need more than a power nap."

"Nah. Just a power nap and I'll be fine."

"Look, I have shit to do all day anyway," I said. "I ain't riding tonight, but I do have to show up to the rodeo opening. We're picking bulls tonight."

Tonight was all about showmanship and kicking things off—building the excitement. The first stop on the tour was the only one we usually drew bulls at. It always drove things sky-high for the crowd. After that, we were randomly matched.

I didn't ride until tomorrow, but there was no way I could miss tonight. Not unless the world came to an end. But West didn't need to be there for that.

"You sleep," I reiterated. "You don't need to be there for that shit."

"Yeah, but I came here to do all that boyfriend stuff. I can't sleep through all of it," West muttered. I held my tongue at the boyfriend comment. This wasn't the time for that conversation. *Though, hearing him refer to himself as my boyfriend made my fucking day.* "Power nap."

"Baby, you need your sleep."

"I'm fine," he snapped once more. I fell silent, staring at my watch to count the minutes of quiet. West made no effort to continue the conversation. It took no more than three minutes for him to completely pass out on me. *Power nap my ass.* He'd be out for hours.

But I also knew how bad he'd feel if he missed anything, so I set an alarm and wrote him a note with instructions for when he woke up. If he slept through the alarm, at least I tried.

CHAPTER 82

WEST

I hugged the coffee close to my chest as I wandered through the rodeo. *Fuck, it was insane.* All the interviews and event replays I'd seen couldn't encompass this shit. My skin crawled painfully, and I wanted nothing more than to fucking leave. The number of people who had bumped into me, the level of shouting, and the amount of alcohol around had me fucking dying.

But I was doing this for Jackson.

I hadn't seen him since I passed out in his bed. Hell, I couldn't remember a damn thing past trudging into his room. Driving all day and staying up all night with horses had taken it out of me but the dealing with all the people part had fucking done me in.

I didn't understand ninety percent of the shit going on around me as I made my way over to the stands. I just wanted to sit down away from it all to watch the bull draw, but Jackson sent me to a specific stand. I did it because I wanted to make him happy.

And it would've been okay if it wasn't for the six young-as-fuck women sitting where I was supposed to sit. Glitter, itty bitty cutoff shorts, and cowboy boots. *Jesus fucking Christ.* He sent me to hang out with his buckle bunnies.

"You must be West!" a tiny blonde thing exclaimed. When she got to her feet, I took an instinctive step back in case she tried to hug me. She looked like the kind of girl who used hugs as a way of greeting. There was no way in hell I could handle that—not even to be nice to Jackson. "Jackson told us to expect you!"

"Yeah." I nodded slowly. *This hadn't been in the note.* "Hi."

"Hi! I'm Darla—Jackson's best friend," she said. I stared at her like she'd grown a second head because Jackson didn't have friends let alone a best friend. *Correction: I was supposed to be his best friend* "This right here is Opie—her full name is Ophelia, but we call her Opie. It's way easier. And that's Wren, Sutton, and Willa. And the one over there lookin' like a tiger starin' at some sheep is Birdie. Her hair don't move."

That last part was said in a hushed whisper like it was a secret I wasn't supposed to know. I just nodded again because what the fuck was I supposed to say to that. *I didn't have the right kind of people skills for her enthusiasm.*

"Come! Sit!" Darla pointed to a spot on the bench and walked over to a different spot.

For a hot second, my heart stopped in my chest. *Fucking hell.* I didn't want to be in close quarters with them. I didn't even know them. But glancing over my shoulder, I realized it was either sit snug with them—people Jackson trusted and sent me to be with—or sit with a bunch of drunk as fuck strangers.

Neither option was fucking appealing.

I made myself sit down. But as I did, the six girls moved around like they'd practiced for this shit. I ended up with a wide bubble of no one in my space.

"Don't you worry, doll face," Darla whispered behind me. "Jackson made sure we got you."

Those words wrapped around my heart like barbed wire, and I sucked in a sharp breath. I glanced at the space around me—more than a generous one-person space in every direction. *Jackson really had fucking thought of everything.*

What Jackson failed to fucking mention was how goddamn boring the bull draw would be. There were twenty-four fucking riders. Twenty-four. Both nights. Which fucking meant we had to do the goddamn bull draw three times. The first time was to determine the pecking order with each rider picking a number. *But no.* They couldn't just pick a fucking number. No, it was a whole goddamn show—one the crowd ate up.

It sure as fuck didn't help that the woman holding the fucking hat was scantily clad and damn near showing it all in her country girl pride. No one gave a shit about the pot-bellied middle-aged announcer hanging out with her narrating the whole event.

I needed a fucking drink.

By the time it was Jackson's turn to pick a number, I'd lost count and track of what the fuck was happening.

"Well, now!" the announcer began as he clapped Jackson on the shoulder. "There's no need to pick your number tonight, is there, Jackson? All the slots are filled and that puts you in as the twenty-fourth rider! How's that make you feel?"

"Well, you know what they say." Jackson grinned as he leaned in closer to the mic. *Yeah, this fucker was about to say some stupid shit to piss people off.* "You always save the best for last. Let me show these boys how it's done."

From the overdone and righteous indignation on all their faces, it worked. That was the other thing driving me insane: the fucking antics. Did they all hate each other that much? Or was it all a fucking act? At this rate, I hoped to hell they were paying Jackson as a goddamn actor too.

"You doin' good, sugar?" Darla asked. I glanced at her, nodding. "Good! Sutton and Wren are goin' to get us all drinks. Jackson said you don't do alcohol, but can they get you anythin' else?"

I almost said coffee but thought better of it. I didn't need to be hopped up on caffeine. Not when I was dying on the spot.

"Water is fine," I replied. "If you don't mind."

"Oh, honey, we don't mind at all!" She laughed, but I failed to see her humor. "You're important to him, so you're important to us."

Yeah, I would never understand it.

The night crawled on with water refills and the eventual bag of pretzels. I couldn't sit still in my spot. My legs bounced with an insatiable need to get the fuck out of there.

Jackson's first pick was some bull named Burger. *Who the fuck named a bull Burger?* That was borderline cruel was what that was.

When they started the second day, the first rider pulled a name I hadn't heard. Though, I hadn't been paying close enough attention to have a good grasp of what was happening.

"Are they only picking from twenty-four bulls?" I asked Darla.

"No, each bull is used only once an event," she said. "I ain't got a clue why, so I can't give you that answer."

I made a sound and filed that away as something to ask Jackson. *Maybe.*

The third draw didn't go by any faster than the first two. In fact, it felt even fucking slower. It'd be rude to fucking leave. I kept that thought at the forefront of my mind to keep from bolting.

"Oooh-weee! That right there, folks, is the unlucky draw!" the announcer damn near shouted when Jackson grabbed the last piece of paper from the hat. The wild response around us was deafening. I frowned. *What the hell was happening?*

"Oh, no," Darla whispered behind me. I glanced over my shoulder at her, wondering what the hell she knew.

"For his second ride, Jackson Myles will be facing down the one... the only... *Rampage!*"

Anything else he said was drowned out by another uprising in cheers. Jackson ate up the excitement with such enthusiasm that it made everyone all that much louder.

"Why the hell do we not like Rampage?" I leaned back just enough for Darla to hear me.

"Honey, Rampage is the meanest son of a bitch they got," she whispered. "He ain't the bull that riders are hopin' for. He ain't no one's Everest. He's the goddamn boogeyman."

"Oh..." I didn't understand half the shit that came out of her mouth. "What the fuck does that mean?"

"Most of the cowboys who get on Rampage, they don't walk away," she explained. "They get carried out or..."

I didn't need her to finish that sentence to know what the fuck she meant. The sense of dread weaving through me said it all.

CHAPTER 83

JACKSON

"OH, C'MON NOW." I chuckled, maintaining my unbothered attitude. "Rampage is just another bull. It's all about how you ride him."

"You say that *now*," the interviewer began with a little giggle. I was pretty sure she worked for the local newspaper, but I couldn't be sure. I'd talked to so many fucking people. We all had.

"Now, look, honey," I took off my hat as I spoke, "I know Rampage has got one heck of a reputation, but it's just talk. That's all. All bulls get a good toss and trample in from time to time."

"But none like Rampage," she pointed out. I ran a hand through my hair to keep from clipping at her too quickly. All anyone wanted to talk about was Rampage's destruction—like I wasn't aware how dangerous the bull was. But the thing of it was, he was just another fucking bull. I refused to let his track record fuck with my head like it did everyone else's.

"Well, he ain't ever come up against me," I said with confidence. *Was I talking out of my ass? Maybe a little.* But I wouldn't let a bull get the better of me before I ever got on its back.

It took me another ten minutes before I managed to escape her. *That was ten minutes too many.* Interviews came with the territory, but fuck, I was over them. I had an opening night party to get to and West to spend time with.

West, despite the clear line in the sand keeping our relationship quiet, stood along a nearby fence just waiting for me to finish up. After five interviews, he hadn't moved. Not once. He didn't even fucking smoke. He just stood there listening and fading into the background.

I hated that last part—though, I had a feeling he didn't mind being ignored by everyone.

"We're escaping now," I said in a hushed voice as I strode right past him. He hurried after me. "If I do one more goddamn interview, I might start fucking lying just for the hell of it."

"Amy would fucking love that," he replied gruffly.

"Amy would eat me for fucking breakfast." I laughed. We made our way through the parking lot, and I kept my head low just to avoid more people. "Granted, I might just do that shit to fuck with her."

I wouldn't. I didn't need bad press.

"Are you worried?" West asked quietly. I blew out a long breath as I shoved my hands in my pockets.

"Maybe," I admitted. I could tell West anything—there was no concern there. "I know Rampage is a wild fucking mess with a bad reputation. But I don't want to get ahead of myself, you know?"

He made a small sound. *Who was I kidding?* West didn't have a clue about bull riding. I had to assume Darla and the girls told him about Rampage's reputation.

"Hey." I stopped, turning and stopping in front of him. His jaw set tight as if waiting for some kind of backlash. I knew it was instinct for him—years of expressing something and having it used against him—but that didn't make it suck any less. "I'll be okay. I've done this hundreds of times."

"On a bull like Rampage?" He cocked a brow, clearly not buying a word I said.

"A bull is just a bull," I told him. Glancing around us to make sure we were alone, I stepped closer and placed a lingering kiss on his forehead. "Besides, we both know I love a fucking challenge."

"That's what I'm afraid of." The words came out so softly that I almost missed them. But hearing that West was afraid for me was almost enough to make me pull out of the event.
Almost.

CHAPTER 84

WEST

Jackson was in his element. That much was clear as day as I watched him dance with a group of cowboys and bunnies—one of those line dances or some shit. I didn't have a clue what they were doing, but he did. His smile was wide, his laughter was loud, and I had a feeling nothing would stop him from enjoying the night.

This Jackson was different. So different I almost didn't recognize him. I knew from following his career that he was more lighthearted while on the circuit, but I hadn't anticipated this.

But me? I stuck to my seat, doing whatever I could do to stay invisible on the sidelines. My nerves burned, misfiring left and right until I couldn't sit still. The restless energy funneled into my legs, leaving me bouncing anxiously. It was too loud. Too chaotic. Too much.

I wasn't cut out for this lifestyle.

I wasn't cut out to keep up with Jackson like this—not when I wanted to crawl into a hole where not a single fucking person could bother me.

There wasn't a hole I could crawl into, but I did walk my ass out the door without letting Jackson know. He wouldn't notice anyway, and I didn't want him to. He didn't need a night where my stupid bullshit swept in and ruined it all.

The knowledge I had of Rampage made me curious. Enough so that I fucking broke into the animal holding area. *They needed better fucking security.* Considering the value of the animals in the pens, I shouldn't have been able to walk in like I did.

Rampage's pen was set away from all the rest, which did nothing but solidify the stories about him. Still, I leaned on the metal gate and studied him. The Bushwacker bull just stood there.

He watched me.

I watched him.

Neither of us moved.

My heart bled for him. This wasn't some vicious wild monster in front of me—not like they made him out to be. He was broken and hurting. He had nothing left to give anyone.

"How'd I know I'd find you here?" Jackson asked, amusement lacing his voice as he strolled down the aisle toward me. "If you wanted to leave, all you had to do was say so, baby. I don't mind."

"How long did it take for you to figure out I was gone?" I replied.

"I watched your ass walk out the door," he told me. My gaze flicked in his direction, surprised. "If you think I wasn't watching you all night, you got another thing coming. Took me a hot minute to say goodbye to everyone. By then I thought I'd lost you."

"How'd you figure I was here?"

"You like animals more than you like people. You've spent all fucking day around people. It don't take a genius to figure out you'd look for a few animals to spend time with."

He had me there. Admittedly, I liked that he knew that about me.

"I see you found Rampage," Jackson said, and I nodded.

"He's sad." I stared at the bull all over again. I wanted nothing more than to open the fucking stall and take him with me. He didn't belong there.

"How can you tell?"

"It's in his eyes." Without hesitation, I stuck my hand through the metal slats, offering it to Rampage to smell. The bull didn't move an inch. No anger. No interest. Not a damn thing.

He just didn't care anymore.

"He's the most dangerous one in here," I commented quietly.

"We already talked about his reputation," Jackson replied. "I know what I'm in for."

"I don't think you do."

"And why's that?"

"When you spend your whole damn life being hit, you start to expect it. And the anger... they just go hand in hand," I whispered. "And it just stays there and festers and fucking builds until you can't hold it in no more. One day you just... snap."

Jackson leaned against the gate next to me, scrutinizing Rampage—trying to see what I saw. He never would. He didn't know what that was like.

"He don't look it," he said. "He's got no fire in his eyes. Not like some of these other bulls."

"It's not the fire you want to look out for. If they've got fire, they've still got something to lose." I tried once more to make a connection with the bull but had no luck. "You want to look for the broken one... the one without a fire in him... the one with nothing behind his stare. That's the one that's got nothing fucking left to lose. That's the one that'll explode because the fallout doesn't fucking matter. Not anymore. There's nothing left to save."

Rampage had nothing left to save. It was in his face. I recognized that look. I'd seen it for years whenever I looked in the fucking mirror. Maybe less lately, but it was still there.

Jackson's silence was uncomfortable and the weight of his gaze on me was a heavy burden I didn't want. I could see from the look on his face that he was worried about me—that he was drawing a few too many conclusions. He didn't need to go down that road.

"I'm fine," I said quickly. "It's just a thing to know."

"Right." He cleared his throat and stepped away from the fencing. "We should go before I end up in the tabloids for breaking in to hang out with the fucking bulls."

"Yeah," I agreed. One more time, I tried to bridge the gap with Rampage. I held my hand in front of his snout and hoped for some kind of response. I wouldn't force it, but I couldn't help but be disappointed when the bull didn't budge.

I wanted more for him. Better. He didn't fucking deserve this.

"Do they sell the bulls here?" I asked as we made our way to the exit.

"What do you mean?" He stopped to stare at me, and I shrugged. "Are you wanting to buy a fucking bull?"

"Maybe," I admitted. I glanced back at Rampage, wishing I could take him home right now. "He deserves better than the fucking monster they say he is. Someone has to show him that."

In two quick steps, Jackson closed the distance between us, dragging my face to his in an intense kiss.

"You're too goddamn good, you know that?" he whispered.

"I think you're the first fucking person on the planet to believe that," I scoffed.

"But I'm right," he said. "And I love you all the more for it."

My throat clogged up with a wild wave of emotion. I merely nodded and kissed him again because fucking words.

CHAPTER 85

JACKSON

As expected, West was too wound up to sleep. It took some coaxing and reassurance, but eventually, the two of us lay in bed just talking in the dark. No more than five minutes into the conversation, West's fingers found their way to my pulse.

"Why the fuck are you asking my favorite color?" he demanded.

"I told you I'd come up with a list of talking points," I reminded him, grinning, even if he couldn't see me.

"What do you think is my favorite color?" West countered.

"Black ain't a color, baby," I said.

"It's a fucking color!"

"It's the absence of light."

"That's bullshit," he scoffed. I could damn near hear the eye roll in his voice. It only made me chuckle.

"That's Google science," I replied.

"Do you believe everything you read on Google?" He scooted closer, and his knees bumped into mine. I waited for him to pull away, but he didn't. The closer proximity made me happy. I'd never push it with him, but I couldn't deny that I enjoyed whatever physical contact I could get with West.

"You'd believe everything on Google if you had a fucking smartphone." *Yeah, I poked at the bear with that one.*

"I don't need a fucking computer in my pocket."

"You have a flip phone!" Him and his damn flip phone. "It's ancient. There's one in a goddamn museum somewhere. You need an upgrade."

"It works just fine. Next question, cowboy. You're not buying me a phone," West said. I was going to replace that fucking fossil of a phone. How I planned to do that was just the question.

"Tell me about your tattoos," I said instead.

"I have them."

"Fucker." *I both loved and hated his smart-ass answers.* "Why the angel wings?"

"Next question," he snapped.

"West." I frowned, wondering what the hell his resistance to the question was about. I wouldn't push it, but I wanted to know.

"When my mom died, she said she'd send an angel to protect me. Obviously, that didn't fucking work," he began with a sigh. "So, I got drunk and decided it'd be a great fucking idea to have my own wings. I'd protect myself since no one else was going to fucking do it."

My fucking heart.

"You shouldn't have been allowed to get a tattoo drunk." I decided to focus on the thing that wouldn't push his buttons—which also happened to be a safety fact. While I didn't have a tattoo, I'd gotten drunk once and tried. They turned my ass away real fast. Something about my inability to give legal consent or some bullshit.

"A guy I knew did tattoos for anyone under any circumstances as long as he got paid." *Well, that sounded shady as fuck.* "He did most of it while I was passed out drunk."

"That sounds unpleasant." It bothered me more than I wanted to admit that someone had done that to him. *How fucking unprofessional.* "Did you get rid of your first tattoos?"

His first tattoos had been two phrases on his inner wrists. But with his full sleeves, they weren't there anymore.

"No. The asshole covered them up without asking."

"That asshole," I said. Then, just to fuck with him, I added, "Want me to punch him?"

"Yeah, I fucking do," he replied. "But I don't have the fucking money to bail you out, so we'd get to see what you look like in orange."

"Don't work with my skin tone," I retorted, chuckling softly.

"Why doesn't that fucking surprise me." His fingers trailed up and down my arm slowly. Every pass was agonizing in its own wonderful way—burning a path along my skin that surged through every inch of my body. It never ceased to amaze me how the little things he did affected me. "Do I want to know what colors work with your skin tone?"

I grinned. The only reason I even knew this shit was because of Darla. She said it helped me look good for my interviews.

"Deep greens, reds, browns, coppers..." My voice trailed off. There was no way in hell I was saying the last one.

"Oranges?" West guessed.

"Not a chance in hell," I retorted. I opened my mouth to say something more, but West kissed me, effectively shutting me up. His tongue slid over mine, the taste of him making me moan.

Everything about him rushed to my head—a feeling I desperately wanted to crash into. *But I couldn't.* It was selfish. I had too much shit on my plate with the rodeo to be fully present if he spiraled because of something we did.

"West," I whispered, breaking away from him.

"I don't want anything else," he muttered against my mouth before I could say a word. "I just want to kiss you, cowboy."

I wouldn't argue with that. I traced the curve of his bottom lip with my thumb and felt his hold on my forearm tighten. Not to stop me but rather with anticipation. My fingers trailed over the coarseness of his beard and tangled in the curls at the back of his neck as I claimed his lips with mine.

I took my time—savored him.

Tasted him.

Shared his breath.

His fist wrung in the front of my shirt and dragged me closer, holding me against him.

"I..." West faltered, his breath fanning across my face as I waited silently. "Jackson, I..."

There was a part of me that had a strong feeling about the words he wanted to say—the words he probably didn't know how to say. Words I'd wait forever to hear from West and never once be bothered if I never heard them.

"I know, baby," I told him softly and kissed him once more. If he was ever ready to say them, I'd be ready to hear them. Until then, just laying in the dark kissing him and knowing some part of West loved me was more than enough.

CHAPTER 86

JACKSON

B ANGING ON THE DOOR pissed me off. I rolled away from West—*thank fuck it hadn't scared him awake*—and glanced at the clock. Six. It was six in the fucking morning.

"Jesus fucking Christ," West grumbled as it kept going. He dragged a pillow over his head. "Make them go the fuck away."

"I'm about to fucking kill someone," I retorted. I stormed to the door, disheveled as hell and not giving a fuck. When I threw open the door, the man standing on the other side gave me pause. He was well put together in a designer suit with perfectly trimmed hair and a perfectly shaved face. "What the fuck do you—"

"Have you seen the news this morning?" he demanded instead.

"No, considering I've been up all of five fucking seconds," I growled. "Who the fuck are—"

"*Gay cowboy brings his convicted murderer boyfriend to a family-friendly event.* And that's a direct title," he snapped. *Ah, fuck me. That wasn't the kind of press I wanted.* To make matters worse, the man held up a printout of an article, complete with a picture of me and West kissing after breaking into the bull-holding area. "My favorite part is where you broke into the animal pens to make out with said convicted murder."

"Fuck," I muttered. I hadn't even seen anyone else in there with us. "Who the hell are you?"

"Your new agent and the man who gets to clean up your mess." He offered me a hand. I took it, a little dazed by the idea of a new agent on such late notice. *No notice was more like it.* "Nathan Stark. It's nice to meet you."

"What the fuck happened to Amy?"

"I removed her as your representation effective immediately," Nathan said. "And then I came here to deal with this mess."

"Why you?" I asked, unable to help my curiosity.

"It's my firm that represents you, Mr. Myles," he told me. "When you look bad, it makes my firm look bad."

"Solid reasoning." I opened the door further to let him in. He wandered in while West sat up in bed, yawning. *Fuck, I wished I could've let him get more sleep.* That wasn't happening.

"And I assume this is the convicted murderer of a boyfriend?" Nathan sounded a little too amused as his gaze raked West over head to toe. *I didn't like that look on his face.* And I sure as fuck wasn't entertained by his antics.

"I'd watch the next fucking words out of your mouth, Stark," I warned. "You leave him alone, you hear me?"

"While I appreciate the bravado, I'm here to save your career, remember?"

"And I'll torch my career if you dare to treat him like crap."

"It's fine," West cut in before either of us could say anything. "Convicted murderer can hold his own."

"You weren't fucking convicted because it was self-defense," I reminded him. I fucking hated hearing him call himself that—especially not with everything I knew about the situation.

"Was it?" Nathan raised a brow. "That's good information to have. I can work with that."

"I was already in jail for armed robbery when it happened," West said.

"That makes it harder."

"Why don't you go get something to eat?" I suggested to West. Anything to get him the fuck out of here. He didn't need to be a part of this.

"That's a bad idea," Nathan interjected. "Him? Going out in public? The story is just spreading. I don't need more bullshit happening."

"I'll text you the house the girls rented," I told him, ignoring my agent. "And I'll let Darla know you're on your way."

"I can hold my own," West snapped.

"I know, but let me come up with a plan. Please?" I didn't want to put the pressure on him, but this was my fucking career. Even if I only had a few good years left, I didn't want them burnt to a crisp by gossip if I could avoid it.

Things were awkward as fuck with Nathan just standing there as West grabbed some clothes and disappeared into the bathroom. Admittedly, I wasn't looking any fucking better, considering I was in nothing but a pair of gray sweatpants. Not that I cared if I made him uncomfortable either.

Maybe I did a little, considering what he was about to deal with to help my career, but I was still pissed about how he talked to West.

I didn't say a fucking word as I fired off messages to Darla, giving her a brief update, talking her down from murder, and letting her know I was sending West her way to lay low.

When he came out of the bathroom, West's expression was unreadable. He grabbed my baseball hat off the dresser and started for the door. I went after him.

"It'll be okay," I promised.

"I'm sorry," West muttered. Curling a hand around the back of his head, I pulled him close enough to place a kiss on his forehead.

"It'll be okay, baby," I murmured against his skin. "Okay?"

"Yeah." He nodded as he backed up, pulling my hat down low over his face.

"Let me know you get there," I said. He made a sound but said nothing else. As I watched him leave, shoulders slouched and head dipping low, I sent another message to Darla because I had a feeling West wasn't planning to go to her house.

CHAPTER 87

WEST

The guilt wouldn't leave me alone.

Gay cowboy brings his convicted murderer boyfriend to a family-friendly event.

Fuck. That wasn't the kind of publicity Jackson needed. And that was my fault. That was the shit I brought to the table. No one gave two shits about anything I did now. This was fucking karma coming to bite me in the ass. This was what I got for letting myself get comfortable with Jackson. For wanting something more with him.

But he and I were done. That writing was as clear as day on the wall. I wasn't good for his career—his agent would remind him of that much.

I should've gone to Darla's house, but I didn't. No, I plopped my ass at the bar. The breakfast crowd started to wander in, and with the rodeo came alcohol. Nothing was off the table.

I stared down at the glass of whiskey, swirling the amber liquid. I hadn't drunk any—couldn't quite convince myself to do so. *It'd make dealing with this shit easier, so why the hell couldn't I do it?*

"It ain't worth breakin' your sobriety, darlin'." I frowned at the sound of Darla's voice. I only spared her a quick glance as she slid into the spot next to me. "Trust me."

"What the fuck do you know about it?"

"Honey, all my drinks are virgins." She leaned a little closer, and I pulled back before her shoulder could bump into mine. She grinned as she added, "Unlike me."

"Right," I scoffed. "You trying to tell me you party with a bunch of fucking cowboys and bunnies while sober?"

"For about two years, drinkin' was all I did," Darla said. "And I made some real bad choices, and a lot of those choices I don't remember. You ain't got a clue what it's like wakin' up, naked in a room with no idea what the hell they did to you and only hearin' the stories later."

"I wish I didn't remember," I muttered mostly to myself.

"*Oh,*" she let out softly. Something crossed her face—something that looked a lot like pity.

"You can fuck off with that whole feeling sorry for me bullshit," I snapped quickly. "I don't need it, and I don't fucking want it."

"Either way," she continued as she took away my glass. She damn near climbed over the fucking bar—ass in the air and all—to put it as far away from me as possible. I scowled but made no move to grab it. "One stupid headline ain't worth breakin' your sobriety. Jackson will figure it out, handsome. You ain't got a thing to worry about."

"He shouldn't have to fucking figure it out," I shot back. "I did this, and he doesn't deserve me ruining his life."

"Jackson's tough," she said. "The men around here can be real mean—not most of the time, but they can be—and he's always good about handlin' them with that big fuckin' smile on his face. This? This ain't nothin'."

"Yeah, but still..."

"You got a hell of an ego, y'know that?" She cocked a brow as I stared at her, scowling. "You think anyone can do anythin' to Jackson Myles' life without his permission? No fuckin', Sir. Look, if you were ruinin' Jackson's life, he'd have kicked you to the curb already. If you're here, it's because he wants you here. The rest is just bullshit and speed bumps, baby boy."

"Just bullshit and speed bumps," I repeated under my breath. "That's the story of my fucking life."

"Mine too." She gave me one of her too-big-for-her-face smiles. "But don't it make life more interestin'?"

I rolled my eyes.

"You and I have very different definitions of interesting."

"Then we just need to redefine your life to one that don't involve drinkin' alone in a bar when you should be making bacon with me. I make a mean omelet."

"What is it with all you damn people and trying to feed me?" I asked.

"It's a love language. So, you ready to stop mopin' about that article?"

"No." I didn't know how to let that fucking article go. It was only the start of many. I could feel that much in my bones. Jackson deserved better than my messy past.

"Did you really kill someone?" Darla asked, leaning as close as she could without touching me. *Thank fuck.* I stared hard at her as I contemplated what to tell her.

"Yeah." I went with the simple one and offered nothing more.

"How do you like your bacon?" *This girl needed to come with a whiplash warning.*

"I don't," I said.

"What do you mean you don't?" she exclaimed.

"I don't like bacon."

"Who the fuck doesn't like bacon?"

"Me."

"Obviously," she retorted as she slid off the stool. "All right, get on up, ponyboy."

"Ponyboy?" *What the fuck was this shit?*

"You have a way with the ponies, I hear," she interrupted. "Now, get on up, I'm goin' to make you a damn good breakfast and tell you about the gator incident in Louisiana two years ago. It was not inflatable, by the way."

"What?" I made a face. *What the hell was this girl going on about?* The only thing I did understand was why Jackson liked her. They shared the same fire. That single thing about her made it easier to trail after her and give in to the idea of her feeding me.

CHAPTER 88

JACKSON

WE DECIDED TO ROLL with it and retaliate by feeding specific information about West's history to news outlets. *Of course, I slowed the fucking process by demanding it all be run by West first.* Nathan was ready to fire away without hesitation—try to get ahead of it all as much as possible. But me? I wasn't about to do anything West didn't want, even if it meant torching my career.

West didn't hesitate. Maybe he felt guilty or maybe he trusted me to make sure it was handled properly. I wanted to say it was the latter, but in my heart, I knew it was because he felt guilty.

And Nathan had a good point. We either released the correct information or the press could have a field day making up whatever shit they had with their half-assed information.

West wasn't a convicted murderer and that wildfire I wanted to put out quickly. He'd been through enough. I worried about what would happen to him when he headed back to Double Arrow while I continued on the circuit. The least I could do was make sure some of this shit was handled right.

All of that filled my fucking day until I was left standing and waiting for the bull riding event to start.

"You're in fringe," West commented. I refused to look at the fucker. He was judging me. "I mean I... I watched you on TV but shit... it's so much fucking worse in person. And assless chaps."

"I look fucking good like this, thank you very much," I retorted under my breath. "Besides, we're all wearing them."

"I know you think that makes it better, but it doesn't," he replied. I glanced at him. The far-off expression on his face as he stood with his arms over his chest tight bothered me.

"You good?" I asked quietly. I knew the rodeo was loud and full of cluttered noises. I didn't understand much about what got to him, but I knew those two things did.

"Yeah," he replied. "I just... you'll be safe, right?"

"I always am."

"Okay," he whispered. I watched how he nodded slowly and could see the wheels in his head turning. What I wouldn't have given to know what the hell he was thinking. "I'm going to find the girls."

"Hey." I stepped in front of him when he tried to leave, speaking quietly because we were surrounded by people and prying eyes. "I'm coming back to you, baby."

"You better, cowboy." His lips quirked slightly at the corner for the briefest moment. *I would've killed for a real smile out of him in that moment.*

I watched him head toward the bleachers for as long as I could before drawing in a deep breath. I had to get my head in the game. Burger may have been stupidly named, but he was a damn fierce bull.

And me? I was aiming to impress tonight.

CHAPTER 89

WEST

Watching a bunch of guys get flung around like fucking rag dolls and knowing Jackson's turn was coming did nothing for my nerves. I knew what he did for a living. Fuck, I'd watched him on TV. But nothing could prepare me for watching it live and in person. My heart was in my throat and Jackson hadn't even gone yet. Watching every other idiot get thrown around only made the anticipation of seeing Jackson do the same was anxiety-inducing. My leg bounced violently in the bleachers, getting worse with every rider.

"Calm down, ponyboy," Darla said from behind me. "Your man's damn good at what he does."

"Why do some of them wear helmets?" I asked her. More than half of them were, but a few wore only their cowboy hats.

"Anyone born after ninety-four has to," she replied. "Anyone born before can pick."

"He doesn't wear a fucking helmet does he?" *Because it was a very Jackson thing to do to not wear it and choose that stupid hat.* I never actually hated his love for that hat—until now.

"Jackson?" She made a sound of frustration. At least I wasn't the only one who felt this way. "I fuckin' wish he would."

"Does he wear any protective gear?" With the way these fucking idiots were getting tossed around, it felt like protective gear should've been mandated. Fuck, I'd have Jackson wrapped in fucking bubble wrap if it'd help.

"All of them wear ballistic vests," Willa said, joining in the conversation. *Fucking hell. Ballistic vests?* Why the fuck did Jackson think this was a great fucking career? "They help protect their vital organs."

"Fucking lovely," I muttered.

"Better than the alternative," she quipped. "I've seen lots of pictures."

"Why the fuck would you look that shit up?" I demanded as I glanced at her. She sat on my right in the same spread-out position they had been the day before. She was completely unfazed by the sentence she'd said. Who the hell would want to look at pictures of cowboys being trampled by bulls?

"I'm going to school for nursing." *Well, that explained that.*

"What do all the numbers mean?" I asked because again, I didn't understand shit about what was going on around us.

"Like how they're scored?" Darla hummed. "You really don't know a damn thing about bull ridin', do you?"

"I know there's a bull and there's a rider," I snapped with a little too much sarcasm.

"Jackson told me you were a sassy one," she commented, earning a laugh from the other girls. "See those two over there? They're the judges. They judge things kind of like you do."

I held my tongue before I lost it on her, my anxiety almost getting the better of me.

"The two of them individually judge each rider based on a few things: how well he controls the bull, how well he stays centered, and if he throws a bit of style in there, y'know?" *No, I didn't fucking know.* How the hell did a cowboy have fucking style while being thrown around like a goddamn toy? "And then there's the eight-second rule."

"The eight-second rule?"

"Their big goal is to stay on that big boy for eight whole seconds—one hand free," she told me. *Jesus fucking Christ. That sounded impossible.* "They train real hard to make that eight seconds, y'know? Still, it's real fuckin' hard to do with how rough those bulls are."

"Only maybe forty percent of riders hit the eight-second mark," Sutton chimed in.

"Then what's the fucking point?" I asked. All the girls responded at once in an overwhelming way.

"To be able to say they did it."

"The adrenaline rush."

"It's hot."

That last one was Birdie—to no one's surprise.

I returned my attention to the event and wondered what Jackson's reason was. I knew that for him he was meant to be a bull rider but why? Maybe I'd add that to the actual list of late-night conversation topics he kept just in case. *The little things Jackson did still floored me.*

By the time it was Jackson's turn, the atmosphere was electric. Four riders had made a qualified ride—with pretty damn good scores too. While I was still a little lost on shit, I was catching on to a few things here and there. The only thing I did know was that Jackson would have to do real fucking good to win the night.

My whole body was a livewire as I watched him climb in the chute and mount the bull. I could hear his laughter as the bull reacted, practically slamming him into the metal.

"Fuck," I let out. He hadn't even started yet and I was drowning in fear for him. Darla hopped over the seat to sit next to me.

"May I?" She held out her hand. I eyed it warily for a moment before accepting. When I took it, she said, "First time is always the worst—for you, not him. Jackson's fuckin' magic. You'll see."

I hoped to hell she was right.

I lost sight of everything as the chute opened and the bull lurched out, bucking violently. Jackson held on with one hand in the air.

One.

Two.

The way he leaned and swayed with every abrupt twist of the bull was fucking mesmerizing.

Three.

Four.

My heart lodged in my throat as I held my breath.

Five.

Six.
Jesus fucking Christ. Time never moved so fucking slow in my life.
Seven.
Eight.
The crowd went wild, and I cringed at the sheer volume of the noise. Nonetheless, I was on my feet with everyone else, clapping hard.

Jackson threw himself off the bull with a kind of grace that shouldn't have been possible. Two pickup men were right there to herd the bull in a different direction while Jackson lived up the excitement.

When his gaze zeroed in on me, he winked. And me? I fucking smiled because I couldn't help it.

Jackson was magnetic. The look on his face and the high that followed was damn near addictive. I stood on the sidelines as he ate up the compliments and talked with everyone. I was good where I was at. I didn't need anything else, and I sure as fuck didn't want to take away from his moment.

I caught the way he occasionally glanced in my direction. Each time, I offered a tight smile and did my best to look reassuring. I was fucking overwhelmed. Words couldn't begin to express how fucking proud of him I was, but I wanted out of the goddamn rodeo. Too many people. Too much noise. *Just too much everything.*

When another person tried to talk to him, he dismissed them, striding right on by with a quick response and making his way toward me. I pushed away from the fence and opened my mouth to say something. Before I could, he wrapped an arm around my waist and kissed me hard. It was short-lived as he smiled all over again.

"Let's get the fuck out of here," Jackson whispered.

CHAPTER 90

WEST

WE WERE ABOUT TWO feet in the door before his mouth was on mine. His adrenaline and excitement from the night bled through me. His tongue swept over mine as I used the front of his shirt to drag him close.

"Are you sure?" he asked, his mouth barely leaving mine. I pulled him back in for another kiss and enjoyed the way he groaned. Kissing him with that damn hat was a feat. *Fuck the damn cowboy hat rules the girls insisted I learned.* I knocked it off his head and tangled my fingers in his hair. "West... I ain't going to be around tomorrow..."

I understood his concern—I did—but I didn't want him second-guessing me. *I hated how that was even a thing.*

"Yeah, I'm fucking sure, cowboy," I said and dragged his shirt over his head. I ran my hands over his sides and muscular back with a newfound appreciation as he kissed me once more.

"For the record, I ain't prepared for this," Jackson told me as I walked him back toward the bed. His knees hit the bed, and he fell back, catching himself on his elbows. Fuck, he looked good like that—hair a mess, chest heaving, and the hunger in his eyes matching mine. My cock strained behind my zipper.

"Good thing I am," I replied while grabbing lube out of my bag. *Yeah, I'd packed it in case.* Honestly, I didn't know what the fuck I was doing anymore. My body was in uncontrolled chaos. Some days the idea of doing anything with Jackson had me hard and damn near close to coming. On other days, it made me want to hop on a horse and run away. I was just stuck for the ride.

But I was trying like fuck to embrace the ride. I wasn't good at it, but sometimes I could make it work in my favor.

"Pants off, cowboy," I ordered. As I pulled my shirt over my head, Jackson undid his belt and opened his pants. Watching him strip naked had my cock aching. I wanted him so fucking badly, and I wanted not to fuck this up. I didn't want to be the reason he couldn't focus on his second ride.

I focused on him as I got undressed—on the miles of muscles he'd molded for himself. On the slight spattering of golden chest hair he had. On just how goddamn blue his eyes were. *Jesus fuck, he was handsome.*

"What're you thinking over there, baby?" Jackson asked gruffly.

"A lot of things," I told him honestly. There were a lot of things tumbling through my head, but I couldn't pinpoint a single one of them if I tried.

Instead, I crawled over him as I gently pushed him back on the bed. I kissed the curve of his hip and swept my tongue over his abs. He tasted like sweat and smelled like leather. The combination was oddly intoxicating. The rough pads of his fingers trailed over my arms, sending a shiver down my spine.

I kissed my way up his neck and scraped my teeth over his ear lobe, enjoying the groan he let out. His fist tangled in my hair, and he dragged my mouth to his, his tongue driving through my lips—hungry and demanding.

"*Fuck*," I rasped when his hand wrapped around my dick and his. My hips thrust forward, driven by a desperate need for more. Root to tip, he stroked both of us in long passes. Pre-cum leaked from his cock and mine, sticking to our stomachs. My nerves were a livewire and sparked with his every touch. I admitted breathlessly, "I want you."

"Your stables, your rules, West," Jackson reminded me, his tone gentle. With anyone else, that phrase would've been condescending. *But with him?* It weirdly grounded me—gave me a sense of control that I needed. "Whatever you want, baby, just tell me."

I kissed him hard as I swiped the lube off the nightstand. Deep down, I was terrified that I'd lose it again if I waited too long—if I drew it out.

Before I could do anything, he took it from me. I shuddered at the cool sensation of his hand as he slathered my dick. My head dropped to his shoulder with a loud moan.

"You keep doing that..." I gasped out, unable to finish the sentence. The small chuckle he let out as he got comfortable underneath me shot straight to my balls. *God, I loved that sound.* "You're going to be the end of me, cowboy."

"I sure as hell hope not," Jackson muttered. "Not with all the damn horses you've brought home."

His legs hitched around my hips as I lined myself up and slowly pressed the head of my cock past that tight ring of muscles. His groan matched mine for very different reasons. I rocked into him, pulling in and out almost completely each time as I pushed a little deeper with each thrust. I took my time as the sensations washed over me. That familiar tug—dark and threatening—ebbed its way through my brain.

"I'm okay," I let out, my voice strained. *Fuck, he was so goddamn tight.* It was so much. Too much. "I'm okay."

Lifting off the pillow, he kissed me. His teeth dragged lightly over my lower lip, and his tongue danced with mine. *His taste, his scent, his touch.* He was overwhelmingly intoxicating without doing a damn thing.

"God, you feel so goddamn good," Jackson whispered.

"Keep talking, cowboy," I practically begged. I needed his voice to ground me.

"Do you want to stop?" he asked.

"No." I shook my head. "Just... keep talking. I want this... I just..."

I just needed help keeping the demons at bay—needed something to cling to that wasn't in my own head.

"Keep going, baby," he ordered, gentle but firm. His fingers wove through my hair and tightened slightly. *Just enough to keep my gaze on his.* "Eyes on me, West."

I did as he told me, letting him be the clarity I needed to hold my headspace. Adjusting my weight, I braced myself and gripped his hip as I picked up my pace.

"That's it, baby," Jackson whispered. "A little faster for me."

I drove into him faster like he asked while he lifted his legs a little higher on my sides. The sound he made was a goddamn aphrodisiac, going straight to my balls.

My gaze flicked down between our bodies as he fisted his cock. I watched with rapt fascination as he stroked himself. *Fuck me, why was that so hot?*

"Do you like watching me stroke myself while you fuck me, West?" he asked. I caught his mouth in a heated kiss, using that to verbalize what I couldn't. "Faster, baby."

I did so eagerly, needing some kind of release. The heat in my spine was fucking unbearable, molten hot and threatening to ruin me. His hand matched my pace until he was coming in thick spurts across his stomach and mine.

"Fuck, cowboy, I'm..." I squeezed my eyes shut as my release became too much to cling onto.

"Don't close your eyes, West," he said quickly. "Eyes on me when you come."

That blue gaze became my anchor as I tipped over the ledge. My muscles seized up painfully tight as I drove deep inside him, coming hard. A jumbled mess of swears fell off my lips as the intense waves crashed over me endlessly until I was spent and damn near shaking.

But I was okay.

I was more than okay.

I mostly felt good—a little disoriented but good.

I was okay.

"You did so goddamn good, baby," Jackson praised, his lips brushing against mine in simple kisses. "You good?"

I nodded, consumed and drowning in the intense emotions washing over me. My forehead tipped to his as I breathed him in and tried to find the words to tell him how I felt. But every time I opened my mouth, nothing came out.

Those were words I didn't know how to say.

CHAPTER 91

JACKSON

I WAS A BUNDLE of nerves. The prospect of taking on Rampage weaseled its way through me. *This was really fucking happening.* Suddenly all the words I'd said about him just being a bull didn't feel quite as reassuring.

I stood apart from the others, fussing with the brim of my hat. *My lucky hat.* I also had on my lucky socks that no one was allowed to know about—they were teal with cows on them. Sure, it was superstitious but I always did better with both. That hat was the only reason I refused to wear a helmet—couldn't wear both at the same time.

"You've got this, cowboy," West said softly as he came up behind me, catching me by surprise. I expected him to be in the bleachers by now. Maybe it was for the better. His handsome face was a comforting sight.

"I fucking better," I muttered.

"You do."

"You sure?"

"You're Jackson fucking Myles." His lips quirked slightly at the corner. *Why did I adore that so much?* "I'm fucking certain that if we racked up the damage you've fucking done over the years and put it alongside his, you'd win every fucking time."

That managed to pull a laugh out of me, and I shook my head.

"All you have to do is go out there and show them how it's fucking done," he continued. The confidence in his expression bled through me. *If West thought I could do this, then I could fucking do this.* "Maybe shout fuck retirement or some shit after eight seconds is up."

"Jesus fuck," I replied. "I'm not doing that."

"Eh, I would. No one's asking you if you want to retire after tonight."

"No, they ain't." *After I rode Rampage for eight fucking seconds, no one would be asking about my fucking retirement.* I dropped my hat back on my head. "Okay. I can do this."

"You can do this," West agreed. "Just know, I'm over here doing the harder shit by sitting with Birdie all goddamn night."

I fucking lost it, turning away to try to compose myself. Birdie was a fucking character, and I could only imagine how she was around West—Mr. Tall, Dark, and Toss Me Around Daddy. Just the thought of that had me laughing all over again. *Maybe the nerves were getting to me.*

"What the fuck are you laughing at over there?" West demanded.

"The fact that she called you Mr. Tall, Dark, and Toss Me Around Daddy the first time she saw you," I said.

"What the actual fuck?" he demanded. "What the fuck is wrong with her?"

"It's the hairspray."

The announcer said something that I didn't catch, but I knew it meant the event was about to start. I closed the distance between us and kissed him briefly. And then again for good luck. I didn't touch him, hug him, or anything else. His body language was defensive, and I'd take only the kiss he let me have. "I'll see you soon."

"Damn straight you will," West replied gruffly. "Give them hell, cowboy."

I would.

I watched him disappear, hating the hole his absence left behind. But I couldn't dwell on that. I had a bull to conquer.

"I've got this," I whispered to myself as I made my way over to join the other riders.

CHAPTER 92

WEST

THE OFFICIAL DECISION WAS that bull riding was boring unless it was Jackson riding. I didn't give a flying fuck about any of the other riders. The ideal event would be just watching Jackson and then I'd get to fucking leave. *And I wasn't about to start in on the fucking rodeo clown they brought out in between shit to entertain people.* I had opinions on that too.

My nerves were shot from the volume, the clutter of noises, and the high energy in the air. I wasn't cut out for places like this.

All of that faded away when it was Jackson's turn. Unlike every other bull, Rampage was utterly still in the chute. Even when they tried to provoke him a little, he remained unmoving. My heart raced in my chest, and I inched forward in my seat. *No one would understand just why that bull was so fucking dangerous.*

Yet again, Darla hopped over the seat to sit beside me. When she offered me her hand, I took it without thinking.

"Our boy's got this," she whispered.

"Fuck yeah, he does," I murmured. I just had to keep reminding myself of that. Jackson was a damn good bull rider. Always had been. He was made for this.

When he nodded that he was good and ready, the chute opened. Rampage flew out in a wild frenzy.

One...

Jackson's hat flew off as Rampage twisted and bucked violently.

Two...

"C'mon... c'mon..." Darla damn near chanted next to me. Her hand tightened in mine or maybe it was the other way around.

Three...

Of all the goddamn bulls I'd watched, none moved like Rampage.

Four...

I saw Jackson's hand slip. It was a fraction of a second but it happened.

Five...

He flew off the bull's back and crashed into the ground—his head snapping off the dirt.

Six...

My heart stopped.

Seven...

Jackson never stood a chance as Rampage trampled right over him.

Eight...

CHAPTER 93

WEST

You could hear a pin drop as pickup men managed to push Rampage away from Jackson.

He wasn't moving.

He just lay there.

Not. Moving.

The breath shot right out of my lungs as the temperature in the arena skyrocketed.

Jackson...

I lost sight of him in the rush of people helping him. I was only vaguely aware of how the rodeo attempted to distract everyone at the other end, but I couldn't look away.

He needed to move.

He couldn't die. This couldn't be it. I didn't know what I'd do if something happened to Jackson.

"C'mon, West." Darla's voice was fuzzy in my ears. Fingers touched my cheek, and I flinched—reality crashing back into me.

"What?" I let out. I blinked, only vaguely aware that Jackson was gone. They'd taken him away, and I'd missed the whole thing. "I don't... what?"

"C'mon, baby boy," she whispered and took my hand. "We need to get you to the hospital."

I nodded because it was the only thing I could fucking manage to do.

My boots were rooted to the sidewalk. I stared up at the hospital sign, but I couldn't bring myself to fucking move. *I couldn't go in there.*

The last time I'd been in a hospital it was a fucking nightmare. The grating of handcuffs on my wrist. The inability to get comfortable. The lack of pain medication. The food that made me sick. The doctor's insistence that touching me *that* way was for my own fucking good.

The bottom of my stomach dropped.

I couldn't fucking go in there.

But Jackson was in there.

Jackson was in there, and I was out here.

I had to make it in there.

Panic clawed at my chest, making it difficult to breathe as I tried to talk myself into it—to tell myself I'd be okay. My brain stalled. The dull screams in the back of my head took over everything, making it fucking impossible to think. I couldn't get anything to work how it was supposed to.

"West?" Darla stood a few feet away, keeping the automatic door open.

"I can't." I barely managed to get the words out.

"What?"

"I can't," I said again, shaking my head. I ignored how she called after me as I escaped—ran like a fucking dog with my tail between my legs.

CHAPTER 94

WEST

I ENDED UP AT a liquor store down the street. If I was going to get my ass inside that hospital, I needed to silence the screaming in my head. *Pathetic.* I knew just how pathetic I was, but I didn't know what else to do.

Sagging against the alley wall behind the store, I uncapped the cheap bottle of vodka and forced myself to drink several gulps. The familiar burn trailed down my throat, and I squeezed my eyes shut against the rising guilt.

I had to walk my ass into that hospital.
I just couldn't do it alone. Jackson deserved better than this.
Better than me.

It took me almost an hour along with half a small bottle of vodka to get my ass inside the hospital. By the time I did, the waiting room was full of cowboys and bunnies along with other random people—probably people who knew Jackson. The devastated mood seeped through my numbed skin as I dropped into an open chair next to Darla.

"Liquid courage?" she asked. From the tone of her voice, she already knew. She scoffed, "Good God."

"Don't pretend like you know a goddamn thing about me, princess," I snapped. The sheer number of people in such a small space did nothing to help my mood. *Why the fuck was the waiting area so goddamn small?*

"No, I don't," Darla retorted. "But I do know that Jackson deserves better than you. He deserves someone who's goin' to show up, not drink himself into a fuckin' hole."

"That makes two of us," I muttered under my breath. She made another sound that grated on my nerves, but I said nothing else.

"In case you fuckin' cared, there's no update," she said. "His mama is on her way out, but it'll take a few hours. His agent says she has power of attorney."

Power of attorney.

Fucking hell. That didn't sound good in any way. My eyes burned, and I quickly shut them, refusing to cry in a room full of fucking strangers. I didn't want Mrs. Myles to show up. I didn't want to talk about power of attorney or healthcare options.

I wanted Jackson to walk out with that cocky fucking grin of his and tell me it'd all be okay.

I needed Jackson to be okay.

CHAPTER 95

WEST

When Mrs. Myles had shown up with Mickey, she all but dragged my ass out of that waiting room. She saved me from drowning in the overstimulation of everything and everyone. I was hanging on by a thread and grateful when his agent pushed for us to have a private waiting area.

And when Jackson was finally out of the OR and put in the ICU, Mrs. Myles made sure I was the first one in there to see him. *Because I mattered more to Jackson than anyone else there.* I almost broke down right fucking there when she said it—the emotions and everything getting to me.

I thought waiting to find out if he was okay was the worst it'd get, but I was fucking wrong. *Seeing Jackson was.*

He had fractured ribs and broken ribs, a punctured lung, a broken skull, a broken nose, a dislocated shoulder, several broken fingers, his left hip had been shattered, his left femur had broken in four places, his left knee cap had been shattered, and his left shin was broken in two places. He was bandages and wires, bruises and cuts everywhere.

The doctors had done everything they could to stabilize him and wait until he woke up—*if he woke up*—to move forward with an orthopedic specialist. His agent had already tracked down the best one in the country to take care of him. And above all, there was a good chance he'd never walk again.

Days passed in a blurry haze of alcohol and stress. Or maybe stress and alcohol. I couldn't tell. I was a fucking mess. We were stuck in an infinite cycle of waiting for Jackson to wake up. Whenever Mrs. Myles spent time in his room, I disappeared to drink. It was the only way I could cope with being trapped in the hospital and with knowing there was a chance Jackson might never wake up.

Sometimes I dropped in and out of a fitful nap as I waited by Jackson's bedside for something—anything—to happen. Every fucking beep of his machines chipped away at me, breaking down my sanity until I couldn't think straight. A never-ending headache throbbed in my temple. Nothing touched the pain. I was fucking stuck with it.

I was drowning with no hope of finding shore.

On the fourth day, fingers brushed through my hair as I rested my forehead on the bed. My head snapped up as I blinked through the bleariness.

He was awake.

The instant flood of relief knocked the wind out of me. I took his hand in mine, brushing his knuckles across my lips as gently as possible.

"Marry me," Jackson rasped. The world came to a screeching halt around us.

What the fuck did he just say?

"What..."

"Marry me," he repeated, his voice a gruff mess.

He couldn't mean that. I searched his face for some kind of doubt—some kind of indication that he wasn't serious.

And as I stared at him, some version of a future together played in my head—one full of panic attacks, relapses, flashbacks, and all the demons I didn't know how to fucking conquer. I could see the hopeful look in those blue eyes, but I couldn't meet his expectations. I wasn't the man he thought I was.

Fuck, I wanted to be, but I wasn't.

"I can't," I whispered. The flash of pain on his face fucking broke me, and I swallowed back the visceral desire to just say yes and give him whatever the hell he wanted. I couldn't. *Not like this.*

His fingers pressed against my lips before I could say more, effectively ending the conversation, and I watched as his eyes drifted shut all over again.

Marry me.

Marry me.

Marry me.

The words played on repeat in my head as I numbly wandered the halls alone. Each word was a stab to the heart.

I wanted to say yes to him. Why? I didn't have a fucking clue. I didn't have anything to offer him. Anything good to bring to the relationship. My demons were too much. How many times did I have to hurt him before I realized that Jackson was better off without me?

I sank down in a chair, my knees giving out. And as I sat there, I struggled to get out my wallet. Tucked away in the back was the same picture I'd kept in there for seventeen years. It was old and worn, thoroughly aged by time.

That picture I'd taken with me the night I ran away had become a lifeline—a reminder of better times. *A reminder of a world where maybe Jackson and I had a future.*

I didn't recognize the kid in the picture. Deep down I knew it was me, but I was so far removed from that kid that he could've been a stranger. But that big smile he wore as he slung an arm around Jackson's shoulders? I wanted to feel that kind of happiness again.

I wanted that carefree feeling. I was so fucking exhausted. The weight of everything was too much, and I didn't know what the fuck I was supposed to do.

Had it always been this heavy?

A sob ripped through me, bursting through every attempt I had to hold it back. I pinched the bridge of my nose as I broke down—ugly and uncontrolled.

I didn't want this life anymore.

"May I sit down?" A woman's voice barely cut through the haze I battled. She didn't wait for an answer as she eased into the chair next to me.

Fuck. I wiped my cheeks and tried to get rid of the tears, but they just kept coming.

"I'm Dr. Hawthorne," she said. "I'm the head psychiatrist at the hospital."

I made some kind of sound. It was about all I had in me to give her. I couldn't hold a fucking conversation if I tried.

"Would you like to come to my office and talk?" she asked softly.

For the first time in my life, I considered that question. I stood at a crossroads with my life. One path was full of my demons and darkness—all the bad things I couldn't conquer alone. The other path led to a life with Jackson. A life where all my bad shit didn't follow us around and ruin everything. Where I could smile and feel happiness again. A life I wanted so fucking bad that it hurt. One I couldn't have if I didn't do something different.

My whole world was burning down around me—a raging inferno I had no control of. I had a choice: get the help I desperately needed or stay bound by my past and let it destroy me. To a normal person, the right answer was obvious. But to me the flames offered consistency. I knew them. I knew what to expect. I had no idea what would happen if I accepted help.

The uncertainty felt worse. But nothing would change if I didn't change it.

"Yeah," I whispered, choking on the word. "Yeah, I do."

CHAPTER 96

JACKSON

I LOST ALL SENSE of time. Morphine was a damn good friend, but fucking hell, I was so far gone—which was probably a real good thing, all things considered. Try as I might, there were so many pieces missing.

I remembered climbing on Rampage's back.

I remembered the bell and the chute opening.

And then I remember thinking I was dead the split moment before his hooves came down on me.

I remembered asking West to marry me and him turning me down. Should've seen that coming.

Everything else was a blurred mix filled with doctors, nurses, my mom, Mickey, the understanding I probably wouldn't ever walk again, and the *Friends* theme song.

"You better not be watching that goddamn show again," I growled, my throat uncomfortably dry. *Fucking Mickey*. I didn't even have to open my eyes to know the old man was watching reruns on my hospital room TV.

"It ain't like they got anythin' better to watch," he retorted.

"It's a stupid fucking show," I snapped. "Turn it off."

I blinked slowly, trying to bring everything into focus. My mom motioned to the TV before sitting on the bed next to me. She did so slowly, doing her best to not move the bed. It didn't fucking matter. I couldn't feel a goddamn thing. Not even my teeth.

"How are you, baby boy?" she asked. Sitting this close, she swam in my vision. *Fuck, these drugs were so strong.*

"Where's West?" I replied instead. My question was greeted by utter silence. Fuck. That was so goddamn telling.

"Baby boy," Mom began carefully.

"Don't." I shook my head. My heart was already shattering. I didn't want to hear her say the words. It wouldn't do me any fucking good.

"No one has seen West in four days," she continued anyway.

I shut my eyes against the burn and ignored her attempts to comfort me. While deep down I knew West never intended to stay—was never mine to keep—a part of me had hoped I'd change that for him.

What a fucking idiot I was.

CHAPTER 97

JACKSON

eight months later

"Jackson. Door!"

I rolled my eyes and ignored my mom. There was no way in hell I was answering the goddamn door. I didn't want to see a single fucking person.

"Jackson—"

"Tell 'em to fuck off!" I practically shouted back. I ignored whatever the hell else she said. She was all about being polite whenever I had visitors. I was not. I was so far down a hole that I didn't want anyone to see me.

Not in this fucking chair.

Rampage had ruined me. I'd been a fucking idiot to think I could ride that bull and last eight seconds.

Instead, I probably wouldn't walk again. My hip had been replaced, and my left leg was all metal plates and screws. They wanted me to do physical therapy and work toward some semblance of walking again, but I didn't fucking want to. Everything hurt, and pain meds did jack shit to fix the problem.

My mom came into the room and shut off the news, eliciting a scowl from me.

"There's someone here to talk to you, Jackson," she said.

"Tell them to fuck off," I snapped.

"You need to talk to him."

"Unless it's Peter or Mickey, I don't want to fucking talk to anyone." I spent months in and out of the hospital between surgeries and recovery. At first, the visitors were in excess—riders, bunnies, my agent, and other random people I knew. But I didn't want to see any of them. The only person I wanted to see had left me. With the way my mood grew increasingly angrier, my list of guests dwindled. *Not that I fucking blamed them.*

"Jackson Ford Myles." She put her hands on her hips as she leveled me with a menacing glare. *Except I didn't give a fuck anymore.* "I raised you better than that."

"There's not a damn person—"

"Either you go to the kitchen to talk to him, or I'll bring him out here," my mom threatened. She'd fucking do it too.

"Fine," I muttered.

"Do you need help—"

"I can fucking do it," I interrupted angrily. "I don't need my fucking mother wheeling me around my own goddamn house."

With Peter's help, my entire living room had been pushed around to make sure a wheelchair could be navigated through. The couch had been outfitted for me to sleep on—much to my mother's dismay, but I refused to sleep in the only downstairs room I had. I refused to take over West's room. *I refused to fucking open the door to his goddamn room.*

Pissed that I even had to do this shit, I wheeled into the kitchen, making sure to take the turn slow. The whole propped-up leg thing was fucking annoying.

Standing in my kitchen was Charles Hart, West's attorney. *Fuck.* He gave me a well-practiced smile when he saw me.

"You're looking good, Mr. Myles," he greeted.

"Bullshit," I retorted. I looked like fucking crap. I'd stopped shaving, I hadn't washed my hair in God knew how long, and I knew I looked tired as fuck. *Because I was.* "What do you want?"

"May I sit?" He gestured to the table, and I nodded. Putting his briefcase in front of him, he sat down. "I'm here on behalf of Mr. McNamara to settle the issue of Double Arrow Ranch."

Good. *Then I could be done with West and every painful fucking feeling his name incited.*

"Now, before you say anything," Hart continued, "I have been made aware of the agreement you and your foreman, Mickey Hughes, had about Mr. McNamara's requirement to work the ranch."

"Whether it's by sale or by forfeiture, the land is fucking mine," I said. "I don't fucking care how I get it. I just want to be done with this shit so I can take care of my ranch."

Or what was left of it. I wasn't sure I had a business left anymore, but what did it fucking matter? I couldn't ride. I couldn't walk. Why not lose my fucking business too?

"Three months ago, Mr. McNamara appealed his father's will and the conditions put on his inheritance." *He what?* Hart opened his briefcase and began laying out papers on the table. "After taking into consideration Harrison McNamara's behavior, the judge granted his appeal and awarded Mr. McNamara his full inheritance of Double Arrow Ranch.

"With that being said, Mr. McNamara has signed over the entirety of his half of Double Arrow Ranch to you. This document here covers the transfer of land while this one covers the transfer of the business and all its assets."

"He could've just waited the fucking contract out and we would be exactly where we are now," I said.

"He didn't do it for you," Hart replied. "He did it for himself."

Why the fuck did he do that?

"And then there's the matter of Bailey, Thunder Jack, and Betty," Hart continued. *Right, the fucking horses.* He set out another piece of paper and an envelope. "While Mr. McNamara is uncertain of when he can retain the rights to take care of his three horses, he has hired me to be the middleman of their care. This is a contract stating the horses will continue to be cared for at Double Arrow Ranch but at the expense of Mr. McNamara. There's a check in the envelope to cover the expenses of each horse going back to eight months ago and extending through the rest of the year. At the start of the year, I'll make sure you receive another check. If any emergencies do arise, Mr. McNamara will cover those costs as well. You just have to—"

"Contact his attorney?" I finished bitterly. "And what if I don't want to take care of the fucking horses?"

"We request one month for Mr. McNamara to find alternative boarding and care for the three of them," he replied. Placing a pen on the contract, he pushed it in my direction.

Who the fuck was I kidding? Of course, I'd take care of the goddamn horses. I grabbed the paper and signed it. At this rate, I'd never be rid of West.

"Is that all?" I demanded.

"Mr. McNamara asked that I give you this." He set another envelope on the table. I recognized West's handwriting on the front. "It's a letter explaining why he left."

"I don't fucking want it." I didn't need to know that shit. I'd spent too many nights trying to figure out why he'd left, but I no longer cared. He was gone and that was that.

"He is aware that you may feel that way," he said. Closing his briefcase, he stood. "And now, I'm off to track down a firefighter captain in Merillville for him. Thank you for allowing me the chance to give you everything."

"Not like I had a fucking choice," I grumbled. I remained in my spot as he made his exit.

"For what it's worth, Mr. Myles," Hart began, pausing in the doorway, "I'd read the letter if I were you."

"Yeah, well you're not me, are you?" I snapped.

"No, I suppose not, but it might just give you the answers you're looking for."

Hours later, I sat on my porch with that stupid letter in my lap. West's handwriting taunted me. One-half of me wanted to open it. The other half of me wanted to feed it to my bull and call it a fucking day.

Yeah, I'd bought the fucking bull that trampled me.

When Mickey had told me in the hospital that they planned to put him down, something inside me broke. He was just a bull turned into a monster for entertainment. He didn't deserve to die for that. It took a little convincing but Mickey managed to secure the sale for me.

Bringing Rampage back here hadn't gone over as well as I'd hoped. None of my guys wanted the bull around, so I had Mickey put the bull in my yard. Was it my best fucking plan? No.

But the bull was so goddamn happy for grass and space to run that he quickly became the easiest animal to care for. Peter spent a lot of time with Rampage. He could say it was for work but no one believed him.

Oh, but I didn't call him Rampage no more. I renamed him Ferdinand because the first five days that he was in my yard, he was glued to the corner where my mom's flower beds were. He didn't eat them. He just stared at them like he'd never seen them before. Maybe he hadn't.

Ferdinand wandered to the edge of my porch, resting his head on the rail as he stared at me.

"Would you fucking open it?" I asked the bull. His long tongue stuck out as he attempted to lick me from where he stood—and thankfully couldn't. "That ain't helpful."

The front door creaked as it opened.

"Did you know?" I demanded when my mom joined me. "Did you know where he was?"

"I did," she said. She took her time pulling a chair up next to mine, but I refused to look at her. Disappointment and anger bled together inside me. *Why wouldn't she tell me?* Why the fuck did my mom get to know where he was and I didn't?

"How long?"

"He told me before he left the hospital," she answered honestly. I wished she would've fucking lied as my anger spiked.

"Then why the fuck wouldn't you tell me?"

"Because he asked me not to tell you."

"And why the fuck does he get to be the one who decides that?" I snapped. "He left me. Not the other way around."

"Because he wanted to tell you when you were ready," my mom said.

"Ready for what—"

"You have to understand something about West, baby boy," she cut me off. "West has been crawling through barbed wire most of his life. The world may offer him brief reprieves but he can't escape it."

"And what? Running away from me was the escape he needed?" *Fuck, I even hated saying the words.* Had I really been that bad for him?

"Maybe... just maybe, Jackson, this isn't about you," she replied. "Maybe West is just tired of crawling over barbed wire as a way of living."

Standing, she combed her fingers through my hair and pressed a kiss to the top of my head.

"Read it or not, baby boy, that's up to you," she whispered. "But I think you need to read what's in that letter."

She left me alone sitting on the porch to stare at that stupid letter. I traced the lines of my name over and over as I debated it. I didn't have a clue how long I sat there, but eventually, I opened it.

Jackson,

    I hope this letter finds you... well, I hope this letter finds you in general. I know there's a good chance I'm writing this just for you to burn it without ever reading it. But on the chance you are, I hope you're doing as well as you can be.

    I know this letter can't make up for the way I left, but I'm hoping it'll give you some answers. You deserve that much. I owe you that much. I'm not expecting anything from you. I just want a chance to say what I need to say.

    First off, I'm sorry I left you when you needed me most. I know you needed me, but I couldn't be that person for you. Not when I could barely help myself. The truth is, I'm so fucking tired of living this way. I want more out of my life. I deserve more.

    But I didn't know how to get there. How to do that for myself. I needed help, Jackson. I still do.

    I met a psychiatrist at the hospital. She helped me when I needed it most. When I broke. She helped me get into a clinic in Washington. The clinic is primarily for domestic violence survivors—a place for them to get the help they need and to start over. I've been fortunate enough that they let me take part in their inpatient program.

    At some point, I'll transition to their outpatient program and learn how to live on my own like a functional adult, but I'm not there yet. Right now, I'm working with a psychiatrist and a therapist for help. I've learned that time doesn't heal everything. Sometimes, time just makes everything worse.

I've spent my whole life burying everything I've ever felt and just hoping it'd go away. That's not how shit works, even if I did have myself convinced I was just fine.

But you changed my life. You broke me, Jackson. And not in a bad way — don't think that. You broke down all the walls I'd built for myself to keep those things out and to bury things I should've dealt with a long time ago.

I'm working my ass off to deal with those things. I've made progress — at least, most days I tell myself I've made progress. So far what I do know is this:

1. Harrison was a brutal parent. What he did shaped everything I know and think about myself.
2. My mother committed suicide in front of me. I never should've seen that, and it's impacted me more than I can put into words right now.
3. When I was nineteen, I was raped by nine men in prison. I'm still struggling to work through this one, and I don't know that I'll ever be able to fully.
4. I was sexually assaulted by a doctor in the hospital during recovery and was told it was normal.
5. I don't know who I am. I know what I became because I had to survive.

6. I don't know how to relate to people or be in a relationship with anyone.
7. I don't know how to cope with anything I've been through or how it's affected me. Drinking was coping, but as soon as I tried to get sober... it just made everything worse because I didn't know how to help myself.

    It sounds simple on paper or maybe I'm diminishing it... I don't know... but it's fucking hard. Some days are more brutal than others, but I'm trying. I'm sober and doing my damnedest to stay that way.

    I see the psychiatrist here every month. She's diagnosed me with cPTSD - complex post-traumatic stress disorder. She says it's more than just a single-incident PTSD kind of thing. That cPTSD alters the way the brain develops and functions. There's a whole list of ways it changes the brain that I won't bore you with, but apparently, when I say 'I'm fucked in the head,' I wasn't wrong.

    I'm on medication to help my anxiety, my depression, and my insomnia. It sucked at first, but I like the way they help me now. I work with a therapist a few times a week to unravel all of this shit. I hate therapy if I'm being honest, but I know it's good for me. I don't know how to deal with anything right now without it. There's a family not far from here—The Harveys—that let us come onto their farm to take care of the horses as a part of my therapy. Equine therapy. It helps. It makes the harder days easier to talk through. Not sure my therapist appreciated the day I helped a horse give birth though.

When you asked me to marry you... I didn't say no because I didn't want to. I said no because I didn't want the life I was living. I didn't want that for either of us. You deserve better, but so do I.

I'm not asking you to wait for me, Jackson, but I want you to know I'm trying. I'm trying to take back my life and trying to figure out who I am. I want to know who I am when I'm not stuck trying to survive.

If you want to, I included the information about the clinic I'm at. You can't visit, but you can send a letter. If you wanted. You don't have to do anything.

Whatever you do, I respect it. I hope you have a good life. I know recovery will be hard, but I know you'll do it. You're too stubborn for anything less.

Thank you for showing me that I could be more.

West

West,

Do you know how hard it is to be mad at someone who puts themself through what you're doing right now? Really fucking hard. I'm still struggling with the fact that you left and that you didn't tell me, but I'm proud of you. More than I know how to put into words. You deserve better than the life Harrison paved for you and I'm happy that you're looking for it.

As for how your letter found me... does grumpy count? I don't know. I just feel angry all the time right now. I hate this stupid wheelchair. I hate the way I feel stuck in it. My doctor wants me to start physical therapy to try and get me back on my feet again, but I can't bring myself to make the call.

I don't know why. I just... can't. Maybe one day, but I don't know.

You'll get a kick out of this or maybe you'll appreciate it. Maybe both. I bought Rampage.

Yeah, you read that right. I bought the fucking bull that put me in a goddamn wheelchair and ended my career. But the funny thing is, he's the sweetest thing I've ever met now that he's away from everyone hurting him. He never should've been a bucking bull.

  I renamed him Ferdinand because he loves flowers. He's obsessed with my mom's flower beds along the fence. He loves them so much that Peter put in fake ones when the season turned just to give him something to look at.

  I haven't written a letter in years —at least, not one that didn't involve yelling at Amy for doing stupid shit —so I'm not sure what else to say.

  I do hope I hear back from you. If not, just know that I'm real proud of you, West, and I hope you find what you're looking for.

Jackson

Jackson,

Get your ass out of the house and get to physical therapy. I know you're scared, and I can only guess just how much it's going to hurt, but don't you quit now.

You're Jackson Fucking Myles.

You can do this.

We've been working on dismantling my triggers in therapy. We're working our way through the color yellow right now. My job is to buy a yellow shirt. I keep telling myself I will, but I can't bring myself to do it. I couldn't bring myself to go into the store. I tried twice before making my therapist take me back to the clinic.

You go to physical therapy and I'll buy a yellow shirt. How does that sound? We can do this together.

I'm not going to lie, I'm glad you bought Ferdinand. Though, I can only imagine how your mother feels about it.

Also... are you keeping a bull in your backyard?

West

West,

    I'm so grumpy I made my physical therapist quit. Twice. Well, two of them. This third guy informed me right up front that he's a retired drill sergeant and that he's meaner and grumpier than I'll ever be. I'm trying real damn hard not to have a challenge-accepted moment with this goddamn man. It wouldn't help, right?

    I fucking hate physical therapy. I'm just putting that out there. No one has even tried to make me walk yet, but the body conditioning alone... my leg doesn't feel like my own anymore. I don't know if it ever will. And what if I go through all this bullshit and still can't walk? What am I supposed to do then?

    Mom did hate Ferdinand at first. But she's also living in my house for free and driving me nuts, so I don't fucking care what she thinks. I don't mean that. Not really. She's been good at taking care of me. I just feel bad. I'm sure this isn't how she wanted to spend her retirement. She gave up her apartment at Sandy Oaks to be here. I feel bad about that.

    Though, Mickey does seem to be coming around a lot more. And sticking around. And spending a lot of time with my mom. There's a lot of quiet conversation and laughs...

Fuck, my mom is secretly dating Mickey, isn't she? Goddammit. And he pokes fun at me for HR issues. Dating the boss's mom has to be an HR issue.

We're about to reintroduce the breeding program here to try and build back up the ranch. We survived last season by the skin on our fucking backs. I sold off some of the land after getting the transfer of land papers. While I had to let a few guys go, it was more than enough to get us back on our feet for a bit.

Now, we just need to build again.

Your turn, West. Did you buy the yellow sweater?

Jackson

Jackson,

Channel all that frustration about your physical therapist into physical therapy. It'll be a good outlet for that. Besides, it sounds like the new guy can take whatever you throw at him. It's okay to be scared. I've learned that much. But don't let your fear be the driver. You are. You can do this.

And if you don't walk again, it'll still be okay. But if there was anyone who was going to walk away from this, it's you.

You can do this, Jackson, and I'll keep believing that for the both of us until you do.

I did buy the sweater... but I can't make myself put it on. I did hang it up in my room where I can see it. I'm trying really fucking hard to be okay with it.

I don't feel great right now, but my therapist says that it's normal to struggle with what we're doing. That it can happen when pushing hard on things that trigger us. We're going to the farm later today. No talking, just horses. I need it.

How are my horses?

West

West,

Drill Sergeant Dan put me on the parallel bars. I sent you a picture. Take that fucking picture to your grave but I did it. Well, I sort of did it. I can't walk yet. Fuck, I'm not even sure if I'm even standing or just using my arms to hold myself up.

It still counts, right? I'm still counting it. It's fucking progress in some capacity.

And guess what? We have five pregnant heifers. It's not much, but it's a start. Now, ask me how they got pregnant. Because it sure as fuck wasn't our doing. No fucking Sir. Not a single cow we inseminated is pregnant.

Ferdinand got out and made some fucking friends— literally.

Including Daisy.

The fucker knocked up my girl.

As for your horses... Thunder Jack misses you. I've never seen a horse sulk the way that horse is. I was worried that he wouldn't handle others caring for him, but he's doing well. Peter has taken a lot of time with him. It helps that Bailey likes Peter. I think Thunder Jack follows her lead. Blind Betty is good. She's become a hell of an escape artist and made friends with all the cows. At this point, I don't know why the fuck we bother putting her in a stall. She always gets out anyway.

Now... put on the sweater, West. You can do it. I believe in you for the both of us.

Jackson

Jackson,

    Your picture is hanging at my desk. Just for me, no one else. I'm fucking proud of you. I know it sucks, but you're doing it.

    I put the sweater on. And I've worn the sweater for a week. Not consistently but you get the idea. I included a picture for proof. I'm still not sure how I feel wearing yellow... it's not bad. I'm still working through it.

    I sat down with the clinic coordinator, my therapist, and my psychiatrist yesterday. We've decided it's time for me to move out. We have a whole list of things to help me get through the transition. The clinic works with a small apartment complex nearby, so I'm not going far. It's right down the street. And I'll still be here every other day for group or individual therapy.

    I'm nervous. I've never had a home on my own. After I got out of prison, I sort of floated. I did a halfway house for a while but I couldn't stand living with so many people. I had this cheap trailer I rented for years. It didn't even have a working bathroom or shit. It was truck stops for showers, bars for bathrooms, or whatever. It worked, but I wouldn't call it a home.

Nothing has ever felt like home. I don't know how to build a home. I'm scared I'm going to fail at something everyone else can do. This is supposed to be an easy thing, right? Living on your own? Everyone does it so why does it feel so fucking hard?

I don't know... I feel stuck in my head about it.

West

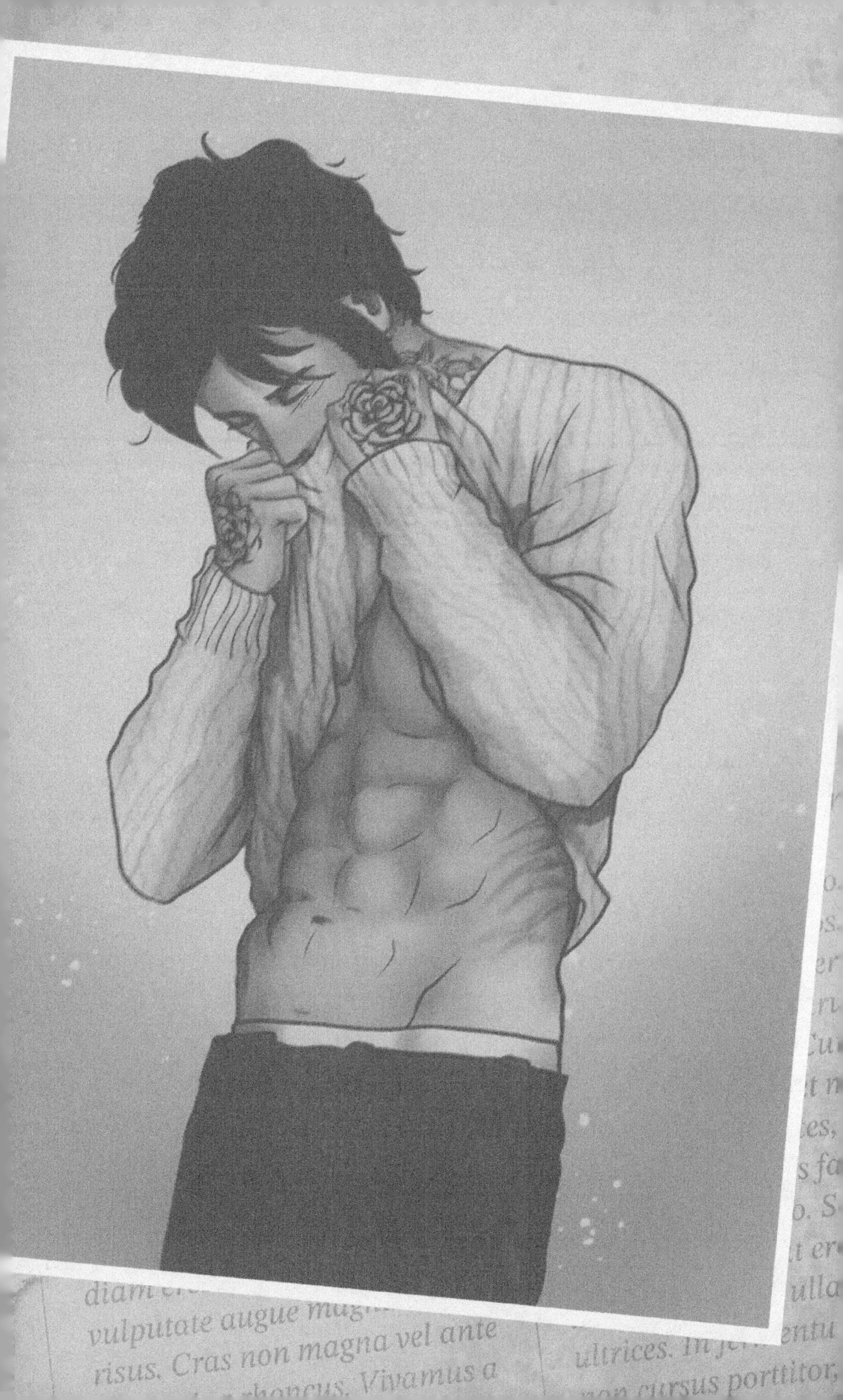

West,

    A first apartment is a big deal. It's more than reasonable to be nervous about it. Everyone goes through it. When my mom decided to move out and signed the house over to me, I didn't know what to do with it. I hadn't lived alone either, and that house was big for one person. The first night, I ended up calling Mickey and made him come keep me company. I didn't say that, but I'm sure he knew.
    It's going to take time, but you've got it.
    I'm including the first thing you can put in your apartment: a picture of pregnant Daisy. I'm in fucking trouble. There's no reason for any cow to be this damn adorable. I may be a little pissed about Ferdinand knocking up my girl, but damn she's extra cute right now.
    I now have a bull and a cow in my yard. She's extra clingy so I moved her here with me. I'm going to end up with a calf living there too. I'm going to need a bigger yard. Hopefully, Ferdinand stays on all fours and I don't end up with more babies from him in the future.

Jackson

Jackson,

Do you know how much shit you need to fill a fucking apartment? A one bedroom, small as fuck apartment? Why is it so much? I don't know where to begin.

I did hang up Daisy's picture. It's the only thing here that's really mine. The rental company included some basic furniture and stuff — a bed, a couch, a table, pots and pans. That sort of stuff.

I don't know where to begin with everything else. It's too much. I don't even have sheets. But how do you pick the right sheets and blankets? I just... it's a lot.

The woman who lives across the hall brought over a giant gift basket to welcome me. Do people really do that? It has all sorts of snacks and shit. I made her take back the champagne, but I think I upset her. Maybe I should've told her I'm an alcoholic instead of telling her I didn't want it.

I'm not good at this people thing.

And it's really quiet here, Jackson. I don't know what to do with the quiet. I've been drawing to fill the time, but I can only draw so much. I don't know how to fill my time.

West

West,

You draw? I didn't know that about you. Maybe one day you can show me some of your drawings.

I'm sending you the pictures I should've sent first — of Thunder Jack, Bailey, and Blind Betty. Those belong with you. I'm not real good at photography, but I tried to get some good ones for you. Hopefully, they work.

I'm proud of you, West. I know it's hard right now and I know it's stressful, but you're doing it. That's a big thing. An incredible thing. You should be fucking proud of yourself.

I took my first steps today. The pain is fucking awful and my whole leg feels like shit, but I did it with some help. That's my big thing.

It's only uphill from here for both of us.

Jackson

Jackson,

    I'm sorry it's been a while. I relapsed and I'm back at the clinic for now. I don't think I can do this.

                                      West

Keep going, baby. You can do this.

Jackson

West,

It's been a while since I've heard from you. I hope it's okay that I'm sending this, and hopefully the clinic gives it to you. I managed to drag myself out to the stables and drove Peter nuts as I dug around for these. And whoever thought letting a crippled guy handle a metal drill was okay was an idiot, even if I am their boss. I damn near took off a finger. I didn't but almost.

The horseshoe is from Thunder Jack— it's one of the horseshoes you took off him when he finally let you. The twine making up the string I hung it on is woven from a few of Betty and Bailey's tail hairs.

Hang that up, West, and when you look at it, I want you to realize what you're capable of. You can do anything, baby. You did the impossible with Thunder Jack and Betty. You took a violent bucking horse and showed him what it was like for him to be loved and cared for. You saw him when no one else did. You took grumpy little Betty and gave her a chance at life when no one else was willing to. She may be a little escape artist, but I ain't ever met a horse sweeter than her.

You loved them fiercely and changed their lives because of it. That's a good thing.

It's time you love yourself the way you loved those horses. It's time you believed in yourself the way you believed in those horses.

Keep going, baby. I'm rooting for you from here.

Jackson

Thank you for the horseshoe, cowboy. That doesn't seem to encompass what I feel when I look at it. I have it hanging in my apartment where I can see it from just about anywhere.

I'm doing this again. I can do this. Before staying in the apartment, we worked on decorating it as a part of therapy. On making it mine. It feels weird calling anything mine, especially something this big.

But I want this, and I just have to keep reminding myself of that.

And yeah, I like to draw. The truth is, I'm trying to figure out who I am. What I like and all that shit. My doctor says that kids who go through the abuse that I did struggle to create an identity for themselves. We create an identity we hope keeps us safe. I spent so much time trying to not piss off Harrison that I never focused on me.

Everyone knows I love horses. I like to draw. I'm learning that I like to cook, and I'm learning how to bake. I picked up the guitar, but I'm not that good at it. I'm not sure if I'm going to stick with it, but that's a part of figuring it out, right?

I added in one of my drawings for you in case you wanted to see. Or you can throw it away. It's up to you.

I'm sorry I took away from you taking steps. I'm so fucking proud of you. How does it feel?

West

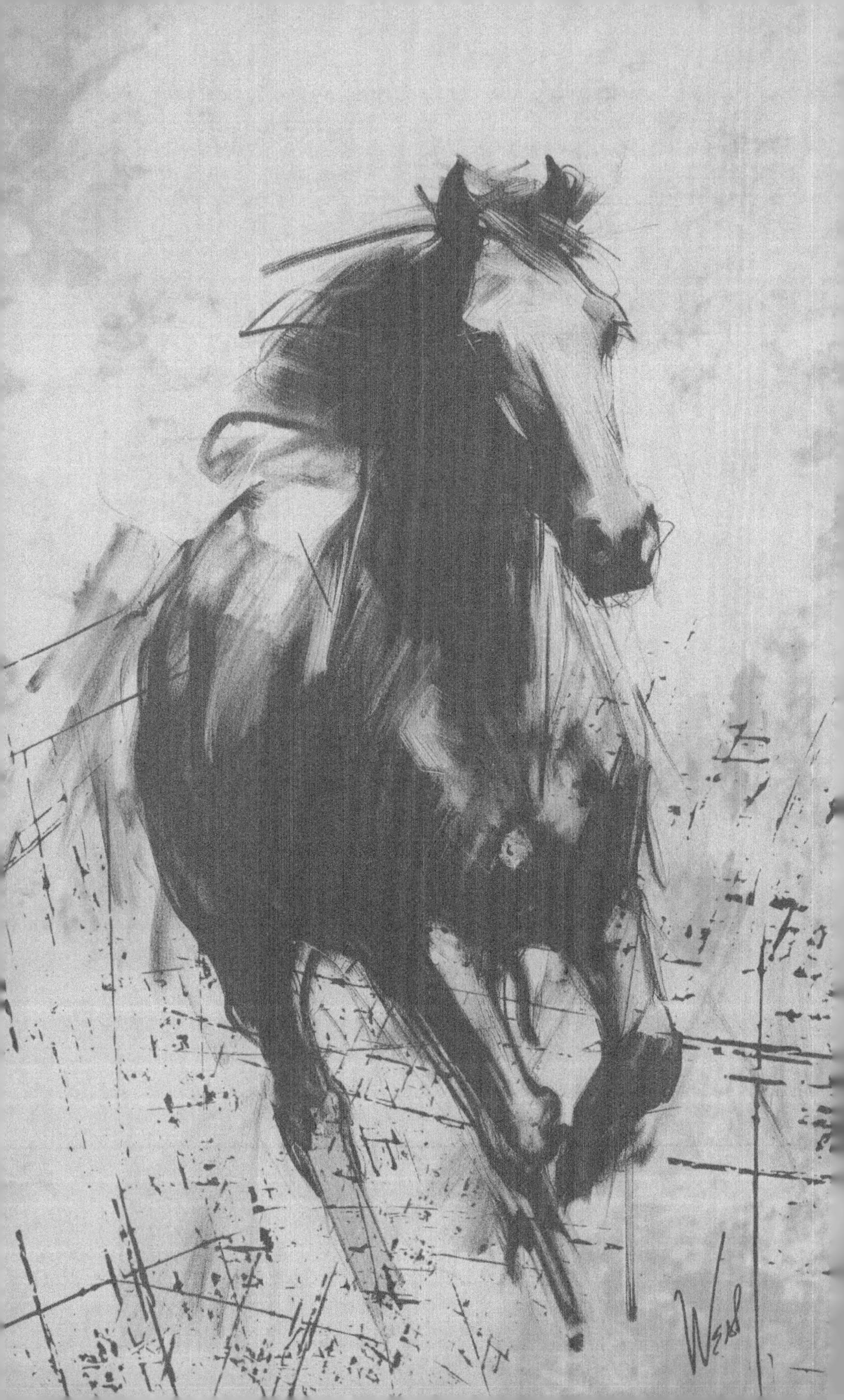

Baby, you have no idea how proud of you I am. All the work you're doing is inspiring. You should be proud of yourself.

And your drawing? You're fucking talented, West. You really are. There's no way in hell I'm throwing that out.

I took a small walk by myself on the ranch yesterday. It's funny how much my appreciation for this place has changed when I can finally walk it. Peter kept close by with one of the UTVs, and I didn't go very far, but it's better than not going at all.

There's an ache when I walk, but I'm not sure if that's ever going to go away. The cane helps.

This place is rebuilding just like me. There's something incredible about witnessing that.

I got invited to the opening event for the rodeo this year, not to ride— that's something I'll never do again— but to make an appearance and help with the picks. I don't know if I want to go.

Jackson

Hey, cowboy,

My neighbor Cait came over to help me upgrade my phone. Yeah, I got a smartphone just so I could watch the rodeo live. I watched you last night help with the picks. You looked good — real good. And you looked happy. Have you thought about maybe teaching? Was that job with Abernathy still open? I don't have a clue what teaching bull riders entails except probably a lot of yelling at them, which we both know you'd be good at.

I got a job in construction. It's nothing too big, only a few days a week, but they weren't scared away by my record so that's a plus. It feels good to be doing something with my hands and keeping busy.

So... there was something I wanted to share with you and it's okay if you don't want to.

I'm graduating from the clinic in four weeks. Me. I never thought it'd happen, but it is. We all think I'm ready. I think I'm ready. I feel ready... mostly. I can do this.

The clinic does this thing they call a birthday party — it's the first day of the rest of my life. It's a small thing with just the women and staff at the center, but I'm allowed to invite one or two special people to celebrate.

I understand if you don't want to, but if you do... I'd love to have you there, cowboy.

West

CHAPTER 98

JACKSON

The *Hope in Healing Clinic* was a one-floor building in a small town that rivaled Wood Springs' tiny size. The town was about an hour outside of Olympia, meaning I had to rent a car after flying to Washington. Driving for that long wasn't the most comfortable thing in the world, but for West, I had no problem doing so.

For almost seven months, West and I exchanged dozens of letters. Some were long and extensive, sharing deep things neither of us ever had the chance or courage to bring up, while others were simpler and to the point. Despite the distance between us, I felt closer to him than I had in a long time. The way he peeled back the curtain and showed me parts of him that he'd never been able to before was something special.

I leaned on my cane as I stared at the unassuming building. It felt a little surreal that after all this time, I was about to see West again. A small part of me was worried. What if he'd changed so much that we didn't fit together anymore? I knew I'd let him go in a heartbeat if it made him happy. I wasn't about to pull him back into his own darkness, but the idea of losing him all over again hurt.

"You must be Jackson." A middle-aged woman opened the front door, standing and holding it open for me.

"Yes, ma'am," I replied. Leaning on my cane for support, I limped toward her. The ride over had fucked with my hip, making it harder than usual to walk. *Still, I was fucking determined.*

"My name is Elizabeth," she told me. She stepped aside to make it easier for me to get inside. "I'm the clinic coordinator. We've been looking forward to meeting you."

I nodded, not sure how to respond to that. I knew West talked about us in therapy. I just had no idea how far all that knowledge traveled in a clinic this small.

"This way, but take your time." She gestured down a hall as she walked alongside me and matched my pace. "We have a few rules here at *Hope* that we ask our visitors to also follow. It creates a safer atmosphere for our patients."

"Of course."

"We ask that you don't swear." *Ah, fuck.* I hated that rule already. I'd follow it without question or argument, but fuck, I hated it. "And we know that physical contact is a way to express affection, but we ask that you refrain from all physical contact with West while with the group."

Well, he didn't like being touched anyway. Besides, I wasn't real sure where he and I stood on our relationship. That wasn't something we talked about. We were close—closer than friends—but that was it. Everything else was up in the air.

"I can do that," I told her. I wouldn't fuck this up for West.

"I'll have you wait in this room right here," Elizabeth said, stopping at a door. "We let our patients visit with their guests here before the party starts. As long as the door is closed, we allow things like hugs and whatnot. We know it's an important aspect of reunions. So, I'm going to leave you here while I go and fetch West for you."

"Thank you," I replied and wandered into the room as she left me alone.

The room was comfortable with a soft couch and an oversized chair. There were blankets everywhere, and the lighting was soft and warm. I couldn't help but wonder if this was one of the rooms where West talked through things. It looked like the kind of room that would make therapy easier.

Minutes passed slowly and I occupied myself with trying to find a comfortable way to stand. I considered sitting, but I knew I wouldn't get back up anytime soon if I did.

"Hey, cowboy." *That voice.* The sound of it sent my heart soaring long before I ever turned around. West stood in the doorway, hands in his pockets as he watched me. An easy, brilliant smile lit up his handsome face—something I'd never seen on him. There was life in those gray eyes, genuine and vibrant. His hair was longer but styled while his beard was trimmed short. He looked happy and healthy, put together and comfortable in his skin.

And he wore a pale yellow dress shirt, the sleeves rolled up to show off his tattoos. No one would ever pull off yellow the way West did. That much I was convinced of.

Closing the door, he crossed the room and hugged me. I returned the gesture, holding on tight as I lost myself in the moment. He no longer smelled like horses—a fact I sort of missed—and instead, a light, spicy musk clung to his skin.

"You look good," I whispered when he finally pulled away.

"I feel good," West replied with another heart-stopping smile. *God, what a fucking sight that smile was.* He nodded at my cane, teasing, "And someone thought weaponizing you was a smart idea?"

"I don't need it," I lied. "I just like threatening people with it."

"Sounds about right." He laughed—the sound so damn real it took me by surprise. "How are you doing? Honestly?"

"I'm okay. Some days are worse than others, but I can get around just fine."

"Good. And today? You doing okay?"

"Yeah, I'm good, West," I said.

"Okay," he replied. "Up for another walk?"

"Lead the way." *Yeah, I'd still follow West anywhere.* All it took was one look to know that much was a fact.

CHAPTER 99

WEST

Jackson was here. The fact that he was made me unbelievably happy. Him showing up had been a point of anxiety for me. After all of our letters, I wanted to believe he'd accept the invite, but that little voice in the back of my head had offered other suggestions. It was something I was working on with my therapist.

I'd participated in several goodbye birthday parties at *Hope*, but to be attending my own was surreal. We sat at a small round table in the community area. A yellow birthday cake sat in front of me, complete with a lit horse candle. There were only four women staying at *Hope*—Gabby, Mia, Beverly, and Alessia—along with the therapist, Karina, and the clinic's psychiatrist, Clara, and Elizabeth, the clinic coordinator.

Everything was first names here. It was easier that way. Some of the women who came through *Hope* were on the run from abusive partners. I'd listened to their stories and they'd listened to mine. The little things we did here to protect each other were important.

"If anyone had asked me last year if I'd be standing here with my own cake, I probably would've called them crazy," I said. *No, I definitely would've.* "When I came here, I didn't have a clue what I was looking for or what I wanted for myself. I was lost in every way a person could be lost. I just knew I wanted a better life for myself."

I drew in a deep breath as I tried to figure out what to say. Emotion clogged my throat. This was a big fucking moment. Sure, it was just a grocery store birthday cake in a community room, but it was a big deal. And having Jackson here with me? Even if I didn't know what was happening with us, the fact that he could celebrate this moment with me was important.

"I don't know how to say thank you," I whispered. "I'll never have the right words—I'm just not good with them—but thank you for opening your doors to me. For believing I could do this when I didn't. I don't know where I'd be without any of you."

But I did know. I would've been somewhere drowning in another bottle trying to silence the demons in my head. I would've been miserable and hopeless.

I cleared my throat. Emotions were encouraged, but I didn't want to get emotional. Not today. I just wanted to enjoy the afternoon. I glanced over at Jackson, trying to gauge his response. I felt a lot of things when it came to Jackson—a lot that I still had to work out. Insecurities, worries, fears. *One thing at a time, right?*

He gave me a small wink. Just him doing that released a tiny bit of the tension in my chest. He was still Jackson, I was still West. Whatever the hell came next, that fact made the stress of it all a little more manageable.

"Thank you," I whispered to Elizabeth, "for taking a chance on me."

It was obvious that *Hope* was a women's clinic, even if it didn't explicitly say so anywhere. When Dr. Hawthorne had called Elizabeth to ask for a favor, there were a lot of reservations about taking me in to be a patient. *I qualified, sure, but what about the safety of the women who stayed there, considering I was a man?* They took a chance on me, and I'd never be able to repay them for that.

"May I?" she asked as she opened her arms.

"Yeah," I replied and sank into the hug. Touch was far from my favorite thing but my brain didn't instantly panic at the contact anymore. Rubbing was still a no-go, and on my off days, I couldn't handle being touched, but it didn't incite panic anymore. And I had a laundry list of coping mechanisms to prevent things from getting to the point of panic.

"I'm proud of you, West," she said softly. "And you should be proud of you too."

"I am." *And I was.*

"Good." Elizabeth pulled away, and I took a healthy step back. "Our doors are always open to you if you need anything. And just remember, having a hard time doesn't mean you failed. It just means you're human."

"I know," I replied. *I was still working on that.* "Thank you again."

"You're very welcome."

I watched as she went back inside and stayed until the door was locked behind her. As I watched her go, it hit me that I'd made it this far. *I'd fucking done it.* Fifteen months ago when I decided to talk to Dr. Hawthorne, I never imagined that I'd end up here. I was happy—a little nervous but happy nonetheless.

Jackson waited at the other end of the parking lot for me. *Fuck, he looked handsome.* His hair had darkened some, losing that sunkissed blond quality from a lack of working the ranch. He'd grown it out though. The long waves brushed his shoulders, and I wanted to know if they were as soft to the touch as they looked. He looked leaner overall. I knew it had everything to do with not training for the rodeo anymore. Seeing him lean on that cane though? That hurt. I knew from his letters what he'd gone through to get to this point, but a part of me still held onto the guilt that I should've been there.

Still, just the sight of him made my heart race with excitement. There was a lot of uncertainty where Jackson was concerned and we had a lot to talk about, but I chose to focus on the fact that he was here.

"Fuck, fuck, fuck, fuck." I hurried to join him as he leaned against his rental car. "Fuck, fuck, fuck, fuck, fuck."

"What's wrong?" Jackson frowned, making me chuckle.

"Nothing," I told him with a grin. "But Jesus fuck, I've missed swearing."

"Dumbass," he said.

"Only on days that end in y," I replied.

"That's all of them."

"Exactly."

"Jesus fuck." He laughed, and I loved the sound. *How I'd missed it.* "So, what now?"

"Now," I drew in a deep breath, "you're going to follow me down the street to my apartment, so we can park your car, and then we're leaving."

"For where?" Jackson asked, and my smile widened. This was the only part of the day that I had a solid plan for.

"I'm taking you on a date, cowboy."

CHAPTER 100

JACKSON

West was something else. He laughed, he smiled, he cracked jokes. When it was just us, he was relaxed and open. Even with the restaurant staff, he wasn't anxious or put out. He was more reserved, but it passed when they left. All of it was a bittersweet reminder of everything that had been taken from him. It was also an impressive testament to what he'd been able to achieve. I was so fucking proud of him, and I'd never find the words to express that.

"It's not much," West was saying as he fished out the keys to his apartment. *His apartment.* He'd come a long way from sleeping in my stables.

"Don't diminish it," I said. "It's yours, and that's a big deal."

"Yeah." He nodded slowly. His nervousness was kind of adorable, but I understood it. I knew just how big this moment was for him. "Okay."

He opened the door, and I followed him inside. The apartment was small and simple with gray walls, plush furniture, and soft lighting. There were sketches pinned to the walls everywhere—horses, plants, cows, and more. A yellow knit blanket was tossed over a chair along with an array of black and gray ones. There were a lot of fucking blankets. A little coffee table was covered in sketch pads and used pencils. Through their open doors, I could tell the bedroom and the bathroom matched the yellow, black, and gray aesthetic.

"You kept it." I nodded to the horseshoe hanging on the support beam between the kitchen and the living room.

"I told you I would," West replied. He stood in the middle of the living room with his hands in his pockets, watching my every move as if trying to figure out what I was thinking.

"I like it, West," I told him. "You don't need to worry about that."

He drew in a deep breath, his head bobbing slightly as he didn't say a word. I could see the wheels turning in his head and decided to wait him out. Whatever he wanted to say, he'd say it when he was ready. *Funny how some things never changed.*

"I want to say I'm sorry," he said quietly.

"You don't have to say—"

"I do, though," he interrupted. "I do need to. I know I apologized in my letter, but I need to say it out loud. I'm sorry I wasn't there after you got hurt. I should've been, or I should've said something to you sooner about where I went."

"You never have to apologize for taking care of yourself, West," I assured him. I was over my anger at him about walking out. It was clear that he needed this so much more than how I'd wanted him there with me. "I get it, and I see what you've done for yourself. You don't have to apologize for that."

"And there's something I should've said sooner." He took a step closer. "You know, I suck at this whole feelings thing. I didn't have the best examples in my life of good relationships, and I just..."

He swallowed hard, and I realized what he was trying to say. *But the thing was, I didn't need him to say it.* Knowing how West felt wasn't hard once I understood the way he expressed himself. It was in all the little things he did—the little ways he cared for me. Those things mattered too.

"I know," I said to help alleviate the stress. "You don't have to say a thing, West."

"No, I do," he insisted and took one more step toward me. "I love you, Jackson. I loved you growing up, I loved you long after I left, and I still love you. I'll always love you."

I knew it—I had known it for a while—but hearing him say the words still made me smile. Two more steps and his hands were on my face as he kissed me. *Confident and emotional.* Every nerve in my body reacted instantly, coming to life in a way only West could manage to coax out of me.

His tongue brushed along the seam of my lips. I tilted my head slightly as I opened to him and kissed him deeper. My fingers curled into his hair while his traveled down my back, sending a shiver down my spine. *God, I'd fucking missed this. I missed him.*

"Drop the cane, cowboy," West whispered against my mouth. His arm wrapped around my waist, anchoring there and supporting my weight. "I've got you."

How the hell was I supposed to argue with that? I set my cane aside and leaned into him as he walked backward toward the bedroom. There was no frenzy. Everything he did was meticulous as he mindfully moved with me—dragging my sweater over my head and working with me to peel off his dress shirt while still holding up my weight.

But Jesus fuck, how unattractive was it watching me ease into bed because my fucking hip and leg didn't work the way they should. And yet, West was undeterred. The look of want and need on his face made my heart pound with anticipation. He was so fucking sure of himself—of us. It was a wild change in him.

Without his shirt on, it was clear he'd started working out. His shoulders were broader and his muscles more defined. But what caught my attention was the new tattoo over his heart. *A cowboy hat and a horseshoe.*

"Is that a..."

"Did I brand myself with a tattoo for you?" West asked. "Yeah, I did."

"Jesus Christ, West," I muttered. I felt how my cheeks heated up at his words. *Jesus fuck this man had me blushing.* "That's one way to put it."

"I've always known what I wanted, cowboy." He kneeled between my legs and caught my mouth in another heated kiss. "I just never thought I deserved you."

I kissed him harder. The way he used past tense to talk about those feelings wasn't lost on me. His hand skimmed down my chest and stomach, leaving a trail of liquid heat in their path. But when his fingers touched the buttons of my jeans, I grabbed his wrist.

"It's just..." I gripped his hand a little tighter as I struggled to find the words.

"Do you want to stop, Jackson?" West asked. *There was an irony in this moment.*

"Not a chance in hell," I retorted. My cock would probably riot if I did that. I hadn't been this goddamn hard in a long time. "But you should know that I'm a fucking mess after all the surgeries and everything."

Mangled mess was more like it. There had been no good way to put me back together without leaving a whole goddamn disaster behind. I was scar tissue upon scar tissue going from my hip to my shin. It wasn't fucking pretty.

"Your scars don't matter, cowboy," he said. After a heartbeat, he smirked and added, "And I'm happy to fucking hit anyone who says otherwise."

"Yeah, still need bail money for your dumbass," I groaned. I dropped back on the bed and lifted my hips as he helped me out of my jeans and boxers. To my surprise, his lips brushed over the scars on my shin. I drew in a sharp breath, tensing under the contact.

"Does it hurt?" West whispered against my skin.

"Not really," I admitted. "Just more..."

"Uncomfortable," he finished for me. I nodded because it was. That touch pain had long since subsided but the damaged nerves bundled into all the scars left everything extra sensitive—something West understood intimately.

He took his time kissing every inch of scarring on my leg. The gesture was so tender that it had my heart in my throat with an overwhelming flood of emotion. When his tongue ran up the length of my cock, all of that melted away with the loud moan I let out. My eyes slid shut as his mouth lowered around the crown of my dick—hot and wet.

Yeah, it'd been too fucking long.

"Get undressed, baby," I ordered, my voice strained. "I want you inside me."

His mouth popped off my dick, and he shot me a cocky grin. From that single fucking look I could tell I wasn't ready for confident-in-bed West.

"What happened to patience is a virtue?" he teased and went right back at it.

"Patience and blue balls don't go hand in hand, baby," I grunted as the head of my dick hit the back of his throat. "You keep doing that..."

Anything else I planned to say was fucking lost as he gave my balls a light squeeze. Without thinking, I grabbed his hair and pulled him off my cock.

"You keep doing that and I'm going to come before we even get started," I told him. As the words left my mouth, I realized the hold I had on his hair and let go. I tensed as I waited for the backlash, but he just smiled. *Gorgeous and undeterred.*

"Watching you unravel? Yeah, that's not the threat you think that is, cowboy." Still, he slid off the bed to get undressed. I watched with rapt appreciation as he stripped. "Lube is in the nightstand drawer."

I went to grab it but came out with an empty bottle. I frowned. The second one I grabbed was empty too. So was the third one.

"West," I began, trying not to laugh, "why the hell are there three empty lube bottles in your drawer?"

"Well... I used them, but clearly, I forgot to throw them away." He grinned. The pride in his face was hard to argue with. Settling over me, his lips drifted up my neck and his teeth scraped over my ear, sending a shiver down my spine. "I worked really fucking hard to get comfortable with my body. Maybe a little too hard. I should probably throw those the fuck away."

"Later." I dragged his mouth back to mine. I wasn't about to fault him for that shit. With anyone else, three bottles of lube would've been ridiculous, but with West, it was a thing to be proud of. Maybe I'd ask questions later, but I honestly didn't care. I liked the level of confidence and comfort he had with himself.

It took several minutes to figure out a position that didn't tweak something painful in my hip. Through all of it, West was patient and doting. He kissed away the frustration I felt with my own inhibitions. It wasn't lost on me how much the roles between us were suddenly reversed.

The stretch and burn as he pressed the head of his cock into me had me holding my breath. And when that first piercing of his stretched me further, I froze slightly.

"Breathe, cowboy," West whispered against my mouth. "I can feel how tense you are."

"It's been a while," I muttered. *Since the night before my accident.* He kissed me again, his tongue stroking mine. My body loosened under his as he took his time, pulling in and out gradually. With each light thrust, he pushed deeper inside me. When he was buried to the hilt, he paused to give me a chance to adjust.

"Fuck, you're so goddamn tight," he let out through a groan. The burn slowly subsided, leaving me with a need for more of him. He braced over me and started slow—too slow. My hands trailed down his back and grabbed his ass, encouraging him to go faster.

We melted into a frenzy driven by passion and fifteen months apart. *Completely and utterly intoxicated by one another.* West's fist wrapped around my cock, stroking me at a pace that matched the way he drove into me. I did everything I could to keep from coming. I wanted to savor this. I wanted to savor him.

I touched him every place I could—running my hands up his sides, teasing his nipple piercings, kissing his neck. The way he reacted was encouraging. *Little moans, gasps, pleas to repeat what I'd done.* It was discovering him all over again. The pressure of his barbells with every thrust was euphoric in a way that I'd never get used to. And while I did my best to stay present—to focus on him—I was fucking soaring and crashing head first into everything he elicited in me.

"Don't hold back, cowboy," West said. His fist skated faster over my cock until I dropped back on the pillow, panting and right there on the edge. He grunted and groaned over me, his body tensing. I grabbed his forearm with a need to cling to him.

"*Fuck.*" The single word was drawn out as I exploded, painting my stomach in thick ropes of cum. West tumbled over the edge with me, pushing as deep inside me as possible when he came. His hand slipped from my dick and braced on the sheets as he breathed hard.

Those gray eyes met mine, and he grinned—real and utterly wrapped up in the moment. That smile on his face roped around my heart like barbed wire, digging in and sticking where it was. *Exactly where West belonged.*

CHAPTER 101

WEST

I LEFT JACKSON IN bed after he didn't wake up with my alarm. As much as I wanted to stay next to him, I had shit I had to do. I stuck to a strict routine with my medication and even with him here, I refused to deviate from it. I was determined to make this work.

I felt good—really good—after last night. While my therapist and I had worked a lot in unraveling all the complicated feelings and triggers I had revolving around the topic of sex, I hadn't actually *had* sex with anyone. Not only did I not want the complexities of a new person in my life, but I only wanted Jackson.

Taking Jackson out to dinner had never been about sleeping with him. It wasn't even a thought I'd entertained. It was just where the night ended up. *And having done so?* I felt good about it all. There was no residual guilt or shame. There was no building panic inside. It was a tiny testament to my progress in therapy.

I was mid-bite of toast when Jackson came out of the room, leaning on his cane and wearing only a pair of boxer briefs—and looking ridiculously attractive. No one should look that fucking good rolling out of bed. In the early morning sunlight, I took a moment to study him, my gaze sweeping over him. While his boxer briefs covered the scars on his hip and upper thigh, I could still see the rest. They tangled their way over the rest of his thigh, wrapping around his knee, and trailing down his shin. I swallowed hard. *Fuck, he'd gone through it with recovery.* Just seeing them made me all that much more proud of him for kicking his own ass and walking again.

That sleepy smile he gave me as he joined me was enough to pull me from my thoughts.

"Sorry," I apologized after I swallowed. "I'll make a real breakfast, I swear. I just have to take my medicine at six, but if I don't eat with them, they make me fucking sick."

I was rambling a little and I knew that. I wasn't used to having to explain my routine to anyone who wasn't my therapist or my doctor.

"You're fine, baby." He yawned as he limped over toward the kitchen table. "I don't think I've seen six in a long fucking time. Not without nurses coming in to poke and prod me."

"Sorry." The guilt of needing to get up early hit deep, and I drew in a steadying breath. *Fuck, I was doing it again.* I cleared my throat. "I'm not sorry that I had to get up, but I am sorry if I woke you."

There. My therapist would be proud.

"You're fine, West," Jackson repeated. "You can make it up to me if you want by feeding me something that isn't my mother's scrambled eggs with ketchup and burnt bacon on the side."

"That's a fucking monstrosity," I whispered. No one belonged eating any of those things let alone every fucking morning. I began digging through my cabinets and pulling out pans. "What do you want? I'll make you anything."

Thirty minutes later, we sat at the table with omelets, toast, and fresh coffee—the real stuff because apparently, my homemade cappuccinos weren't real coffee. *He was a fucking heathen, and I loved him all the more for it.*

Jackson ate with a slew of happy expletives, but I just picked at everything. My brain was all over the place as I tried to organize my thoughts. For as much as my therapist and I had practiced the exact conversation I needed to have with him, I still wasn't prepared to have it with him in person.

"Do you want to talk about it?" Jackson asked softly, leaning back in his chair. Those blue eyes watched me closely—reading me. Once it would've made me uncomfortable but not anymore. He wasn't observing to scrutinize me. He was watching because he cared. That distinction made a difference.

"I should've made us have this conversation last night," I muttered. I pushed my plate away with a sigh and sat back. My heart pounded anxiously in my chest, and I crossed my arms to keep from fidgeting.

"Take your time, West. Whenever you're ready."

"My stables, my rules?"

"I think this time it's your apartment, your rules," he teased. "Unless you're hiding horses in here."

"I wish." I missed my horses so fucking much. The ones at the Harveys just weren't the same as mine. "There's... something we need to talk about."

"I figured."

"I'm not..." The words got stuck in my throat. Damn it. The guilt was intense. I should've had this conversation with him last night before anything happened between us. That would've been the right thing to do. "I'm not coming back to Double Arrow, Jackson."

There. I'd said it. Jackson's eyes narrowed slightly, but he said nothing. I could do this.

"This thing is... I'm not cured—there's no cure for this," I told him. "It's a lifetime thing I have to maintain."

"I know," he replied.

"I have a routine I stick to, and my medication helps make everything easier to manage. I can handle touch more than I could but not always," I continued, trying to rush through everything before I lost my nerve to tell him. "Some days are good and some days aren't. They're not bad like they were before because I know how to take care of myself, but it's never going away."

"You know that don't bother me, right?" he asked.

"My doctor and my therapist are here," I said instead. "My AA group is here and the clinic is here if I need them. And I love... I love being with you, Jackson, but I can't go back to Double Arrow. I can't go back to all those memories. I can't go back to a town where everyone fucking knew what Harrison was doing and didn't do a damn thing about it. I don't want to drown again. I don't... I don't want to leave here. I found a nice big plot of land that I put a bid in for. I should hear back in the next few days. I'm going to build a house and fence it all for the horses. And I just... I can't go back to Double Arrow with you."

I shut up because the expression on his face was unreadable. *It fucking killed me.* What the hell was he thinking? His jaw ticked as he nodded slowly and picked up his cane. Without a word, he got up and started toward the bedroom.

"What're you doing?" I called after him, my heart pounding faster. *Fuck. I'd screwed this up.*

"Going to email Colter Lexington and find out if the offer to buy my ranch is still on the table," he called over his shoulder.

He was... what?

"What?" I turned fast in my chair as he stopped in the doorway.

"I told you once, West, and I'll tell you again," he began, "you're my priority."

"I know but—"

"And if that means selling my family ranch to be with you, then I'm selling my goddamn ranch," Jackson continued. *He what?*

"You can't do that," I told him stupidly. He couldn't give it all up for me, especially not after all the work he'd put into rebuilding it over the last year.

"I aim to do just that," he replied. "But we'll have to figure out space for the horses."

"Yeah."

"And Daisy and Ferdinand."

"Obviously."

"And probably a few of Daisy's friends so she don't get lonely."

"So, we'll just move the ranch," I said. My chest tightened as my eyes burned. *This man.* The simplicity in which he treated the situation was more than I could've expected—more than I truly deserved. "Are you sure you want this, Jackson? I wouldn't be mad if you didn't."

"I told you that if you'd asked me years ago to leave with you, I would've," he replied seriously. "You mean more to me than that ranch ever will, West. Always have, always will."

EPILOGUE PART 01

JACKSON

five years later

I DIDN'T HAVE AN alarm clock. I didn't fucking need one. Instead, I had a needy as fuck bull who liked to push open the sink windows and bellow until I showed up to feed him.

"You're a pain in my goddamn ass, you know that?" I grumped as I limped my way into the kitchen. When West built our house, he kept everything low enough to the ground to make it easy to access for me. There were no stairs or ramps anywhere. But then, this fucker decided that instead of putting a glass window over our sink, he put in a few half-sized barn doors. They opened inward and allowed the cows to pay us a visit whenever they wanted. At first, it was fun, but then Ferdinand figured out how to open them and demand lettuce whenever the fuck he wanted.

The bull bellowed and stuck out his tongue, trying to reach the fresh bowl of lettuce leaves on the counter. I braced against the sink and ran a hand over his snout.

"You're lucky you're fucking cute," I said and handed him the biggest leaf I could find. I smiled while he munched on it. "Sleep well last night, buddy?"

He made a sound, and I continued to feed him. Only when he was completely satisfied—including a vigorous round of pets—did the bull leave my kitchen. I made my way through the house toward the back door, grabbing my cane before joining him outside. Most days, I could wander around without my cane, but I didn't dare go outside without it. Not with the way our animals trampled around the yard. While we had a stable and a sectioned-off pasture, most of our animals had free range of our entire property. We had our horses and cows but over the years we'd added chickens and goats along with another collie to keep Tess company.

Colter had leapt at the chance to buy Double Arrow from me. He gave me the time I needed to shut down but also gave us the time we needed for West to build a house in Washington. The transition meant more months apart, but instead of letters to get us through, we traded phone calls and video chats. I still hated the distance, but I knew the end result would be worth it.

My mom had strong feelings about me selling Double Arrow and not in the way I'd expected. There was a pride in her that I couldn't describe, and she was more than thrilled for me to start this next chapter of life with West. Unfortunately, that goddamn conversation was done over burnt bacon and scrambled eggs with ketchup. She also used that as a chance to tell me that she and Mickey were getting married. I still had mixed feelings about their whole thing, but she was happy, which was all that mattered.

Before the final move, we made use of the northern ridge one last time to get married. Mickey and my mom joined us along with Peter. West was late and showed up on the back of a horse, wearing a yellow dress shirt and a smile that blinded the sun. I knew he'd be late after rushing over to talk to his former sponsor in Merrillville, so I wasn't even bothered in the least. But that was the thing, I'd wait forever for West without hesitation.

And then we left Double Arrow in the past. A part of me would be forever grateful for that ranch because it gave me West, but I was more than ready for the next phase in our lives. We named our farm West Haven because this was truly West's safe place as he forever dealt with the shit life had handed him. We had good days and bad days. West couldn't bend or sway. He stuck the line. He had to. The uncertainty of not knowing what would happen next was often too much on his fight or flight.

But I could.

And I did.

Happily.

There wasn't a damn thing I wouldn't do to make the war against his own mind a little easier. Some people said it wasn't fair to me—that I deserved better than everything he went through. But they didn't see West the way I did. They'd never see him with his guard down when he felt safe and comfortable. They'd never understand how fiercely that man loved me in all the little ways that mattered. They'd never see under his armor.

And I was okay with that. I didn't need anyone's validation about our relationship. Loving West McNamara wasn't hard. Watching him fight a war that I couldn't protect him from was.

And so I just loved him. And kept on loving him. That part was easy. That part I firmly believed I was made for.

Every year in May we went on vacation. We took the worst day of his life and filled it with new memories of places he wanted to go. We'd gone to Italy, Canada, Mexico, London, and Ireland. The pictures were all over our house—a happy reminder that we didn't have to stay bound to the past.

I wandered toward the stables in search of my husband, attracting a small crowd as I did. Ferdinand became my shadow as did our goats Taco and Granola. We didn't fucking name them that crap. They came pre-named and answered to those goddamn names.

Sure enough, West was moving bales of hay inside for the horses—shirtless and in a backward hat. I leaned against the fence and enjoyed the show because him doing farm work like that was one of my favorite fucking things.

When he saw me, a smile lit up his face and did things to my heart. West's smiles always did. I loved being on the receiving end of them.

"How do we feel about selling baby cows?" West demanded, huffing out a quick breath when he joined me.

"How do you feel about fighting my fucking cane?" I retorted. No one was selling my baby cows. He grinned as he braced against the fence, those gray eyes holding mine. I was all too aware of the careful placement of his hands—close but not touching. I filed that little piece of information away. *It was one of those days.* "You have horses, I have cows."

"Except my horses aren't fucking horny all the time."

"Damn it, Ferdinand!" I glanced at the bull, but there was no shame in his adorable face. "Who now?"

"Daisy and Poppy," he replied. "Maybe if you stopped naming your cows after flowers, the bull who loves flowers would stop fucking them."

I opened my mouth to say something but closed it, making West laugh.

"You know I'm right," he said.

"Can you stop fucking all my heifers?" I snapped at Ferdinand. The bull didn't give two fucks—well, he had and that was why we were having this goddamn conversation. "Think we can ask the Harvey's kid to sterilize him? Ain't that one a vet?"

"You want to neuter a bull?"

"That's the best I've got."

"Okay." West took off his hat and ran a hand through his hair. "I guess I can give him a call later today and find out what he says. I ain't getting my fucking hopes up."

"We'll figure it out," I told him. *Hopefully.* Fucking Ferdinand was living up his best life with all the snacks he could find and treating my girls like they were his snacks too. We had nine baby cows from him in six years.

"Do you want to go for a ride?" he asked.

"I have to be at Abernathy's facility in a while," I reminded him. I'd taken Beau Abernathy up on his offer to teach future bull riders—finally. I'd hemmed and hawed over the decision for five years. But after years of attending opening day as a guest, I was ready to do more. I'd never be able to ride, but I wasn't done. As West always said: I was Jackson Fucking Myles, and I was still a goddamn legend. I was ready to see what more I could do, including training the next generation of bull riders.

"I know." His lips quirked at the corner, and I bit back a sigh, knowing full well he was up to shit. "And I plan to be there with popcorn. I'm going to sit there and watch you yell at a bunch of young kids. They don't fucking know what they're in for."

"You're terrible."

"Tell me I'm wrong, cowboy." *I couldn't.* He leaned across the fence and kissed me quickly. "Let's go for a ride. When we get back, we can shower, I'll make you breakfast, and then we'll go."

"A short ride," I corrected. "Not one of those six-hour rides you sometimes drag me on."

Drag was a stretch of a word. I was a willing captive to whatever adventures he took me on. It didn't matter where the fuck we went. As long as West was there, I was happy.

"That was still one ride," he told me with a laugh, "but we'll make it a short one. I promise."

EPILOGUE PART 02

WEST

As a wedding present to Jackson, I'd taught Zeus how to be mounted from a lying down position. His accident may have taken a lot from him, but I refused to let it take horseback rides from him too. *From us.* To say it made him emotional was an understatement. I'd never tell just how hard it had been because every minute of fighting Zeus had been worth it to watch them gallop through the back fields of our home.

I lived for these moments with the open sky overhead and the wind in my hair. The hoofbeats on the earth beneath me were grounding—centering me in a way I'd never be able to explain. These moments calmed my heart and brought peace to my soul.

And there were moments in the quiet as I rode Thunder Jack when I was floored by the life I had. *The life I'd built for myself with Jackson.* An impossible kind of gratitude would take over—the kind I felt deep inside. There were no good words to describe how I felt about what I had.

Years ago, I never would've thought a life like this was possible for me. I let the demons and the darkness take everything from me. I couldn't see beyond any of it. *How could someone like me be worthy of anything so good and pure in the world?* The answer had always been so simple: I wasn't.

And that wasn't to say I hadn't fought for it. I had. Every fucking day for fifteen months I fought for it. And I still did. But it was worth it. The good days far outweighed the bad ones. I knew real happiness—the kind of happiness that had once been a pipe dream. The kind of happiness I never believed I was worthy of. I felt comfortable in my own skin. My body wasn't a stranger to me, and my mind... well, it was a work in progress, but even that didn't scare me because I knew I couldn't fail.

I'd survived my worst days.

I could survive whatever else life threw at me.

"You good, baby?" Jackson asked, his deep voice pulling me from my thoughts. He nudged Zeus a little closer. I smiled at Jackson—at the man who inspired me to be better. Who showed me just how good my life could be and saw me, even when I couldn't see myself.

At the man who so fiercely believed in me that I knew I could do anything.

"Yeah, I'm good, cowboy."

And I was.

I loved our life at West Haven.

I loved Jackson.

But most of all... I loved me.

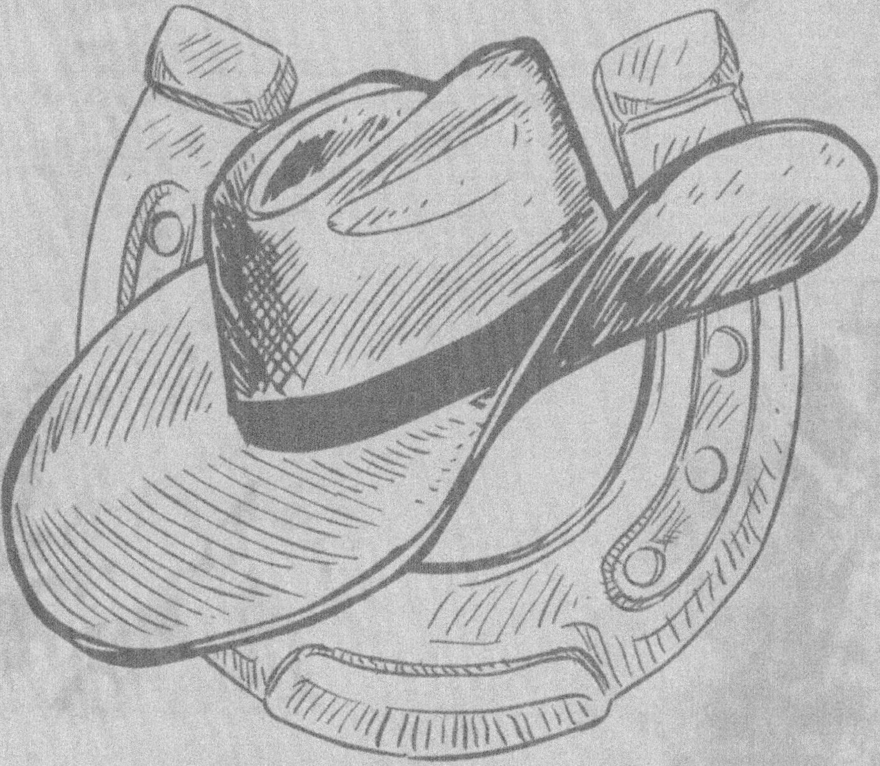

ACKNOWLEDGEMENTS

This book was nothing short of a labor of love. An emotionally taxing one. I couldn't have done this one alone even if I tried. I want to say a very special thank you to my team for taking on this emotional toll with me and helping carry me through to the finish line.

To Sierra... thank you for being my rock to get through this one, for listening when I needed it, and for always being gentle with me when I was struggling to be gentle with myself.

To Dominique, Alissa, Jade, Jayna, and Kirsten, Maygan, and Savannah... thank you for shedding a million tears with me along the way.

To J & Dani... thank you for being my cheerleaders and my sprinting buddies.

A. WINCHESTER

And to Michelle... thank you for loving my boys the way I do and helping me bring them to life through art.

ABOUT THE AUTHOR

My *About The Author* section is turning into... collect facts about Winchester with every book you read. Here are three more random facts about me since I never know what to put about myself in things like this:

1. I grew up in the Chicagoland area.

2. *Don't You Dare* by CE Ricci and *No Tomorrow* by Carian Cole are tied for my favorite books ever.

3. My favorite dinosaur is the T-Rex from Jurassic Park / Jurassic World.

I'd love connect with you on social media. I can be found on Instagram @awinchesterauthor

I also have a Facebook VIP group as well—Wanderlust Haven: A. Winchester's Reader Group

It's a great place to grow and connect with me on future projects and more.

OTHER WORKS

The Wayward Sons
The Wayward Sons: Back to the Beginning: *Available on Amazon*
The Wayward Sons & The Wichita Werewolf: *Available on Amazon*
The Wayward Sons & The Seattle Sirens: *Available on Amazon*
The Wayward Sons & The Vampires of Fortune: *Coming March 2025 to Amazon*

The Byrne Boys
Escaping Expectations (Declan's Story): *Available on Amazon*
Wrecking Love (Killian's Story): *Available on Amazon*
Hunting Destiny (Finn's Story): *Coming to Patreon January 2025*

Stars & Players
Halloween Fumble: *Available on Amazon*
Game On: *Coming April 2025 to Amazon*

Standalones
Chasing Wilde: *Available on Amazon*
Every Tomorrow: *Coming May 2025 to Amazon*

Made in the USA
Monee, IL
11 March 2025